Maximus SHOCK

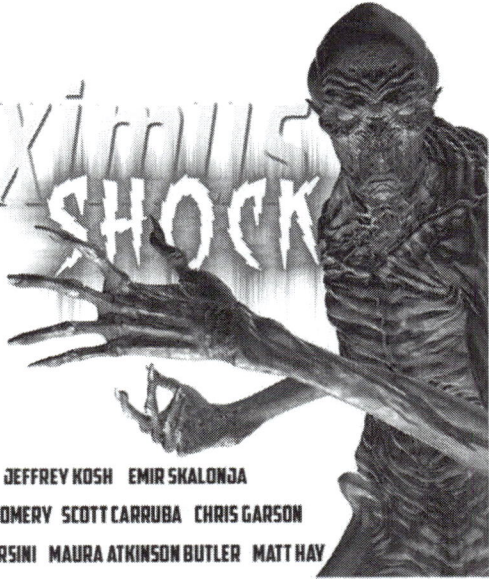

RICKY FLEET   JEFFREY KOSH   EMIR SKALONJA

KEITH MONTGOMERY   SCOTT CARRUBA   CHRIS GARSON

LORRAINE VERSINI   MAURA ATKINSON BUTLER   MATT HAY

LEON BROWN   WK POMEROY

EDITED BY
CHRISTINA HARGIS SMITH

Maura Atkinson Butler

MAXIMUS SHOCK
©2017 Optimus Maximus Publishing
First Edition
Edited by Christina Hargis Smith
Cover art and Interior Art by Jeffrey Kosh Graphics
Published by Optimus Maximus Publishing, LLC

ISBN 10: 1-944732-20-9
ISBN 13: 978-1-944732-20-2

FOREWORD

by
CHRISTINA HARGIS SMITH
Editor and Publisher of OMP

Dear Reader,

Welcome to Maximus Shock, our first collection of short stories, which we have decided to release to mark the first anniversary of our publishing house, Optimus Maximus Publishing.

When I created the company, as another way to channel my lifelong love for books, I really wanted to have as close a relationship with our authors as possible. We made it our purpose and our promise that every author we work with feels like family.

It is my honor to bring these masterful writers together in this anthology, which is a perfect combination of seasoned and never-before published writers. Each storyteller brings a unique tale to Maximus Shock, from psychological thriller to terrifying monster stories to scare the bejeezus out of you.

It truly is a work of love and collaboration, and I am so very proud to have all this talent in my "family".

We hope you'll enjoy Maximus Shock as much as we do.

Happy reading!

Christina Hargis Smith

TABLE OF CONTENTS

Maximus SHOCK

OPTIMUS MAXIMUS PUBLISHING
Brick, New Jersey
2017

Collected tales of Madness and Terror

Maximus SHOCK

An OMP Magazine

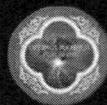

MAXIMUS SHOCK 1

Issue No. 1

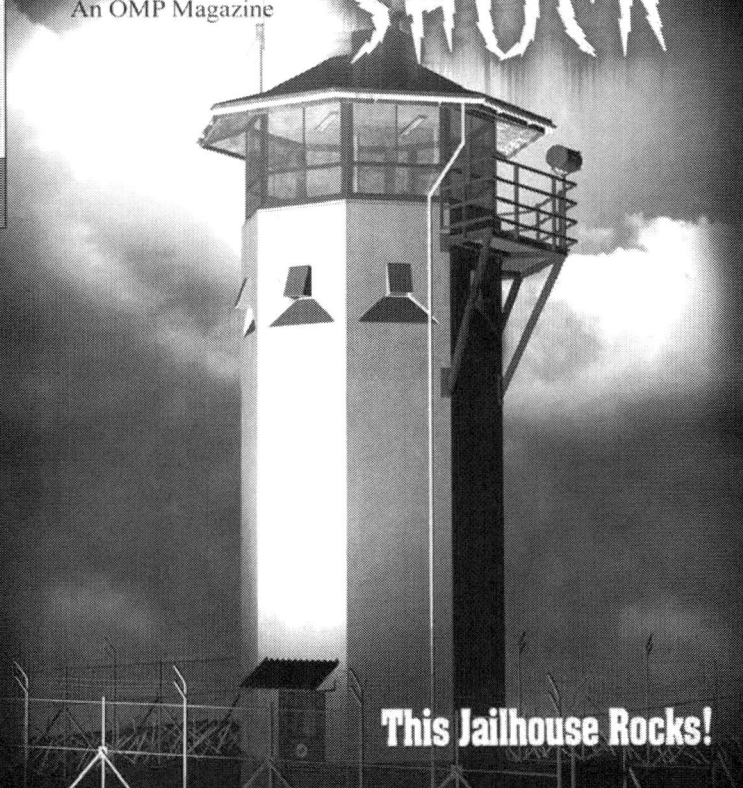

This Jailhouse Rocks!

MONKEYS IN THE PALACE

Chris Garson

The screams of dying guards and inmates and sirens blaring on the towers sounds like an Auto Tune masterpiece. Today's mayhem is compliments of Hector Escandia, leader of the Latino gang in this backwater penitentiary located on a patch of swampland between Pensacola and Mobile. He started this riot, which has already and will undoubtedly continue presenting numerous opportunities to satisfy my unusual urges, for which he has my undying gratitude. Someday perhaps I'll thank him personally. For the moment, all my efforts are focused on escaping his attention entirely. You see, Hector is one bad hombre with reason not to like me. He's a lifer, a rapist, and murderer ineligible for parole. They nailed him for his landlord's wife and kids but that was just the one they could prove. He made his bones many times over — you don't climb to the top of the slag heap handing out marshmallows. Being in the joint hasn't slowed him down one bit. He has as big an army here as he did outside.

I'm in the inner yard, flat against the wall, surrounded by the dead and dying. The orange jumpsuit I'm wearing is splattered with someone else's blood. As much as I want to drink in every note of these death wails, I can't stay here and risk Hector finding me. I have to survive until order is restored. That will take hours, less if the feds get involved. My chances are better inside, where hiding is simpler. Even so, it won't be no picnic. The monkeys have invaded the palace.

It's no wonder to me that I landed in a prison. You might have been surprised, had you known me before today. I do respectable quite well though I do have to work at it. The truth is, I've always known that prison is the perfect place for me. It's the only place, really, where I can safely satisfy my peculiar appetite. Were I to drink from the fountain of my particular pleasure on the outside, the public

3

would be aghast. Its sensibilities are easily offended, but not here. No one really cares what happens here.

My mother was the first to realize my truth. It was hard to get anything past Elise, unless she'd been drinking to escape my father's beatings, and she drank more than she should have, more than anyone should have. I was too young to drink. So, I found other ways to forget, like pulling wings off butterflies. In fourth grade, I microwaved Cinnamon, the neighbor's cat, an orange, overly puffy creature resembling a deep sea anemone on the Discovery channel. Elise knew I'd done it and why. She kept quiet, even when Johnny Mortenson was blamed. There's nothing like a mother's love, is there?

They sent Johnny away. Elise went on a three day binge, leaving me to take the brunt of it on the home front, just me alone with dear old dad. Right before he'd hit me, the beast would tease me by calling me Brandy.

Ocean cats and butterfly wings were stepping stones to bigger and better things. In junior high, I learned quite by accident how much better it is when you can hear the pain. Butterflies don't talk and if Cinnamon was meowing for her life, I couldn't hear over the microwave's sputtering fan.

Chad Bennington was my favorite kind of playmate. Chad was a squealer. I've had all types, from wailers to stoically silent warriors. Many sob hysterically, but the best squeal like pigs. Chad taught me another lesson – you can get away with murder, or damn close to it, if the other person starts it, which Chad did by taunting me with *that* name. I broke three of Chad's fingers before he passed out. Each cracking bone brought an unbidden smile. I learned something else that day. Girls take a back seat to pain.

Afterwards, I was sent to the vice-principal's office, where Mr. Cahill paddled me three times and then lectured on the importance of eschewing violence. Silly, ironic man. It was never about the violence, it was always about the pain. Mr. Cahill didn't understand. Chad, however, was sent to the principal's office, suspended for a week and never bothered me again.

Fond memories of Chad fade. I am in the midst of a prison riot and to reach the relative safety of the building, I must cross the crowded yard without being noticed. Cons are everywhere, settling longstanding grudges and battling outnumbered guards armored in vests, helmets, and shields who hold the outer gate like Spartans at Thermopylae. Staying inconspicuous is the most essential element of my plan as Hector isn't my only enemy here, just the meanest. Right now seems like a good time to make my dash. No one is paying any particular attention to me; I'm just another bloody orange jumpsuit. I glance at the towers above. Snipers are always there, but no barrels are glinting in the afternoon sun.

I sprint for the door. When I'm almost there, a figure holding a Bennelli Super Black Eagle II shotgun with a satin walnut finish steps out of the shadows to fill the doorway. "My, my, Brandy. Don't you look sweet all covered in orange and red?" It is hard to hear over the sirens and gun fire.

JaJuan Jefferson Lincoln, or J3 as the massive black man demands to be called. Why? Because it rhymes with Jay-Z. J3 is the strongest inmate in Cell Block B. He once ripped the toilet from the floor and hurled it at his cellmate for snoring, breaking the aforementioned cellmate's nose, which of course made the snoring worse. J3 thought he had a real future as a rapper. That's only because everyone was afraid to tell him that lifting heavy objects and breaking things were his only real skills. He'd been the breaking half of a B&E team and got sent upriver when his partner rolled on him. Hector used him as muscle sometimes.

"It's Brandon, not Brandy." I am furious. No one has called me Brandy since Chad, not even the beast. After my father met with his accident, he left me alone.

"Shut yo mouth, bitch. I'll call you whatever I damned feel like." Then he pumps the shotgun twice. "Not another step, Brandy."

Lincoln is no killer. It takes a certain kind of person to kill another human being in cold blood. I know one when I see one. Lincoln won't shoot. He might break my jaw or crack my ribs or body slam me to the ground, but he won't shoot. It's not his style. And, he has nothing to gain. He's a short-timer, due for release next month. "J3, my man. Put that down."

"Shut up, man."

"You don't want to shoot me, J3." I take a step forward.

"I said don't move." He waves the Bennelli. In his huge hands, it looks like a toy.

I stop. "Okay. What now?"

"I don't know. Just shut up and let me think." Beads of sweat are running down J3's face.

The Bennelli triggers an awful thought. Ordinarily, Lincoln's no killer, but he is holding a shotgun. What if he's already killed someone? Mistakes happen on a day like today. If he has, all bets are off. "Where did you get that shotgun, J3?"

"What?"

"The shotgun. Where did you get it?"

"I found it, man. I found it in the laundry. Shit, Brandy, what does it matter?" Lincoln looks at me like I'm crazy. If only he knew how crazy, which raises an interesting question. Does the very awareness of one's own insanity render the person in question sane? If so, then I am as sane as you. That, I admit, is a terrifying thought. For I must conclude that if I am, as has been posited, sane, and also, as I am willing to stipulate, devoid of any true morals or conscience, then I must be evil. Some might heap pity on me and blame the beating beast. They would be wrong.

6

Elise knew. If you're considering showering me with your pity, save it for poor poor pitiful J3. I don't deserve it.

"Did you see Deering there?" The Bennelli was Deering's Christmas present from his wife. The other guards all use Mossberg 500 pump actions.

"Yeah."

"Did you …"

"No, man. I wouldn't shoot him. Deering was all right. He was alive, last I saw him."

Thank God or my Lucky Charms. The latter is more likely. They say we're all God's creatures, but no God would admit to me. I'm betting on the breakfast cereal. My concern has nothing to do with Deering. This is all about Lincoln and how to handle him. He hasn't crossed any lines yet so his release is still in reach. That's all I need to know. "I have a big stash inside, J3. We can do this easy."

"What you mean, Brandy?"

That was the fourth time. "You get out soon, don't you? You ain't done nothing to mess that up, have you J3? I could you set you up, my man. I could set you up real fine. You know I got the goods. You know I'm the man. Let's do this easy."

The barrel wavers. "Where's yo stash, man?"

"I'll take you to it." I take a step forward.

"I ain't said yes yet, Brandy. Don't come any closer."

Yes you have. You said the magik word. Yet. "If you kill me, you'll never find it."

"How much we talkin bout?""

"Lots, J3. Enough to make your record."

"No shit?"

"No shit. I been here a long time, man. Let me take you to it."

"Well, all right then, but don't try nothing. I still got this shotgun and even without it, I could squash you like a bug." J3 waves me into the hallway with the Bennelli.

Shadow gobbles us. The main power has been cut and only the emergency lights are working. I move past him. Now, the Bennelli is trained on my back. We keep walking.

"Do you know how Hector pulled it off?" I ask him.

"It was McGriff. McGriff and Slikowski. Hector bragged about it."

The tower guards. So that's why there weren't any snipers. "How did he get them?"

"Cash. Cash and women. Hector's bitches took good care of them."

Slikowski is nothing. He does whatever McGriff tells him. McGriff is the prison's most corrupt guard. Today he entered the halls of overachievement. I'd seen Escandia's main squeeze. She is a tan, dark haired beauty with a mouth filthier than most cons. Every month she drives up from Pensacola, sometimes with a friend or two, and goes into the last visitation chamber on the right. Hector does her good while the guards look the other way. The going rate is a carton of smokes. I sometimes watch through a peephole. "I never heard about her messing around with any of the guards."

"That's the beautiful thing about it, Brandy. They hooked up on the outside, where no one would find out. Now, let's get this over with. Take me to your stash and," he holds the Bennelli menacingly, "It better be worth it."

Now that we're too far down the tunnel for anyone in the yard to see, I decide that JaJuan Jefferson Lincoln has outlived his usefulness. Despite being outweighed nearly two to one, I'm not worried. I am small and quick and he is big, slow, and clumsy and not nearly cautious enough. I've studied human anatomy in ways that few people ever have. I know fifty ways to kill a man and which of them hurts the most. Also, I have a real knife, eight inches of stainless steel in the form of a bone-handled Damascas Skinner Hunting Knife, not some homemade shiv made from a filed down toothbrush.

A noise sounds from down the hall and Lincoln turns away for just a moment. I draw the knife. It fits the palm of my hand perfectly. I strike. The blade flashes up and into Lincoln's armpit, where it nicks the axillary artery. I stop short of severing it completely, I want him to bleed out slowly. He slumps onto the floor. I told you, not everyone is cut out to be a killer. It takes one to know one.

His eyes open wide in fear as his life spills out. "Shit, Brandy. What'd you go and do that for?"

"For the pain, J3, for the pain." I straddle his chest and hold the knife over him. He is already too weak to stop me. "Now the fun begins, take a good look JaJuan, I'm the last thing you'll ever see." I jab the point into his left eyeball and transparent goo oozes out. Lincoln is still screaming, not quite a squeal but it'll do, when I take his other eye. "You ought to thank me for taking your eyes first. You won't want to see what comes next."

"You're a sick mother fucker, Brandy," he chokes out. "You belong here."

I lose my patience and stab him in the chest eight times, once for each Brandy. "Don't. Ever. Call. Me. Brandy. Again," I say while stabbing him. He's dead too soon, even before I can get off.

Goddamn it. I lost my cool. I hadn't meant for him to go so quickly. I wanted him to linger. After coming so far since Cinnamon and Chad Bennington, you'd think I'd show more restraint, but the Brandies got to me.

I take the Bennelli and leave Lincoln in the hallway. I march deeper into the prison, knowing I just have to wait it out a few more hours. By then, Lincoln's body will be just one of many. They'll never connect it to me.

I edge past the heavy steel door leading to the guard towers. It is open and in the blinking emergency lights, I see a body sprawled on the steps. There is a gaping hole in the back of McGriff's head and grey matter is spattering the walls. Hector has paid him well. There is no sign of Slikowski.

I pass through Cell Block A and into the laundry room. Deering is lying on the floor next to a large industrial dryer. A cut femoral is spraying a fountain of blood from his thigh. Across the room are the remains of Carponelli, a three-time loser car thief and Beckham, an embezzler who worked for a big bank on Wall Street. The Bennelli had blown both of them apart - Deering hadn't gone down without a fight.

"Johnson, help," he moans. Lincoln told the truth. Deering is alive, a condition I will soon rectify.

"I'm coming, Deering. Hold on."

"Pressure … stop … the bleeding." His words come out slowly with labored breathing between each.

Deering will be dead in minutes, with or without my intervention. I can either hasten his demise or slow it. I choose the latter, to better savor his end, but I don't have a belt. Prison jumpsuits don't come with belts. There are too many ways to use one that don't involve pants. I make a tourniquet by tying two pillowcases together.

"Thanks … Johnson," Deering croaks.

"Does it hurt much?" I bask in his death throes

"Don't feel … much. Cold," he shivers. "So cold."

"Let me see what I can do," I say. I brandish my Damascan steel. Lincoln's blood is still dripping from it. "Maybe I can help." I make a slit in his stomach like I'm a surgeon doing a C-section. Deering gasps and I drink in his pain. If you cut in the right spot, to the right depth and peel away the muscles and tendons, you can reach into a man's gut and pull out his intestines in one piece, if you're careful. The last of Deering's tugs free with a pop. He squeals, finally a squeal, and then his eyes go blank. This one's so much more satisfying than J3! I really do owe Hector. I haven't ever had a day like this.

After leaving the laundry I make my way past Cell Block B and down the main corridor. My place of refuge is close. All I have to do is cross the shop room floor.

"I see you homeboy. You're mine," Hector calls out from behind the light blue '93 Oldsmobile they are rebuilding. "I owe you, man. I owe you big time."

I'm armed now, but so is Hector. He has one of the Mossbergs. If I wait, he'll start shooting until he hits something. He blames me for his time in the hole, never mind that he stabbed Gonzalez, not me. As for what happened once he was in solitary, I proudly take full responsibility for that.

I see a way out. The lever activating the fire control system is nearby. I reach out and Hector steps into view. He's Cheech Marin, but covered with scars and tattoos and not nearly so funny. He shoots and misses. The buckshot ricochets off an empty oil drum. I pull the lever down. A siren goes off, then jets of water and flame retardant foam pour down from the ceiling. I dash for the far door.

"That won't do you any good, homeboy. I'm coming for you."

I barrel down the hallway. At the end, I open the door. My name is spelled out in black letters on the frosted glass – Warden Brandon Johnson. I slam the door shut, sit in my chair behind my desk, with the Bennelli on my lap, and wait. I hear footsteps.

To Jeffrey Kosh, who included me into his literary world.
In him I found not just a new favorite author, but also friend responsible for lighting the fire of writing in my heart. He never once faltered in his encouragement or belief in me.

Everyone calls me Sunny.

Everyone, except my parents that properly christened me Sunshine Ellory Woods. Obviously, my parents are Grateful Dead-listening, pot-smoking hippies.

To all my friends, I am just Sunny.

Friends, ah! This is Senior year at Elmore High School and, being very smart, I am required to take all advanced classes; which translates to being friendless. I exist in a very nondescript way as it is my goal to become invisible. It isn't about my looks. Because I am attractive in that all-American, girl-next-door way: bright blue eyes that only require the barest of makeup to enhance; a small scatter of freckles that add character to my countenance; silky, shoulder length hair that hangs straight as a razor in a style that takes others hours in the morning to replicate. But rather than call attention to myself, I disguise it all in black or gray hoodies and hats that are pulled down as far as possible without losing full visibility. It is easier for me to hide than speak. My shyness dictates that I only talk when commanded, and even then, it is in a soft ghost-like whisper. That's because I am afraid of the world. My parents still hold on to the notion that we live in a *love your neighbor, people are inherently good, do no harm* world. We don't. No matter how many times I try to enlighten them to the horrors I face throughout my school career, all the time light refuses to dawn on their marble heads.

And then came the day that I was proven right.

***

It started like every other day: I was shambling through my pitiful existence, wishing I were anywhere or anybody else; the Senior hallway was as packed as usual and I had to squeeze myself through the masses. While navigating toward my locker, I clocked the *'Stepford Girls'* and noticed that I was going to come in direct contact, so I quickly adjusted my trajectory. With the close call averted, I managed to eke a passage around, as they would never have deigned themselves to make room ... for anyone.

This is going to be another fun-filled day, I groaned inwardly.

Finally, I reached the end of the hall, where my locker was located. Turning the dial, 28 left ... 16 right ... and back to 43 left, I then lifted the lever.

"What the ..." I squeaked as I pulled my hand away, as if the metal was scalding hot.

Gum.

Someone had stuck a chewed up purple wad of bubble gum onto the underside of the handle.

"Damn it," I huffed while tugging the sticky mass into a slimy strand that stuck my fingers to my locker in an absurd parody of a tacky grape spider web. Laughter sounded out from somewhere behind me. Quickly, I whipped around and ... what a non-surprise! There they were: the *'Stepford Girls'* in their gaggle pointing, whispering, and, of course, laughing.

"Bitches," I whispered to myself. It was always best to not let them hear you. Nobody was capable of withstanding a confrontation with those girls; chances of an unscathed survival were nil. The commotion that would have ensued would have been loud, mean, and very public. Knowing this, I chose to remain beneath the radar, stay out of their crosshairs, and to continue to dwell in my cloak of invisibility. I was used to shutting up and dealing. So, I yanked the hood of my *Serenity* sweatshirt down further, attempting to camouflage as much of my face as would fit.

It seemed that the imminent threat of humiliation had passed, so I hefted my olive drab backpack higher onto my shoulder, turned back toward my locker and opened its door. My goal, at that moment, was to retrieve a scrap of paper with which to disengage the nasty purple wad. Instead, every book and personal belonging cascaded onto the floor. Someone, somehow, had gotten in and had magically stacked anything left in the locker up against the door, so that when I had opened it ... crash! I unleashed a waterfall of books, papers, and clothes.

That's it! I drew in a deep stuttering breath, squared my shoulders, yanked my hood back and whipped my head around to glare daggers at Kristen and company. As I started to make my way directly into her face, I fingered the Bic in my pocket and worked the cap off. As I came to a halt, my nose was inches from hers; I snatched out the ball point pen, like I was unsheathing a sword. Raising it high above my shoulders, I swung my arm down in an arc, jamming the end directly into Kristen's left eyeball. The squelching pop was like nothing I had ever heard before. A wicked smile slowly crept across my face. God that had felt good! There was stillness and silence before the screams of horror ensued. That was a whole different sound experience for me. Chills raced through my body in an almost orgasmic release.

It was then that I crashed back into my reality with the slamming of a nearby locker. I hung my head in shame and disbelief. I wished I possessed the courage to confront those bitches. I would have loved to see the look on Kristen's face with my pen sticking from her eye socket. Instead, I froze while the entire hallway erupted into gales of unsympathetic laughter. No one rushed over to offer aid. No one asked me if I was OK. No one cared that I was going to be late to homeroom. The last thought rolled through my mind as the bell rang. The overzealous mirth quickly ceased and the herd of students bee-lined toward their classes. I just continued to stand there, unmoving, staring at the chaos at my feet. A single tear tried to slide down my cheek, but I would never give them the satisfaction of seeing me cry, so I swiped at the lone traitor determinedly. I bent down, dropped my backpack aside the mess and started gathering my crap to cram it back into the locker, in its disheveled state.

I don't know how they got the combination, I thought, *but I know the 'Stepford Girls' are responsible.*

The nasty girls that I collectively referred to as the 'Stepford Girls' all wore identical clothing styles, expensive and tiny. They not only sported the exact same hair color, but precisely the same cut as well. Those carbon copy bitches were named Kristen, Kelly, and two Katies. They were obviously the product of some horrible lab experiment gone awry. And of course, they were the most popular students in the whole school. Their boyfriends were exact reproductions as well but of the male variety: gorgeous, muscled, and well-dressed Varsity football players. Two of them were even brothers. Robbie, Steven, Michael, and Ricky. Robbie and Ricky were the dynamic duo from the same family, each dating a Katie. *I always wondered if that created confusion.* Steven and Michael - *never Steve and Mike* - were paired with Kristen and Kelly respectively.

I know you probably thought they were cheerleaders … but you'd been wrong. Those girls were the stars of our undefeated girls' Varsity lacrosse team. Those four couples, like sets of bookends, moved together in a pack, like hyenas. If they ever chanced travelling solo, I never witnessed it. They also always arranged to have all their classes together. One unfortunate guidance counselor once made the mistake of culling Kristen from the pack, for she should have been in a more advanced math class. The ruthless foursome had descended on Ms. Gardner's office like *Dementors* from *Azkaban*. The air had turned so icy you could practically see your breath. The unholy screeching that had emanated from behind that door could've been heard throughout both the Junior and Senior hallways. After the tirade had finally would itself down,

Ms. Garner had backpedaled frantically, bowing, scraping, and apologizing profusely. She had switched Kristen back immediately.

Did I forget to mention that Ms. Gardner was the lucky soul we were supposed to report *'any and all incidents of bullying?'* After word of that debacle spread school-wide, everyone confided in her to handle exactly nothing!

At that point, I was almost finished with the reorganization of my locker when a pair of brown loafers appeared in my peripheral vision. Sliding my eyes to the fancy shoes and then slowly upward to the face that loomed above me, I gulped audibly.

It was Steven. As in Kristen's Steven.

He suddenly bent down and collected the last of my personal effects from the floor, neatened the pile, and handed it back to me. I was stunned into utter silence. I bobbed my head like a crazed owl and tried to mumble an intelligent, "Thanks."

"You don't have to take that," Steven said conspiringly, in a low rumbling voice.

"I don't … I mean … take what?" I managed to eke out in response.

"The shitty way the girls treat you. For the record, I had nothing to do with this. I never get involved in their shenanigans," vowed Steven earnestly. "I've tried discussing all this crap with Kristen. She never listens. Actually, she has given me the silent treatment for an entire day, just for bringing it up."

"It's ok," I valiantly tried convincing him, "It's not that bad."

Not that bad! Those girls have literally haunted me since seventh grade. In the After School Special version, we were probably besties until they discovered popularity on the first day of Junior high. But again, that'd be incorrect. There has never been a day that I haven't felt the hate emanating off the four robots. Those vipers have always been thin, gorgeous, and vicious. But as far back as my recollection of the hateful venom goes, I know that my feelings for Steven have spanned a much longer past. Since, Kindergarten, I have been in awe of this beautiful boy. Maybe Kristen has always been aware of my pitiful crush and it has fueled her hate-fire toward me … or maybe it's due to the simple fact that I have continued to draw oxygen. I'll never know.

Steven had always been, by far, the kindest and most pleasant of the group.

He had a soft-spoken voice that always made my insides feel all warm and fuzzy.

One Saturday, when I was walking to the library, I spied him, safely from behind a tree, coaching *Peewee football*. He was patient and kind to the boys; whenever they made an error on a play, he calmly gathered the kids together and re-explained each individual's responsibility over and over.

I also remember the precise moment I had fallen in love with him. It had been in Mrs. Warner's Kindergarten class, during art. The whole group had been scattered about eight round tables. We had been given the task of coloring Mother's Day cards and I had asked the kids at my table for a purple crayon. Every single one had looked up, had stared at me for a second, and then had resumed scribbling. Not even one child had responded. Steven, sitting at the next table over, had apparently heard the snub. He had stood up and had marched that violet beauty right over to me.

"Here you go," he had stated with a smile.

I had looked up into those angelic periwinkle eyes and the rest, as they say, had been history. I was totally and utterly twitter pated. Anyone who has seen the *Disney* movie *Bambi,* would understand. That torch has been secretly carried and nurtured since that day.

I returned to the present and realized that he was standing there, staring at me as I was strolling down memory lane. *Say something, you idiot! Talk to him.*

Too late. Steven shrugged his shoulders, shook his head, then turned around and began his retreat to his classroom.

"Steven wait," I called after him. He halted midstride, pivoted back in my direction. Now, standing face to face with the boy of my dreams, I reached out and rested my hand on his shoulder. "I'm sorry. I didn't mean to blow you off like that," I stated.

"Don't worry about it, are you ok?" he inquired. His eyes were filled with concern as he stepped even closer to me. Slowly, Steven reached up and pushed my hood back just enough to reveal my eyes. My breath was caught in my chest. I couldn't breathe; I couldn't move; and I definitely couldn't speak. The only sound I heard was my own spastic heartbeat. With an intimate look and a smile, he readjusted my hood and dropped his hand.

My vision cleared just as Steven's back vanished into his homeroom.

I needed to snap out of it; it was just another fantasy.

Shoveling the last notebook into my locker, I took out my Spanish textbook and then rushed across the hallway to my own homeroom. I was extremely tardy. Mr. Walsh glanced up from the attendance book, witnessed my late arrival, and insisted I stayed for a quick minute after class.

Great. What had already started as a stellar day was just getting better.

I then proceeded to my chair, battling the urge to sprint from the room bawling.

The bell signaled the end of homeroom and the beginning of the five-minute travel time to first period. The synchronous sound of everyone standing at the same moment sounded rehearsed and comical. "They are all a bunch of automatons," I chuckled to myself.

I stayed in my seat until the room cleared. Slowly, I hefted my backpack as if it weighed a ton and shuffled up to Mr. Walsh's desk. I stared at the floor so that my hood and hair hung like a privacy curtain. I maintained this pose, just waiting for the inevitable questioning of my tardiness. Instead, Mr. Walsh surprised me by saying, "I heard what happened this morning. Actually, I saw most of it. Are you ok?"

I remained rooted in my spot and started blinking at him like I was transmitting Morse code. Finally, I managed to stutter, "I'm fine." Hoping that this lame answer would satisfy his urge to get more involved.

It didn't

"If you are being bullied by *'those girls'*—" He had even gone as far as to use air quotes.

I couldn't refrain myself and finished that tripe for him. "You need to report it to Ms. Gardner, I know."

Right. As if that is gonna change a thing, I continued in my thoughts.

Mr. Walsh gave me a queer look, then he opened his mouth. "Why would you continually allow them to torment you?"

"If you know what has happened ... *is* happening ... why you don't do something about it?" I asked incredulously.

"Oh ... well ... It's not my department," he stuttered out.

I slammed my fist down on Mr. Walsh's desk and leaned over the pile of papers and folders. Reaching up, I grabbed his necktie by the knot and dragged him forward onto the workspace. Slowly, I twisted the tie until the color of his face began to change. First, it was a pink blush; then it changed into a deep crimson. All the while, his arms were pin wheeling, trying to find purchase on his chair. Desperately searching to disengage himself from my murderous grip.

Mr. Walsh cleared his throat.

Whoa, not again. I've got to get a grip on these insane daydreams.

I could see his embarrassment in his lack of action and the uncomfortable silence. Well, it did not surprise me that Mr. Walsh was as afraid of those vipers as Ms. Gardner and the rest of the school.

"May I just have a pass to Spanish class? I'm going to be late," I requested dejectedly.

The entire conversation was then dismissed by a few scribbles of his pen. I took the pass, shoved it into my sweatshirt pocket, and slinked back out to the hallway.

Right into the Stepford Girls.

I literally smacked into Kristen's back. This caused her to careen into the other three.

I withered under the glare from the four pair of eyes casting hateful rays directly into my soul. I scurried around them and headed off down the hall. I sensed all four girls turning with the precision of the Marine Corp Drill Team, marking my retreating progression.

Just as I was about to go around the corner, I locked eyes with Steven. Of course, he had seen the whole debacle. But unlike his earlier behavior, he instantly diverted his eyes, showing absolutely no recognition. Why would he? He was back with his boys.

I was never going to catch a break.

The rest of that day went mostly unremarkable; I made through it without any additional cripplingly embarrassing events. It was almost a reason for celebrating.

I repacked the books I'd need for homework and made my way out of school. The buses were out front, filled with riders. The Senior parking lot resembled a tailgate party minus the grills and foam fingers. Everyone finished up socializing, scurried to their appropriate rides, and then began the mad dash to the lot's exit.

I was walking home alone, as usual.

Thankfully, I lived close enough that I was not forced to use the school transportation. Yet, I was not lucky enough to have a vehicle of my very own. My parents believed that had I wanted a car, I could pay for it myself. Babysitting just hasn't afforded me that privilege, yet.

I had just started the ten-minute trudge home, when I was caught completely unaware by the blue *Challenger* with black racing stripes pulling up beside me. It was Steven, and he was uncharacteristically alone. He had his window down, and was leaning partially out on his elbow. "Sunny, could I talk to you?"

I hesitated, and furtively glanced around looking for the ambush. Surely this had to be a set up. Where were the cameras? Where was the rest of the clique, ready to pounce and beat the crap out of me? I saw nothing alarming so I slowly stepped off the curb and closed the distance to the muscle car.

"Get in, let me drive you home," he stated more than asked. I shook my head, but my feet decided to make the trek around the front of the car on their own. Steven reached across and unlocked the passenger door. I hesitantly pulled it open, tossed my backpack on the floor, and slid onto the cool leather seat.

"Seatbelt," he demanded as he was already reaching across and pulling the strap across my body. I froze again, until I heard the click and he replaced both hands on the steering wheel. Then, he steered the car in the direction of my house. We cruised, slowly and silently, until, to my disappointment, we reached our destination. Too short, too fast.

We were sitting in front of my house; the car was in park and the engine idling. I stared down at my bag wedged between black *Converse*.

Steven expelled a very audible sigh. I peeked out from under my curtain of hair and hood and noted him gazing down into his lap.

"Do you have to go in? Can we go somewhere private to talk?" he asked in a hopeful voice. I gulped and nodded, not trusting myself to speak. He must have taken that for a *yes*, for he pulled down the street, pushing a CD back into the player. The car filled with music. No longer traveling in silence, the lyrics from Bon Jovi's *Bed of* Roses would be forever ingrained into my brain.

Roughly ten minutes from my neighborhood, Steven pulled into the woods, down a dirt road that I had never noticed before. Nervously, I peered around the trees looking for anything familiar in the gloom. I wasn't sure of what was happening: it was all too good to be true.

I waited for the trick to be revealed. I was probably being lured to that secluded spot and the whole Stepford gang would be there, ready to kill me.

Noticing my obvious anxiety, Steven reached over and clasped my hand. "Relax, there's nothing to be scared of," he chuckled. "I'm not a serial killer or anything." It was almost as if he were reading my mind. "I just wanted a chance to talk to you without *them* seeing us." He stressed the '*them*'. "I come down here with my dad. We fish here all the time." As he confided this, I noticed that we had indeed arrived to the edge of a pond. The still water was as dark as night and trees stood around like sentinels in the faded sunlight. Running out of the dirt road, Steven stopped the car and turned off the engine. There was an instant silence.

Then, he caressed slow circles on the back of my hand; I realized that he hadn't let go.

Slowly, he turned his body toward mine and tugged gently on my arm, turning me toward him. Any further attempt at breathing or maintaining a regular heart-rate was history.

"I want to start by saying how sorry I am. The way Kristen and her... our friends treat you is horrendous. Although I don't participate in their actions, I also do nothing to stop them either." Steven's voice was filled with emotion as he stared down at our entwined hands. "Sunny, I've wanted to say something to you for so long, but was afraid of the hell Kristen would unleash on me when she found out."

I was blown away.

Feeling a tad more courageous, I placed my other hand on top of his.

Our eyes met. Daylight was weakening and it appeared as though his eyes were glowing from some inner source. He freed his hand and reached up to push back my hood, just like he had done in my daydream. He then tucked an errant strand of my hair behind my ear. I just continued to stare at him, like I had turned into a department store's mannequin. With his hand then resting behind my head, he gently drew my face closer to his. I felt the soft brush of his lips on mine.

We both pulled back with a surprised look.

My head was spinning and butterflies were on fast-attack mode in my stomach.

Unexpectedly, he dragged me closer once again and kissed me as though he could steal the air from my lungs. It worked, because I couldn't breathe; I couldn't move; and I hoped that moment would never end.

I tasted Heaven, and it tasted like cinnamon.

Lost in that bliss, it took me a second to realize that the moment had indeed ended. I snapped open my lids, and searched out Steven's eyes. As I sat, breathing raggedly, I noticed that Steven had not escaped unscathed: he was also breathing hard. Without letting go of me, he was staring down at the console. I pulled back slightly.

"What is it? Did I do something wrong?" I stammered out, addressing his confused expression.

"No, I ... that was ... I'm sorry I started that. I can't do this. Kristen would kill you, and then me," he mumbled.

"I wouldn't say anything. We don't ever have to tell her. She never has to know," I rushed out in a torrent of words that broke my heart as I had uttered them. The very reason for getting out of bed; the very reason for returning to school day after day, despite the torment; the very reason I drew breath was in hopes of experiencing again what I had just had.

Steven looked up at me with that million-dollar smile. "Really, you wouldn't say anything? ... To no one?" he asked me.

I considered.

Then, I inquired, "If she is so awful, why are you still with her?"

Steven's smile faltered. His voice took on a hard edge as he responded, "It is what it is!"

Thinking that I had pissed him off, I quickly backpedaled, "Never mind, forget what I said."

The smile miraculously reappeared and I exhaled in relief. Lifting my hand to his lips, he pressed them against my knuckles, and kissed the delicate skin between the joints. He replaced it onto my lap before turning back to the steering wheel. Steven's car responded with a throaty rumble, as he twisted the ignition key. Reversing, he managed to turn the car around and headed down the dirt road. In the short time that it took to return to my house, Steven reclaimed possession of my hand and singed along with his Bon Jovi CD as if he had not a care in the world.

Meanwhile, I turned the conversation over and over again in my head, as if on an endless loop. I couldn't figure out what had happened.

The *'I'm sorry'*, the kiss, the angry tone, then back to the smile.

I quickly decided that I didn't care; I could keep a secret. If that meant the kiss would happen again, I'd take it to my grave. As long as Steven continued to look at me that way, I would have done anything.

"See you soon," were the last words he said.

Leaving the car, I floated into the house and cruised through dinner on autopilot. My parents didn't question my silence, as it was expected. They didn't ask about my day because they couldn't interpret my mumbling.

I excused myself and attempted tackling my homework.

***

The next day was the first time I was actually excited for school. I couldn't think of anything besides the taste of cinnamon. Speed walking, I made it to the building in record time. As I scanned the Senior parking lot, I discerned the blue *Challenger* in its usual spot. Eight bodies clustered around it in groups of two.

Damn, he was with *her*. He was kissing *her*.

I quickened my pace, breezed through the front door and beelined to the bathroom. Secured in a stall, I struggled to catch my breath as I was crying too hard, yet endeavored to do it silently. Then, I composed myself as best as I could and yanked down on my black watch cap until the rim rested at half-mast, over my eyes.

I dreaded the walk to my locker.

I knew that I was going to see Steven and the Stepford crew. I knew he'd be holding her hand or have his around her shoulders.

It sucked.

And there they were.

I steeled myself as they sauntered by. I fully expected the complete lack of recognition, yet I was unable to keep from peeking up at Steven's face.

He winked.

I couldn't believe it, he winked at me!

My heart soared.

***

This bizarre behavior continued for weeks.

Some days would bring a wink or the soft touch of a hand lightly trailing across my back. Twice, I found notes shoved into the vents of my locker, with just a time scribbled on it: I knew I was to be outside my house, standing behind the hedges until I heard the rumble of his car; then we would return to our pond for a tryst.

Then there were the cold shoulder periods, when Kristen was the recipient of Steven's full attention, causing me such heartache.

Logically, I understood. I was the other woman, the secret, the one that never got to be seen with Steven in public. I had agreed to this. Had I known how horrible this …

Bullshit! I would continue to do whatever needed doing in order to keep seeing Steven.

***

We were sitting in the car, surrounded by the trees. I was staring off into the murky pond while music played softly and Steven held my hand. We were silent, lost in our own thoughts.

Then, with a vulnerable look into his eyes that broke both my heart and the silence, he asked, "Do you love me?"

"Of course, I do," I swore. "What can I do to prove it?" I probed innocently.

A slow smile erased the sadness from his eyes and inched across his face. "We have to get rid of her," he rasped out, leaving no room to misinterpret who he was speaking of. "I can't continue this way any longer. Having to pretend to love her, while craving to be in your arms … I won't do it anymore. Either we kill her, or you and I are done."

Of course, that request - that plead - shocked me. He loved me. He practically admitted as much, but ... killing Kristen? I know I dreamed of harming her, but could I actually go through with it?

Yet, at the same time I had tasted Heaven; it tasted of cinnamon and I wasn't going to let that craving fade for anything in the world. I wasn't going to lose Steven now.

"What do you have in mind? Do you have a plan?" I surprised myself asking. Hell, I was really going for it!

That hard edge returned to his voice and his eyes gleamed wickedly as he reached across my body, popped open the glovebox and, shuffling papers around, he retrieved a large leather sheath. "Here's what we'll do," he said revealing a big serrated blade within.

"Tomorrow, I'll collect you right after school and bring you back here. I'll drop you off and head directly to Kristen's house. I'll tell her that we need to talk. That should make her nervous enough to come willingly, without asking too many questions. The few times I brought her here, she hated it. 'It's too dirty, it's too dark, there's nothing to do,' she whines. I'll explain that I just want to have a conversation that wouldn't be interrupted. When we arrive, I'll get out and lean against the back of my car. This will ensure that she gets out too. In the meantime, you'll be hiding behind that double trunked tree, right there." He pointed out the passenger side window. "I will make sure she is standing with her back toward you."

I saw where he was going, but I let him talk.

"I'll start some sort of argument, so that our raised voices will mask any sound you could make approaching. Just slide behind her, grab a handful of her hair and yank it backward. This will expose her throat."

It was bad, really bad, I had to stop him to go on, but I felt excited.

"Just jam the knife against it and drag the blade as hard as you can from one side of her neck to the other. If it is quick enough, she won't be able to scream. But prepare yourself; there will be lots of blood."

Could I really do that?

"When it's done, we just weigh her body down with rocks and toss her into our pond. I'll have a change of clothes for us in the trunk. Then, after making sure we are all cleaned up, we just leave."

I was both frightened and impressed by this murderous outline. And I was scared on two accounts: first of all, did I think I was capable of this? I mean, we were taking about killing someone. Secondly, and more importantly, would we get caught?

I apparently addressed my first fear by having the second.

The impressive attention to detail was what gave me the confidence that the plan would succeed. No one knew about Steven and I, so they certainly wouldn't link me to Kristen's disappearance. More, they would have to find the body to prove a murder. So, everyone would just think she was missing. Since nobody knew about our trysts at the pond, and Steven admitted that Kristen hated coming here, why would they even think to look in there?

And, after an appropriate length of time, Steven and I would be finally able to be seen together in public.

No more hiding.

"I'm in," I exclaimed as I reached for the knife. I fumbled into my backpack, pulled out an extra shirt and rolled the edged weapon up in it, then tucked it into the bag, out of sight.

After running through the details over and over, Steven drove me home. Before I stepped out of the car, he planted a kiss on my lips.

"Soon, we can do that whenever we like," he promised before leaving.

I would do anything for him.

Anything.

***

That night and the next day were all blurred together. I went through the motions, staring at my watch as if I could speed up time. I rushed home from school, emptied my bag except for the rolled-up t-shirt and knife, and resumed my lookout from behind the bushes. Again, I heard the muscle car before I saw it, and was standing on the curb as Steven pulled up. I jogged around the front and hopped in. The excitement of what I was about to do, paled considerably to the thrill of being released from the secrecy of our relationship. Pulling down the dirt road and bringing the vehicle to a stop, Steven grabbed my face and roughly kissed me.

"See you soon," he growled at me, practically shoving me out the door. He took off so fast, the tires kicked up huge sprays of dirt. I went to my hiding place behind the tree. Resting my back against the trunk, I slid down until I was sitting on the ground. I opened the pack, pulled out the shirt, and unrolled the knife, so I knew I would be ready.

After what seemed like hours, I heard the throaty roar of Steven's engine.

Quickly, I stood, but I didn't risk peeking, in case Kristen was looking out the window. Hearing the doors open and close, I still maintained my cover; I decided to wait until I heard the arguing ensue. Almost immediately, I heard voices raised in anger.

That was it. I started my stealthy approach.

Upon nearing the car, I quickly registered that something was wrong.

Kristen didn't have her back toward me. In fact, she was still yelling at Steven, yet she was staring directly at me, grinning wildly. Her nonsensical words trailed off as she continued leering at me. I tightened my grip on the hunting knife, almost forgetting what its purpose was.

Kristen glanced down at my right hand and laughed out loud.

"You bitch! You really would have tried killing me? Not today sweetheart." She laughed again, noticing the confusion on my face. "Oh Sunny, how pathetic. You thought Steven was falling in love with you?" she taunted. "You did. Oh, this is priceless. Every single word he said, everything he did, was because I told him to. You thought you are here *to get rid of me*'? Well, guess what? We are here to get rid of you."

I stumbled backward a step or two, hoping to put some distance between us.

What a fool! I had totally fallen into it. My nerdish sixth sense had tried to warn me from the start, but no; I was too taken by a dream, by the illusion that a guy like Steven could be mine. In my hunger for love, I had swallowed it hook, line, and sinker!

But I certainly didn't want to make this easy for them.

Besides, I still had the knife. Rather that achieving the space I needed, I crashed into the tree in the back of me.

No, not a tree, a person. Michael was behind me.

Before I could do anything, he locked me up in a bear hug, pinning my arms to my side. Another person appeared in my peripheral. Wresting the knife from my grip, Kelly came into view with the weapon. She was also laughing but trying to hide her mirth beneath her hand. One by one, the whole crew materialized from amongst the trees. Steven didn't just pick up Kristen. He had brought the whole band.

"Why?' I uttered, feeling totally betrayed.

Again, I was answered with laughter. "You probably think I'm angry and just getting even for screwing around with my boyfriend. You're wrong. I loved it. I loved watching you walking around all starry-eyed. I loved sitting in Robbie's car across the pond and observing Steven's magnificent performance. I got off on it. Did you really think you are actually important enough to even make a ripple in my world? Well, you aren't. You were only given a taste of our lives to make you so malleable, so open to suggestion. We needed you to behave erratically, even more so than normal. We needed you to keep up the secrecy, couldn't have anyone making the connection between Steven and you. But most of all, we needed you to fully trust Steven." She paused to reach in through the car window. Pulling out her own backpack, she dove in and began passing out more wickedly serrated blades. Steven popped his trunk and removed a long length of coiled rope, while the two Katies stepped aside to reveal a mound of rocks.

"We are doing this, well ... because we can ... because we enjoy it ... because we haven't been caught yet," he said, grinning.

Everyone began cackling maniacally, like some perverted evil laugh copied from some cheesy horror movie.

Gradually, Michael's grip got tighter and tighter, crushing my lungs so that inhaling became impossible. Dark spots began swimming in my peripheral vision.

I can't breathe… I'm blacking out…I can't brea—

***

I'm breathing. I thought I was dead, but I'm breathing.

I slowly open my eyes.

I'm in a hospital bed with the privacy curtain fully surrounding me. The lights above are blinding and send shooting pain through my head as I try to assess the damage. A thin white blanket covers my body. I try pushing myself into a sitting position, but I can't move my hands. I wiggle myself enough that I uncover them from the blanket and …

There are big leather cuffs around my wrists.

31

I am restrained to the bed. I try kicking off the covers and realize my feet are secured as well.

"What the hell is going on?" I begin to call out, hearing how rough and scratchy my voice sounds. "Oh, my God! They were trying to kill me!"

I start crying, and screaming, as the realization takes hold. Loud wracking sobs that cause my chest to heave and my nose to run, begin to emanate from my mouth like an air-raid siren. "Someone ... Anyone... Help me!" I screech.

Finally, a nurse appears as she parts the curtain. "You're awake," she states in a monotone voice as she quickly takes my vital signs. I bombard her with questions.

"What happened? How did I get here? Where did the others go? Why am I tied down?"

She ignores all of them with a curt - and chilly - statement. "The police are waiting to speak with you." Then, she vanishes through the single open in curtain.

The police?

They must have interrupted the Stepford gang's plot to kill me.

A strange man, wearing a rumpled navy suit with a gold badge clipped to his belt, appears, dragging a chair with him through the fabric doorway. He doesn't bother glancing in my direction once. Instead, he places the chair in front of the bed, in an almost delicate fashion. Sitting down, so that he directly faces me, he begins rifling through his pockets.

A small leather notebook appears.

He flips pages until he finds what he is looking for. Then, he looks for a pen. When he finally seems settled, he raises his stern face, dominated by hard brown eyes, and levels his gaze to meet mine.

"Ms. Woods, I am Detective Ash Murphy. I would like you to explain to me why you were found unconscious next Steven Barnes' dead body ... with a knife in your hands ... down by Old Miller pond?"

32

"Steven's dead?" I gasp. "How?" My question hangs between us like noxious smoke from a cigarette. "Where did the others go?" I prod further.

"Others?" He looks and sounds puzzled. "There was no one else there. No signs of others on the scene."

"Kristen, Michael, Kelly … the rest of Steven's football buddies and their girlfriends. They were going to kill me!" I'm shaking with a mixture of fear and outrage. "They have been torturing me by … forever. Steven pretended to be attracted to me. He lured me to the pond! He then left only to return with his gang … They all had knives … I was pinned down, I couldn't breathe, I blacked out … I thought I was going to die! Then, I woke up here, restrained to this bed!"

The cop looks at me like my head had just cracked open and a flying saucer had come out of it. He looks down to his notebook. Then, he gravely says something that sends cold shivers down my spine.

"Steven Barnes was on the football team, yes. But he had no friends, no girlfriend … besides you, according to your classmates. He was a loner. Exactly how they described you. You stabbed the 'love of your life' sixteen times. That's where you were found, lying next to his body, covered in his blood."

No friends, no Kristen?

They aren't a figment of my imagination. I didn't make this all up …

Or did I?

The implications of that thought send me off screaming again. It's a long-tormented animal-like wail that sounds alien and distant, as it is not coming out of me, but from someone else; someone I don't know. It makes me mad. I want it to stop! Someone has to stop that horrible cry!

It's endless.

Until the nurse reappears, rushing in with a syringe. She jabs the needle into my shoulder.

The last thing I hear before fading into a much welcomed oblivion is the voice of the cop reading something on his notebook.

"… having daydream-like delusions for quite some time now."

"To the Lord of Washing Up - Don't ask"

'You, *whore*!' Agnes bellowed, jabbing a finger at the obscurity. 'You, evil grotesquery whose thirst has no end. You just couldn't leave him alone, could you? All those men you lured to your bosom...there just wasn't enough of them, was there? You had to have him as well. And now? Do tell me... How does that make you feel, uh? Are you cheering, deep inside, at yet another conquest, or have you ditched him and moved on to your next target already?'

The silence returned no answer.

Agnes sat down, unscrewed the bottle, and took another large swig of the whisky she had brought with her. The cap slipped from her trembling fingers. 'Argh! Shit!' she spat as her hand felt around under the seat. She quickly gave up, opting instead to revel in warmth brought on by the alcohol. She thought her courage would increase tenfold. She was wrong.

A flood of tears welled up in her eyes.

'Do you care how *I* feel?' she choked. 'Probably not, ha! Well, let me tell you...' Agnes paused, summoning all the strength in her to say it, to face the reality she had been avoiding all this time.

'You have killed me too.'

And like a dam breaking, rage and despair hurled out of her, ripping her body to pieces.

There. The truth was out. Those tough scales she had patched herself up with, that fake display with the face of a woman full of fortitude and resilience despite being struck hard by the loss of her husband, all had tumbled like a tower of cards. This tiresome game of pretence was no longer necessary. And suddenly, not from the effects of drinking but from the sheer violence of coming to terms with the fact that her own life too had been robbed from her, Agnes collapsed, sobs rippling through her body in endless waves.

'Oh, Georges,' she mumbled, 'how could you do this to me? I was your wife, your sole family, your one and only true friend. And you dumped me at every opportunity to be with your other love. I never stood a chance, I should have known. But no, like a sick puppy, I trailed behind you, and begged for the attention that was due to me, in vain. I supported you, comforted you, and took blow after blow, not once biting back. How pathetic of me, I see that now.'

Nausea started to make her insides uncomfortable. Agnes shifted to her side and, her head propped on her left arm, she caressed the wood with the pad of her right index. Very easily, Agnes conjured up a vision of Georges' weathered face, the image as flat as the floor. Her digit slowly moved along the largest wrinkle on his forehead, and lovingly stroked his temple. Then it stiffened, and she dragged her nail across his cheek until it drew blood. A scraping sound broke the lull.

'It's a real shame I only grasp now how badly love screwed me, unfortunately. I should have whipped your backside into taking better care of me right from the start, Georges.' Her jaws tightened, and full of conviction, she groaned, 'So bad you'd have never strayed again.'

The satisfaction of finally uttering the words she'd refrained from saying for so long mingled with the heat of the spirit swirling through her veins, and sent her head into a spin. Agnes closed her eyes until the sensation subsided. At least, in her current position, she was in no danger.

'How did it all come to this, Georges? I remember the day I first set my eyes on you. You paid me no heed for quite a time, while I stared at your toned arms working the ropes that moored the *Gaoithe Sidhe*. Something must have eventually told you I was there, and that smile you flashed got me whirling on my heels and running away from a sight I have cherished for the past forty-seven years.

'That smile, you flashed it again when I said "I do". When I promised myself to you, body and soul, for better and for worse. I was yours, Georges, but were you ever mine?' she chuckled. 'There was only ever one love in your life. She was your passion, your obsession, your vice, your strength and your weakness. And, sadly, she wasn't me. Was there something I could have done any different? What did I do to make us take that direction?'

Unable to formulate an answer to her own question, Agnes resumed her tirade. 'Mother told me that was our lot, us women. We had to be good-hearted and kind, to tend to men's every fancy and need, to bake their bread, to raise their kids, to accept everything and never moan. Can't say I wasn't aware of what I had signed up for. Was it simply too much to ask for an "I love you" in return? Just one? No, because you'd have been the laugh of the town, right? "Emotions are for sissies," you kept saying – oh no, Big Strong Georges surely wouldn't be one of them!

'And so I was left to live my life with a marble slab for a husband, a life of the kind I would have never aspired to. I did my best to please you, Georges. And I certainly believed we'd be happy. But your coldness shilled me to the core—and you didn't once make an effort at kindling the dormant embers, until the fire died out. My body, my home, and my bed, all blasted into the Ice Age by your indifference. So, tell me, what was the point in our union, really?'

The discomfort of her screaming old joints seizing up on the hard surface disturbed her stream of thoughts, so she leaned on her back. Above her, the skies were putting on their best show; stars twinkled like diamonds in the darkest of the night, while angels called her to join them in their graceful dance.

'Haha! Give me a minute, my darlings. I'm not quite finished yet.'

The mirth in her laughter was genuine. Agnes couldn't wait. Surely, the world beyond was a thousand, a million times better than this one. Even Hell would be.

But first, she had to wipe the slate clean. That burden weighing on her conscience would only prevent her ascent.

Georges' trial had to take place; her plea had to be heard. And to be able to do this, Agnes had to shake the drowsiness that wrapped her in cotton wool. She propped herself on her elbows, and sat up, hoping gravity would somehow help her to remain alert.

Or maybe not. Upright being a more suitable position for drinking, she fished for the bottle that was lying beside her, and guzzled down what alcohol hadn't spilled in her fall. She coughed, cleared her throat, and clarified her voice before she continued emptying her bucket.

'A charming partner, a swarm of noisy children, smoke coming out of the chimney, and the lovely smell of stew emanating from the kitchen windows. That's what you wanted, and I wanted it too. If only they knew how you started to treat me when you realised I was not quite what you had hoped for! I'll admit it: I was young and inexperienced. But I was willing to learn. You slowly killed that enthusiasm with your grunts. "The bed sheets are rough", "There's a speckle of dust here", "Why haven't you dealt with that stain yet", and the most offensive one, "You smell, did you take a shower today?" *Gnagnagna.* How can I not say I'm not glad, sometimes, that your boisterous voice has been silenced for eternity? But why do I miss you so much, then?'

Agnes' fingers curled into a fist, and she raised it in front of her. 'Argh!' she rasped, 'I should have grown some balls and hurt you just as much! Maybe that would have knocked some sense into you!'

Now was too late, though. And regrets would not change the past. It was just her, and the present. Agnes inhaled deeply to bury her anger, and her trembling muscles relaxed.

'All along, I believed I had pushed you away. I thought it was my fault, Georges. But who could ever say it was?'

she asked. 'I know you loved your freedom and enjoyed your solitude; I saw how distraught you could become when you weren't in your element. We were supposed to be married, but what married life did we have with those long disappearances of yours? I was always on my own. Even when you were here.

'And I really longed for children, you know? Little cherubs that I would have cherished to no end, and who would have loved me back. Who would have filled my days with activities until I was exhausted, my heart with joy to the point of bursting, and my thoughts with worries and much needed hope. They didn't happen—how could they, anyway, since you were never around? You had once shared that same dream with me, but something changed shortly after our marriage. Did you realise that building a family would remind you of what you didn't have yourself, as a child? Is that it? But in that case, what did *I* do to deserve the consequences of your selfish decision? Why didn't you give it a chance—if not for yourself, for me? We could have made it work. We could have patched what was broken in you, I'm sure of it. We could have been happy, Georges. Ah, you and your stupid stubbornness!

'Or maybe I'm just fooling myself – your other love...she blessed you with the fruit of her womb aplenty, didn't she? Were you so content with her that you had no use for me? What was it, Georges? I've tried to ask you, but you kept withdrawing in your shell. Wasn't I worthy of an answer? What I wanted was for you to let me in, for me to be a part of you, as you would have been a part of me. But all I ever met was a wall. And endless confusion.'

Argh! You silly, rambling woman. Even though he's out of your life, you're still trying to understand him. That reasoning is falling on a deaf ear and you're heading nowhere. If you still don't know now, you're never going to. You're here for a purpose, after all. Don't forget it!

Agnes could no longer deal with the bitterness that had crippled her all that time. Against her better judgment, she needed to let it all out, then make peace with Georges. Had it always been that bad? She wasn't sure, but reminiscing over the past was not helping.

She could shrug it all off, maybe it was just one of those things. Sometimes, no matter how hard one tries, life has a way of not panning out the way one hoped. At least, she could absolve herself from any wrongdoings, and shed the guilt.

'Georges, I did care. Always. You weren't a bad man; you did well for yourself. Started from nothing, built a business, brought money home, provided for me. Except the one thing I needed the most. And believe me; I'd have tossed anything else for it without thinking twice. That's how much you meant to me.

'But *she* was the one that occupied your heart and thoughts. You came home to me, but you were counting the minutes before you could get back to her. You listened, but your mind was always in another place.

'So many times, I visualised myself packing my bags and leaving you. Waving goodbye to a life I abhorred. Getting free of that prison, walking away from it, and not once looking back. And then you'd pass the threshold, find an empty place, and fall to your knees, at a complete loss. Gah! Damn you, misleading dreams, for making me stay!

'It's all clear as crystal now. I was never a match. She was more beautiful, more understanding, less demanding. She never aged, never turned bitter, never questioned you or barked at you. She mesmerised you with her blue eyes, lured you with her song. And she always welcomed your presence with open arms, even when you had become a wreck of a man in your final days.'

Agnes wiped the tears from her face and snorted.

'Georges, I can't deal with the fact that you wouldn't have me by your side when you died,' she added. 'That you preferred to go it alone.'

Going around in circles was excruciating, yet pointless. So she decided to draw her own conclusion— the less painful one, the less enduring one. The torment had to come to a stop—that was her only way out.

'Maybe it wasn't you, Georges. Maybe you just weren't that strong after all.'

And summoning up all the goodness in her heart, a genuine 'I forgive you' escaped her lips.

The deed was done. Agnes sighed the lingering remainder of the tension away.

But instead of inner peace enveloping her, the fury emerged again from the depths, electrifying every cell in her body. And almost mechanically, the target shifted. Her husband had been innocent in all this; Agnes had determined so. That didn't mean she wasn't right in feeling that she'd been unfairly treated. Justice still had to be exacted.

'She had cast a spell on you, the bitch, and she knew you were hers. Look at her right now, sniggering at me!'

Lithely, Agnes jumped on the sitting bench as if to gain height before addressing her audience. She couldn't see who would receive her vocal message, but *she* would be among them.

'Well, I say it's time we finally get acquainted, don't you think? I was scared of you, but I fear no more—I wouldn't be here if I did. You were the shadow looking over my shoulder all along, but time has come to turn the tables!'

After the few seconds needed to find some sort of balance while her head spun around like the arms of a frantic clock, she brought the neck of the whisky bottle to her lips, tipped it up, and waited.

Nothing came. Her insides erupted. 'Sod it!'

With all the might left in her aged limbs reinvigorated by a newfound purpose, Agnes lifted her arm over her head, arched her back, and, like a spring suddenly uncoiling, threw the bottle as far as she could. Its descent was accompanied all the way by the shout of a warrior entering the battlefield, until her lungs gasped for air. The distant splash of the landing wasn't nearly as satisfying, but would do for now. It was only the beginning, and Agnes had a much better weapon.

Her own self.

Taking a deep breath, she straightened up, her posture tall and dignified. Her long, white hair floated in the light breeze that had appeared out of nowhere.

'Ha! If that's all you can throw at me, you're done,' she spat, before raising her voice. 'If you think that's going to make me run...well, let me tell you this: you're mistaken! I was a victim for too long, but now, I'm coming for you! Gone will be the days where I turned a blind eye to the power you had over my husband. You were a thorn in my side all my life. However, I'm going to die right here, and from now on, and for the millennia to come, I'll be the one in yours! I'm going to haunt you, and pester you, and make darn sure no one else ever goes through what I have. Mark my words!'

Agnes let out a boastful laugh. In response, the bench started to wobble. She anchored her feet to the wooden board and relaxed so her body absorbed the movements.

'Come on! Surely you can do better than that? Aren't you supposed to be temperamental and unforgiving? And you only manage to come up with ninny tricks that wouldn't frighten a newborn? Show me your wild side, I wish to go with a bang!'

Agnes waited a while for her ending. But no bang came.

That was the worst kind of insult.

'Fine, then. I'll do it myself!'

And with a flick of her foot, Agnes sealed her fate. The lamp fell to its side, and the glass smashed. Immediately, the oil was set ablaze.

Agnes observed, silently, as the flames licked the hemming of her nightgown then ignited her like a torch. She clenched her jaws, cast aside the pain, and determination filled her. She would deny her the enjoyment of her own suffering, if that was the last thing she would do. She had provided her with enough of that already.

Water, water everywhere... Nor any drop to quench the fire, Agnes thought, not quite sure why, as she invited death. *Good old Georges, you'll always be in my heart.*

As if summoned, a blurry shape appeared. Agnes narrowed her eyes to see better, and slowly, it came into focus. A dashing young man dressed in a navy-coloured Aran sweater and a yellow rain jacket walked to her, his right hand held out. Looking straight into her eyes, he flashed a smile.

Agnes climbed down from her makeshift pedestal and tiptoed over to him, her heart swelling. She felt her facial muscles loosen, and the corner of her lips moved upwards. 'Georges?' she chanced.

'I've missed you, Agnes,' he replied.

'It hasn't been that long, Georges,' she retorted, 'but it's been an eternity at the same time.'

'I heard you, Agnes. And I'm so sorry.' The guilt in his voice sounded genuine. 'Will you come with me?' Georges asked as he stepped to the side and swung his left arm to reveal a spot of bright light at the end of a long path.

'Where are we going?'

'To the most wonderful place you will ever see.'

Agnes stared at his open palm, intrigued and enticed. She delicately placed her dainty fingers inside it, and watched as he brought them to his lips. Then she looked up to him, and saw the smile widen, turn brighter, before he placed a kiss on her knuckles.

Georges nodded. 'Shall we?'

And together, they climbed over the edge of the rowing boat, and ventured on the path. It wasn't the ending Agnes had envisioned for herself, but she'd be damned if she threw away the chance of finally getting what had been due to her.

***

It was too dark.

In a thundery noise, the wave crashed, engulfed her, and sent her spiralling downwards.

Agnes punched and kicked and thrashed. Looked up to the surface, but the weight of her wet dress kept dragging her further and further into the depths.

She valiantly fought the urge to breathe. Until it became impossible to resist. In one big swoop, water invaded her lungs, the salt searing her bronchi. She coughed, and ingested some more.

And in the short moment before death dawned, Agnes realised that once again, *she* would make sure Georges and her would be separated.

Once again, the sea had won.

But Agnes wasn't ready to concede defeat just yet. The next battle was awaiting.

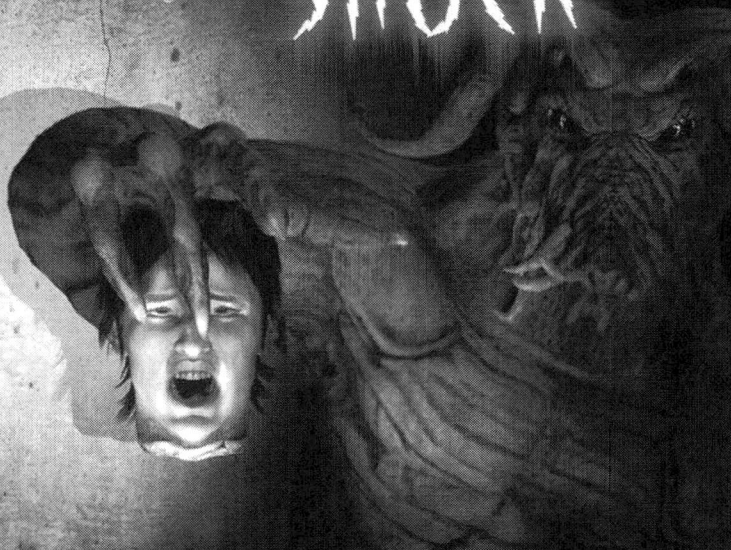

Daniel ran, his shoes slapping against the unyielding concrete, the muscles of his thin legs burning.

"I'm going to get you, you *faggot*!"

Daniel panted as he ran, chest heaving. He darted down an alley, then another, until he came up against a wall. He looked around, trying to see something in the darkness, some route of escape, but he was trapped. He turned just as Cameron came into view. The larger boy grinned.

"I've got you now, *faggot*!"

Daniel had always been the smaller of the two. Puberty had been much kinder to Cameron, leaving Daniel skinny and short.

"I know you miss me in the showers at gym. You probably jack off to me at night, don't you?"

Daniel stared at Cameron, trembling. He scanned the area again. The walls of the buildings were tall and shrouded in darkness.

"You ain't getting out of this one," Cameron pressed, then he reached for his belt, unbuckling, "You know you want it, so you're going to get it."

Daniel readied himself to make a stand.

There came a sound and then something else moved into the darkness with them. snatching at Cameron while making a low growl.

Daniel stood in shock, eyes open wide. He had seen *something*, some discernible shape in the darkness, something black and shiny. He wanted to run, but backed into a wall instead.

Cameron screamed once, a sound of pure terror, and then fell silent. Daniel crouched, staring into the darkness toward the sound of ripping and tearing, and then the shadow retreated. Cameron's headless body fell to the ground in front of Daniel as if flung at his feet. He screamed, then screamed again, tearing at the wall behind him in panic until he managed to free himself and run as fast as he could, hands clenched and outstretched as if to ward off an attack.

He did not stop until he got home.

***

Daniel silently watched as the police walked out of the small apartment. He had told them what he had seen and what he hadn't. There had been a statement after his father called the police, but now, or rather still, it was the same questions. But he had not seen anything, not really, and there was nothing that he could add. The fact that he had no blood on his hands seemed enough to satisfy the police that he had been witness as opposed to the attacker. At least for now.

"So many rumors about you, boy."

Daniel started and replied with a stare.

"I've tried to endure them, look the other way, be supportive, but it's just all about rumors with you."

Daniel continued to choose silence.

"I don't think it's natural, but if you want to be gay, then so be it, but now I hear these rumors of you doing something terrible to that other boy. Is this some jealousy thing?"

"I didn't kill Cameron," Daniel muttered, then added, "I'm not gay, either."

His father just stared, then rose from the meager table in their small kitchen and walked out of the room.

Daniel sniffled as he left the apartment and wandered the nighttime streets, his sense of sadness eclipsing any thoughts of fear. He gave no heed to the shadows, his hands tucked into the unneeded light jacket, eyes cast downward. He finally looked up when he saw the crackle of flames. He had somehow managed to wander into The Ward, an area of the city uncomfortably close to his own home, a place that had been taken over by transients. He noticed gatherings here and there, some areas that even looked as though bartering or socializing might be afoot, like some modern-day version of a gypsy camp.

He came up short when a thin girl spoke to him. She stood in what looked like dark rags, her hair as black as pitch, hanging in oily threads about her young face. She was filthy, but it was obvious she was female. Her voice sounded breathy, as though speaking barely above a whisper held immense difficulty. It took him some moments to realize she was propositioning him, offering to trade sexual favors for money.

His words stumbling, he refused and walked on.

A young man accosted him next, offering the same. Daniel shook his head and picked up his pace, moving deeper into the area and then stopped, exhaling deeply. Looking around, he realized he had become lost. He turned sharply when he heard the noise, a sort of odd scraping. He heard another noise, this one more like a rattle. He tensed, knees bending a bit, preparing to run, but he hesitated. Then came another noise, like whispered laughter, and he bolted.

"Where are you off to?"

He came up short to find a handful of the local denizens had somehow surrounded him.

"Hey! Why are you here?"

Daniel pushed, trying to flee from this small crowd.

"Watch it!" came one call.

A firm hand grabbed his arm in an iron grip, the bedraggled glove revealed the man's dirt-encrusted fingers.

"What's your problem, kid?"

"It's coming," Daniel managed.

"What?"

"It's coming," he repeated desperately with an effort to extract himself from the man's grasp. "It's coming."

"Bring him into the light."

The small crowd watched as a woman approached, a woman who despite her rags gave an impression of nobility.

"So, it's coming, is it?"

"You have to believe me."

"Oh, I do. I do." The woman nodded. "You're safe here."

"What?"

She offered him a benevolent smile.

"You're safe."

"I need to get out of here."

"Where will you go? There are shadows everywhere."

"What?"

"This may sound strange to you, but I know about a lot of things that most people don't," she began. "I know this life is just as much a curse as it is a blessing, but it's not always both at the same time. Karma isn't fickle. Karma isn't out there at all. People who try to put some morality on the universe are just fooling themselves. Do you think the lion is bad because it eats the gazelle? Is a typhoon bad only when it hurts people? Karma is for narcissists."

The small crowd offered murmurs of agreement, though Daniel had all but forgot they were there.

"What does this have to do with anything," Daniel asked, staring into the darkness.

"You know it's out there. You saw it, didn't you?"

"I just saw … the darkness."

"It's in the shadows," she offered, and he gave a shaky nod.

"What - what is it?"

"I don't know, but it's been here for a long, long time. Some say they've seen it. I never have, but it's been described as looking like an octopus or even a panther. Makes no sense. Seems silly, don't it?" She cast a smile on him, and he saw in her eyes that she didn't think any of this was silly at all. "Not from this earth, I think, and this is its haunt."

"It's a ghost?"

"Oh, no," she slowly shook her head, "This is its *hunting* ground."

"Wha-why?," his voice caught, "it hunts us?"

"Oh, yes," she answered with a slow nod, "It takes the head."

"Wh-wh-why?"

"Maybe it feeds on our dreams."

"I have to go." Daniel tried to leave.

"Not safe out there."

"I have to go anyway.

"You know where to find me." She nodded.

"Okay," Daniel muttered, turned and walked away, looking fearfully behind him.

"Keep those eyes peeled, boy."

"I will."

"Stay in the light, boy!"

***

The next morning, Daniel wandered into the kitchen, ignoring the half-full pot of coffee. He had barely touched his cereal when his dad came into the room.

"Where were you last night?"

"I was here," Daniel muttered.

"You went out, then you came home late. I'm a light sleeper." His eyes studied his son, waiting, but Daniel said nothing.

"Where were you?"

"I just wanted to take a walk. I- I needed to clear my head."

"The police were here," his father shot out.

"Again?"

"There was another one last night."

"What?"

"Another victim, another body found without its head. Last night. While you were out.

"You think I did it?" Daniel asked, his voice cracking toward the end.

"Where were you?"

His father stared silently, as though seeing him for the first time.

"It ...," he began, his voice catching in a hitched breath, eyes moving away.

"What?" his dad demanded.

"It wasn't me," he tried. "It was- it was something in the shadows."

"Something in the shadows?"

Daniel looked up fully into his father's face, steeling himself, "It was a monster."

"A monster," his father repeated.

"Yes." Daniel looked at his father. "I was talking to some woman and she said ..."

"A woman?"

"Yes, a homeless woman."

"A homeless woman told you there is a monster."

"Yes, she did," Daniel replied hopelessly.

"Go to your room."

"I didn't do it! You don't believe me."

His father sighed, "I don't know what to believe anymore."

"I swear! It wasn't me. It's some kind of monster."

His father silently pointed in the direction of Daniel's room.

"Dad?"

Weeping, Daniel retreated to his room, closing the door behind him, his eyes searching his room fearfully. He stared at his collections. One area showed six playing cards, displayed face out, all of them of intricate designs; another portion of a shelf revealed a small bowl packed tightly with exotically colored marbles. There were his science fiction action figures, and beside them rested seven polyhedral dice bearing ornate markings. In one place stood his grouping of three glass figurines that were made to look like ghosts. These were not scary, or even made to look realistic, with their lack of feet and necks, but the glass allowed them a translucency, their innards done to appear greenish, otherworldly. And one was gone.

Daniel froze. His father would not have taken it. With the same sense of certainty, Daniel knew the creature had done it. The monster had come into his room and stolen the figurine. A thing of shadows, a hunter of humans, had snuck into his bedroom and kidnapped a ghost.

Daniel stood there, fighting the growing fear, the threatening tremble. The thing knew where he lived, and he was left wondering if it had come while he had been out or when he had been in here sleeping.

He wanted to hide, but where could he hide outside the reach of shadows?

The old woman had offered safety and it seemed to Daniel, an explanation, however bizarre. At least she had believed him.

Opening his door silently, hearing his father from the next room, he tiptoed out of the apartment and ran back to find her, searching wildly. But he was found instead.

"What do you want?"

He stopped in his tracks, looking into the grizzled face of one of the men who had accosted him during his prior visit.

"I …," he began, but then the man was shoved out of the way, losing his footing and toppling to the ground. Another man stood there, this one taller, dark and lean in aspect, the layers of denim and leather on him seeming more a proud uniform than the tatters of refuse.

"Come with me," the man commanded, walking away, and with a glance to the other who still held place on the ground, Daniel followed.

They finally stopped in a somewhat secluded spot. The Ward was still quite visible, but they held sufficient isolation to warrant a measure of privacy.

"Alright, so you seen it," the man said.

Daniel stared back into the man's eyes, trembling.

"Well! Have you?"

"I s-saw *something*. I didn't get a clear look."

The man nodded.

"It looked like the shadows come alive, didn't it?"

"Yes!" Daniel's eyes went wide as the forced exhalation of breath carried the single word.

"I don't know if it come from Hell or some secret government lab or another planet, maybe even another dimension. That's stuff for Madeleine. I just know that it's dangerous, real dangerous, and it's here to hunt us, and I aim to kill it."

"Madeleine?"

"She's the one who saved your skinny ass last night. The one who took you in."

Daniel hitched, fighting the burn of growing tears.

"It's given you the *fear*. I can tell just by looking at you. It's gonna let that simmer, but it won't forget you. Being that thing's plaything is worse than being its snack."

"Stop it!"

"Look, there's a lot to take in, lots of history here, and I don't have time to tell you all of it. My name's Aldegar. What's yours?"

"D-Daniel," Daniel sobbed, "Aldegar? That's an interesting name."

"It means old spear. You'd have to ask my momma why she gave it to me."

"It's - it's pretty cool," Daniel wiped at his face with his fists, eyes shifting to the man and away.

"Daniel," Aldegar summoned, gaining the boy's focus, "I've been hunting this thing for years. Too many damned years, if you ask me, and it's marked you, so now, you're going to help me find it. And then we're gonna kill it."

"We are?"

"You look really scared."

"I am."

"Good, you should be." Aldegar nodded.

"What do you want me to do?" Daniel managed.

"It's marked you, I said. Think of it as a curse. It *likes* you, and that's not a good thing. It's going to come after you again, and we'll be ready for it. So, you do what I say, and you'll be alright."

"You want to use me as bait!" Daniel accused.

The man stared. "Not many choices you got here."

"And you really think you can kill it?"

"I don't got many choices neither." Aldegar shrugged. "Walk with me."

Daniel followed uneasily.

"I've been plagued by this damned thing for most of my life." He stopped, looking back at the trailing lad, squinting his eyes.

"I was around your age," he said, resuming the walk. "The police won't help, but I've got enough information of my own. I've seen the places where it's struck, put 'em on a map. I know its haunt."

Haunt ... there was that word again. And it had taken his ghost. Lost in his own thoughts, he almost passed his guide before he realized the man had stopped.

"What are you doing?"

"It's gonna rain," Aldegar predicted, looking up into the darkening sky as a shock of lightning coursed through the heavy clouds, the thunderclap announcing itself short seconds afterward.

Daniel looked up to see those strange eyes boring into his.

"Should we call it off?" Daniel asked.

"We don't get to call it off," came the quick reply, "Come on."

And the hunt continued.

A loud report of thunder sounded, and Aldegar jerked his head around, looking back from where they had come. "Shit!" Aldegar cried, and he reached out, grabbing at Daniel's arm, then with this tenuous hold, he took off at a run.

Daniel had trouble keeping up, stumbling behind and then being pushed into a nearby building. Aldegar shoved Daniel further into the small space, and then shoved the door closed, trying to secure it.

"What is it?" Daniel panted.

"It's out there!"

"Outside?" Daniel squeaked.

"I heard something and looked back, and there it was," Aldegar continued, "Hiding in the blasted shadows. Thing'd been tracking us for no telling how long, curse it!"

Daniel pressed further back, face pale and eyes staring.

"I'm going to check outside."

"No, don't!" Daniel panicked.

"This door still has a bolt, so don't worry," Aldegar gestured to the rusted piece of metal, "I'm just going to look out the window."

Aldegar, tall as he was, had to stand on his tiptoes and grip the frame of the opening to pull himself up enough to get a good look.

"Be careful," Daniel whispered quietly.

Minutes passed. Thunder rumbled. Illumination shattered into the room on the heels of lightning bolts.

"Aldegar?"

The pitched whisper garnered no response.

Daniel reluctantly walked to where Aldegar stood at the window.

"Hey?"

There came no answer.

Daniel touched Aldergar's shoulder, causing the man to fall from his perch, his body tumbling to the ground.

Daniel darted back but he managed to strangle the pending scream. Most of Aldegar's face was gone, leaving behind what looked like ground meat. The thing may not have taken the entire head, but it had taken enough. The skull was empty.

"A-Al-Aldegar?" Daniel pointlessly whispered.

Daniel looked at the window. The bars were still there. The darkness still lurked. Was the thing just outside, munching its meal, ready for a second course?

He had to get away, but how? How could he escape the shadows? How could he avoid the screams?

Daniel heard a heavy *slither* against the concrete wall.

Being that thing's plaything is worse than being its snack.

There came the sound of laughter from outside of the building.

He dropped to his knees next to the corpse, patting over Aldegar's clothes. He was not surprised when he found a knife. It looked sharp and ready. Perhaps he *could* fight. Daniel looked at what was left of Aldegar and then at the window, his hand shaking.

There once again came the guttural sound of laughter that seemed an echo in the darkness. Daniel held the knife, unsure of what to do with it, his chin resting on his chest as he sobbed, while outside the rain pelted down, uncaring.

How long he knelt there he could never say, but he screamed when the door finally burst open. The police moved into the room, following the lead of their flashlights and pistols, finding him there – a young boy, holding a knife, kneeling beside a man with hardly any face left.

***

55

He resisted but it was a paltry effort. Time began to bleed together, feeling less and less distinct. He finally snapped out of it when he realized he was in restraints, being walked down a brightly-lit hallway. He should have found the lack of shadows comforting, but something rose in him, a sharp bite amidst the constant gnawing. He tensed, planted his feet, pushed back.

"Come on, Daniel," one of the large orderlies chided him in an oh-so-friendly and casual way, as if they were the best of friends.

He was locked in the room, his protests fruitless. He looked around, and he noticed how much darker it was in here than the hallway. He didn't see any lights.

There was a window high up on the wall, too far for him to reach, but it did allow light to pass through. But what would happen when the sun set?

"No, no, no, no," Daniel said, then wailing, "no, you don't understand!"

Was that a slither? Did he hear a gurgling giggle?

The sun continued its inexorable march to the horizon, and Daniel screamed as the shadows joined him inside of the locked room.

*This story is dedicated to all of the people over at Zombiefiend who have supported me
in my writing for the last few years & also; to the people who were a part of the first ever online
Role Play that I participated in as that was the inspiration for the world this story is set in.
A special mention to Joy Killar, without whom there wouldn't have been a platform for me to write on..*

PROLOGUE

Strange noises and movement came from the shadows of the mostly empty building site. These were the sounds of feral creatures on the hunt for fresh meat. Growls, moans, and shuffling steps going over a dusty and rock strewn floor went unnoticed by the lone security guard on shift that night, Graham; who was sat flicking through his social media profile on his smart phone, headphones on and rap music filling his ears. A normal routine for him on the night shift since nothing ever happened on it. There was nothing exciting, nothing strange and nothing offensive...just nothing.

So the skinny nineteen year old would sit and do what nineteen year old's did in the digital age, blind themselves to what is going on around them with their phones, tablets, and computers. The growls slowly grew louder as the footsteps drew closer, but Graham was deafened to it by his music.

When zombie apocalypse scenarios were mentioned in film or literature and the idea grew popular, people argued that 'someone would notice it surely?' and 'They are too slow and clumsy to cause a *real* problem'. But of course, the irony of this was that these comments were made on viral videos online by people who didn't see what was happening outside their windows.

By now, the hands of a creature that *was too slow to be a problem*, were reaching through the open window of Graham's booth, clasping him and dragging him towards a gaping, stinking maw. More emerged from the shadows, the groaning getting louder and the feeding frenzy growing in number. It was too late. Graham's screams went unheard because he was the last living soul left in this town. If only he had glanced up from that screen...

CHAPTER 1

Sam stood and looked around the campfire, waiting for the adulation to pour in from the teens in his youth group.

"We wanted a horror story, mate, not a bloody cautionary tale," one of them said.

"Yeah, we live in a zed-apoc as it is, do we really need a reminder of how it happened?" another chimed in.

Groaning, they collectively got to their feet and wandered back to their homes in the safe zones of Salvation City, the only place left in Britain with living people still inside that he knew of. Sam ran a weekly youth group to try and give some of the surviving teens something to look forward to on regular basis. Everyone here had a job of sorts and it was held together by Mr. Raymond Saunders, a man who had been rich before the turn. He had seen it coming in the years before it happened, despite people calling him crazy, and erected a huge wall around his three thousand acres of fields and farmland surrounding his family manor in the country. Once that was done he built this entire city inside it.

The man's wealth was vast, but to achieve this feat, he had sold his stakes in all of his family's many businesses, and thus created the first self-sustaining community in the country using a combination of solar power and a large wind farm setup. Filled with housing, commerce, and entertainment; Salvation City was to the naked eye, exactly like the world before the turn. Sure, it lacked chocolate and exotic fruits and other things they took for granted, including cars, they instead got around on these weird electric golf cart things, but it was a safe haven among the dead and Sam loved it here. Sam doused the campfire with water, and watched as the flames went out to be replaced with steam and smoke. Perhaps it was a little silly to use some of the reality of the turn in a 'horror' story, but this was the first one of his sessions to go badly for him so it wasn't the end of the world....well it was...maybe it was things like this that made him a bad storyteller?

Sam had returned home to his flat in the heart of Salvation City. The very center of the city was where accommodation was built and surrounded by its own walls, just like a gated community that only the wealthy used to occupy before the turn. Mr. Saunders believed that if the walls were breached, it was the outskirts that would suffer first. Since there were so many children and families housed here, he wanted to ensure their safety in that event, one of the many reasons he was revered as a hero by the occupants here. Because of this, the middle of the compound was like a gigantic estate filled with flats and houses of all sizes. In some ways, it resembled a holiday park with chalets and walkways connecting the properties together, which in the beginning Sam found hard to navigate, and built a real sense of community among the many residents. It was a great place to be and reminded everyone of the way the world was and could be again. It was these thoughts that eased Sam to sleep that night.

An alarm woke him the next morning at 6am and he rolled over to stop the ringing when all of a sudden it stopped.

"Rise and Shine," a voice said cheerily, almost causing him to fall out of the bed in shock. Lucy, the first person to talk to him when he arrived in Salvation City, was stood over him. She had a big smile that made her nose crinkle in a cute way and her red hair was tied up into pigtails and she wore her usual grey hoody, ripped jeans, and converse shoes.

"Get up, we've got work to do!" she added tapping him on the cheeks and flouncing out of the room.

Reluctantly he rolled out of bed and went about his morning routine of wash, dry, and dress. He opted for a black t-shirt and joggers today and pulled on his socks and shoes, electing to take one of his morning breakfast bars instead of cereal and grabbing his old Chelsea football club cap off of its hook by the door before leaving the house.

"So where too today?" he asked, putting the cap on over his bald head and stifling a yawn.

"Where else?" Lucy said, nudging him in the ribs playfully as they walked out of the community gates.

"Of course," he said rolling his eyes, "Ya know, this shopping centre will be the death of me?"

In response, Lucy just smiles brighter than before and they head towards the outskirts of the city.

It was their turn to do guard duty for the next forty-eight hours in a shopping centre just outside of the city where, when necessary, they screen new arrivals and ensure they are safe, healthy, and above all else, uninfected before they get to come into the sanctuary of Salvation. And it was the most boring job on the planet…...until today.

A quick stop at the guard post before they left the city walls saw them equipped with stab proof vests, sidearms, and their preferred weapons. Sam picked up his favourite shotgun, a Remington 870 Express 12 Gauge, despite being warned that it was terrible for long range. He had never needed it for distance yet, and that was due to Lucy's weapon of choice being a PSG1 sniper rifle.

She was a crack shot and usually covered him from afar whilst they were out looking for more survivors to bring in to safety. That is a job that Sam would rather be doing over the next couple of days, but no, they were stuck in the screening centre where nothing had happened for over three months now. No survivors had shown up or been found, meaning the place was becoming known for being just a boring patrol and lookout post in the wastelands outside of Salvation.

Sam and Lucy encountered nothing on the way there, a testament to the effectiveness of today's patrol? Or a point in favour of it being one boring day ahead?

They were greeted by curt nods from the two people manning the entrance, M16's over their shoulders as they took watch over the desolate car park surrounding the centre. They entered into the building and went straight up the now still escalators, down a side corridor, and then arrived outside the security office, knocking once and entering. The room was filled with TV monitors that hooked up to the CCTV system, occasionally switching to different feeds in an autonomous fashion; right now they were showing the delivery bays in the back of the building. Sat at the desk in front of them was a middle aged, balding man called Carl. He never left this place unless he was called to meet with Mr. Saunders himself.

"Lucy, looking lovely!" he said genially as entered, "Sam, have you done something with your hair?"

"Haha," he responded sarcastically. Carl was always partial to poking fun at people which he found made peoples day it a little brighter.

"How'd the group go last night?" he asked.

"Not so great, tried something different and it didn't work."

"Ahhh, well you can't win 'em all," he said cheerily giving him a pat on the shoulder.

Ain't that the truth, Sam thought to himself.

"Well, Sarge, where you want us?" Lucy asked brightly.

A question Sam was sure he knew the answer to....

Sure enough, Carl had put them on patrol throughout the building, to check on the other people on duty, and be filled in on the goings on over the last week. This roughly translates to; go and see everyone in the massive old shopping centre and be told the same thing until you get back to the security office to tell Carl, "Nothing new to report". Which is exactly what happened.

"Three hours," Sam muttered to himself as he left the security office for the second time, "Three hours it took to be told nothing at all."

"Quit ya moaning," Lucy said rolling her eyes. "We get to go on the roof now and keep a lookout!"

"Great news, now we can actively *see* nothing happen," he said with sarcastic thumbs up.

For the first few hours he was completely right. Sat on the roof and looking out over the empty car park, they saw nothing but a stray fox rummaging in one of the big bins below. Lucy was having a whale of a time though, picking out details on the trees that bordered the edge of the western most side of building. They were around an hours walk away from Salvation City and about fifteen minutes from a small village, which always made Sam wonder, *why the hell would anyone build a shopping centre way out here in the middle of miles of fields and woodland? It can't have made much money before the turn surely?*

"Hey ho, what's this?" Lucy asked, binoculars up to her eyes and entirely unaware of what Sam had just said. He didn't bother looking up, reckoning it was nothing more than a badger or something coming out of the woods. But then... "That's an actual person," Lucy said in awe.

"You sure it's not a dead one?" Sam said, still not endeavouring to get his hopes up.

"Nope, definitely a breather."

"Let me have a look," he said, getting up and dusting himself off. He took the binoculars up to his eyes and looked in the direction Lucy was indicating.

"Holy crap you're right," he said, spying a woman emerging from the tree line. Picking up the radio given to them by Carl, he thumbed the send button, "Breather incoming from the west. Female."

"She certainly doesn't look like nothing," Lucy said happily as the boys below acknowledged the message.

***

Far from sitting down, Sam was now pacing the roof in frustration. The first thing to happen here in three months and they didn't even get to see it? The woman had made it so far towards the men on the door below before collapsing, which caused them to rush to her aid. Once she had been carried inside, that was the last they knew of what was going on.

"Calm down fidgety man," Lucy said, with a mild look of concern. "I'm sure she's okay down there."

But Sam didn't hear her, he had checked his watch and someone should have been up ten minutes ago to swap shifts, but just then roof door opened and two of the women from his first round in the building walked out.

"Time to tag out," the older of the two said. Sam moved quickly down the stairs with her calling after him, "Don't you wanna know where you are next?"

But Sam wasn't interested. He and Lucy spotted this woman and he would be damned if they weren't in on what happened next. They had set up a makeshift infirmary in what was once a pharmacy, and that is where Sam was guessing the woman had been taken.

Sam arrived at the Infirmary ahead of an out of breath Lucy who had been struggling to keep up.

"Alright hold up a second," she panted before he put his hand on the door. "What exactly do you think you're missing in there?"

"Let's find out," he said impatiently but Lucy put a hand on his shoulder to stop him.

"Do you really find the job that boring?" she asked, her freckled face crinkling in concern.

"Here? Yes," he replied shortly and pushed the door open.

Carl was standing next to Dr Stephanie Burns, a friend of Mr. Saunders from his youth whom he had convinced to move to Salvation before the turn took place. He wanted her to care for the people in his newly established community and she was one of two people with medical experience currently residing Salvation City and the only one ever stationed in this building. Right now, she was giving the new arrival a check over.

"No bites, or wounds to speak of," she was saying as she examined the woman. "However, she does appear to be severely malnourished and dehydrated. There's no telling how long she's been out there alone."

"So she's clean...figuratively speaking," Carl added, noticing the grime and muck covering the woman's hands.

"Yes, and she needs to rest. When she wakes she will need food and water."

"Wow, full TLC from Doc Burns. Maybe I should stop eating for a day or two," Carl joked, giving her an overplayed wink.

"I wouldn't recommend it," she responded, clearly missing the joke as she finally noticed Sam and Lucy standing in the room, "Can I help you?"

"We were the ones who spotted her, thought we'd drop in and check on her," Sam said calmly, "See if we could lend a hand."

"Only because you find...," Lucy began but Sam cut her off with a stamp on the foot. "Ow!"

"New people interesting, you're right, Lucy," he finished her sentence for her.

"No respect for peoples toes though," she said pouting and bending down to massage her foot.

After a search of her pockets, Dr. Burns discovered a driver's license that told them the woman's name was Jane Smith and she had lived in London before the turn. It had been over a year since then, and yet people still kept things like wallets and identification with them, maybe out of habit, maybe out of a sense of hope that the world would right itself. Either way, it made it easier to identify people or prove who they were. It didn't help them wake up any sooner though.

Sam had been instructed to check the medicine stock in the back whilst Lucy assisted in keeping the unconscious Jane's temperature down. He realised quickly that this was no less boring than before and was mentally been kicking himself for being so curious. But maybe the wait would pay off when this Jane woke up again. It was an hour before the stock check was completed and Sam, his head was whirring with all the different drugs names like *Co-Drydamol* and *Amoxicillin*, ventured to the good doctor to see how things were going.

"Stock check is done, and your numbers seem okay," he reported. "Plenty of antibiotics and painkillers from what I could gather. Don't ask about the rest of it though, I couldn't tell a lot of the names apart."

"I'll look through the check list later," she responded idly and sat herself at her desk. "It's the first time I've had anyone in here helping since that last load of survivors from Yorkshire showed up last year, so anything is appreciated. "

"Really?" Sam responded in slight shock.

"That's awful," Lucy said looking up angrily.

"Oh, it's fine really, nothing but some scrapes and bumps since then to treat," she replied waving the notion away like a bug buzzing around her head. Jane stirred and mumbled something incoherent causing everyone to look round at her. Then, just as they thought she was settling down again, she sat bolt upright and grabbed Lucy one handed by the throat...

CHAPTER 2

As quick as a flash, Jane had gotten behind Lucy and restrained her, one arm under her chin in a sleeper hold and her other hand restraining an arm. She moved lightning fast and with precision, clearly trained in what she was doing and still strong despite her undernourishment.

"What's happening?" Jane asked in a hoarse voice, "Where am I?"

Sam had whipped out his sidearm, as his shotgun was too far away by Dr. Burns desk, and had it trained on the pair in front of him.

"Put the gun away, there's no need for it," Dr. Burns said calmly. "My name is Doctor Stephanie Burns, and this is Sam Cooper. You are at Salvation City's outer screening centre. You collapsed outside the building, so we brought you inside to help."

The woman looked scared, her eyes darting between Dr Burns and Sam, who had now sheathed his pistol and put his hands up to show her his empty palms.

"If we're making introductions, the person you're choking is Lucy Turner," Lucy piped up in a slightly strangled voice due to the arm around her throat. Jane let her go slowly, keeping her eyes on them as she did so, clearly still wary.

"Sorry," she said in her hoarse voice. "Couldn't take the risk.....being followed....water."

Dr. Burns crossed to her desk, took a bottle of water off it and handed it to Jane who gulped it down like she hadn't drunk in years.

"Who's following you?" Sam asked as Lucy coughed slightly and massaged her throat. The look that Jane gave them in response sent a cold shiver down Sam's spine; it was a look of pure hatred....

Jane, after taking a deep breath and appearing to swallow the hatred down, started right from the beginning. "I was in London when the turn happened; with friends in a high rise block of flats.

We survived there until the power grids went out and then we knew we needed to move on. There were six of us to start with, but as the months rolled on that number dwindled. We lost John to the dead, Kim to infection, and Caroline killed herself."

Sam could see that these losses were affecting her deeply. He had lost his friends too, but he hadn't seen it happen before his eyes. Jane, it seemed, wasn't so lucky.

"The three of us left kept on moving, but we were low on food and water and it wasn't long before it ran out completely, that's when we came across them. They were a roving band of survivors that preyed on others. They had weapons, supplies, and numbers. They got us while we slept. Beat us, tortured us, then took our stuff. We thought they'd left us for dead, but really... they were giving us a head start. That was a few days ago." Jane paused for minute, looking down. Was she ashamed?

Sam was willing to bet that these people were the reason they'd stopped seeing survivors around here. But did they know about the screening centre?

"They've been hunting us. They got Craig yesterday and then Will gave up... judging by the screams, the dead got him. I don't know how far behind me they are, but they're coming," she finished, looking upset but determined at the same time.

Sam, Lucy, and Dr. Burns exchanged looks at this and then Sam left the infirmary, heading at a run to the Security office. It seemed like Jane hadn't come alone, she'd brought a shit storm with her....

***

Carl called back the patrol currently in the wastelands out of precaution and by 6pm that evening the watch on the roof had been bolstered and the front doors barricaded. Lucy was the best shot there, so she had been put upstairs too.

Dr. Burns' infirmary had been locked down and she was moved up to the security office with Carl for protection. Jane was offered the same treatment, but she

67

refused. Far from scared of the prospect of these people showing up, Jane had been eager to confront them if they broke in; keeping herself on the ground floor. Sam, however, didn't know how he felt. He had wanted something less boring to happen, not have an armed band of thugs trying to storm the place.

The plan in place was to keep their heads down whilst being vigilant for the group that Jane had encountered. The screening centre, from the outside, looked like the abandoned Shopping Centre that had been before they occupied it. Carl hoped that would be enough to have the gang pass it by if they came across it, but Sam was dubious. If he was part of a roving band of survivors and came across a place like this, he would have ransacked it for supplies. But here he was, on the ground floor with a few other men and a furious, scorned stranger armed with the shaft of a sweeping brush.

If she was going to take them on hand to hand, then she was more pissed off than Sam had been in his entire life. But even if he was boiling with rage, Sam knew he'd still prefer his 12 Gauge to take a large group on. Carl's voice came through his walkie.

"Heads up people, we have some zed's incoming."

Jane lifted her head suddenly, staring hard at the door, "Ask him if they have guns," she said.

"The Zeds? Why would they have…" he began

"Just do it," she snapped back.

"Carl…do they have guns with them?" he asked, thumbing the send button

"Why would they have…..yeah they do," he replied, his voice heavy with confusion.

"Then brace yourself," Jane said. "They're here."

***

It was truly agonizing waiting for the group to approach the building, but Lucy reported from the roof that they were committing to their zed act, shuffling forward slowly, weapons slung over their shoulders. She didn't want to draw attention to herself though so had only been able to peek over the side, opting not to use her rifle scope. Carl had no zoom function on the CCTV system and could only see them when the right camera feed was displayed. Sam was listening to the steel grey haired ex-army veteran that was with them on the ground. Sam thinks his name was Steve but he couldn't really remember.

He was whispering orders to the small group of three that would be the first line of defence against the people outside. Jane was at the forefront of the group, next to Military Steve, her makeshift staff gripped tight and ready.

Suddenly there was a thumping on the doors. They were testing them, seeing how sturdy they were. At least that's what Sam thought at first. Then the banging kept on coming, joined by more on the boarded windows with groans coming through in a low drone.

"Wow, they really are committed to this act," the younger of the two other guys said, almost impressed.

Sam slowly approached the doors, and peered through one of the boards across the glass. Snapping jaws and rotting flesh was all he could see through the gap. Holstering their sidearms, the lads approached the doors to peer through as well. It was then, without warning, that Jane struck.

Sam turned around in time to see the broom shaft strike Steve in the temple, dropping him like a rock. He tried to raise his shotgun but a swift swipe knocked it sideways and a loud blast sounded off, a shot hitting one of the others square in the chest.

With expert precision, Jane followed up her attack by sweeping Sam off his feet, his gun clattering to the floor, then launching a kick in the face of the remaining man.

Sam was dazed and his vision blurred after he hit his head off the tiled floor, but he heard the snapping noise and the thud of a body dropping next to him. He raised his head and tried to blink his vision back into focus, but a sharp pain erupted in the side of his face as Jane's boot connected with it.

Then blackness.

CHAPTER 3

Sam awoke, his vision still blurry and the right side of his face full of dull aching pain, and if he wasn't mistaken, was one of his back teeth missing? He was in the converted living space for the people on shift here, an old furniture shop full of beds and sofas.

"Ahhh you're awake," came a familiar voice from beside him. "I thought you'd never come to."

Jane then drifted in focus as his vision started to return to normal, that's when he realized he was tied to the bed he was on. He looked around and saw the other men also restrained; only they weren't themselves anymore. Snarling through gags in their mouths, these men had joined the legions of the dead. Sam struggled against the zip ties holding him in place.

"I wouldn't bother, you're not gonna get out of 'em," Jane said casually, walking around the side of his bed and sitting down in an armchair. "You're probably wondering about the cameras aren't you? Their feed is down. Nobody knows you're here and I've been feeding Carl reports with your walkie talkie," she said.

Sam couldn't bring himself to say anything in response to the woman, instead he just glared at her.

"Oh you're no fun," she said suddenly getting to her feet. "Usually people ask *why* or say *you'll never get away with this* or something. You're just boring." She walked over to the door of the old shop and opened it up, "I think

I'll go pay a visit to the security room. They might be a bit more exciting."

As the door swung shut behind her, Sam struggled once again against his restraints. He had to get out of here…

***

Twenty minutes of struggle had netted him some sore wrists, with some friction burns from the zip ties, but he was almost free with one of his hands. The man turned zed he had inadvertently shot through the chest earlier had managed to spit his gag out and was now snarling angrily in his direction, snapping his jaws in a fruitless effort to chew on Sam's flesh from the bed across from him. *Why had Jane tied them to the bed? Was she hoping to scare the crap out of the next people to stumble across the place by having a room full of zeds tied to beds in some freakish post mortem orgy looking situation?*

Finally, his left hand wriggled free and he rolled over, taking the zip tie on his right hand between his teeth. The zed next to him had started to rock violently now, his bed scraping and banging as he did so, but Sam didn't stop. Several minutes of grinding and chewing later and he was completely free of his captivity. Unfortunately, the violent lashing of Mr. Chestless had rocked his bed onto its side, the headboard breaking on impact with the floor, freeing the zombified man.

Instinctively Sam reached for his sidearm, but it wasn't there. "Of course it isn't," he cried in frustration as Chestless grabbed his leg and sent him sprawling to the floor.

With his former friend clamping his leg with a vice like grip, Sam struggled and kicked out with the other one. His foot connected with the zed's face twice, then three times before he relinquished his grip. Rocking forward into a sitting position, Sam then threw himself backwards into a roll that took him to his feet as the zed also rose clumsily and began shambling towards him.

Picking his spot carefully, he waited for the zed to lunge for him, then grabbing its wrist and putting a foot into what was left of the abdomen, he used the momentum to monkey flip the abomination and land on top. Sam began lashing out and punching the thing as hard as he could but to no avail. He was freshly turned and unlike those outside who'd emaciated and rotted, his bone structure and flesh was still sturdy.

Remembering something he'd seen in an old zombie movie, Sam took a chance and dug both of his thumbs into the eye sockets as it continued snapping at him, then finally something in there gave way and he penetrated straight through and into its brain, nails first. He kept going as the creature beneath him began to convulse before finally going still. Sam rolled off and onto the floor, panting heavily. He caught sight of his blood soaked hands, noticing the brain matter and had to swallow the bile rising in his gorge. There was no time to be queasy; he had to stop Jane from doing whatever it was she had planned.

Sam took one of the broken pieces of wood from the busted headstand and gave his two former comrades some mercy before leaving the makeshift living quarters. Jane had had a huge head start on him which meant that he needed to move fast. Running past the entrance where zeds were still banging to get inside, Sam bolted up the escalators and down one of the side corridor offshoots and to the security office. It was locked.

"Carl!" he called out, knocking on the door, "You in there?" The lack of response caused feelings of worry to settle firmly in his midriff. Were they still in there? Were they unconscious? Dead? Or had Jane moved them entirely?

Sam flew towards the access stairs to the roof, taking them two at a time and reached it quicker than he knew was possible. He burst out into a massacre, like a scene straight from a horror film, like most things are these days. There were bodies scattered across the roof, some still and being feasted on by the others, now reanimated. How the hell had one person managed this? The rest of them had been up here, ten people in total. How had one person managed to kill that many people on their own?

With a fresh spark of horror, he remembered that Lucy had been up here!

Without thinking he started forward, towards one of the nearest reanimated guards and shoved the sharp piece of wood he was still holding through its ear, a squelching sound erupted as it lodged itself in the skull. This got the attention of two more of the things and now Sam had no weapon. He didn't care, he charged forward, launched a thrusting kick into the chest of one of them, sending it careening into the one behind, the two of them falling off the roof and leaving a small silence until.....splat.

Three of the things remained, all of them ignoring him as they gorged on one body on the far side of the roof. He looked around and saw a crowbar on the ground, he didn't care how it got there, Sam took it and swung a vicious shot at one of the grotesque creatures, the spiked end going through its temple, causing it to crumple. The others didn't care; they were still intent on feeding. He wrenched it out and repeated the attack, dropping the second into oblivion and finally, the third looked up at him. Her pig tailed, red hair was blood soaked, gore dripped from her mouth onto that familiar grey hoody. Lucy snarled at him as he raised the crowbar again and struck...

CHAPTER 4

Sam would sit there for a good half an hour, the sun setting in the sky as he gazed down at Lucy's corpse. She was one of the kindest people he knew, wouldn't hurt a fly, and here she was now on the ground, in a pool of her own blood. She'd been murdered by a mad woman and left to feast on her friends as she continued existence as a monster.

"Hello, Sam," came voice from inside the building. "Are you still with us?"

He got to his feet, gripping the bloody crowbar tightly and ran back inside, down the stairs, and out the corridor. He didn't stop until he was looking over the balcony of the upper level of the former shopping centre and scanned for the woman who'd called to him, the woman that had taken his friends away.

"Oh there you are," Jane said again, and Sam realized that the voice was coming through the PA system.

"How's Lucy doing? She's been up there a while, she might be quite hungry....Too soon?" she added as Sam sprinted back towards the security office he had just passed, throwing himself at the door shoulder first and crashing straight through.

"You won't find me in there, Sammy boy," Jane's voice said, full of evil mirth as he frantically checked every monitor for even the slightest sign of her.

"You sadistic bitch," he muttered furiously as he glued his vision to the screens in a single minded quest to find her. He scanned them intently, waiting for the feeds to change, and as he did so he failed to notice the movement behind him. A sharp pain erupted in his shoulder as the teeth of a now dead Carl clamped down on his flesh.

He cried out with pain and swung an elbow back into the face of the former head of security, feeling a chunk of his shoulder tear off into Carl's mouth.

The creature dropped to the ground as Sam felt blood trickle down from the bite sparking a rage in him. He flew towards the downed zed and began kicking and stomping on its head. No humor or jokes to be heard from the mouth of Carl now, just a garbled, strangled groaning and snarling as his face started to cave, the nose popping like a cherry and the skull started to give until... squelch... Sam's foot went straight through, coating his shoe in fresh blood, brains, and bone fragments.

"*Now you're being fun!*" she laughed mercilessly as Sam tried to staunch the flow of blood from his gushing shoulder.

Tearing a sleeve off Carl's shirt (not that he'd be needing it now) and using some duct tape; Sam fashioned a makeshift bandage. He knew the infirmary had real ones but he didn't really have the time to get there. He needed to find Jane and stop her from doing this to anybody else. It was clear to him that Jane was nothing more than psychopath. She was thriving on the pain of the living and using her abilities to help bring that pain about seemed to be her sick calling.

Sam knew that he didn't have much time; the infection rate varied from person to person, but once bitten there was no cure, not even in Salvation City. The taunts over the PA were coming frequently as he searched, growing weaker as the sick game of Marco Polo continued until it hit him.

There were only two places in the centre with a PA mic, but Jane couldn't have known where to find it on her own, she'd been too busy killing and tying people to beds. Dr. Burns was still alive.

"You're getting warmer," Jane said teasingly over the PA as Sam went through the infirmary and into the stock room. When the place was just a shopping centre, every shop took deliveries through the warehouse out the back and you could get to this through any of the shop's stock rooms. There was another security office out there that hooked up to both the PA and CCTV systems, something that anybody who had spent extended time here knew. He reached the door to the warehouse and grabbed the handle.

"Let's see what's behind door number one!" Jane's voice sang out like some kind of demented game show host.

He opened the door and stepped out into the bitter cold of the docking bays where lorries used to be parked. Now it was completely empty and devoid of life, except for the thin woman standing just outside of the security office, a shotgun leaned against the wall behind her. Her lank hair had been tied back now and she had stripped herself of the overly large jacket she had been wearing when they *saved her*. He could see that her wiry frame was well toned, and he suspected that the gaunt face was due to choice rather than under nourishment like they previously thought.

"What do you think?" she asked, giving a twirl.

"I think you're a psychotic bitch," he snapped back and she gave him a look as if he had hurt her feelings. He now spotted Dr. Burns in the window of the office, but he couldn't tell if she was restrained.

"That's just mean," she said pouting. "I meant my body, not bad for a diet of wild animals and protein supplements eh?"

Sam had had enough. He charged forward and threw a punch as hard as he could, all thoughts of being infected and the feeling of weakness melting away as adrenaline surged.

Jane parried the blow easily and drove her elbow into his gut, forcing him to double over and stagger backwards. "You'd really hit a woman?" she asked in a mocking tone as she bent over him. "Not much of a man are you?"

Sam threw his head up and struck her under the chin; it took her by surprise and sent her reeling. He regained his bearings in time to see that Jane had blood trickling from her mouth.

The mocking ceased now as rage adorned the woman's face. She wiped the blood from her chin and flew at him at lightning speed, fists balled as she attacked mercilessly. He tried to keep his guard up but she was so fast that he didn't know where exactly to block. It felt like bricks were raining down on him from all sides now and he realised that this woman was bloody tough.

She'd backed him into a wall and was striking as hard as she could.

He did the only thing he could think of at this point and lifted his leg, stamping down hard on one of her feet. It was enough to create an opening and he used it to push her two handed by the shoulders, sending her sprawling.

He tried to press his advantage but she swept out his legs from beneath him and rolled atop. Jane took a knife from inside her boot and raised it, her knees pinning his shoulders down and preventing him from fighting back.

He was helpless.

"I was going to spare your friend and kill you quickly," she said fiercely. "Now, I'll just." She raised the knife above her head and Sam closed his eyes, waiting for it to plunge him into dark-ness.

BANG!

The weight on top of him was thrown off backwards in a spray of blood and brain matter, Jane's head was completely eviscerated. Sam opened his eyes and looked back to the security office door a few feet away where Dr. Stephanie Burns stood with his shotgun.

"I see why you like this thing now," she said in wonder, "bit of a kick though."

EPILOGUE

Fortunately for them, the commotion in the delivery bay had drawn the zeds to the back of the building, making the front entrance clear for an escape. As they began the journey back to Salvation City, the weariness had set in. It was dark now, the moon high in the sky and casting a bluish glow over the landscape. It was beautiful.

Sam felt the life draining from him with every step, a fever settling in and a dizziness starting to overcome him, but he focused on the task at hand. He needed to get Dr. Burns back to Salvation.

They didn't utter a word to each other, neither knowing what to say. The reality was that only one of them was going back into the city, and they both knew what had to be done. The spotlights from the city guards illuminated the ground before them as Burns identified herself, then the gates opened and a figure came out and straight over to them, embracing the doctor in a tight hug.

The man started to lead her back towards the gate and as she went through it, he looked back.

Raymond Saunders looked him in the eyes and Sam shook his head slightly, which was all he could muster. His whole body felt heavy and his skull felt like it was full of water.

Mr. Saunders bowed his head respectfully, a sad expression full of understanding on his face before looking back up.

"Thank You," he said in a deep, eloquent voice.

Sam nodded in response, saying nothing as Raymond Saunders turned around and went back inside the gates. The spotlights snapped off a moment later and from inside Salvation City's limits, as Saunders escorted Burns back towards his home, a single shotgun blast rang out. Birds flew from the trees and into the night sky as Sam Cooper joined his friends Lucy and Carl on the other side.

Collected tales of Madness and Terror

Maximus
SHOCK

An OMP Magazine

Issue
No. 6

IN DEATH, THE SPIRITS' CALL

The Horrors of War!

Emir Skalonja

To my wife, Nicole, for constant support and love.

Russia, 1943...somewhere near Stalingrad.

It rained hard. It was coming down much worse now than earlier that day; the sky had split open and let it all out; as if the Heavens wept for all the lives that came to an abrupt, bloody end.

Henrik saw it all in those few hours, more than he could ever wish to see. He was with his group earlier that morning when they stormed one of the Russian trenches and what was supposed to be a hard-fought battle, quickly turned into a one-sided slaughter. Burkhardt, easily the most blood thirsty son of bitch he had ever had a displeasure of meeting, opened fire on the Russian soldiers that had already dropped their weapons and fell to their knees to beg for mercy.

Burkhardt mowed them down one by one without even flinching; his face was stoic, no expression in his lifeless eyes as he held the trigger down and dispelled the hot lead into their bodies, shredding them to pieces. Only three soldiers fired their weapons while others looked on in horror.

The trench was filled with about a dozen bodies in a matter of seconds. They were all piled on top of each other. Those who tried to conceal themselves under their fallen comrades met their demise when Burkhardt began overturning the corpses, looking for survivors. Some of them, he even shot twice, even though they were long gone.

Henrik just stood there at the edge, his machine gun heavy in his cold hands.

"Something the matter?" Burkhardt called from the distance. He was crouched by one of the dead soldiers, emptying the Russian's pockets and in effort to find something of value.

"N-no..." Henrik stuttered as he tried to grip his gun tighter.

"You can do your duty, soldier, and make sure there are no dirty Communists hiding anywhere."

Henrik, after a moment of hesitation, nodded insecurely and fixed his helmet.

Burkhardt walked over to him, stuffing his pockets with whatever he had found on the dead soldier. "Have you lost your ability to speak, soldier?" Burkhardt asked and leaned closer into Heinrich's face.

His eyes were so blue, so perfectly blue, that Heinrich wondered if they were even real. There was something about him, he thought as he felt the man's hot breath on his skin. Henrik shook his head.

"Then answer with your damn words, you idiot," Burkhardt snarled and slapped the young soldier's helmet.

"Yes, sir," Henrik finally replied.

"Take two men and look for the enemy further down this fucking trench."

"Yes, sir," Henrik repeated and nodded. He fixed his helmet again.

"If I have to say it again, I will shoot you myself," Burkhardt said and gripped his weapon tighter.

It was at that moment that Henrik felt something wrong with the place, and knew that Burkhardt, even though a violent and sadistic individual, was driven by something else. There was a strange, dark force in him, something grim and sinister, though Henrik couldn't explain it even if he tried. He looked at his superior for a moment longer and nervously walked past him.

"You and you," Burkhardt shouted, "Go with him! *Now!*"

The two men he pointed at joined Henrik at once.

The young German soldier could see that the guys he was tasked with clearing the trench with had been just as nervous as he was. He didn't know their names. Was he supposed to? Why did it matter?

It hadn't been long before they ran into a scared Russian soldier who was curled up in a fetal position. He was a sole survivor; it looked like, what appeared to be German shelling, that might have happened mere moments before Henrik's division stormed into the trench.

The Russian's clothes were torn. He was covered in blood from the wounds on his arms and the side of his exposed ribs. The breaths that the man tried to catch were short, frantic and as Henrik came closer to him, his gun pointed up, he saw the wounds weren't serious enough to put his life in danger. They were merely flesh wounds: scratches and burns from the grenades.

"Get up!" one of Germans Henrik was with shouted. "Get up!"

The Russian slowly turned his head in terror and gazed upon them. It was now that Henrik saw the man had been missing one of his eyes. Well, he wasn't exactly missing it; it was ripped free from its perch and hanging loose outside of the socket, dangling there.

Henrik lowered his gun, chills running down his spine.

"You can't hurt me," the man said in a broken German. "You can't hurt me with your weapons. A bullet does nothing more but provide a mere wound upon my flesh," he continued and shook his head.

"What are you talking about?" Henrik asked, almost under his breath, not loud enough for the man to hear him over the gunfire that was sounding off in the distance, but somehow, he did.

"Once you look into the darkness of pain, you realize evil has been here all along. It holds us in its grip. We are but puppets in this sick game for its pleasure." The Russian had managed to get on all fours, then rose up on his knees to face Henrik and the other two soldiers. Henrik saw the knife the man was holding in his hand, just half way tucked behind his back.

"You would be better off to run away from this place…away from the evil that will consume you if you stay any longer." Tears ran down the man's face as he spoke, "I saw great destruction today of your men. It knows nothing of the colors of a uniform." He now slowly raised his knife, but not at Henrik. "Heed these words and save yourself," the Russian man said and then with one quick move, stabbed himself in the throat and fell on his side. He convulsed there as blood shot from his neck in thick and heavy spurts and when he bled out just enough, his movements subsided.

And then, as if his world turned upside down, Henrik saw what the man was talking about; his words were now a reality as the gruesome images played out before his eyes, a projection of horrors from his mind right there in front of his face. He saw the pain and suffering, the dismembered bodies, torture, and never ending grief. In a brief moment as he watched the dead man lie still, he saw soldiers shooting each other on a battlefield; men cutting off their own limbs, prisoners committing suicide by placing their pistols into their mouths and squeezing the trigger. Their heads exploded from the back, sending blood and pieces of skull and brain flying through putrid, disgusting air.

What disturbed him the most was the fact that they were all laughing as they committed these brutal atrocities upon themselves; they all died with smiles on their faces. Others had let themselves be tortured and killed by their fellow soldiers, some even willingly surrendering to the enemy.

"Is everything alright?" one of the soldiers called to Henrik. He made no reply, but only continued to stand there, staring at the dead Russian. Something was wrong with this trench; there was a strange and evil force about it, as if it was warped in another dimension, different from the one he was in. Now that he paid closer attention to it, there were no more sounds of battle. There were no grenades flying above the trench, no screaming of the dying soldiers, no bullets flying by, no tanks whirring about…

Everything somehow came to a standstill.

"You must end it," the voice came, and it didn't take Henrik long to realize that it was coming from the Russian soldier. Yes, his mouth was somehow still moving, his single eye blinking, staring back at him. "It is the only way out, if you not wish to be trapped here for an eternity."

Henrik nodded, now more calm, his nervous jitters long gone. His heartbeat had steadied. He turned around, aimed his machine gun at his fellow soldiers and fired. The quick burst of bullets went right through their heads, blowing bits and chunks inside their helmets.

The bodies fell down to the muddy ground right before him. Wasting no more time, he made the trek back to his other brethren where they had first entered the trench.

They were all there, sopping wet, exhausted. Some stood by Burkhardt's side, others sat on in the mud away from the pile of corpses. Henrik saw them looking upon this ghastly scene in terror. Many of them were contemplating desertion; he could see this on their faces. They were scared of Burkhardt. Hell, *most* of them didn't want to be here anymore.

This war wasn't what they expected; there was nothing heroic about it, the stories were all false, misleading. There was no fanfare, no sons of victory, just grim days and cold nights, both drenched in blood.

"Where are the others?" Burkhardt asked as Henrik walked to the pile of the dead Russian enemies. Burkhardt approached him and leaned in his face again, "I asked you a question!" Blood rushed into his face, seething with anger. He raised his machine gun and hit Henrik with the butt of it, sending the young soldier to the ground.

The hit didn't faze him. He slowly got back up and turned his attention to Burkhardt.

"Do you want to get shot?" Burkhardt asked as he pointed his weapon at him, his finger lightly touching the trigger, ready to squeeze it in a blink of an eye. "I will shoot you, but I will aim to maim, not kill. Then I will drag your body with me back to camp and will perform unspeakable things to it and you will watch me. I will keep you alive just so I can inflict more pain upon you as each day passes."

Burkhardt was possessed too, Henrik thought. Yes, it was the trench; even though Burkhardt was a violent and evil man, who only joined the army so he could satisfy his penchant for blood and killing, it was this place that was giving him that extra nudge to play out his most vile fantasies.

"So, you will answer my question,"

"No," Henrik said calmly then casually aimed his machine gun and fired the first shot. The bullet hit one of the soldiers sitting in the group away from the corpses. Burkhardt never took his eyes off of him, as if he didn't care about the death of his own man.

The others were confused at first, caught by surprise, but then pointed their own guns at Henrik. Henrik squeezed his trigger again and the machine gun blasted the bullets in all directions, shaking violently in his hands as the fiery lead zipped and ripped through the bodies of the soldiers standing before him.

And all while he continued to shoot, Burkhardt kept staring at him, not even blinking once. The expression on his face was disturbing, almost dead, devoid of any feeling or emotion. It was as though he wasn't himself, as if his body was a vessel for a far greater evil. The man probably enjoyed it, Henrik thought as he shot the last of men that were trying to crawl over the other side of the trench, toward Russian lines.

Their screams slowly subsided and then there was silence again. There continued to be no other sounds of war coming from anywhere. The air was still again, putrid and heavy. As each moment passed, this reality he was in, weighed on him more. It was as if this place was closing in and was about to crush him.

But there was something lurking outside this gutter, he knew it, and it was going to be there soon. It was far more terrible than the sadistic nature of man that he bore witness to over the years. He couldn't explain the feeling of dread; that something was out there, slowly squeezing in on them. The thought of it made his skin crawl. If he was still there by the time it got to the trench, he would meet a far worse end than at the hands of an enemy soldier. He might as well kill himself.

Yes, that was probably a good idea.

He could hear it coming. It was the ruler of this domain and nothing that crossed into its world stayed alive for too long.

Burkhardt looked at him blankly and spoke, "It's just you and me, you idiot. You will suffer now." His voice was flat, lacking any sort of emotion, as if something else was speaking through him. It could have also meant that he had come to terms with this place and that this was where he belonged.

The thing was close. It was almost there, the smell of it becoming stronger. Was that…sulfur? It had to be. Henrik's eyes itched, his throat was dry. He swallowed hard, whatever spit he had left, and clung to his machine gun.

"Your skin will be peeled very slowly, you idiot." Burkhardt smiled now and licked his lips. "Pain…like you could never imagine…" He shook his head and began pacing. "It will never end, until it becomes all you ever knew."

Henrik felt the sickening, demonic presence, but couldn't see it. It had perched itself on the edge of the trench and though he thought it was there, as a singular entity, he felt it everywhere, like a cold cloak of enclosing darkness, pain, and suffering. Those bloody images began to replay themselves again. Terrible stories of brutal torture and dismemberment where everyone was rather happy to cut up their bodies and willfully be shot in the head.

Henrik brought the weapon to his chin, but felt himself restrained, as if the dark force was holding him captive.

"You don't understand," Burkhardt said. "This is home. This is where we finally rest. It won't let us leave. You have to accept it. This is where we stop seeing with our eyes and start seeing with our mind. What the eyes don't behold is what the mind makes up, and for that matter, it is much…much worse. It is the absolute bliss."

Henrik finally managed to lift his weapon all the way to the bottom of his lower lip, and broke off the sinister hold. He looked at Burkhardt one last time and squeezed the trigger, fiery bullet blowing through his face, separating it from his skull in a quick burst.

He woke suddenly, from the morbid nightmare, hiding behind the wall of a destroyed building.

His heart racing, he glanced around to see his fellow soldiers from the trench there, all hiding and holding their rifles and machine guns.

Burkhardt was there too. He was on the ground by the window, a bullet hole in the middle of his forehead, his gun and helmet on the floor next to him.

Henrik watched him there for some time, briefly exchanging looks with the others. None of them knew. He carefully peeked behind the wall and at the trench in the distance, their ultimate destination.

It was there, waiting for them…

MAXIMUS SHOCK 7

Collected tales of Madness and Terror

Maximus SHOCK

An OMP Magazine

Issue No. 7

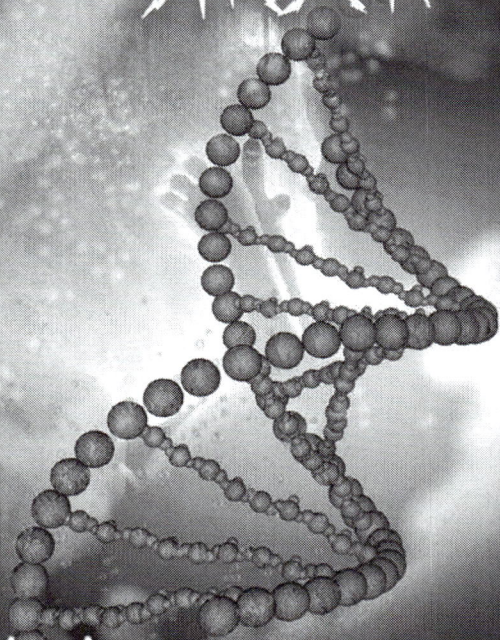

Mystery Science!

PROJECT 84

Ricky Fleet

Marc rubbed at his grainy eyes and let loose the yawn which had been building for the past five minutes. The genetic sequences laid out on the computer monitor were refusing to obey his direction. After their recent success, the board had ordered further splicing of transgenic material. His team had been working day and night for several months but had been unable to replicate the earlier experiment. As the time passed in a blur of data and failure, Dr. Borden was beginning to conclude that it had merely been a fluke. Needless to say, the upper echelons of the company were less than satisfied with the diagnosis. Their demands had grown into thinly veiled threats of funding withdrawal and promises of never securing tenure in the industry again. Each member knew the vast reach of their employers and the links to the highest levels of government.

"Please," he begged, crossing his fingers, "This time."

The DNA coding came back as invalid and Marc sighed, rubbing at the stubble on his chin. Christ, when had he last shaved? Two days ago, by the feel of the bristles under his touch. Only one more double shift lay ahead and the thought of a warm shower and a meal with his wife, followed by an early night in his own bed brought a weary smile. Being alone didn't help with his research, but with several of the other scientists breaking under the strain he had no choice. Four colleagues would arrive in about six hours and the sharing of ideas could commence again. Silence lay like a shroud on the laboratory and it was easy to go stir crazy in the sterile environment. Thoughts of leaving the building to find he was the last man on earth were an increasing burden and before he knew what was happening a handset was pressed to his ear.

"Is there a problem Dr. Borden?" Neil asked.

Momentary bewilderment at the unexpected voice led to a pause and the security guard asked with more insistence.

Marc shook the fog from his head and replied, "Yes, everything's fine. Sorry, Neil. I was just wondering if you want a cup of coffee?" It was a bizarre question and he could have kicked himself for even asking.

"No, I'm fine thank you, sir. Are you sure you're ok?"

"Yes, I'm sure. It just gets a bit lonely in here," Marc replied, feeling embarrassed by the admission.

A note of sympathy entered the guards voice when he answered, "Well you know we aren't permitted to enter the labs unless there is an emergency, but please feel free to pop into our office if you need a break, sir."

"I may just take you up on that. Thanks, Neil."

"No problem, sir. You know where we are."

The phone line disconnected and Marc felt a pang of despair as he replaced the receiver. God, he really was going stir crazy.

Picking up the plastic coffee cup, he was amazed to find it ice cold with a shiny film floating on top of the remains. Had it really been that long since a caffeine fix? No wonder he was exhausted. Standing up and taking the dregs, he swiped his card and exited the room with a hiss of pneumatics sealing the door behind. Navigating the corridors with the immaculate white walls and polished floor, his mood lifted a little with each pace toward the vending machine.

"Come to papa," Marc grinned as he approached the glorious chrome creator.

Tossing the dirty cup in the waste bin, he roamed his fingers over the buttons. Was he in a latte mood? No, that was a rare, milky pleasure. Feeling the subtle, but increasingly heavy pull on his eyelids, he opted for two cups of espresso and pressed the selection. With a whir and click, the internal mechanisms dropped a new plastic cup into the holder. In seconds, the black liquid started to bubble and froth into the container with promises of rich flavour and bodily rejuvenation. Rising tendrils of heat wafted into his nostrils and he breathed the aroma in deeply. Taking the cup, he pushed the selection again and sipped at his first beverage as the second begun to pour.

"Damn," he hissed, sucking in air to cool his burned tongue.

Blowing ripples across the surface of the boiling liquid, Marc started to think of what they could have missed. An oversight, a missing piece of the puzzle, anything that they could be doing differently. It was an inner dialogue he had been engaged in for weeks with no discernible progress. Removing the second coffee, he jumped in fright as the claxon started to shriek its incessant warning. Waving his scolded hand to cool the skin, a voice came over the speakers.

"Containment breach in sector 3B, all personnel are advised to stay in your designated safe zones until the situation is under control."

Neil's voice was all business with none of the earlier warmth. It was easy to see why and Marc's stomach was doing somersaults. Terror traced icy fingers down his spine at the thought of that *thing* being loose in the building. His laboratory was only eighty feet away but the door to the cages lay between them.

"Oh God, oh God, oh God!"

Feet surrounded by a black lake, his heart hammered and his hands visibly shook. The liquid holding him in its grasp could have been a prehistoric tar pit; he was no less trapped than the ancient beasts whose fossils were still being recovered to this day.

"Get to safety, Dr. Borden!" screamed Neil, racing past with three colleagues. Each had the Heckler and Koch MP5 raised and sighted down the long hallway.

"Sir, now!"

Neil had turned and rushed back, pushing him forcefully towards the exit. The contact broke the bizarre fugue and he blundered away, unfeeling of the burning sensation from the, now crushed, second cup in his hand. Squealing in shock, Marc felt desperately for the wall. Something had caused the lights to blow and the red emergency bulbs bloomed into life in the ceiling. In his dread addled mind, the halos of crimson were like hellish spotlights guiding him to the underworld. Slamming into the reinforced door, he swiped his card over the reader and wrenched on the handle. Illuminated by the ruby glow, Marc was unable to see if the lock indicator was staying red, or completely dead from the lack of power. Trying again and again, he was denied freedom by the security system. At least the wailing cacophony had also stopped with the power failure.

"Someone let me out!" he screamed, hammering on the door and waving to the camera mounted in the ceiling. If anyone was watching they were either unable, or more likely unwilling, to let him out. Knowing what roamed free, he couldn't blame them.

A series of shouts were followed down the corridor by the loud cracks of automatic gunfire. Relief surged through Marc at the sounds of lethal finality. It would mean an end to the research and give them a perfect excuse to get out from under the boot heel of their employer. There was no way they could be expected to continue trying to replicate the mistake, was there? Screams and more gunfire reverberated down the twisting passage and the terror clasped his heart in its clammy grip once again. Silence returned and the only sound Marc could hear was the blood coursing through his veins.

"Neil, are you there?" he called out quietly.

There was an answer of sorts, but too quiet to be understood. It could have been a cry for help, so Marc took a step forward on leaden legs. Closing on the first corner, he tried calling again. This time the reply was unmistakeable, and definitely not Neil.

Backing away, his eyes never left the corner of the wall and the white paint. A faint scuff was visible from the passage of a piece of equipment and it became a focal point, a talisman that could hold back the horror. If he so much as blinked, the spell would be broken and the creatures of Hell would pour forth to consume his eternal soul.

"I just want to go home," Marc whispered to the small blemish in the plaster.

In the periphery of his vision he noticed the straight edged silhouette of the male bathrooms. Sidestepping through the doorway, he imagined he could still see the mythical scratch. His eyes were starting to ache from the drying membrane and only when he backed into a cubicle did he dare to blink. Closing the door with exaggerated care, he then climbed onto the rim of the bowl and waited. Marc closed his eyes and concentrated on breathing through his mouth slowly. To his ears, each exhalation sounded extraordinarily loud even as his scientist mind tried to rationalize it as the enhanced perception of the human 'fight or flight' response.

A dreamlike trance descended and seconds seemed to stretch into hours as Marc crouched on the porcelain, staring at the cubicle door. His left leg started to twitch against the rim, making an almost imperceptible squeaking sound. His state of abject terror turned into paralyzing horror as the shadow of the outer door moved across the bathroom floor. A steady patter of droplets fell into the toilet water below, but he was heedless of the source being his own bladder. The heavy thud of footsteps rebounded in the confines of the room, accompanied by a deep, guttural snorting. Marc was trembling so hard he fell in a heap from his perch. The door crashed inwards, slamming into his shoulder and throwing him back onto the toilet.

Staring up into the inhuman eyes, Marc whimpered, "I'm so sorry. We didn't mean to make you."

Screaming once before he was torn apart in blinding agony, his dying mind thought of his wife and the meal that would never come. Then nothing.

***

"Sergeant Rankin from four nine two, come in. Over."

Sergeant Rankin sighed and pressed the transmit button on the police radio attached to his vest, "Delta Lima four nine two, receiving. Over."

"Four nine two, we have received reports of a disturbance at Pearson Global Technologies. A member of the public reports hearing an alarm and then screams from inside the grounds. Could you swing by and have a look while we try and reach their security team?"

"Received. ETA ten minutes."

Turning to his trainee, Rankin sighed in frustration, "There goes our peaceful evening."

"Screaming and an alarm? Could be interesting," replied Constable Walton with a grin.

"At this time of night it's probably just some kids doing shrooms in the woods which border Pearson Global. Wouldn't be the first time they've started hallucinating."

"It's happened before?" Walton asked.

"Twice during my shifts," Rankin confirmed, turning the ignition, "They start spooking each other around the campfire and the next thing you know they swear blind that monsters are real."

Shifting into gear, the squad car pulled away with a shriek of rubber and flashing blue lights.

"What do these folks do over there anyway?"

"I have no idea, but the security is tight and they have several layers of fence plus more cameras than a Paris Hilton paparazzi convention."

"So it's high tech stuff then?"

"No, they store furniture," Rankin replied, sarcasm dripping.

"Must be antiques then," Walton fired back with a chuckle.

The two men were chalk and cheese, but somehow the partnership worked. Rankin was a twelve-year veteran of Hampshire Police, and Walton was fresh out of university. Rankins education came from studying villains and patrolling some of the toughest estates in England, meeting people from all walks of life. Walton's degree in business management, however, had been designed to land a high-flying job in the city of London. The fierce competition for any work, even entry level, had been fierce. After spending every penny of a loan from his parents, he had accepted defeat and moved back home, filled with despondency. A suggestion of attending a police recruitment drive had borne fruit and within months he was finished with the training.

Rankin looked across at the Cheshire cat grin spread across his face and scowled. In a few years, and with the new fast track career policy for graduates, Walton would be his boss. Wouldn't *that* be a laugh. From snot nosed rookie, to upper management in a decade. Whatever happened to rising through the ranks based solely on arrests and hard work? What was it his wife used to say? The world's changing and he needed to adapt?

"Bollocks."

"What's that?" Walton asked.

"Nothing, just thinking out loud. We're nearly there."

At two in the morning the traffic was non-existent and they made excellent time. No cars waited in the laybys next to the wall of forest which partly surrounded the facility, so if it was youngsters they were on foot.

"It's really dark," Rankin mused as he turned into the access road.

"It is the middle of the night."

"I know that, smartass," Rankin replied, "But the place is normally lit up, even at night."

"Strange," Walton agreed.

Cameras silently watched their approach and the lenses flashed intermittently from the reflected headlights. The high set lamps which ran the length of the road were all out which only added to Rankins growing unease.

"Wait, look!" Walton said, pointing through the windscreen.

"Thanks for the tip, Poindexter. I never would've noticed the flashing torch beam waving at us to slow down."

"You know I'm going to be your chief inspector one day, don't you? How does permanent custody duty sound? All that sick and faeces to clean up."

"You can kiss my hairy ass."

"You won't be able to speak to me like that," Walton chuckled as they slowed for the guard.

"Oh, sorry. I mean you can kiss my hairy ass, sir."

As the signalling guard approached, they could see a second guard inside the gate pacing back and forth with a gun of some kind. A look passed between the officers and Rankin pressed the button on his radio.

"Delta Lima four nine two, are you receiving? Over."

"Four nine two, we're receiving, over."

"I have just seen a firearm. Can you scramble armed response to our position asap?"

"Four nine two received. The commander has ordered you to fall back and hold position until they arrive on scene. Over."

"Received. Over."

"We'd better get out of here quickly," Walton muttered as the shadowy figure approached.

"Shit, I can't turn around or I'll hit him," Rankin hissed as the man reached their window.

94

A cheerful face peered in, illuminated by the flashing blue lights. There was no malice in the eyes, but both men could see a pensive quality to the expression as he kept shooting glances back to the gate. Rankin sighed and pressed the button to drop the window and a cold gust of wind blew inside the car, pulling the smell of the recently smoked cigarette in with it.

"Good evening, gentlemen," said the guard, "I'm Bob Camoletto, head of security. What can we do for you?"

"We were just patrolling the area and I forgot this was a private road. We'll be leaving now, sorry," Rankin replied.

"Really? The sign at the entrance is pretty hard to miss," remarked Camoletto, "It's eight feet tall and twenty-five feet wide."

"As I said, I missed it," Rankin replied firmly, staring at the smiling guard.

"Look, there's no need to be coy. I know your protocols upon suspecting a firearm is in play, but we all carry here," he explained, showing a holstered sidearm, "We are fully licensed by the Home Office as a government contractor. I have all the relevant paperwork inside my breast pocket if you will allow me to reach for it."

"You're the one with the gun," Rankin replied with more sarcasm than Walton was comfortable with.

Seeing the disapproving look between the junior officer and his superior, Camoletto held his hands wide in conciliation, "You have nothing to fear. Your bosses response is understandable in the circumstances. If we meant you harm, we would've already opened fire."

Breaking into the disarming smile again, he withdrew the relevant licenses and handed them over for inspection. They were all in date and signed by the Home Office administration. Satisfied that everything was in order, Rankin handed them back and relaxed a little. Holding a finger up to silence Camoletto, he reached for the radio.

"Delta Lima four nine two, are you receiving? Over."

"Four nine two, receiving. Over."

"Stand down the armed response units. Further inquiries have shown all firearms to be fully accounted for and licensed by the relevant authority. Standby for an update once we have spoken to security. Over."

"Order received. Over."

"Thank you, sir. I didn't relish the idea of having a dozen guns pointed at me," Camoletto stated, placing the paperwork back into his pocket.

"I get the impression it won't have been the first time," Rankin suggested, "You've served?"

"The full twenty-two. Parachute regiment," Camoletto replied, "You?"

"Same. Twenty-two years in the Royal Marines before joining the police force."

"A commando?" Camoletto nodded appreciatively, "Pleasure to make your acquaintance."

The two ex-soldiers shook hands and Walton held out his own. Ignoring the proffered palm, Camoletto asked, "So what really brings you out to our dark corner of the countryside?"

"We had a report of a disturbance and screams from a member of the public. Do you know anything about that?"

"I certainly do. It was my men shouting to each other as they checked the generators."

"The member of the public specified *screams,*" Walton challenged, feeling insulted by their unspoken bond.

"Out here your mind can play tricks on you, junior. I can assure you they are mistaken."

"Then you won't mind us taking a quick look around will you, sir," bridled Walton.

"I'm afraid I can't allow that, gentlemen," sighed Camoletto, "This is a highly sensitive installation and our work is top secret. Only those authorized by the National Security Secretariat are permitted to enter."

"For a highly sensitive installation, I'd have expected better maintenance of the electrical system."

"And the generators too," added Walton.

Camoletto chuckled, ignoring the insinuating tone, "Tell me about it. The head of facilities is on his way in and I'll be tearing him a new asshole as soon as he arrives."

"How about an old favour between two veterans?" Rankin coaxed with a wink, "Just so I can tell my governor that we can close the job down as a simple misunderstanding."

"When I say that I would not only lose my job, but end up in prison for twenty years if I let you through those gates, I'm not exaggerating. Sorry."

"What if we came back with a warrant?" Walton pressed.

"Then I would be obliged to let you inside," Camoletto replied, eyes narrowing.

"We won't take up any more of your time. Have a good night and I hope they get the power back on quickly," Rankin interjected and they shook hands once more.

"I hope so too," he replied.

Neither policeman could miss the hint of fear in the words, but they didn't push the issue. Pulling a U turn, Rankin watched the figure dwindle in the mirror, staring after them and speaking into a handset. The glow from the rear lights cast a red hue over the guard, lending him an ominous quality.

"What was that all about?"

Rankin left the road without answering and came to a stop half a mile away.

"Boss?"

Finally acknowledging the question, he turned on the interior light and pulled out his phone. "I have no idea, but there is more going on than we know."

"What's with the phone?" Walton asked, seeing a web browser open.

"I want to see what the internet has to say on Pearson Global Technologies."

Hidden beneath pages and pages of corporate jargon and nonsense about a multinational ethos and global responsibility was a small newspaper article from one of the founders written in the nineties. With each passing line, Rankin's unease grew.

"What is it?" Walton asked breathlessly. It was the first time he had seen his superior rattled.

"Our friends back there are involved in some really shady stuff. Virology, biological warfare, chemical warfare, and genetic engineering to name but a few."

"And?"

"And… there's no way that a facility like that would ever risk a power failure. They would have backups for their backup's backup. Something's wrong here. Very wrong."

***

Alan's eyes shot open in the darkness. Was it a noise in a dream he had heard or something in the waking world? Nothing else manifest so he decided it was the former.

Staring at the ceiling, he could tell it was around three thirty in the morning by the depth of shadow. A farmer for fifty years, he was accustomed to early starts and would have been getting out of bed within the next hour anyway. Settling back onto the warm pillow, he turned to feel the space his wife once occupied. She had passed away over two years ago, but he still found comfort in gently rubbing the covers and talking to her.

A series of bellows came from the barn and he was out of bed and dressed in moments. The guttural protests were unmistakably his herd of milking cows in distress and he flew down the stairs two at a time, never once needing the light to find his way through the familiar cottage. Snatching the shotgun from its illegal hooks by the front door, he slid two cartridges home and snapped it shut. If the local police ever knew it was kept outside the gun cabinet he would lose his license, but every second counted if someone was trying to hurt or steal his herd. A close friend a few farms over had fallen victim to a trough poisoning and had lost fourteen cows before the cause was discovered.

"Bastards. Let's see how some buckshot feels, shall we?" Alan snarled, pushing through the door and running across the yard.

For an older man, he was still remarkably fit which was partly his diet, and partly the miles and miles of walking he did every day between pastures and fields. The commotion was now in full frenzy and it would be suicide to try and enter with the sheer strength and weight rebounding in the barn. Ethical farming had been a source of pride for his family and the beasts weren't individually stalled. Instead, they could roam freely inside the massive building which kept them happy and content. Standing carefully to the side of the huge entrance, he pulled the bolt and threw the door wide. A stampede of muscular cattle surged from the hidden danger and Alan's stomach twisted when he saw the blood. Some were wounded; large gashes and punctures in their flanks. Others were just coated in crimson liquid, which saturated their white hides.

"I'm going to kill you all, just see if I don't," Alan whispered through streaming tears. Someone had hurt his girls and they would pay the ultimate price.

When the danger of being trampled subsided he dodged around the doorframe and stood against the wall. His chest ached with the pain of counting the escapees and realising over thirty were too injured to get clear of the barn.

"Show yourself you sons of bitches!"

The beam played over the scene and it seared into his memory like a branding iron. A slaughter house was the first thought that came to mind, with twitching meat and blood running in torrents from their torn remains. Some still lived and their big eyes stared at him, begging their friend and keeper for an end to this bewildering agony. Though not unintelligent, the bovine creatures lacked the awareness to know they were dying. Great racking sobs escaped Alan as he gave up all pretences of stealth. Stumbling over chunks of viscera and slipping onto his bottom twice from the blood, finally he reached the other end of the barn. No blade wielding nemesis waited to do battle. In fact, there were no other people in the barn at all.

"Where are you?" Alan yelled.

Flashing the torch around, his confusion at the inexplicable attack grew. The light picked out a previously unnoticed detail and he jogged over to investigate, slipping over once again in his desperation. A large hole had been forced through the corrugated iron siding of the building, much bigger than any man would need.

"I'll find you!" Alan screamed through the hole.

Grief gave way to a frown of deep thought at the sight. The only footprints were his own as they approached the breached wall. Shining the torch around, every other imprint was hooved, including a set of tracks that came through the hole from outside.

"What the hell?" Alan whispered and heard a grunting noise from behind.

Ready to usher one of his girls back out to safety, he turned. The blood-soaked creature stood before him was not one of his own, and he had to crane his neck to stare up at the sulphurous eyes. Dropping the gun from hands which would no longer respond, he could only tremble as he was appraised. The gaze seemed to bore into his very soul, judging him for misdeed and sin. Unable to help himself, Alan started to giggle. It was an unhealthy discord more worthy of the depths of an asylum than a dairy farm. Letting loose an inhuman roar, the monster pounced but

Alan had already gone to safer places within the maze of his own mind.

***

"Nine, nine, nine. What service do you require?"

"Oh God, all of them, send everyone you have. Police, paramedics, the army, everyone!"

"Please calm down, sir. What seems to be the problem?"

"There's so much blood. I've never seen anything like it."

"I'll connect you with the police. One moment, sir."

"Please hurry!"

"Hampshire Police. What's your emergency?"

"Blood. So much blood."

"Sir, have you been involved in an accident? What's your location?"

"Not mine. Theirs. Everywhere. So much blood."

"Sir, I need you to tell me your whereabouts. Please focus."

"Bowlees Farm. They're all dead. Send everyone."

"Sir? Are you still there? Who's dead? Sir?"

***

"Sergeant Rankin from four nine two, come in. Over."

"Delta Lima four nine two, receiving. Over."

"Four nine two, we've just had a call from someone at Bowlees Farm claiming that there is blood and bodies everywhere. It's probably just a prank, but can you check it out just in case? Over."

"Delta Lima four nine two, we are off shift in twenty minutes. Is no other unit available? Over."

"Four nine two, I'm afraid not. The road traffic accident on the M3 motorway has most assets tied up. The

101

commander says he will sign off on double overtime pay. Over."

"Received. Over."

Rankin downed the last tepid dregs of his coffee and replaced the cup on the thermos flask.

"Do you really think it could be a genuine call?" Walton asked.

"Of course not, it's all a bunch of shit. I've known Alan from Bowlees for over ten years and since his wife died it's only been him living there. Unless he was having a party and someone has killed all the guests which is just as ridiculous. He's going to have a right old laugh at this."

Dawn had broken and the first commuters were on the roads. Most gave way willingly, but there was always one who was still half asleep. No matter how loud the sirens or bright the lights, they would fail to notice the police car and yield which always brought a torrent of expletives from the sergeant.

"What's that?" Walton asked, leaning forward to peer through the windscreen.

A blur of fluorescent was running towards them, waving its arms in the middle of the road.

"Lester?"

"Who?"

"Lester, the milkman," Rankin replied as they converged in the country lane.

"Isn't Bowlees a dairy farm? Why would they need milk delivered?" Walton asked with a frown.

"It's called supporting your friends. Lester is a lovely old guy and people refuse to put him out of business by saving a few pennies at the supermarket."

"Oh, I see," Walton replied, dubiously.

"Lester, get in," Rankin ordered and the sweating, gasping man climbed into the back seat.

"Thank God it's you John. Something bad has happened at Bowlees. It's a slaughter."

"What are you talking about? We had reports of blood and bodies everywhere?"

"There is, it's awful. Most of Alan's cattle have been slaughtered and I couldn't find him anywhere."

The whole story finally clicked and shifting into gear, the sergeant accelerated aggressively towards his friend's farm.

"Slow down, there are a few roaming around the area. I only noticed them after I reached the house," Lester warned.

Rankin did as instructed, and on the approach road a couple of cows wandered aimlessly, grazing at any loose grass. Dried blood coated the beasts and as they got closer to the barns they could see more bodies of animals that had succumbed to their wounds.

"Didn't you see those as you turned into the farm?" Rankin asked.

"I was in a world of my own when I got here," Lester offered weakly, "I still hate early mornings."

"You could've picked a better career then," Rankin said, bringing the car to a full stop just outside the farmhouse.

"It's empty," Lester said, reading the officers minds as they stared at the open front door.

"Where's Alan then?" Rankin whispered, scanning the outbuildings and fields for any sing of human movement.

"Shall I call for backup?"

"Yeah. Tell them we need the armed response for real this time too," Rankin replied, "Whoever did this is a fucking lunatic."

As his trainee set to summoning the relevant assets, the sergeant climbed out of the car.

"Where are you going?" Walton hissed.

"I'm going to look around. If Alan's hurt, he may need my help."

"Ok, boss. I'll get an ambulance here too, but order it to hold back until ARU have given the all clear."

Nodding his agreement, Rankin closed the door and looked towards the barn. Both doors were wide open and a trail of drying blood showed the escape route of the cows. Someone had opened them, and knowing his old friend so well, it must have been Alan going to help his herd. Staring down the outer length of the building, more pools of claret had formed, flowing under the walls themselves. Jesus, for it to reach outside there must have been countless litres of it spilled. With trepidation not felt since the battlefields of his youth, Rankin took out his torch and banished some of the shadows within the barn. It was a charnel house. Bovine corpses lay scattered across the ground in varying states of evisceration and dismemberment. Studying the closest body, it was clear that no knife had been used. The wounds were numerous and varied, with wild slashes laying open the internal organs and legs torn off leaving shreds of muscle and tendon. The most curious were the wide, circular puncture wounds which were abundant on every carcass. That they were stab wounds was obvious, but the size and depth were totally baffling. Circular, with a diameter of around four inches, the only time he had ever seen anything similar was when an accident victim had once impaled themselves on a wooden fencepost.

"Fuck me," gasped Walton as he entered.

Vomiting the recently eaten sandwich all over his feet, the young recruit nearly fainted. The coppery smell of the blood found its way into his nostrils and the officer stumbled away, retching.

"Get back in the car, but don't you dare puke on my seat!" Rankin hissed and Walton gladly complied.

"Alan, are you in here?" Rankin called out, emboldened by the growing clamour from the approaching armed vehicles.

A cackling laugh echoed in response and the small hairs stood up on the back of his neck. Backing away carefully, the sound came again and Rankin paused midstride. The timbre of the mad giggle was familiar and Rankin found himself moving deeper into the barn again. Like a lightning bolt, he suddenly understood it was his friend making the awful noise. Jumping over scattered chunks of carrion and pools of indescribable gore, he reached the source of the childlike snickers.

"Alan! Thank God you're ok!"

The policeman tried to help his friend stand up but he only shrieked and pressed further against the wall. Cradling a broken arm, the old farmer backpedalled furiously on the floor as if he could push himself through the barrier and out of this world completely.

"Alan, you're safe now. Everything's going to be alright," Rankin said quietly, trying to calm him.

A moment of clarity twisted Alan's face and he grabbed the outstretched hand of the officer, "Going to be alright, is it?"

"Alan, let go. You're hurting me," Rankin begged, attempting to prise the vicelike fingers from his own.

"Demons walk the earth and they visited me last night. They'll come back and take me to Hell soon, you'll see!" Alan started to laugh hysterically and rocked back and forth in his own filth.

"What in God's name happened here?" Rankin asked himself, looking at the deep scratches in the wall.

Hoof prints marred the muddy ground, but set amongst the normal sized impressions were a much larger pair. One set was facing into the barn through the peeled back steel siding, and the other was facing the other way, showing where the creature had left. Something not of this world had attacked this place during the night and Rankin crossed himself and whispered a prayer.

"That won't help," giggled Alan in the corner.

***

Gazing thoughtfully out of the window, Quinlan watched the small yachts and boats pass on the River Thames. A gentle rapping on the door brought her back to the present and she turned back to the desk.

"Come."

A young woman strode in, full of self-confidence. Long, blonde hair framed a stern, unsmiling face. What she lacked in warmth, she more than compensated for with efficiency. Quinlan valued her above all other aides and she smiled as she placed a file on her desk. Stamped on the top corner were the words 'Top Secret' in red ink.

"It's all there, ma'am."

"Thank you, Paula. That will be all."

With the ongoing danger of cyber attacks on the government networks, certain sensitive information was kept only in paper format and locked away in the deepest archives of the Houses of Parliament. Leafing through the documents, Quinlan read it with emotional detachment. As the UK's Home Secretary, she was well versed in state secrets and the research that took place 'off the books'. It was a well-known fact that across the globe, despite treaties opposing the practice, chemical and biological experimentation were commonplace. Anyone not partaking in the clandestine race were not moral crusaders, but fools. Certain nation states would gladly unleash viruses capable of killing billions of people and it was only through espionage that they had been prevented from doing so already.

On her desk, the intercom bleeped and she pressed the button to speak to Paula.

"What is it?"

"Ma'am, the CEO of Pearson Global Technologies is here. Shall I show him in?"

"Please do so."

In moments, the door opened and a man entered, politely declining the offer of coffee from the aide. Striding across the room, he held out a hand and Quinlan shook it warmly.

"George, it's been too long."

"Indeed it has, Brenda. How's the family?"

"Growing up fast. Patrick is nearly finished at university so I will need to find him a bag carriers job with a fellow member of parliament."

George smiled and nodded, "Following in his amazing mother's footsteps I see."

"He's already talking about becoming Prime Minister," she replied with a chuckle, "Anyway, let's get down to business. What on earth is going on at your Midhurst facility?"

Collecting his thoughts for a few seconds, George chose his words carefully. "I'm afraid we had a containment breach."

"And what does that mean? Did that *thing* really get out of its cell?"

"I'm afraid so."

"Bloody hell!" Quinlan shouted, pressing the intercom button, "Paula, I need that coffee. And make it strong."

"Yes, ma'am."

"Please tell me you've managed to capture it."

"We are taking all necessary steps to facilitate the reacquisition of the asset."

"Oh cut the horse shit, George. I assume by that you mean it's still free to roam the laboratories. Is there any way it could reach the vaults and break any of the equipment?"

"No, the storage areas for the most dangerous chemical and biological threats is still mechanical."

"Thank goodness for that," Quinlan sighed. The last thing she needed was a worldwide epidemic of Ebola or other catastrophic disease. Seeing the wary look on his face, she leaned forward, "What are you not telling me?"

"It's not just free to roam the laboratories," George finally admitted, "This was a targeted hack by an enemy of the state and they shut down everything. Power, backup systems, and took over all security feeds."

"You mean to say it got out of the bloody building?" Quinlan was apoplectic and George, despite being a powerful man in his own right, cowered away.

"Yes. We lost seven members of the security team and two of our best scientists. Whoever did this used the electronic door systems to guide it to freedom."

"Oh, Christ," Quinlan sighed, slowly shaking her head.

George knew that she was just gathering power for an eruption in the same way a volcano does and quickly responded. "We have four teams on foot following the creature. A farm was attacked an hour ago, so we are assuming it's moving directly away from the facility. It's only a matter of time until we catch or kill it."

"How many died on the farm?" Quinlan demanded.

The door opened and Paula could see the barely repressed anger in her employer's eyes. Placing the cup on a coaster she beat a hasty retreat and closed the door.

"No human casualties, thankfully. The farmer was assaulted by the creature before it fled. He's now being treated under sedation following a minor mental break. A great number of his dairy cows were slain, though."

"Why kill the animals but not the man?"

"It could be that the creature didn't feel the same intense hatred for the farmer that it did for the staff in Midhurst."

"And the animals? Why kill them?"

"We simply don't know." George shrugged. It was a mistake.

"Then you'd better bloody well find out!" Quinlan beat her fist on the desk, "If a single member of the public perishes because of your negligence, you will be held fully accountable!"

"I don't think that's fair," George replied, defiantly, "I don't think I need to explain the economic benefit we bring to the United Kingdom."

Quinlan glowered across the desk. "Are you attempting to blackmail me?"

"Not at all. I was merely reinforcing the mutual advantage we share by having our European operations based here. I'd hate any unhelpful recriminations to affect the long-term viability of that arrangement."

"How dare you?" Quinlan snapped, "Remember the funding you receive from us. Threats work both ways, George."

He stood up and shrugged again, "There will always be governments willing to pay top price for our work. I sincerely hope it won't become necessary, though. I'll be in touch as soon as we resolve the situation."

Quinlan watched him saunter out of the office and promised herself that she would mention Pearson Globals recklessness at the next security briefing. She knew their value to the country, but that wasn't to say she couldn't make life uncomfortable for a while.

Looking at the photograph in the file, she shuddered.

***

"Sarge, can we call it a day now? I'm exhausted," Walton whined.

The attitude of the younger generation never failed to annoy Rankin and he ignored the plea. Gone was the sense of duty, to be replaced by a clock watching mindset and refusal to go above and beyond.

"We're on duty until the job's done."

"But the chiefs already stopped our overtime after the last call. Why bother?"

"I'll tell you why," Rankin fumed, rounding on the youth, "Because one of my friends lost his whole livelihood today, and probably his mind too. Whatever is out there is psychotic and dangerous and needs to be stopped."

"But what can we do against it?" Walton continued, betraying the real reason for the desperation to go home; fear.

"We have our pepper spray and Tasers. It doesn't matter if it's a man or an escaped animal, neither will enjoy a face full of chemical or a fifty-thousand-volt shock. Besides, AR units are out in force and will probably find it first anyway."

"I sure hope so."

"Remind me to leave you in the car on the more violent calls in the future, just so you don't get put in harm's way," Rankin sneered. The conduct of his subordinate had been poor before this incident and with each passing day it became clear he was more suited to an office than the streets.

"That's not really fair. Have you forgotten those cows and how they were ripped apart?"

Rankin grunted, grudgingly agreeing with the point. It didn't detract from their duty to protect the public though. If the thin blue line put personal safety first, then anarchy would rule the world.

"Sergeant Rankin, from four nine two, are you receiving? Over."

"Aren't you going to respond?" Walton murmured after ten seconds of silence.

"Sergeant Rankin, from four nine two, come in. Over."

Walton reached for his own radio and Rankin stopped him with a single glare. "They will put us on reprimand for ignoring the radio."

"Don't be daft. They have to prove we willingly ignored it first, and if you keep your mouth shut they'll never know."

"Why aren't you answering, though?" Walton demanded.

"Because I know where the bastard's going."

"How?" Walton asked, anxiety twisting his stomach into knots.

"Look," Rankin laid a map on the centre console and started pointing, "The tech facility is here. The attack on Alan's farm was here and the car crash was here."

"How is the car crash related to it all?"

"Think about it. No other cars involved, clear morning with no rain or ice. The skid marks indicate a sharp twist on the wheel and loss of control. What was she trying to avoid?"

"We can ask her when she regains consciousness."

"We will, but after we capture or help kill this thing. Lastly, we had the report from the two hikers who claim to have seen a large animal loose in the woods. It scared the hell out of them. These incidents follow a north by northwest trajectory."

"Shall we call it in then?" Walton asked, hopeful for backup for any coming confrontation.

"No," Rankin replied, "If I'm wrong, we will pull all units to one location and leave others vulnerable. The thing may veer off and if it does the others need to be able to respond quickly."

"So where are we going?" Walton said with growing dread.

"There." Rankin pointed to a position on the map, "It's an old, abandoned farmhouse. The place is falling apart after the owner built a newer one closer to town. If it needs to sleep it would make a great shelter, though."

"I have a bad feeling about this."

Rankin ignored him and drove away, face set in determination.

***

111

After disabling the sirens and lights, Rankin guided the vehicle up the gravel drive. Nature had largely won the battle and a few more years would see the road returned to its original state, the farm a long forgotten memory. Vegetation slapped against the windscreen as they pushed through and finally reached the house. The concrete yard was proving more difficult to reclaim, with only the hardiest weeds managing to gain a foothold in the cracks.

"Could this look any more like a scene out of a horror film?" Walton groaned sickly.

"Suck it up and load your Taser," Rankin ordered.

Pressing the cartridges into the weapons, they climbed out of the vehicle. A preternatural silence had fallen over the surrounding area which unsettled Rankin. As a child of the countryside, he knew the familiar mating calls of the wildlife, the chirrup of birds as they nested in the trees. That comforting ambience was totally absent in any form, as if the local animals knew something unnatural was nearby. Walton was from the city, but he too could feel the *wrongness* of the scene and looked to Rankin for strength.

"You go left, I go right. We meet at the rear of the property. Stay sharp."

With a nod, they moved away from the safety of their car. Graffiti had been sprayed on every wall and at some point, a firm had been paid to try and secure the dilapidated property. The steel bar fixings had corroded in the intervening years and most of the cages had fallen to the ground to continue their degradation. Every window and door was broken, giving a multitude of access and egress points to the dark interior.

"Keep your distance," Rankin whispered, pointing at the openings.

Walton nodded and gave them all a wide berth as he disappeared around the corner. With each careful step, Rankin listened for any clue from the shattered windows. A scrape, or thud, even a deep breath. Nothing presented itself and he met his colleague without being attacked.

"Anything?"

Walton shook his head. "What's the plan?"

"We go in."

"Are you fucking nuts?" Walton hissed, colour draining from his face.

"Go back to the car then," Rankin sighed, "I'm going to make sure it's not inside."

"It's not that I don't want to," he whimpered and backed away.

Stepping through the back door, the stench of mould and decay was carried past him by unseen draughts. During his career, he had been subjected to many properties in a more appalling state, housing drug addicts or worse. Sniffing at the various scents, none presented itself as an unusual addition to the medley and he moved deeper into the home.

Moisture damage had softened some of the floorboards and he made sure to tread carefully on the joists supporting them. Nothing remained of the furniture or contents that had been moved along with the previous owners which made the search of the ground floor a quick affair. Standing at the foot of the stairs, scuff marks had disturbed the settled dust on the treads. Rankin shone the torch at each imprint, trying to discern the shapes. In his expert opinion, they were all human footprints, most likely kids hoping to get high or have sex away from prying eyes.

If that's the case, why can't I take the first step? Rankin thought, feeling foolish that his trainee's paranoia had polluted his own psyche. Forcing the uncooperative limb to obey, he begun the ascent, keeping the torch beam on the landing above. With each creak of protesting timber, Rankin expected a demon to burst from the corner and leap down the stairs to tear him apart.

Pull yourself together!

He reached the landing and the open doors to the upper rooms provided enough light to see everything was clear. Cigarette ends and broken bottles littered the floor and he grimaced when he noticed a few used condoms amongst the debris. Straining with every fibre of his being to hear anything that might give away their assailant, he went unrewarded yet again. More graffiti marred the cracked lath and plaster walls as he carefully checked each room. Only the bathroom door remained closed, teasing him with its inscrutability.

Surely a demon wouldn't need to hide behind a flimsy door, much less have the ability to open and close it with their hooves. *Knock it off, for fuck's sake!* Taking a deep breath, he twisted the handle and pushed. A scream nearly tore from his throat when a rat screeched and scurried over his foot. The temptation to run after the rat and leave the building was nearly overwhelming, but training and pride took over.

One hiding place remained; the deep, claw footed bath on the other side of the room. From his angle, most of the tub was concealed and he raised the Taser in readiness. Each pace into the room gave him a better vantage point and the sight of dark fabric against the pure white enamel caused his heart to skip a beat.

"Police! Get out of the tub slowly or I will discharge the Taser!"

Whatever was hiding inside didn't stir an inch and Rankin kicked a shard of glass across the room.

"I won't ask again!"

Edging forward, the cloth revealed itself to be nothing more than a stained blanket. Several others lay inside the bath and Rankin lowered the weapon when it became apparent he had only discovered a makeshift bed. Tossing the sheets aside to be absolutely sure, only a couple of bits of burned foil sat at the bottom. Burned foil meant heroin needles were a real possibility so he ended the search.

Relaxing for the first time since stepping over the threshold, Rankin holstered the Taser. Pausing at the top of the stairs, he slowly turned to the left.

How the hell did I miss that?

The attic hatch was partly open; the wooden cover twisted and not sitting flush in its recess. Standing on tiptoes, Rankin was done with stealth. His earlier shouts should have roused any monster above and the fact nothing had crashed through the ceiling was reassuring. He slammed a fist up and the panel went clattering into the darkness. Silence reasserted itself with no shrieking or gnashing of hellish teeth.

Damn!

Maybe old age was throwing off my instincts, Rankin pondered. He had been certain the creature would keep to the route it was following and this was the only uninhabited building in the area.

"Time to think about retirement, you old fool," he chuckled and left the property.

Leaving via the front door, Walton wasn't visible in the car or surrounding area. The passenger door stood open, so he must have just gone for a piss break. Why couldn't he wait until the all clear had been given?

"Walton, hurry up!"

Sliding into the driver's seat, he reached for his radio.

"Please, no," he pleaded at the sight before him.

A pool of crimson was slowly spreading across the ground and Rankin hadn't been able to see it from the front door. Leaping from the car and drawing the Taser, he raced around the vehicle. Whatever had transpired was fatal; no one could lose that amount of blood and live. A cold fury settled over him as he followed the trail towards the dense hedgerows. A wide swath had been crushed under foot, or hoof, and the traces of claret led directly through the cleft. Thinking this was a pursuit, he was running full tilt at the opening when the creature stepped out of the shadows. The military training pushed the terror down deep into his stomach and he fired the Taser into the bristly hide. The barbs sunk into the flesh and the electricity crackled as it discharged into the beast. Instead of going into spasm or collapsing, it clenched the wires and tore them free.

"Dear God," Rankin whispered as he sank to his knees and wet himself.

Letting loose an inhuman roar, the creature charged. Closing his eyes, the thud of hoof on the dry ground was like the bell tolling for his demise. Terrified birds and cowering animals bolted as the chattering cracks of gunfire broke the morning air. Bellowing in fury, the beast hit the ground hard and crashed through Rankin. A horn tore deeply through his thigh in passing and he screamed in agony.

"Move in!" came a yell from the shadows to his right and men dressed in black combat fatigues broke cover.

Unable to talk through the pain and steadily ebbing flow of his blood loss, Rankin was dragged unceremoniously away from the monster.

"Sir, orders?"

"Finish it!"

The roar of pain and fear was almost human in its tone and Rankin clapped his hands over his ears. Eight more shots silenced the mournful lamentations and he finally gave in to the darkness which promised a glorious end to the pain.

***

Waking up, Rankin was momentarily disoriented by the strange ceiling. Lights and storage cabinets made him think he was laid in the aisle of a plane, but the smiling face which leaned over banished the illusion.

"You're going to be ok," said the paramedic, "Just lie still."

"Is it dead?"

"Pardon me?" asked the man with a perplexed frown.

"That *thing*. Is it dead?" Rankin demanded.

"The man that assaulted you is dead, yes," he replied, "It's lucky the armed response officers showed up when they did."

Rankin sat up and looked out through the rear doors of the vehicle. Every man of the paramilitary force had changed into normal armed police uniforms. Who the hell were these people?

"Sir, lay back. You suffered a deep laceration and we need to keep your blood pressure steady."

A gently insistent hand pushed him back into place, but not before one of the men had caught sight of his awakening. It was none other than Bob Camoletto. With a nod, he summoned someone out of sight and started to walk over.

"Can you give us a few minutes, please?"

"I really need to get him to hospital as soon as possible," complained the medic, injecting a small dose of liquid into the cannula attached to his hand.

"We'll be quick. I promise," Camoletto insisted.

"Make sure you are."

As the medic hopped down, a second man joined the disguised head of security. Wearing an immaculate suit which was worth more than several months of Rankin's salary, he held out a hand and they shook. Smiling a smile of purest white, he turned to the rear and shut the doors.

"Sergeant, my name is Harrison Sieger."

"Why are you on my murder scene?" Rankin demanded, "Who are you people?"

"I understand this is all confusing to you, but I can assure you this is all legal and above board. Before I can talk further I need you to sign this document," Sieger explained, removing a file and a gold fountain pen.

"What the fuck is this?" Rankin slapped away the hand and the heart monitor started to bleep in warning. Walton was dead and the insufferable smile was an insult to his sacrifice.

"I understand your anguish, Sergeant, believe me," Sieger pleaded, "But I can't divulge any more information without your signature. It's an Official Secrets Act contract so you can appreciate what's at stake here."

Rankin glared at the man and his perfect teeth. Snatching the items, he snapped, "Give it here!"

"Thank you for your cooperation. I understand you were a Royal Marine for two decades, so I don't need to explain the implications if you break this agreement."

A veil of drug induced euphoria descended on Rankin as the morphine started to deaden his senses. Satisfied the officer knew his place, Sieger smiled and turned away. It had never been his intention to explain the secrets of his operation.

"What was that *thing*?" he slurred, holding up a leaden arm in an effort to stop the men leaving.

Sieger jumped down, but Camoletto turned and the nervous tension was evident in his eyes, "It's better you never know. Your partner's family will be well taken care of, I can guarantee that. Get well soon, sergeant."

"Wait!"

They were gone and the doors latched shut behind them, leaving him alone with his muddled thoughts. Genetic engineering? Biological warfare? Whatever that thing was, it was better off dead. As he lay back on the sterile pillow, looking at the ceiling, he couldn't shake the final moments out of his head. The stricken monster had known it was about to die, but what animal can *speak*? There was no doubt the grunted words which passed through the poorly formed vocal chords were *'Please, kill me.'* It had obviously been gifted with a self-awareness that made it more intelligent than any non-human creature on the planet, but who would have ever conceived of such a creation? More to the point, how was it even possible to play God with such wildly different species.

The paramedic returned and tried to calm Rankin down. Talking softly, he informed the sergeant that he was a hero for ending the madman's rampage across the countryside and there was discussion among the suited gentlemen gathered outside about a bravery award. As the ambulance pulled away from the scene, he started to weep uncontrollably.

Madman? It was no madman that had the cloven hooves and thick, muscular legs which had propelled it towards Rankin. His reeling mind tried to make sense of the horned head, similar in shape to a bull, with wide, gaping nostrils and red eyes that seemed to glow with inner fire. Nothing could conceal the truth of the hairy, humanlike torso, or the way its hairless arms ended with broad, thick knuckled fingers. It reminded him of a story he had loved as a child about Greek mythology. Sobs gave way to laughter and the paramedic couldn't understand the garbled words.

"Can you repeat that, sir?"

More crazed sniggers escaped his lips, "No wonder it was so upset," he giggled, "A minotaur needs its labyrinth."

Collected tales of Madness and Terror

An OMP Magazine

Issue
No. 8

Maximus
SHOCK

Immortality has a price!

THE
DEMON'S
ERRAND

Keith Montgomery

To my wife whose patience, love and tough but fair criticisms have made me the writer I am and my life a nice a beautiful place to be.

Richard Salem wiped his brow as he took a drink of water from his canteen. He checked his watch. He'd been walking around in this disgusting swamp for well over three hours. Whipping out his handkerchief, he dabbed more pouring sweat from his forehead. Damn, was it always this hot and humid in Louisiana?

The CEO of Salem Industries, he was brutally handsome, ruthless, and ambitious. All of it served him well in his rise up the corporate ladder. Father brought him on board after he graduated with his master's in business management. But instead of offering a partnership, he found himself in the damned mail room! 'A man needed to work his way up to truly appreciate when he reached the top', father was fond of saying. What a big fat stinkin' load of crap. Sticking him in that low level bullshit job, instead of giving him his birth right. He should've been rubbing elbows with top executives, not pushing a cart delivering packages and mail like some stooge. Father, in his feeble mind, was trying to teach him a valuable lesson. And he learned well. It took years of hobnobbing, catering to assorted egos and sewing alliances. It was astounding how many enemies father had made in his rise to the top. He'd never forget dear ole dad's face when the board of directors along with key stock holders, all of whom had an axe of their own to grind, voted him out and made Richard the new CEO. The old bastard damn near had a heart attack right there in the boardroom. Good times.

Reaching into his back pack, he grabbed his notebook and opened it to the page he'd marked. This had better work. The money he spent to acquire this information, made him gag. But if the legend was true, it'd all be worth it. Money, women, and let's not forget the glorious power; his position ushered many benefits his way, but the thing he wanted most, not even all his clout could buy. He wanted to live forever. He wanted immortality. To remain young, vibrant and strong for all time; paired with his knowledge, business savvy and cunning, the world would be at his feet.

Science and technology got him nowhere; both miserably failed him, so he turned to magic. Through research, study, and bribery he found the answer to his dreams. A forbidden book, called the Algeus. Oh, there were those who warned him to give up the search for the malevolent text, but give up the chance at possibly gaining immortality? Get real!

After many years and extremely large investments, he at last obtained the thing, and when he held it, he could literally feel energy flowing from the pages as if it were a physical force. His whole body resonated from it. Of course, once he possessed the accursed text, then came the problem of finding someone who would touch the damn thing, let alone translate it.

Pouring over his notes, he studied the map on the page. No way would he chance some two bit magician or other prying it from his grasp. Oh no, he had it locked up tight in his office safe. He slapped at the mosquito pricking his neck. Figures the bayou swamp is where this jaunt would take him. Whatever, if it got him what he deserved, he'd crossed the Sahara Desert on the back of a tortoise.

Stroking his chin, he looked about. According to the map, there should be a path marked by an old hickory— there! Directly to his right was the hickory pine. Just like his notes described, it looked as if a giant ax had split it down the middle. According to the evil text, the tree was struck by lightning as three witches prepared to sacrifice a virgin to some malicious deity. Stowing his notes, he zipped up his back pack and made off down the path.

He was searching for a circular clearing with a pedestal like tree trunk in its center. Legends had it that witch covens performed all manner of unspeakable deviltry there. It was there he would supposedly be able to summon the demon. It was said any who could complete its task, it would grant a wish.

Five bull frogs and two gators later, he arrived at the clearing. His heart hammered against his rib cage with John Henry like force. Tearing his notebook from his backpack, he rushed to the pedestal tree trunk. Carefully setting down his haversack, he recited the incantation then waited. Nothing moved. Nothing happened either. He looked about. No rumble from the sky, no ground shaking, not even a rain drop fell to earth. Carefully, he repeated the spell with the same result. He clutched the paper tight causing it to crinkle. No, this better not be a cheat, not after all he had lost, all this had cost him! Through clenched teeth, Richard once again recited the incantation, enunciating each word. Still, the world remained as peaceful as...

An impenetrable darkness descended upon the clearing as thunder rumbled above. The temperature fell rapidly. Richard hugged himself against the frigid onslaught, his breath coming out in fogs. Out before him, a circular distortion in the air, the size of a dinner plate, formed and began to approach him. He backed away as cold, or was it fear, cascaded down his spine. The anomaly levitated to eye level then faded to black belching smoke. Then he smelled it; sulfur and brimstone. It was all around him, saturating his skin, his nostrils, his clothes. Flames filled the darkened portal. Richard could almost feel the heat.

"Who summons me?" It was as if a thousand voices were speaking as one.

Richard flinched in spite of himself. The voices, they reminded him of a verse he'd once heard in his childhood. 'My name is legion, for we are many.'

"I..." Richard cleared his throat. "I did. I've come far to take on your task, in exchange for one wish, as it was written."

"Bah, waste not my time and patience mortal, you have not the conviction needed to carry out this undertaking."

"I have whatever conviction it takes to get what I want, demon. I will not be denied. I get what I want, no matter what. I always have, always will. Now, tell me what I must do, then you can fulfill your end of the bargain," Richard said with as much confidence as he could muster without wetting his pants.

"Very well, I will allow you to try." Richard shuddered. He couldn't see the thing, but he could sense it was smiling. "Listen well, son of flesh, journey deeper into this swamp, toward where the sun has set. You will find an old shack. Slay the old woman, Seska, and return here with the talisman she wears about her neck."

Kill an old woman? He didn't come to commit murder, but whatever, if that's what it took... In a few centuries, he doubt he would even remember the old bag of bones. Still... "Simple enough, but why do you wish this woman dead? What has she done—"

"Yours is not to question, son of flesh. That is the task, accept it or be gone from me!" The flaming area shrank away and with a muffled pop and puff of smoke, it was gone. The oppressive darkness retreated as did the bitter cold air. The heat and humidity quickly moved to reclaim the clearing.

Richard blew out a sigh. Fear released his spine as he looked about. It was as if nothing had occurred. Returning his notes to his back pack, he zipped it shut and checked his watch. It was already

7:30 pm, he'd have to move quickly, while he still had daylight. No way he wanted to get caught in this hell hole after dark. Slipping his pack strap over his shoulder, he looked about. "Be prepared to grant my wish, demon, I'll be back, with the talisman."

Another hour and a half of walking through the muck and he still had yet to come across anything even resembling a shack. He was all set to give make camp when he saw it. Centered between four trees the shack sat, the flicker of candle light in the windows. Approaching the dwelling from the rear, he crept toward one of the windows. Snap! Dammit, he'd never heard a twig break so loud! He ducked into the brush. The light from the candle continued its ghostly glimmer No shadows or any sign of movement came from inside.

Keeping low, he snuck up to the glass and peered inside. What a dump. No electricity, running water, nor telephones as far as he could tell. The room was peppered with candles; each glimmered with a life of their own. In the far corner, sat an old cast iron potbellied stove. Old wooden furniture sprinkled the room. Against the opposite wall, an oil lantern rested on a mantle above an old stone fire place. A log burned a crimson/orange as a woman sat nearby in a rocking chair.

Reaching into his back pack, he withdrew a large hunting knife. He paused. Was he really gonna kill an old woman in cold blood? To get what he wanted, you damn right he was! He'd be doing the old spinster a favor. With blade in hand, he trudged around to the front. One good kick and he'd go in, knife shank grandma, take the talisman, and present it to the demon. Simple. Hell, the sudden noise would probably kill her before he could get close anyway.

Marching up the walkway, Richard gathered himself and drove his foot against the door. It flew open, hit the wall, and bounced back. As he stood at the threshold, the rocking chair pivoted as if on a swivel. Now facing Richard, the old woman's face contorted into a ghoulish grin. Spindly arms and legs, snow white hair, and hollow cheeks, she had to be the most decrepit old bat he ever laid eyes on. Why waste the energy killing her when one good sneeze could do the job? Around her neck, hung what he'd come for; the talisman. A crystal, golf ball sized sphere, a star burst shaped light pulsated from within. "Welcome

Mr. Salem, I've been expecting you," she said, her raspy voice every bit as ancient as she appeared.

Richard flinched, she called him by name!

"Of course, I know who you are, Richard Salem."

His jaw went slack.

"I am Seska Monroe, please come in. I assure you, it's quite safe." When he stood pat, she rolled her eyes and sighed softly. "If I wanted to harm you, I would've did so when you peered through my window. Please, do come in."

He complied. Slowly, cautiously, he entered. Stopping out of arm's reach, he regarded Seska. She looked even older up close. "If you know who I am, then you know why I've come."

"I know that too." Her eyes traveled down his body. "I must say, the demon's selection of pawns is improving. Of those he's sent to destroy me, you are by far the easiest on the eyes. If I were but a few thousand years younger, I might've let you have your way with me." Seska winked.

Ugh! Richard's stomach curdled. Just the thought made him want to take some hedge clippers to his joy maker and toss it into a blender. "Cut the crap, old woman, if you know why I'm here, why did you invite me in?"

The whistle of a tea kettle interrupted their conversation. "Would you care for some tea, Mr. Salem?"

"No."

With a gesture of her hand, the kettle rose from the stove and levitated to a small tea cup resting on a circular end table next to the old woman. Steam rose from the spout as it tipped forward filling the cup with hot water. "Are you certain you won't have some?"

Richard growled as the kettle drifted back to its place on the stove. "No, what I want is for you to answer the fuckin' question!"

Seska picked up a spoon and stirred her tea as the rich aroma of her brew scented the air. "Earl Grey, it's one of the few guilty pleasures of the outside word I enjoy. I'm afraid I've become a slave to its delightful flavor."

"You're stalling, Crypt Keeper. Answer the question or I'll kill you right now!"

Seska took a sip then set the cup back on the table. "Very well, I want to discuss with you, your future, Mr. Salem."

Richard sneered. "What about my future? Make it good or I'll slit your wrinkly, dried out neck."

"I will tell you, but be warned, fail to heed my warning—"

"I remind you, I'm holding the knife, old woman." Richard countered.

"It is not I you need fear, Mr. Salem. Your enemy lies within you. Its name is lust. It's what led you to seek out the demon. It's what brought you to my door. The question is, what is it you lust after, what has the demon offered you in exchange for my life?"

"You really think I came all this way to talk about me?"

"The demon will use your lust against you, Mr. Salem. I plead with you. For your own sake, leave my home and return to your life." Seska closed her eyes, tilting back her head in concentration. "I see in your future, a beautiful woman. She will become your wife and will bear you three strong sons. You will share a lifetime of joy and happiness and both grow old together."

Richard snorted bitterly. "And at the end of this glorious vision, I die right?"

Seska opened her eyes and met Richard's gaze. "Death is a natural part of life, Mr. Salem. It is inevitable for all living things. Even I, for all my powers, will one day feel death's cold embrace."

"Whatever, so tell me oh great, all-seeing oracle, what happens if I decide to just kill your ass?"

She once more shut her eyes. Her brow furrowed.

Richard watched. His grip on the knife tightened, his muscles coiled. He could do it now. Drive the blade into her chest; she wouldn't even see it coming. Hell, from looking at her, he'd be doing her a favor. But curiosity welded him to the spot. He had to know what the witch would see. What she'd she have to say.

The old woman trembled. Sweat beaded on her forehead, her breaths came in heaves, her chest rising and falling rapid fire. As tears streamed from her eyes, they snapped open. Seska swallowed, composing herself. Slowly, she lifted her gaze to meet his. What he saw in her eyes made his own breath catch in his throat. Whatever she saw left her shaken. "Immortality, you lust for immortality. You will achieve it, but the price…It will come at a terrible price."

Richard threw back his head and laughed. "That was good. And the Academy Award goes to Seska! You must think I'm a fool, old woman. The only terrible price I'm going to pay is taking that little bobble around your neck to the demon, after I've ended you of course."

Seska shook her head and looked upon him with the saddest eyes he'd ever seen. "You shall regret the decision you make this day. All will."

"Regret is not in my vocabulary, my dear Seska. But you're right, there's gonna be a ton of people who'll regret my immortality. As CEO of my corporation, I've made many enemies during my rise. I'm going to take my sweet time destroying each and every one of them. And there is nothing you can do to dissuade me, so don't bother wasting both our time!"

"Then it's time to for you to embrace your destiny, Mr. Salem," Seska rose from her rocking chair with a strength that took him by surprise, given her frail appearance. "I am unarmed, do what you came to do."

Richard eyeballed her suspiciously. "You're telling me you're just gonna stand there?"

"I am old and tired, Mr. Salem. For tens of thousands of years, my family has stood guard over the demon. For the last three thousand years, I've done so alone. I am the last of my line. My strength and powers are failing me. I can do no more. I'm ready to have this burden taken from me, so I can join my family in the next life. Do what you must, grant me my freedom. But whatever you do, you must never give the demon this talisman."

"Anything you ask," Richard replied through a wicked smile. Lunging with the knife, he drove it into her delicate chest. His weight and the force of the blow drove her down to the floor. The blade had gone into her so smoothly that if he hadn't seen it enter, he would've sworn he'd missed. Again and again he plunged the blade into Seska. Madness took him. The more he stabbed, the better it felt. It wasn't until he saw blood flowing from beneath her that he came to his senses. Seska hadn't cried out once. As he withdrew his skewer, the old woman shuddered, her breaths nothing more than a wet gurgle.

Her lips moved. He leaned down to hear her. "Cr..cr..cry...f...for...y...you." The light faded from her eyes. Seska was dead.

Richard looked upon her with disdain. "Save your tears for yourself, old woman. As for this little trinket, it's going to make all this worth it." Wiping the steel on his pants, he yanked the talisman from her neck. Rising to his feet, he grabbed the lantern. Standing at the open doorway, he hurled the kerosene lamp against the wall. Flames leaped as the oil splashed and ignited. The fire spread quickly consuming the dry wood of the shack. "Thank you for your cooperation, Seska, I'll drink a toast every year on this night in remembrance of you!" Pushing the talisman into his pocket, he made a hasty exit.

Richard hurried back through the swamp. Despite the darkness, he made fast time back to the clearing and the pedestal trunk. Setting his back pack down, he tore his notes from his pack and hurriedly recited the spell. With a muffled pop, and the stench of brimstone, the portal appeared as before.

"Who has summoned me?" the thousand voices rumbled.

"I have, demon." He held aloft the crystal orb. "Seska is dead and here is the proof; the talisman you asked for."

"It seems I underestimated you, son of flesh, so many have tried and failed, but you alone have accomplished my task. Now complete the quest, destroy it and surely, I will grant your request. You shall have immortality."

Richard looked about and grabbed a large stone. A smile spread across his face. For so long, he dreamed and planned for this. Now he was so close. Placing the mystic sphere on the ground, he raised the stone above his head and slammed it down, crushing the tiny orb. The portal exploded outward, the force knocked Richard off his feet. Flat on his back and disoriented, his senses were assaulted by a piecing shriek rising to decibels he didn't think possible. Screaming, he clamped his hands over his ears as gore moistened them. Nothing of this Earth could produce such a sound. Mercifully, the shriek subsided.

"For thousands of years, have I waited for a soul with enough darkness to destroy the witch, Seska! One by one I watched them fall," the thousand voices of the demon ranted. "It was her ancestors who imprisoned me and defeated my plans for the annihilation of the human race! Trapped between dimensions, I could do nothing more than wait as they perished until only Seska remained. She was the last of her line and greatest of mine enemies. Glorious, the last of my jailers is no more! Now, as per our arraignment, rise Richard Salem and receive your reward."

He was never so scared in his entire life. Suddenly, the bargain with that thing terrified him. Every fiber of his being begged him to stay down, but he'd after all he'd done to get this far, there was no turning back. Gingerly, he rose to his feet and faced the creature.

His breath caught in his throat. It was huge, with glowing red eyes and a mouth of sharp looking teeth. Its smile as it approached him, nearly caused his bladder to purge. "For your part in regaining my freedom, Richard Salem, I give you eternity!" Richard backed away as the demon's eyes changed from red to black. He was about to flee as two obsidian beams lanced out, striking him in the chest. Once again, Richard was thrown off his feet, landing on his back. Everything moved in slow motion. From somewhere in the distance, he heard a man screaming and realized it was his own voice!

The demon double crossed him. Through the agony, he felt his heart stop, as did his breathing. Writhing on the ground, his suffering continued. Tormented beyond reason, all he wanted to do was die. Die to be liberated from the torture. As suddenly as it began, the pain ceased.

"Rise, Richard Salem, and take your first steps into immortality."

To Richard's amazement, he was able to move. He felt nothing; even the aches of his back were no more. As he got to his feet, he knew it. Something was very wrong. His body looked bloated, like it had been blown up like a parade balloon. His clothes hung in shreds from his body. His body! He held up his arms inspecting them. They were no longer the perfectly tanned arms. They were bone white, pale, and lifeless.

Scrambling to his back pack, he dumped out its contents as the demon watched. Frantically, he tossed items aside until he found his shaving kit. Tearing it open, he looked into the looking glass. That thing reflecting back, it was him. His face was sunken and elongated, as if he were gazing into a funhouse mirror; his dazzling blue eyes were gone. In their place was blackness that filled the eye sockets. His hair long, stringy, and lifeless, hung down to his shoulders.

He simply gazed at the image. Running his enlarged finger over the glass, he tried touching the face that stared back. What did it do to him? Richard dropped the mirror as he sank to his knees. Drawing in a huge breath, he arched back and screamed to the night, in a voice not his own. When he could scream no more, he sprang to his feet and whirled on the demon.

"What have you done to me!?" Richard yelled with as much hate as his soul could muster.

"I have given you what you most desired."

"I didn't desire this, you son of a bitch, you tricked me!" Richard screamed, throwing out his arms.

"There was no deception on my part, Richard Salem. You were warned about the price to be paid for what your heart desired."

"Warned, what the hell are you talking about?"

When the demon replied, it was in the voice of a single female. "Richard, I implore you to abandon this search. Nothing in magic is free. There's a price, a terrible price to be paid for what you seek. It will destroy you and devour your soul. Once done, it cannot be undone." He knew the voice all too well. Minerva was the sorceress who translated the Algeus. It was her notes he carried in his back pack. His obsession ended their relationship. He lost the only woman he ever truly loved. Richard hung his head.

"Do you not recall the words spoken by your former lover, Richard Salem?"

"I paid the price when I lost her. I paid the price when I killed the old woman and set you free. I paid for immortality, not this!"

"You paid for the right to receive immortality, fleshling. Immortality itself has a price all its own. Your arrogance allowed you to believe that you could gain immortality without paying its price. You deceived yourself. You're a fool. And like all fools, your folly has led you to ruin."

Richard sank to his knees, defeated. His chest felt heavy like lead. It was gone, all of it, gone. His wealth, power, and very life were gone. He could never go home, again.

"Our business is at end, son of flesh, as is the age of man." The demon threw up its clawed hands as enormous bat-like wings stretched out from the creature's back. The skies darkened with ominous clouds. The earth beneath Richard's feet heaved and quaked. A fissure opened, expanding as it belched hell fire and brimstone. "Arise my brothers, arise from your slumber and come forth," the thousand voiced demon implored.

With a burst of superheated air, they emerged in waves, Hundreds of millions of demons, fanning out in all directions. Richard watched in horror. The sky was blotted out by their numbers, all screeching and laughing in triumph.

The demon faced him as the multitudes continued streaking skyward. "I thank you, Richard Salem. Without you, our day would not have been possible. I go now to join my brothers. If we should meet again, I shall destroy you and dine on your innards. Farewell." With a flap of its wings, the demon was airborne, joining the stream of creatures headed toward New Orleans.

The demon was right. His obsession had doomed him and the human race. From far away, the sound of car crashes, gun fire, screaming, and cries for help, reached his supernatural ears. It had already begun. The end of the world he knew. The Earth would forever more be a world of demons, flowing with the blood of billions; blood that would never wash off his hands. It was all on him. And he would witness it, forever tormented by the magnitude of his sins. Because of his greed, lust and pride, he would spend eternity on a dead world, trapped in an enormous husk of rotting flesh.

Collected tales of Madness and Terror

Maximus SHOCK

An OMP Magazine

Issue
No. 9

MAXIMUS
SHOCK
9

Here, you are the ...

ENDANGERED SPECIES

W. K. Pomeroy

On the day in question, I checked the trail register heading to Vanderwhacker Mountain not really expecting any hikers. Brown, red, and yellow leaves blanketed much of the forest floor, only a scattered few clinging in sparse clumps onto their branches. I smelled the threat of snow on the breeze, even over the decaying foliage.

I always marvel in the way the tiny roof and slide out drawers almost always keep the registry lists dry even after the worst storms. Since there had been no other car when I drove my official SUV into the pull-off parking area, seeing two names scribbled on the bottom of the registry surprised me. Amy Pray and Amelia Bonder had signed in the previous day, and never signed out. They hadn't filled out the box to show how long they intended to stay, which usually meant a day hike.

I pulled out my cell phone first. For a split second I saw one bar of connectivity. Before I pressed a single button, the bar vanished. Putting my phone away, I unsnapped a walkie-talkie from where it hung on my belt. "Hey, homebase, anyone authorized for overnight around Vanderwhacker?" When I released the button, I heard soft static, nothing else. "Hey, Sandylocks, you there?"

More static in response.

She must have stepped out for a cig, I thought to myself.

I considered the situation. People often forgot to sign out when they went up a trail, especially if they came back a slightly different way.

I knew a few typical camping spots I could walk to within a couple hours, and figured I'd pick up a cell signal or check back in by radio somewhere along the way. I knew this broke procedure. Maybe the late fall sun on my back talked me into it, or because I knew if my search went long, I wouldn't have to eat Maria's vegan loaf for dinner.

I considered walking back to get the bear gun with its rubber bullet ammo from the SUV's arsenal. While there, I could have checked in via car radio since it almost never lost signal, but decided not to waste time. Bears had been active that fall, but not too bad, and if worse came to worst I had my sidearm with me.

Per procedure, I checked each red trail marker as I walked the well-worn path that I knew would fade the further I got from civilization. I came to where an old hemlock had fallen across the established path. From the fresh earth clumped in its upturned roots, I figured it happened during the thunder storm three days prior.

I tried my walkie again by that deadfall, and still got no response. I made a note of it, so we could get a crew in to clear it.

I could see where people had gone around it on the root side of the tree. Those roots formed a vertical wall which would have made a great start for a lean-to. I had used something similar to it during my first survival training in the Army.

Just past the fallen tree I got a face full of cobwebs. I flailed my arms around and spit to get them off me. If someone had been watching me, they would have thought I was some lunatic lashing out at invisible people.

I continued up trail until I came to the spot where experienced hikers often Y'ed off down an unmarked deer path leading toward some of the more remote woods. I'm not like my buddy Hawk who can track people and animals by broken twigs and minute imprints scratched on hardened ground, but even I could see tread marks of size seven hiking boots heading down the deer trail.

I checked my cell, tried the walkie, and again got nothing. If I had been issued one of those new satellite phones the captain and his top guys have, I bet I would have gotten through.

I pulled my Bowie knife out of its ankle sheath and using the dull back side carved an arrow into hardened dirt right next to the path. The tip of my arrow pointed up the deer path where someone on the main path could easily see it, but wouldn't be likely to be step on it accidentally.

I know this didn't follow procedure either, but not being able to contact anyone since I checked when I first got to the region, made me think if I took too long someone might come looking for me.

With a gentle breeze in my face, and stray sunbeams warming me, I got into a mindless walking rhythm. I lost track of time. The deep thunk of my boots echoing on solid ground with each step calmed every nerve. I kept my footsteps loud and even hummed a little so I wouldn't come round a corner and surprise a bear trying to fill its stomach before its winter sleep.

Occasionally, I'd see a hiking boot tread in a spot between the leaves or an even smaller sneaker tread pressed into soft soil along the trail. It made me feel pretty good about going the right direction.

I got to the first spot where I knew a good camping area could be bushwhacked to with a little effort. I detected no indications anyone had gone into the brush there, so I continued forward. Feeling people had to be closer, I transitioned to hunter mode. I tried to keep my footfalls quiet and stopped humming. I might've even made Hawk a little proud of me.

Further down the trail, I paused where beeches, maples, and scrub pines thinned into a clearing. Wilted wildflowers, clover, and canary grass stretched out in front of me. About to step out of the tree cover, movement ahead in the field stopped me.

I focused on it. Something gray, not as big as a bear, definitely bigger than a beaver, slunk forward away from me, keeping very close to the ground. My pulse sped up a bit, not really believing what I beheld.

I've always loved wolves. As much appreciation as I have of nature as an adult, my love of wolves probably stems from watching Lon Chaney movies with my father.

Back when I first became a Ranger working in Adirondack State Park, I learned the number of native gray wolves had dropped so low as to almost be considered extinct. As a result, even though I always wanted to see one in the wild, I never expected to. There had been times, deep in the forest, when I checked remote fire towers or trail markers, I'd heard distant howls, but I chalked them up to coyote, coy dogs, and the yipping of foxes.

I inched forward, trying to verify what my eyes told me. The gray mass stayed very low to the ground making it difficult to see.

I must have made a sound. It snapped its lupine head in my direction.

I froze in place.

A large gray snout rose up above the wild grass sniffing the air. A triangular patch of white fur under its jaw made it almost look like it had a beard.

Adrenaline spiking, my heart pounded, but I held my breath, to not make another sound.

He's so beautiful, I thought, (though I really had no idea if it was a he or she).

He blinked twice before silently lowering his head and focusing on something else. A yearling White-tailed doe, barely old enough to be past the stage of spotted fur, fed at the far edge of the clearing. She bent her head to take in a mouthful of berries; possibly the last remnants of that year's raspberry crop, I wasn't close enough to be sure.

I could just make out the wolf's back as it crawled along the ground. The way it moved appeared smooth, almost snakelike, without the writhing, and faster than I would have thought possible. The wind carried me an odd scent. The smell reminded me of Hawk's hunting dogs, though somehow both wilder and thicker.

The protector in me wanted to cry out and warn the doe. Another part of me watched in rapt fascination as this predator moved in.

The White-tailed deer lifted her head staring in the direction of the wolf. It scanned the field never pausing in its chewing. If she scented anything or heard anything it must not have registered as dangerous. She lowered her head to take another bite.

The wolf sprung into the crisp fall air, much higher than I expected, at least doubling my 5'8" height. Its full weight came crashing down on top of the doe. Jaws clamped down on her neck. The front legs and back legs supported the wolf, while its second and third set of legs wrapped around the young deer holding it in place even as it tried to run.

The wolf twisted his neck ripping a large hunk of bloody flesh in a spray of arterial blood from the doe, then clamping back down to rip again and again. In the quiet after the deer stopped struggling, I heard a sucking sound, like a straw at the bottom of a glass trying to get that last drop.

At first my brain did not comprehend what I had seen. I counted twice, then recounted a third time. No matter how I tried to count it, the wolf had four fully developed sets of legs, eight legs in total.

"Holy shit." The words came out of my mouth before I knew I had been going to say them.

The wolf-thing opened its jaw and let the deer's carcass fall to the ground. It looked directly at me and growled.

Something primal in me twisted my gut into one large fear knot.

All eight legs bent, and not necessarily in the directions one would expect them to. It took a six foot hop in my direction.

I took a cautious step backward.

It showed its teeth to me, sharp and vicious, still bloody from the doe, but it did not come closer.

I took a second step backward.

It made a breathy noise somewhere between a sniff and a snarl. Its knees bent awkwardly as it moved back to where it stood with all eight legs straddling the doe.

My blue eyes and his yellow eyes remained locked the entire time I backed away, until I got far enough back trees interrupted our sight line.

As soon as I got out of its sight, some primitive ape part of my brain told me to run. It is a measure of how panicked I actually felt that the thought of pulling my sidearm and shooting the thing had not even occurred to me. Only my training allowed me to retain some semblance of calm as I trotted (rather than sprinted) back along the deer trail, intending to get to the safety of my vehicle quickly without being exhausted when I got there.

I'd only been on the move a couple minutes when I saw a plump blonde haired girl ahead of me on the path. She held an armload of dead wood, and a guilty grin on her face.

I slowed my pace before I got all the way to her.

"Good afternoon, officer." I'm not a great judge of age, but I judged her as younger than me by a few years, though definitely out of college.

"Ranger, not officer," I corrected her robotically. With that automated response my sense of panic vanished. I remembered what had brought me out this far, and figured out who she had to be. "Are you Amy Pray or Amelia Bonder?"

Her grin faltered. "I'm Amelia. Is everything alright?"

I wanted to blurt out, *no nothing is alright.* Instead I kept my tone calm, "You signed in yesterday and didn't sign out."

"We're doing a four day camp."

I could feel tense muscles in my neck straining as I shook my head from side to side.

"We have everything in order. Our camp and burn permits are back at the tent." I saw her light green eyes focus on the patch over my shirt pocket, where blocky print spelled out my entire name. "Ranger Ameris?"

"You can call me Rand," again my automatic response kicked in.

"What does the T. stand for?"

For a moment what she said and the flirting tone in which she said it confused me, then I realized the patch had my full name on it, Randall T. Ameris.

"My middle name is Terrance."

"Oh that's funny, that's my brother's name, though he isn't in nearly as good shape as you."

"Amelia, you need to get out of here. There's a ...," for a moment the right words wouldn't come into my head, "an animal control issue here, and it isn't safe."

"Oh don't worry, we've sealed our garbage and hung it up high. There's nothing to draw the bears to us."

A mental image of the wolf-creature leaping into the air to grab a plastic bag of garbage in its jaws almost made me laugh.

"Where's your camp?"

"Not too far. We used the side of the ravine as a wind break. Snug as a..."

"Ma'am, put the wood down and take me there, now."

"But I've been gathering it for..."

"Now!"

I don't know if the seriousness of my tone got through to her then, but she put down her sticks, stopped talking, and led me back to her camp.

Under other circumstances it would have been a comfortable safe set up. I saw their hunter-orange tent fifty feet before we got there. A well-built stone ring firepit contained the ashes of a fire. A camp coffee pot sat on the collapsible wire cooking frame over the pit.

"We've got company," Amelia almost sung out as we got close to camp.

A dark haired woman emerged from the tent wearing those square black framed glasses really popular five or six years ago. She gripped a paperback book in her left hand with her thumb holding her place.

Her face reminded me of a school teacher who had been at it a little too long; hard, tired, emotionally beaten. I'd guess she wasn't much older than me, but kinda like some guys I knew in the army, she had that look of having seen things regular people shouldn't see.

"To what do we owe the pleasure, Ranger?"

Her deep sultry voice held all the joy her face seemed to have forgotten about. She probably could have made a fortune hosting one of those phone sex lines.

"Are the two of you here alone?"

Amelia, seeming angry about not bringing back her wood began to chirp, "I don't see what business that is of…"

Amy shut her down with half a glance. "Yes, we're alone."

"Ma'am, I apologize for interrupting your trip, but due to the proximity of a dangerous situation, the two of you will need to leave the area as quickly as possible."

"But we've got the permit to be here," Amelia's whining voice contrasted Amy's deep tones.

"Do we have time to pack up?"

I thought about it. The wolf-creature had a good sized doe to eat. If it behaved like other canines, the meal should satisfy it for a while. Of course as far as I knew, no one had ever seen a canine like it before. The way it looked at me and growled still twisted my innards when I thought about it.

"If you pack up quickly."

She nodded thanks and made a move toward the tent.

"But we've got two more days?"

"Amelia Bonder," the blonde haired woman stood up a little straighter at the sound of her last name, "this man is only doing his job trying to keep us safe. You will not give him lip."

Amelia kicked the tip of her sneaker into the ground like a little kid, but did not argue.

They pulled two large backpacks and one oversized Phantom brand sleeping bag out of the tent.

I began helping them take the tent down. I had just pulled the last stake out when each small hair on the back of my neck stood straight up.

I dropped the stake and spun around. I didn't see anything. I'd don't know if I had smelled something or heard something. I felt sure we were no longer alone.

This time I remembered to draw my gun.

"Quiet."

The two women stopped moving. There was no sound; no birds, no squirrels chittering, nothing.

"Ladies, very slowly, pick up your backpacks."

"What's going on?" For the first time Amelia sounded scared.

"Shhhhhh." Even Amy's hush noise had an element of sensuality; at another time it would have been a welcome distraction.

Its scent reached my nose, that powerful doglike odor made it feel too close. The quiet broke when I heard it growl. I pointed the barrel of my sidearm in the direction of the menacing sound. Even though I couldn't see it immediately, I knew the thing had to be there.

Something moved close to a stand of four white birch about twenty yards from us. It might have been just been a falling leaf. The movement seemed too small to be the wolf-creature.

I tried to keep my voice quiet, while maintaining a command tone. "Ladies, in a moment I am going to fire my gun. When I do, I want the two of you to run back to the road as quickly as you can. Lock yourself in my truck and wait for me there."

Without taking my eyes off the birch trees, I reached with my off hand down into my pocket for the car's key fob. I held it out behind me, like a relay runner handing off the baton. I felt one of the women take it from my hand before I brought the fingers back to steady the other holding my sidearm.

Much closer than I expected, I saw a canine nose poke out beyond the rotted end of a fallen maple. I discharged my firearm twice. I've always been a good shot, and I thought I hit it.

"Go! Now!"

With the echo of the shots in my ears I didn't hear the women moving. I snuck a glance over my shoulder at them, while trying to keep most of my focus on where I believed the wolf-creature had to be. In that instant, I saw Amy with her hand in the center of Amelia's back pushing the younger woman forward as they sprinted toward the deer path.

I felt much more than saw the mass of gray fur hurtling down at me. I know it shouldn't be possible, but I swear I saw the bullet exit the gun as my sidearm discharged. The slug tore through the joint of what would be the equivalent of a shoulder on a human. Hot blood spattered my face, as the creature's weight crashed down into me. My legs gave out, forcing me to a semi-kneeling position. I focused on its snout, the gnashing teeth attempting to get to my neck, the same way it had killed the doe. I shoved the gun into its mouth with one hand. If I could shoot from there, I'd blow its brain out the back of its skull.

Sharp fangs tore into my hand making me lose my grip on the trigger. I felt my skin shred inside the creature's closing jaw. When it tried to clamp down all the way, I heard the painful sound of teeth striking metal. When it reflexively opened its mouth to avoid the gun, I ripped my hand out of its mouth. My blood started to flow, mixing with its blood.

I distinctly felt five of its limbs push off on me, rock hard paws bruising me, nails scratching me, as it bounded several feet away. It shook its head spitting out my firearm and to my satisfaction part of a tooth.

I stayed on my knees in a defensive position, sliding my bowie knife from the ankle sheath.

It started circling me. A strange half-cough, half-wheezing sound, issued forth from deep inside as the creature prepared its attack.

It held its front left paw off the ground, avoiding weight on the injured shoulder. Its extra legs more than compensated for any possible loss of mobility. The white triangle under its muzzle no longer looked like a beard with three different shades of blood staining the fur, the doe's, mine, and its own.

Bright yellow eyes with large black pupils studied me as it circled, moving past the fire pit.

I tried to look strong, not like something it would consider prey.

A guttural growl filled my ears.

The snarling noise didn't come from the creature. My throat had begun producing a sound I had never heard before.

The wolf crouched low flattening to the ground. For a split second I almost mistook it for a gesture of supplication.

It sprung into the air, jaw wide open waiting to chomp down on my neck.

A detached part of my mind noted it had no obvious genitalia where I would have expected to see it.

Against instinct I moved into its leap, getting under it, letting its weight drive my knife into its underbelly and rip down then across, twisting the blade to increase the damage. Blood, organs, intestines, and eleven fleshy eggs the size of golf balls poured over me in spurts and thumps. I kept ripping. Its fangs bit the top of my head. That hollow sucking sound filled my ears. Its legs kept pawing at me battering against me for what seemed like forever, until it finally went still.

I don't know how long I stayed there, watching its eyes glaze over, smelling its death, letting my own heartbeat slow. Tears of relief and somehow loss, sobbed out of me, mixing with the blood and gore plastered to my face, but not washing it off. Eventually, I gathered my strength, forced myself to crush each egg under my boots despite the sickening feel of something wiggling each time.

By the time I got back to the deer path my legs had stopped trembling, though I didn't feel steady enough to run. A few of the yellow sunbeams turned burnt orange in the western sky, letting me know it would be cold and dark before I got back to the SUV.

I came around a boulder and not ten feet away a set of yellow eyes examined me. Smaller than the creature I had killed by at least a season, it bristled. Dark nostrils flared. I heard it inhale, once angrily, then a second time, and its entire manner changed.

If a wolf face can be said to smile, that is what he did. Rather than bounding at me, his eight legs carried him to me with a gait approximating a horse's canter. He sniffed me a third time, before backing away almost playfully. It felt like those yellow eyes expected something. I had no idea what.

He howled.

I howled back at him, though my human throat didn't really make the same sound.

A chorus of answering howls came from too close by, ahead of me, up the path.

I walked slowly willing myself to show no fear. Each member of the pack sniffed me. I don't know exactly how many of the eight legged wolves approached me, at least a dozen. Their sizes varied from a scruffy pup to one with darker gray fur almost as big as the one I killed. Two of them licked me like domestic dogs might when they expected a treat. They used their odd canter gate to keep pace along next to me as I walked, a many legged gray fur escort.

I discovered Amy's body first. It looked like the older woman had been tackled from behind, though her body might have been turned while they had been feeding on her. I would not have recognized the desiccated corpse as her, except some tufts of her black hair still protruded from the shriveled remains of her skull. Where skin remained, it had turned a pale greyish color, and though I didn't touch her I could see the brittle dry quality of it, like all the moisture had been drained out of it.

Amelia's body had been torn to pieces. I'd guess by the younger pups. Blood soaked the ground on one side of her torso, but that was the only indication of moisture. I saw no sign of her limbs, and made no effort to search for them.

The pack looked at me for approval. I picked up the less destroyed backpack from where it had been tossed and continued to move forward.

The pack traveled with me until the sun went down, then one by one they and their yellow eyes vanished into the deepening shadows, and I came back to civilization.

Based on his statement following his emergence from the forest, transcribed above, my subsequent testing, and the results of independent psychological tests, it is my recommendation Ranger Randall T. Ameris be committed to the high security wing of the Upstate Mental Health Facility until such time as a psychological review panel finds him stable enough to be tried for the murders of Amelia Bonder and Amy Pray.

Miles Ooreau
Miles M. Ooreau Ph.D.
New York State Police Internal Affairs Office

Collected tales of Madness and Terror

Maximus SHOCK

An OMP Magazine

MAXIMUS SHOCK 10

Issue No. 10

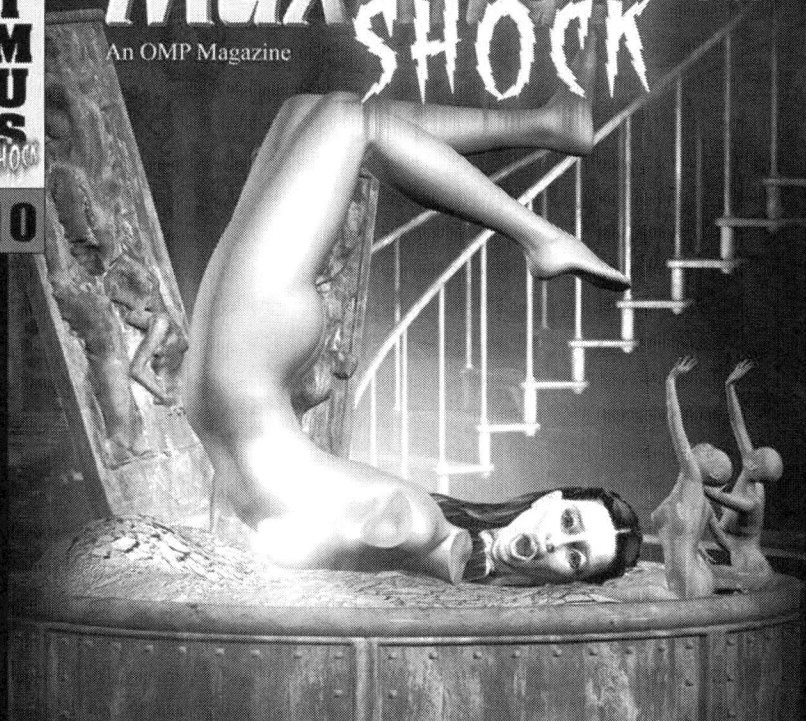

Horror for Sale!

MANNEQUIN

Matt Hay

To Susan, Samantha and Emma, my beautiful girls.
I couldn't have done this without you.
Thank you for putting up with me whilst writing.
You like Mannequin will always have a special place in my heart.

CHAPTER ONE

It was a dark, windy night in the beautiful city of Edinburgh. This was the busiest time of year at MacDougall's Department Store with shoppers staying late to spend their hard-earned money on gifts for their loved ones during the festive period. Children were often left with their grandparents or child minders whilst their parents scoured the shop to try and bring a smile to their faces on Christmas morning.

The store had been closed for a few hours after staying open late to try and tempt the traditional nine to five workers into spending their final salary of the year. A middle-aged man with light brown, receding hair was sitting slumped across a cluttered desk with his head resting peacefully on his drool soaked arm. A quiet, purring snore escaped his vibrating lips as Brian dozed in his office. The end of the month figures were due and he had worked on to get them finished. Sales had been unusually slow this November and he was worried that this would affect his Christmas bonus which was needed to buy presents for his eight-year-old son Keith. A messy divorce in the summer had left Keith living with his mother Lisa. This had caused a mountain of bills which left Brian struggling to find money to live and support his son. The many sleepless nights spent worrying had caught up with Brian tonight as he dozed away, alone in his office.

Scrunched up balls of paper and half eaten chocolate bars surrounded him on the desk. Large boxes of files were scattered on the floor with crumpled forms untidily hanging out. Brian was not the neatest person in the office but he usually got the job done. Over the last three months, the store's declining profits had singled him out as a target from his area manager, Sandra. Each month, she picked the worst performing store and embarrassed its leader in front of everyone else at the meeting. Humiliation and shame were often used as a motivation technique to improve the performance of her team. Brian had been the target of her wrath recently and Sandra had often lost her temper at him which resulted in various office supplies being thrown in his direction.

Stirring from a peaceful slumber, Brian's breathing quickened as his eyes slowly opened to familiarise themselves with their blurry surroundings. The sluggishness was evident as he sat up sharply in his black leather office chair. Absent-mindedly, he picked up the coffee cup, which had been sitting on his desk untouched for the last few hours. The cold, sugary taste hit his palate; the revulsion of the stale coffee caused him to gag slightly. Gulping down the foul liquid to force it into his stomach, this was better than the alternative of the beverage being sprayed over the paperwork spread on his desk. Hurriedly, he finished the remainder of the drink to try and sharpen his dulled senses.

Slowly, Brian relaxed back in his chair, extending his arms out, before letting out a long, tired yawn. The dregs of the coffee had failed to rouse him from his grogginess and a sudden craving for more had fantasies of the luxurious Americano from the Starbucks around the corner entering his mind. Unfortunately, the waiting sales figures brought him back to reality as his mood soured at the realisation that the plastic liquid from the aging machine in the staff room was the only option left.

Easing himself out of his black leather chair, Brian stood shakily before staggering out of the office into the poorly lit hallway. Using the side walls to keep his balance, he headed towards the short staircase to the level below.

At the bottom of the stairway, he continued along the hallway before entering the staff room at the end of the corridor. It was a small room that was rarely used these days due to the emergence of the takeaway lunch from the myriad of choices around Central Edinburgh. Inside the cosy room was a small table with four cheap plastic chairs arranged around it. On it sat a small, brown bowl which contained the remains of a tin of tomato soup. At the other end of the room, the small microwave sat on the work surface with a tiny fridge occupying the corner beside it. To the right of the appliance was the coffee machine that Brian had in his sights on. Standing in front of it was a small, well-built man wearing a long brown overcoat. The bald chap, who was in his early forties, was pouring himself a cup of coffee out of the aging contraption. Upon hearing the larger man's echoing footsteps, he turned to face the store manager.

"Evenin' boss," he remarked with a smile which emanated from his stubbly, rugged face, "You down for a cuppa?"

"Good evening, Joe," replied Brian, "I'm dying for one, mate. White, two sugars please"

"Aye, no bother, boss."

Joe turned back around and punched some numbers into the black, metallic device. Out dispensed a small brown cup, followed by a painful gurgling sound and the black steaming liquid started to pour into the plastic container.

Brian had known Joe for a number of years and Joe was one of the staff that he socialised with. They often spent evenings playing poker or grabbing a pint at the local bar whilst shooting pool or playing darts.

Unexpectedly, the lights extinguished which plunged the room into sudden darkness. From the other end of the room, Joe uttered a small curse as Brian could hear the splash of the hot liquid spill onto his exposed hand. The outline of Joe's figure was barely visible as Brian could see him fumbling about in his pocket in the low light. After a few seconds, an exclamation of triumph came from Joe as he lit the room with a small torch.

"Ha!" called Joe, "I knew this bugger would come in handy one of these days. Looks like the power is off, boss."

"Fuck," remarked Brian in frustration, "I need to get these damn figures in. Are you any good with electrics, mate?"

"A wee bit, boss," answered Joe. "I've dabbled a bit around the house. The fuse box is at the other end of the store in the cashier's room. We could go over and see if we can fix it ourselves?"

"Aye," replied Brian, "There is no harm in trying. After you."

The pair crept down the dark stairway into the shop. A large steel door blocked Brian's exit to the main floor. Despite pushing down on the handle, he struggled to shift the entrance obstructing his path. It soon gave way after he used his stocky frame to force it open. A cool chill greeted them as they entered through the foreboding darkness which provided little respite from the shadow that surrounded them. A low whistle was heard in the distance and the intermittent sound of fluttering echoed around them.

"Fucking hell!" exclaimed Brian. "Some stupid fucker has left the fucking windows open. Come on, we need to get those closed or the damp air will ruin the stock."

Brian squinted in the distance, trying to make out what lay ahead. He could just see the long aisle extending out in front of him with a variety of overpriced cotton tops flanking him. The going was tough as they carefully walked along the rough, carpeted floor. Intermittently, they stepped over numerous garments left strewn on the ground, dislodged by the gusting wind. Stumbling slightly, Brian lost his footing and it took the quick reflexes of Joe to keep him from falling into a heap in front of him.

Minutes seemed like hours as the end of the aisle loomed larger. Brian's eyes were slowly adjusting to the fading light as garment after garment was pushed away to clear the path ahead. A shadowy figure lay blocking their access. Brian motioned for Joe to pass the torch over before examining the body. Jumping back in shock, Brian gasped as the light of the beam reflected on the face of the prone figure.

"You ok, boss?" asked Joe.

"Aye," replied Brian stunned, "There's one of those store dummies lying on the floor in front of me. The way it looked at me was a little creepy. It freaked me out a bit."

"Let me have a look, boss," asked Joe.

After Brian passed the torch over to him, Joe slid past to shine the light down to try and get a better look. "Those bloody things are too lifelike for my liking," said Joe in awe. "Look at that one, it's almost the spitting image of the new sales rep Cathy."

The face of the mannequin reflected in the light of the torch as the long, blonde hair, luscious red lips, and deep blue eyes confirmed his suspicion. Brian turned ashen white as the crude marks of the cheap staples caked in crusted blood separating Cathy's tanned neck from the white body of the display model were revealed to him.

"Joe," Brian stammered at the bald man with a fearful look on his face. "It is Cathy!"

Joe rested his hand on Brian's shoulder to try and calm the shaking store manager down. "Boss," he said softly, "Take deep breaths and say it slowly, mate. I didn't catch what you said there."

Brian bent over and inhaled the cool fresh air. After a few seconds, he relaxed and was able to stand straight again. "Joe," said Brian clearly, "It is Cathy, have a look."

Joe aimed the beam onto the face of the figure before him. The beautiful sales assistant's aging features were instantly recognisable by the usual over application of make-up which was caked all over her pained, tortured face. Joe turned white as he examined the rest of her body, noticing the staples on her neck and limbs. The blood was oozing through the poorly stitched joints and formed a crimson puddle on the floor behind it. A swarm of small flies were buzzing around the fallen figure, feasting on the gore on the floor. A small piece of paper lay folded on the ground; Joe picked it up and started to read.

"Cathy, ten percent," read Joe, "Not good enough."

Brian's face changed to a deep crimson colour, highlighting the anger which was coursing through his veins as he slowly clenched his fist and began pounding it into his hand.

"When I find the bastard who did this, I'll fucking kill them."

"We'll get them," said Joe coldly, "But we have to move Cathy. She's blocking our way, mate"

Brian bent down to lift it but the pungent stench of the blood and gore that oozed from Cathy's limbs caught the back of his throat causing him to throw up the contents of his stomach.

"You ok, boss?" asked Joe.

"Aye, fine, mate," Brian replied. "I caught a whiff of that awful smell just as I bent down. Give me a minute and I'll be ok."

Brian stood with his hands on his hips and took some more deep breaths before bending down again to grasp the torso of the mannequin and drag it to the side of the aisle. He removed a long coat from the railing beside him and used it to cover the face of Cathy before motioning to Joe to continue the weary journey ahead.

A crackling noise vibrated through the speaker system around them, causing him to jump with a start.

"Staff announcement," rasped a robotic voice, "Would Cathy please make her way to Aisle Six, it's a matter of life and death." A demented laugh sounded from the tannoy system, its long, chilling cackle sent shivers up Brian's spine. They stood frozen in shock as the laughter gently faded, leaving them terrified at the taunting they had just heard

CHAPTER TWO

Brian remained frozen as the eerie silence enveloped him, not noticing the clatter of the torch dropping to the floor, the small beam extinguishing as it shattered into tiny pieces behind him. All he could hear was the fading echo of the voice reverberating through his tortured mind, tearing through him like fingernails scraping down a dry blackboard. He jumped as he felt a cold hand on his shoulder, shaking him vigorously to bring him back to the chilling reality.

"Boss, boss," said Joe with concern, "Can you hear me?"

"Aye," replied Brian, shaking as if he was standing in the middle of a small tremor. "Sorry, but that just freaked me out a bit, mate."

"Me, too," said Joe. "I don't know who that is, but they are one sick bastard."

"What happened to the torch?" asked Brian.

"Sorry, boss," replied Joe, "I dropped it in shock. I think it's broken now."

"It's ok, mate," said Brian, "We'll just have to cope without it. The plan hasn't changed. We need to get the lights back on."

The pair cautiously made their way along the rest of the aisle. A gust of wind eased the soft fibres of the flapping, satin blouses onto the exposed cheek of Brian, sending a small chill through his already tense frame. Brian lashed out to try and remove the uncomfortable material from the touch of his body, instead it coiled around his exposed limb. Exasperated, Brian pulled as hard as he could but the blouse held firm, bringing the metallic frame attached to the garment crashing down on top of him. Its awkwardness and the weight of the clothes prevented him from escaping his self-created Prada prison.

Tentatively, he reached out to try and free himself from the clothes rack, causing his hand to rest upon wrinkled, soft flesh that was attached to the sleeve of one of the garments, causing him to slightly recoil. Panting, whilst sweating profusely, it took a few moments for him to steady his breathing as panic began to set in.

"Boss!" Joe called out to him. "Boss!"

"Joe!" wailed Brian, "Get this fucking thing off me!"

"Two secs, boss, are you hurt?" asked Joe.

"No, mate!" he snapped, "But there is something on top of me. I need it off me, now."

A small flicker of light appeared in front of him to reveal Joe's unshaven face, illuminated in a faded yellow flame. Slowly, the light moved along the rack of clothes spread across the top of Brian's outstretched body. Joe stopped and let out a gasp.

"Jesus, boss," exclaimed Joe, "That is just fucking sick."

"What?" asked Brian with dread.

"It's a fucking knob, boss."

"You're joking me, mate?" exclaimed Brian in disbelief. "A penis?"

"It is," replied Joe. "It's bloody and limp. Hold on, there seems to be something on it." Joe moved the lighter closer to the detached manhood, examining what appeared to be black markings on the exposed member. "No balls, no sales," read Joe slowly. "That's all it says."

"I don't give a fuck what it says; can you get this fucking thing off of me?"

Joe reached into the top pocket of his overcoat and pulled a black pen out. Carefully, he flicked the cock off Brian's trapped body watching as it rolled to a stop beside Brian's left ear.

Brian gagged in revulsion as Joe lifted the rack of clothes from him, allowing him to slide to safety. Slowly, he rose, brushing the dust from his trousers, shuddering from the unexpected touch of the detached penis. His office seemed a lot more attractive to him as he contemplated bolting back up the stairs and locking himself away from this nightmare.

Joe tapped him on the shoulder; his already frayed nerves caused him to jump sharply. The shocking events of the past few minutes, coupled with the slight touch from Joe, freaked him out even more.

"Don't do that, mate," he exclaimed, "I'm on a knife edge just now."

"Sorry, boss," Joe replied, "But I think we need to get moving."

They made better time as Brian's eyes were adjusting to the faded light enabling him to clearly see the trip hazards that lay ahead. Carefully, he stepped over each item of clothing, praying that one false move wouldn't send him to the punishing floor below. Without further incident, they reached the end of the aisle. Peering into the distance, they tried to locate the best way to the cash room which housed the fuse box. A route through the kitchenware section, into the perfumery before exiting through the bedding section, etched itself into Brian's head as he planned his next move.

Brian had taken point whilst Joe remained at the rear to cover his back. This meant that it was easier for the smaller man to get past him if he did run into any problems. The extra pair of hands would be useful as he had a feeling that more surprises were lying in wait for them.

Brian slowly eased his way around the corner of the aisle into the murky, chilling path that faced him. Straining, he could hear a faint noise in the distance coming towards him as the floor vibrated causing him to shudder. A trundling sound of scraping metal raked through his body as a square frame shaped before him. The vibrations intensified as the newly formed shopping trolley gained speed before him.

"Watch out Joe!" yelled Brian as he dove back down the aisle to avoid the incoming object hurtling towards him.

Sprawled on the floor, Brian could only watch as the trolley screeched by. A pair of glowing, red eyes stared at him as it passed. The eerie figure slowly transformed into another one of the mannequins as more laughter was heard from the speakers around him. A deep piercing stare locked on Brian as the cart rolled to a stop beside another of its comrades in the distance. The noise faded to an uncomfortable silence, causing Brian to tremble as the fear coursed through him.

Brian's eyes remained fixed on the creepy figure, unable to spot any alterations to it due to the darkness ahead. It winked at him as he sat aghast at the audacity of the demented dummy.

Unaware of the movement behind him, Joe slipped past, sneaking quietly towards the stationary trolley, taking care to remain unseen as its motionless face remained locked on the quivering store manager behind him.

The events of the night had taken its toll on Brian as he remained lying on the ground, unable to do anything but watch the hypnotic eyes of the terror ahead. Cathy's mutilation, the severed penis, and the creepy figure in the trolley had left him scared, to the point where he could only watch as Joe crept closer to the chaos ahead.

Joe was rapidly gaining on the shopping cart as Brian continued to look on, moving quietly, like a panther stalking its prey, getting reading to devour its next meal. Shadowy figures moved either side of him but each time he shifted his eyes, the shape disappeared. The faint sound of clothes rustling was heard to his left followed by quiet, fading footsteps to his right as his mind started to play tricks on him. Too frightened to move, he lay there, not wanting to risk catching the attention of whatever was nearby.

Joe finally reached the trolley, ignoring the dummy on the floor and peered at the creepy figure inside, its eyes fading out as Joe reached out to examine it. A few moments passed as the mannequin remained motionless whilst Joe searched the cart looking for any clue to explain tonight's horror.

Movement from the corner of his eye drew Brian's attention to the model on the ground rising up before sneaking behind the bald storeman. The dark figure repeatedly struck Joe across the back of the head with a long, thick object as Brian watched Joe's lifeless form fall to the unforgiving surface. Unable to move, Brian could only watch in terror as the dark figure bent down, dragging Joe into the darkness beyond. The laughter finally dissipated leaving Brian alone, paralysed with fear.

CHAPTER THREE

The cold air whistled through the desolate, shadowy store. The satin blouses could be heard fluttering in the light breeze as Brian sat with his mouth open, aghast at what had transpired. A small tear formed at the corner of his eye and slowly trickled its way down his cheek. Subconsciously, he brought his arm up and wiped it away with the sleeve of the silk shirt that he was wearing. Another one formed to replace its fallen comrade and it soon fled the battlefield of his dampening cheek. More followed and a large white handkerchief was produced from Brian's pocket which soon became sodden from the river that flowed from his inescapable grief. His eyes soon blurred from repeated wiping which coupled with the surrounding darkness, took the horrifying sight of the mannequin away from his tortured mind. All that remained was the nightmare of Joe's abduction replaying through his fragile psyche, his hands clasping his forehead as he watched his friend's body being dragged away. Rocking back and forth, he muttered random phrases as the pain of losing his friend throbbed through his mind.

It took a few minutes for Brian to regain his senses. The disturbing image seeped into the depths of the memories that he'd temporarily banished from his consciousness. Now alone, he was left to face the hidden terrors in his workplace as he looked around expecting to see the shadows moving nearby but he saw nothing but the emptiness that enveloped him. Turning, he glimpsed movement beside him as shadows of the clothes flapped in the wind, teasing his already fragile nerves.

Loneliness grabbed his fractured mind, playing tricks on his senses, creating shapes and sounds around him. His sanity was almost gone before he realised that he had to get a grip of himself.

A new resolve formed in him as he discovered that the only way to survive the night was to put a stop to the madman who was plaguing him. A determined look formed across his face, a look that said that he was the boss of this store, a look that said that he was going to take his store back and no-one was going to stop him. He was Brian MacDonald and this was his store.

Straightening up, Brian puffed out his sagging chest before striding masterfully towards the kitchen section to find a weapon to defend himself against tonight's horror. There was a number of different utensils which Brian thought could be useful as he rummaged through the drawers looking for a sharp fork or a kitchen knife but he was ultimately left disappointed as nothing matched his requirements.

Brian's footsteps quickened when he resumed his route as more adrenalin burst through him, heightening his faded senses, turning the reduced light to his advantage. The path ahead was more visible as he strode confidently towards the other end of the store.

The adrenalin pulsed through his veins causing him to shiver as his body cooled to compensate for the increased heart rate. His muscles contracted as he eased into a light jog down the dim aisle. The obstructions that littered the path ahead were more visible as he hurdled over sweaters, skirts, and blouses strewn in front of him. It was a black, lace brassiere that sent him sprawling to the floor, the one item of clothing that Brian usually had no trouble removing now lay wrapped around his feet as he squirmed on the ground trying to free himself. A gentle tug finally untangled the offending lingerie after several attempts to remove it had failed.

Once again, the rasping laughter reverberated through the speakers. The long and haunting sound echoed around him before seeping through his soul and tearing his beating heart from his chest. It gradually softened in tone until it faded into the background causing Brian to shudder at the chilling noise. Turning slowly, not sure of what he was about to face, a dark shadowy outline of another one of the dreadful dummies appeared ahead. Imposing, it stood fixated on him as he rubbed his eyes, trying to erase another one of the nightmares from his vision.

Cautiously, Brian edged his way forward to confront the terror before him, focusing on the still head of the mannequin, waiting for a crimson light to glow through its eyes as the laughter around him faded before leaving him in stony silence to face the plastic peril.

Drawing closer, its joints were now visible, stained with the congealed blood of the victim. The scarlet stream of blood could be traced down the fleshy arm of the mannequin, dripping onto its midriff.

Brian forced his head up to examine the creepy figure. Surprisingly, the crude staples that were prominent on its arm were barely detectable in the light, replaced instead by delicate stitching which held its neck in place. No blood remained on the almost seamless joint causing Brian to take a small intake of breath. His eyes elevated towards the face of the mannequin revealing the rugged features of his former colleague Peter. Brian fondly remembered the rapport that Peter had with the customers. The warm smile on his face often brought him sales as the customers all seemed to love it when Peter took interest in their lives, often giving advice on the best things to buy in the store. That grin was gone now, replaced with a soulless image of what remained of the salesman.

Peter's striking green eyes gradually opened revealing the distorted cherry tint around the iris, causing Brian to take a step back in surprise. The mannequin called Peter stared vacantly at Brian, blinking in slow deliberate movements. After the third one, Peter's chapped, cracked lips pursed together but were unable to produce anything that he could understand. A quiet groan turned into a sound that resembled words which were repeated constantly. Brian strained his head forward to try and make out the chilling message but the low whisper could not be heard. Peter's head tilted forward towards Brian, its lips continuing to talk in a low dulcet tone as Brian remained frozen, hypnotised by the piercing eyes of the hybrid salesman.

"Don't run," whispered the Peter, continuing to ease forward, "You're next. The Master knows you are here and you will die if you run."

Continually, Brian heard the words, "You're next," followed by "don't run," whisper from Peter's drying lips. An urge to turn and bolt surged through Brian as he fought with his inner self. It was only his fear that stopped his shaking legs from moving.

The voice faded into the oblivion and a deep smile extended over the face of the dummy. Brian clenched his fist, before lashing out at its mocking features. The force of his punch decapitated the mannequin's head, causing it to fly several yards before settling to a stop. Peter's cold, empty eyes continued to stare at him and a deep rasping laugh emanated from the severed head in front of him. Angrily, he strode towards it and stomped repeatedly until it was mashed into a bloody pulp on the floor.

The flash of a long object blurred in front of his eyes, striking him across the bridge of his nose. Brian slipped into the darkness of his subconscious as his body slumped on the floor in a crumpled heap.

CHAPTER FOUR

Visions of decapitated mannequins flashed in front of him. Blank faces etched into his tortured mind. Each head morphed into someone he knew and loved. His son, with his beautiful blonde locks and blue eyes had blood running down the side of his cheek. He smiled at him and whispered, "You're next." His ex-wife entered into view with her exquisite ruby mane and her soft milky skin tainted by the seeping, open wounds on her cheek. She sneered at him and hissed, "You will die." His mother and father, with their hair soaked in their own gore, spun along his vision chanting, "You're next son, you will die." Every one of his sales assistants faded in and out of sight. Each one with an injury to the face, each more gruesome than the first, mocking him as they passed. They whispered, "Die, Brian, die," as the nightmare continued. His aunts, his uncles, and all of his cousins faded in and out of his vision, laughing and chanting, "Die, die, die."

Brian tried to run, he wanted to escape the horror before him, the nightmare created by his disturbed psyche. However, each time he moved, he only bounced off one of mannequins into the waiting arms of another. Each one was cackling evilly as he was passed amongst the store dummies.

The taunting continued until he was relayed to a tall, well-built figure whose laughter was deep and booming. The large monster was cleaner than the rest but there was still a little blood spattering across his forehead. He looked up to see the face of his fallen comrade Joe attached to the terror before him. Joe flashed a wicked grin at him before winking and shoving him towards the centre of the plastic fiends.

Each mannequin linked hands and hummed softly. They gently moved in a clockwise direction around the stricken Brian. The humming got louder as they moved faster around the circle. He slumped to the ground and pulled his arms over his ears in terror. Brian slowly eased his knees up to his chin and let out a long pained scream.

Brian awoke with a start. He was sweating profusely despite feeling a cold wind nip the tips of his exposed fingers. The screams continued from his nightmare into his now conscious mind. They soon died down as he slowly realised that his ordeal had ended and he was sat on a dark cold floor with no sign of the evil of his hellish vision nearby.

Brian gasped as he felt a small hand gently resting upon his shaking shoulder. Panic shot through him as he faced the fact that he was not alone. Unsteadily, he rose to his feet to face the owner of the hand. As he rose, his knees gave out from under him, losing balance causing him to fall forwards to the hard surface. The previously undiscovered binds on his wrists meant that he was unable to prevent his face from impacting with the ground underneath.

Briefly, consciousness slipped from him due to the severe concussion to his head. The descent into darkness was brief as the collar of his shirt was violently grasped, dragging Brian to his feet to face his captor. Unsteadiness caused by nerves meant that his legs wobbled as the understanding that he was about to meet his assailant rattled him

As his focus sharpened, beautiful deep brown eyes pierced through his heart, killing what was left of his damaged soul as he could only focus on the two orbs of insanity before him. A deep chuckle escaped from his aggressor's blurred lips, the laughter intensified, booming into a familiar sound before fading into the darkness that surrounded him. The blood drained from his face in shock as his vision cleared to reveal the identity of his tormentor. A small pointed nose and a pair of full, pouty lips brought a familiarity about the woman, it was as if he knew the face from somewhere. At first, he thought that it might be Lisa, his ex-wife, but as more of her features came into focus, he saw that it was Sandra, his area manager. What was she doing here? She should be either at home or working in her office in Glasgow.

An inner rage built inside of Brian as his eyes focused more on his tormentor. The white makeup plastered all over her face and arms was streaked with thin red lines of what looked like dried blood. A white silk blouse barely covered her chest as the slash marks across the side of it revealed the edge of a black lace bra. A black knee-length skirt, slit up the middle revealed her perfectly toned, blood stained legs which in any other situation would have aroused Brian but tonight it just sickened him. Gagging slightly, he watched as her elongated tongue darted out to rapidly collect the oozing liquid from the side of her jaw into her eagerly waiting mouth. Satisfaction groaned from her lips that slowly transformed into a familiar chortle which sent more chills down his spine.

"Sit down, you snivelling toad," she commanded. "You disgust me with your pathetic act."

Brian resolutely stood and stared defiantly into the gleaming eyes of his maniacal manager. Trying to appear determined, he stood proudly whilst trying to fight off the cramp that had started to build in his leg.

"Oh, do sit down, you stubborn ass," she snapped at him, "You've caused me enough trouble already tonight."

Kicking out, Sandra extended her long, toned leg into the back of Brian's knee, causing him to buckle and fall once again to the ground as a result of the unyielding pressure from the force of the blow.

Looming menacingly over him, she used the high, pointed heel of her shoe to drive it into the flesh of his exposed thigh. The pain rushed through Brian as Sandra twisted her foot aggressively into him, causing the skin to break which sprayed blood over her as she pushed harder into his thigh. Finally, resistance was met by the ground underneath, trapping him under her weight.

Writhing in agony, it took all of his willpower to prevent his bowels from releasing through his trousers. He looked up, with a pleading look towards Sandra. Ignoring him, she squealed in pleasure as the pain continued to jolt through his weakening body.

"Brian, Brian," she taunted as she pulled a long sharp kitchen knife out from behind her back. "It's time to put an end to this night for you. My team of obedient mannequins await. Do you want to meet my lovelies before you become one of them?"

Sandra let out a shrill whistle which pierced through his ears. Several loud footsteps were heard as three mannequins appeared behind her. The one on the left was the tallest with shocking red hair and a tattoo down its left arm. Its face revealed the features of John, the Kitchen Department Supervisor. Brian prayed for John's two daughters as they now faced a life without their caring father. Beside him stood the next tallest of the dummies with long black curly hair and slim tanned legs, it was Susan, the Head Cashier. He lamented as he recalled the recent time they had spent chatting. She had been a good friend to him, listening to him as he spoke about the end of his failed marriage. The final mannequin was the shortest of the three. Its small pale legs and bald head soon revealed Brian's abducted colleague Joe.

Brian gasped in shock, his face paled further as he vomited up the foul green bile that remained in his stomach. The sight of Joe sickened him to the centre of his soul. He couldn't bear to watch his dismembered friend standing there at the bidding of the maniac in front of him. It angered him but he remained trapped by the fiend before him as he struggled to free himself from her despicable trap.

"Behold," she exclaimed, "My lovely efficient Sales Team, your new colleagues. Now it's time for you to join them."

Sandra's hand pulled back and slashed across his throat, slicing through the exposed artery in his neck. Leaning across, she extended her tongue and gently lapped the flowing crimson liquid that sprayed from his throat leaving him helpless as he watched the sickening act unfold before him.

He weakened as the blood slowly drained from his body with a morbid acceptance that the end was coming for him. Finally, he could be at peace with the world, ready to join his departed parents and watch over his son whilst he lived out his life. With his last moments upon him, he accepted his approaching fate and realised that he had no way of stopping it, leaving himself at peace with the world and forgiving the gruesome act of his killer.

A sudden movement caught his attention as one of the mannequins was slowly moving towards him. Sandra continued to laugh as more blood spurted onto her waiting tongue, her thirst never-ending as the liquid flowed down her waiting throat.

The figure was almost upon them now. Sandra was oblivious to the movement behind her as she continued to greedily feed on his ebbing life. Brian's vision faded further into the light and towards his final breath as the dummy reached out and placed its fleshy hands around the throat of the psychotic fiend. It squeezed forcefully onto her exposed neck causing her to inadvertently jerk away from Brian, revealing the face of his good friend Joe on the body of the mannequin before him.

Joe winked slowly at Brian as Sandra slumped to her demise. A sense of relief came across him knowing that his killer had met her doom. She could no longer torment his friends and colleagues.

Drawing his last breath, Brian surrendered to the darkness, letting it surround him as he accepted his ascendance out of this life. It dissipated to reveal a glowing white light which embraced him before delivering him along the path to his final journey.

The mannequin formerly known as Joe turned, shaking his head at the carnage that had just unfolded. The corpses of Brian and Sandra were soaked in the blood of his former boss and lay lifeless before him. Awkwardly moving across, he lightly kicked Sandra to see if there was any sign of life. After no response, he was satisfied that she was dead and returned to check on John and Susan who both lay a few yards away. During the chaos, they had flopped to the ground helplessly once he had put his hands around Sandra's throat. Again, he nudged each of them in order, checking for any sign of life. Both, lay still, their faces chalk white as no movement was detected from either of them.

Joe understood that he had changed into one of the shop mannequins by Sandra, but didn't quite understand why. Much like Brian, Sandra had consumed his blood until he passed out. When he woke, he had examined himself to find that his head and limbs were attached a plastic torso. It took a long struggle to break the control that she had over him but when he did finally overpower her will; he took vengeance on the puppet master and gave Brian the peace that he deserved.

Joe took one last look around the store and exited into cold night, wondering how he would be able to live out the rest of his life as part man, part mannequin.

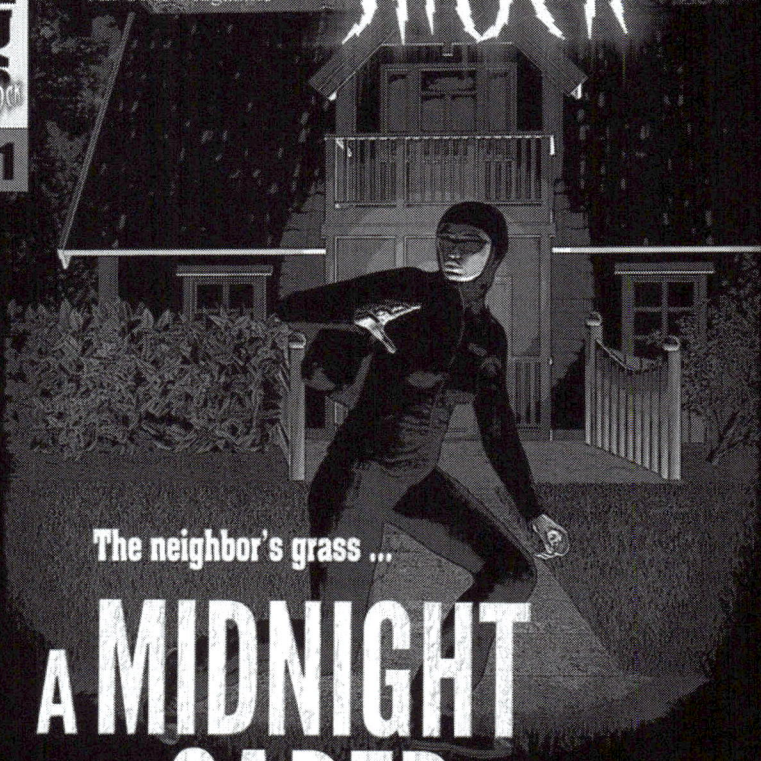

I'd like to dedicate my first story to Christina Hargis Smith.
She invited me into the Optimus Maximus Publishing family as a proofreader
and editor. These are dream jobs in my opinion.

The house stood vacant.

The former occupants, both friends and neighbors, had packed up and transferred their lives to Japan. As I glanced at the empty dwelling, sadness rippled through my thoughts as a hurtful reminder. The pair of handmade Adirondack chairs, missing. The colorful flower pots brimming with summer blooms, absent. The beginning of leaves making an early descent, in preparation for autumn. As I continued to stare vacantly, the brilliant yellow marigolds caught my eye.

Wow, I think, *those flowers have really thrived, even without assistance.*

I remember the day we went and picked them out at a local farm. It was a warm spring day. The sun beating down with the promises of impending summer heat. Upon our arrival, we were afforded an amazing selection of beauties. Wagons brimming with red, pink, yellow, purple, and white blooms, we put our future gardens into the trunk of the car. As soon as we got back to our neighborhood, I immediately got to work planting my floral rainbow. My friend's selections sat on her front porch, still in their plastic square flats, for what seemed like ages.

On our daily constitutional around the subdivision, I teased her mercilessly. Finally, she confessed that she hated dirt and was waiting on her husband to 'commit them into their final resting place.' I gathered from that odd statement, that neither she nor her husband had a green thumb. Being a doctor afforded her husband little time for leisurely activities around the house. What small fraction they eked out of their hectic lives, Rick and Kyra spent traveling. While they were gone, my daughter Lily and I took it upon ourselves to water the dehydrated marigolds and watch the porch for any package deliveries.

Once into the groove of our summer schedules, time passed rapidly. One morning, on our walk, Kyra informed me of their pending relocation to Japan. Not a visit this time, she assured me, but a permanent change of address. I had mixed emotions. As happy as I was for my friend, they truly desired this move, I was equally saddened at the thought of missing them. Though I pretended that life would carry on normally, I couldn't stop the arrival of the packers and movers.

The day finally arrived. We hugged goodbye. I watched them climb into their car, and then follow the moving truck from our street. Lily and I stood on our driveway waving until their car turned the corner, forever removing it from our view.

I stopped reminiscing, and my wayward ideas returned to the healthy marigold bunches still adorning their front yard. The house has remained empty thus far. No new tenants have arrived to fill Rick and Kyra's space. *I want those flowers*, I greedily contemplated to myself. *I helped choose them, and helped to keep them alive. I have a vested interest in their future.* I rationalized. "That's it, I'm going to plan a midnight caper!" I declared, unbeknownst to my husband. *Kevin and I are going to sneak over tonight, uproot those flowers, and replant them in our own flowerbeds.* I even had a maniacal cackle in my thoughts.

Once I decided on this obvious course of action, I just had to convince my husband. This was much more difficult than it sounded. Kevin is a no-nonsense type of guy. Not only does he *not* break the rules, he doesn't even bend them. On the other hand, I am a shenanigator. I thrive at 'stirring the pot', as Kevin is fond of pointing out. He is my moral compass, so to speak. If he had any qualms about what I was proposing, I was either on my own, or the caper was off entirely.

After Kevin's arrival home from work, I laid out my scheme, in detail. He stood for a moment, with his arms folded. After several excruciating seconds, his only response was, "Ok," coupled with a shrug.

Maybe my idea wasn't as illicit as my imagination deemed it. Because my level of excitement was so great, I struggled to get through dinner. After the family was fed, the dishes were done, and Lily was fully ensconced in front of the fifty-five-inch babysitter, Kevin and I gathered up our tools and placed them into the red metal *Radio Flyer* wagon. I had my orange-handled trowel and matching dirt scratcher, my skull printed gardening gloves, and heavy duty *Maglite*. Not only did it function as a flashlight, the four '*D*' batteries inside guaranteed that it also doubled as a defensive weapon. Kevin was standing in the doorway with a regular sized shovel slung over one shoulder, and pair of work gloves half tucked into a back pocket. He was shaking his head and wearing an amused smirk.

It was time!

Actually, it was ten-thirty, as close to midnight as we were likely to get.

I stood on the edge of our lawn, where the grass met the sidewalk and glanced furtively about. My ears straining to catch the sounds of any approaching cars or nocturnally strolling neighbors. I heard nothing other than the wind dancing fallen leaves down the street. "Let's go," I whispered and Kevin and I stealthily slid from the shadowy side of our street into the intense light from the street lamp. I felt so exposed, as if we were just targeted by a searchlight. We quickened our steps and safely reached the shadow on the opposite side of the road. Again, we paused to peer in all directions, waiting for a challenge from a neighbor. Yet everything remained quiet.As we approached the bushes, Kevin and I donned our work gloves and readied ourselves for this late night endeavor. Crouching down, we began to dig around the stems of the flowers, searching for the roots. Suddenly, I grabbed Kevin's arm, "Do you hear that?" I urgently whispered.

"Hear what?" he replied in a normal voice.

"Shh… is that a car engine? Shit, I can see headlights coming down the street!"

Not wanting to explain to any neighbors, or worse yet, to the police, what we were doing, we jumped behind the hedges and laid flat on the ground. The car was driving by so slowly; I was sure we were busted. Holding my breath, my heart racing, I awaited the inevitable shine of a flashlight, and the authoritative voice demanding, '*What are you two doing behind there? Come out with your hands up!*' I could feel my rapid pulse, and hear the blood flowing in my ears.

Eventually, although it seemed like forever, the car drove past our place of refuge, and continued on its way, quite unaware of our presence.

"Damn, that scared the crap out of me," I hissed breathlessly.

"We need to get this done," stated Kevin matter-of-factly. "I'm not explaining to the cops that my wife just wanted to commandeer the neighbor's abandoned marigolds. They're liable to lock us both up until we can pass full psych exams." Pausing for a moment, "Come on," he huffed as we got back on our feet and headed around to the front of the hedges. We resumed unseating the first bunch of flowers, and stowed them into the cart. As we proceeded on to the second set, my dirt scratcher got entangled. I assumed I had snagged some of the roots, so I gently eased the tool from the ground and went about manually removing the dirt. Scooping and scraping out double handfuls of soil, I saw something glinting in the hole.

"What the…? Hey Kevin, there's something buried under this plant."

He leaned over, shined the flashlight into the recess, and reached down to grab the object. Pulling upward, Kevin said, "Weird…I think it's a watch."

As his glove emerged from the hole, he was indeed holding a watch, except... except it was still attached to a hand.

He automatically dropped the grisly surprise, jumped back, yelled "Shit!"

I immediately started scrabbling away backwards on my hands, like some demented crab. I wanted to scream but my breath got caught in my throat. A gurgling yelp was closer to the sound that issued forth. "Oh my God; Oh my God; Oh my God," I continued to chant until Kevin told me to 'shut it.'

I tried, unsuccessfully. "Was that a hand? How did...? Why is...? What do we...? I stammered.

"Don't touch anything else! We need to go home and call the police," Kevin demanded logically. Leaving all our tools, the wagon, and the flowers, we ran back across the street to our house. Just before tearing through the front door, I was stopped by Kevin's hand on my arm. "You need to calm down. You can't go inside acting all freaked out in front of Lily."

Drawing several deep breaths, I nodded my head and tried to put on a 'normal' face. Reaching for the door handle, I noticed my hands were trembling. Placing his hand on top of mine, Kevin helped open the door.

Lily was sitting on the rug, watching some cartoon movie ... *The Chipmunks*, I think. The voices were squeaky and high pitched. Kevin picked up his cell phone and moved back down the hall toward the door. I heard him speaking, but couldn't make out the words. I walked over to the bar. Pulling out the *Jim Beam* and a shot glass, I filled it to overflowing. Tossing it back, I immediately poured another. Kevin came back into the kitchen. Murmuring next to my ear, he said, "They're on the way."

In a fake, shiny voice, I addressed my child. "Lily, it's past your bedtime. Let's go put on PJs, brush your teeth, and get to bed. Kiss Daddy."

I remained upstairs for a total of twelve minutes.

As I came down, I could see the rotating red and blue lights. There were several police cars, a fire truck, and an ambulance. *Won't need that*, the irrational thought caught me unaware and I started to giggle. I physically attempted to squash the laugh with my hand. "Not funny...get a grip!" I murmured.

Successfully controlling my inappropriate mirth, I joined my husband and the group of uniforms on the porch. Kevin was relaying, in detail, all that had transpired this evening. Question after question was being fired at us.

"How well did you know your former neighbors? Did you ever witness any odd behavior from them?"

I didn't have time to process much less answer any. Apparently, my husband was having the same issue. I glanced across the street. Several men were excavating a much bigger hole, throwing the dirt into a giant mound around the opening.

It looks like a grave, the thought flew through my head. As I realized the horrid implication of my accurate assessment I gasped audibly. Everyone stopped talking and just stared at me.

"I'm sorry...I just...this is so..." I rambled incoherently.

We had stepped across our street with light hearted shenanigans in mind and tripped straight into *The Twilight Zone*.

After the incessant questioning, we were asked to walk back over to where the body now lay under a black plastic tarp. Taking a deep breath, I followed Kevin to the crime scene.

"Do either of you recognize this man?" asked the cop, as he whipped away the plastic sheet, in some parody of a grotesque magic trick. I steeled myself, then dragged my eyes over the remains of the human being unearthed from the garden. The wiring in my head must have been malfunctioning. My brain was having difficulties processing what my eyes were communicating. Having watched so many police dramas on tv and in the movies, I thought I knew what to expect. Never have I been so wrong in my life.

There was a corpse all right; it was just an incomplete corpse.

Large pieces of this man were missing.

At this point, I had endured as much as I was capable.

My head was spinning, my vision blurred. I knew it was a matter of seconds before I threw up. Mumbling some version of 'excuse me,' I staggered back to our house and raced my nausea to the toilet. Thankfully, I won.

This isn't happening, was the thought stuck on a loop in my head.

Eventually, the flashing lights were extinguished. The fire truck and ambulance retreated back to their station, while all the police cars remained. Our neighbor's entire house was cordoned off with yellow crime scene tape. Kevin, concerned about my rapid departure, came in search of me. He found me sitting on the floor of the downstairs bathroom, my back against the cabinets under the sink. A wet cloth was draped over my ashen face.

"Are you ok?" he asked, knowing that I was not.

"What happened to that man? Did Kyra and Rick have something to do with it? How could a body be buried within sight of our house, and we know absolutely nothing about it?"

To each question that flew from my mouth, Kevin responded calmly, "I don't know."

The rising of the sun signaled a new day, even though neither of us had gone to bed. We just sat on the couch trying to wrap our heads around this atrocious situation.

Just as I decided to brew some *Dunks* dark roast, Lily came bounding into the room. Her eyes so wide open, in that enormous way that only children seem to achieve.

"Did you see all those police cars? What's going on? Can I go over and see? Daddy, do you know what's happening? Will you go outside with me? Can we have pancakes for breakfast?"

Again, I was having a processing issue. I heard everything she asked, but couldn't form a single answer besides, "No, eat some cereal."

It was going to be hard to distract her from the circus across the street. Other neighbors were starting to gather in groups, whispering their versions of the situation. A few black vans had joined the parking lot that was once our quiet street. Men in coveralls were running about with toolboxes, inside the house now, as well as out. Photographers were capturing every last blade of grass under or near the tarp. Everything lay undisturbed from last night. The body, the hole, our tools, the wagon, all exactly where I remembered them.

Maybe these busy men have uncovered some answers to all the questions that they were firing at us a few hours ago. Having a quick and discreet conversation, we decided that Kevin should go back over, and try to glean some information. Meanwhile, I sat on the floor with Lily and played *Star Wars Battleship*.

After what seemed like forever, Kevin came back into our living room. I can honestly say, I have never seen him look so rattled. He kept running his hand from the top of his bald head and down his face. This action brought into focus his pallor. Again, I don't think I have ever seen him so pale. My anxiety kicked into high gear. The tense knotted feeling in my gut erupted. I began wringing my hands in anticipation of what insidious facts were about to be delivered to me.

"Lily, go clean your room. If you do an awesome job, maybe we'll go out for ice cream later." With this half-hearted bribery issued, Lily bolted upstairs cheering the whole way. With the child otherwise engaged, Kevin sat down on the floor next to me. "It isn't good," was how he began.

"Fuck...just tell me already," I exploded.

"The missing parts of the body were removed with a type of circular saw, something about the marks left on the bone. They went through the entire house and garage with UV lights, looking for any blood, tissue, or bone fragments." Again, his hand traveled the path from his head down his face. "They said the garage lit up like a Christmas tree." Looking down, he shook his head. "They think Rick and Kyra cut off pieces of that man in the garage, and...oh shit... (again with the hand) they think they ate the missing parts."

I didn't think it possible that I could be any more shocked.

I was wrong.

My head flashed back to the day when Kyra and I were sitting on the porch, sipping wine, and shooting the shit. She needed a good chili recipe, she had said. Rick loved a good chili with corn bread, she had said. And naturally, I shared my mother's famous chili recipe with her.

Later, enthusiastically, she had come back bringing over a few *Ziploc* containers for us.

"Try it," she had teased. "I hope it is a good as your mom's."

Dinner that night was Kyra's version of my mom's chili.

It was delicious, but not quite the same.

I wonder...is it possible?

Collected tales of Madness and Terror

Maximus
SHOCK

Issue
No. 12

MAXIMUS
SHOCK
12

Here Comes ...

MR
QUIVERS

Chris Garson

For the first time in his ten years, Sam Spencer held a cat. He managed it rather awkwardly. One hand clutched the scruff of its mangy, white neck. The other scooped its rear legs, which were clawing at the air like a falling rock climber. He could feel its terrified heart beating. The poor thing's eyes glanced about wildly, looking for escape into the bushes of Anna Parker's back yard.

"Not like that, Sam. Here, let me show you." Anna, Sam's seven year old neighbor, took the cat from him in an easy hand-off. Sam was on the small side. Anna was large for her age and a little chubby due to her having to stay inside an awful lot.

The cat purred contently in her comforting arms. A lazy paw reached up to play with the yellow ribbon streaming from her sable hair. Smatterings of white fur from earlier cuddling covered her flowery pink dress. "See. Dander likes being held. You just have to do it the right way."

"Can I try again." Though older than Anna, she knew more about cats. The only pet Sam ever owned was the goldfish he won at the school fair, which didn't count since you couldn't do much with goldfish. You could watch them swim, or watch them eat, or watch them poop, but you for sure couldn't cuddle with them.

"Sure ... ah, ah, atchoo." She wiped her nose on the sleeve of the white shirt she wore under her dress, slightly squishing Dander in the process. The cat meowed.

Sam took Dander from Anna. This time, he held her the way Anna showed him. The cat stopped squirming. Sam bent down to nuzzle Dander with his nose. The cat sneaked a lick, making him squeal with laughter. "Haha. Her tongue is scratchy."

"She's a he, silly." Anna brushed off some of the white fur clinging to her dress.

Sam studied the area between Dander's legs where the fur was thinner. He could see pink skin underneath but no distinguishing anatomy. "How can you tell?"

Anna shrugged. "I don't know. My mom said Dander's a … ah … atchoo, … a boy." She wiped her nose again. Stains from many sneezes covered her sleeve.

***

"Please, Mom," Sam whined while watching his mom get dinner ready. "Can't we keep her, I mean him? Pleeeeease!"

"I don't know, Sam. We'd have to discuss it with your father." Faith Spencer flashed Sam a quick, telling smile. The smile that launched a thousand ships, his father said. "I'm not making any promises, but I think we can work it out."

Sam knew what that meant. His mom could talk his dad into anything. "Yay!"

She folded her arms across her chest, cautioning him against getting too excited. "Now, when your father gets home, don't pester him right away. Let me talk to him first."

"Okay." Sam's foot tapped rapidly against the floor.

"I can tell you're excited, but promise me, Sam."

"Okay, Mom. I promise." Sam crossed his fingers behind his back, just in case his excitement got the better of him.

At six o'clock, Dan Spencer pulled his silver BMW 740 into the driveway. Sam remembered the model number because 7 was for Pistol Pete Maravich and 40 was for Bill Laimbeer, two old time basketball players Sam knew about them from the cards his father collected at summer camp as a kid. He liked that Laimbeer was a "Bad Boy", and Pistol Pete, well, he just had a really cool name.

Sam ran out to greet Dan in the driveway, his promise to Faith instantly forgotten. His dad was a big shot at the company and really good at selling things to people, but being a big shot meant he worked too much and got home after dark most nights. His mom said that Dan was a good looking charmer who could sell sand to a Bedouin. Sam didn't know what league the Bedouins played for, let alone which city, or why they'd want sand.

He gave Dan a hug, careful not to ruin the crease on the grey, pinstriped suit trouser. Dan took pride in his fancy suits. "Dad, Dad, guess what? Anna's got allergies and the Parkers can't keep Dander. Can we keep her, I mean him? Please, Dad."

Dan peeled himself free of Sam's hug and looked down at him with the strangest expression. His mouth was taut and his eyes narrowed, as if he was mad at Sam, but Sam couldn't imagine why that would be … unless his mom had told him about the broken window.

From the doorway, Faith shook her head. "Sam, you promised! Give your father some room. He's not even inside yet, for Christ's sake!"

"Faith, please. Language," Dan Spencer said. Dan was very observant. He went to the Church of the Blessed Trinity at least every Sunday, and often took Sam. Faith Spencer usually stayed home, to prepare Sunday dinner, she said. Sam thought she just didn't like going and that was her excuse. Sometimes Sam used homework as an excuse to get out of church. His dad always made him seek out the confessional and sitting alone in that stale smelling closet with Father Browning watching through the latticework gave him the creeps.

After Dan changed into jeans, the family sat down to eat dinner. Faith made Sam's favorite, spaghetti with red sauce and garlic bread. Everyone held hands and closed their eyes while Dan recited Grace.

Sam sneaked a peek at Faith. Everyone said that he looked like her, with his wavy brown hair and green eyes. Sam thought his mom was pretty. So did Kevin Lowry, his best friend. Kevin said that his dad said that Sam's dad was lucky to have married such a hot, young babe. Sam had heard the story many times, how Dan Spencer was a junior big shot when he met Faith Yormund at the job fair during her senior year. They married right after she graduated college.

"Lord Jesus, our brother, We praise You for saving us. Bless us in Your love As we gather in your Name, and bless this meal that we share. Jesus, we praise you for ever."

And then together, "Amen."

Dan served the pasta. "Now, Sam. What was that about Anna?"

Sam grated fresh parmesan over his spaghetti. "You know Dander, the Parker's white cat?"

"That dirty, flea-ridden stray they took in?" Dan said with enough venom to put down an elephant.

Sam wondered if Dander had scratched his dad. "Dander is not dirty. She, I mean he, is awesome. I held him, this afternoon. Anna showed me how. He was all squirmy till I learned how to do it right."

"You'd be proud of him." Faith beamed. "He's a natural with cats."

"So,anyways. Anna loves Dander, but she's allergic so her dad says the cat has to go. Can we keep him, Dad? Please! Anna says if we don't, they're gonna take Dander to a shelter."

Dan scowled. "Cats are terrible creatures."

"But, Dad, Dander's so cute. When he purrs, he sounds like your Beamer!"

"If you want a pet, how about a dog? I had a St. Bernard when I was your age, I called him Saint Bernaducci. Dogs make better pets than cats, especially the

Parker's cat. It's a stray, Sam. It just wandered into their back yard one day. We don't know where it comes from, if it's healthy, how old it is ..."

"Please, Dad. I really, really want him." Sam thought about crying. When he was younger, that sometimes worked, but now that he was ten, not so much. The older he got, the less convincing his tears were.

Dan Spencer stood and clutched the crucifix hanging from his neck tightly, as if it was giving him sustenance. Jaw clenched, veins on his neck popping, he looked scarier than any Halloween mask to Sam. "Absolutely not, Sam. I absolutely forbid it. We will not have a cat in this house. Not now, not ever, and that's final."

Sam burst into real tears. Dan was never that mean to him. Even Faith looked surprised at his outburst. She slid back in her chair and stared at Dan as if he was an alien. "Take a deep breath, Dan. What's with all this hostility? It's just a cat, for Christ's sake."

Dan's hand moved in the sign of the cross. "You don't understand, Faith. Cats aren't decent."

She walked behind Dan, put her arms around his waist, laid her head on his shoulder and kissed his neck. Sam shut his eyes. Kissing was so gross. He didn't like watching his parents when they were all lovey-dovey. "It means a lot to him, Dan."

Dan pulled away from her. "I won't have it."

"Did you have a bad day at the office, Dan?" She said it all sugary, like she did with Sam when he wouldn't talk to her after school.

"What?" At first, her question seemed to throw Dan. Then, Sam thought he caught on. "No, that's not it. Everything is fine at work, better than fine, actually. We closed the quarter with a new sales record."

Faith poured herself a glass of red wine. "Then what is it? I've never seen you act this way. You always want what's best for Sam."

"That's right," he barked. "And this is no different. This may seem harsh, but it's in Sam's best interest. You have to trust me."

"But, Dad," Sam stammered. "I … I don't want a dog. I want a cat. I want Dander. She, I mean he, already loves me."

Faith wouldn't be put off. She got right back in Dan's face. "Pets are good for children. They teach them responsibility, to be loving and caring."

Dan just about spat. "Be serious, Faith. No one loves cats. They're arrogant, stand-offish creatures, selfish and uncaring. If you were bleeding out in front of one, it would lick its paw and barely give you a sideways glance. Cats don't teach responsibility either. You don't have to walk them. Hell, if you don't change the box, they'll just shit on the floor."

The color drained from Sam's face. "Dad!" His dad never used such language. Dan was equally mortified, as evidenced by yet another feverish sign of the cross.

Faith, never shy about using words Sam wasn't allowed to use, couldn't keep the flicker of a smile from her face. She sipped her wine slowly.

Dan apologized right away. "I'm sorry, son. I shouldn't have said that. That will cost me with Father Browning next Sunday."

"Oh, Dan. Please. He hears worse every day on the playground." Faith was right about that. Sam knew words from the other kids at school that would make his dad's ears burn red.

Dan snapped back, more harshly than Sam thought necessary. "That doesn't make it right, Faith."

Rather than listen to his parents bicker (they called it open communication) Sam lowered his gaze and watched an ant carry a crumb from the garlic bread across the kitchen floor. Kevin's parents discussed parenting behind closed doors. Not Sam's. They always hashed it out in front

183

of him. He sought a warm memory and imagined Dander cradled in his arms.

"That's a conversation for later, Dan. Right now, we're talking about the cat. I gather you don't like them. I didn't know that, but that's fine. I also know that you, and I, always have Sam's best interest in mind, don't we?"

"Of course, dear," Dan said slowly, obviously sensing the same trap Sam did.

Sam relaxed, knowing how it would end. His mom usually got her way. She either sweet-talked or nagged his dad into it. Tonight, he'd snuggle with Dander.

***

The plane descended below the cloud layer. Sam grabbed Kevin's elbow and pointed out the window. "Hey Kevin. Is that where the Fairwell Raiders play?"

Kevin Lowry leaned his stocky frame across Sam's lap. All the Lowry boys played high school football. "Nah. I been to my big brothers' games. That's way bigger."

When the plane hit the runway, the wheels skidded and the brakes shrieked. While they taxied to the jet way, Sam's excitement mounted. Eight weeks was the longest he'd ever been away from his parents. They were planning a barbeque for his first night back from camp with Anna and the Parkers. Also, he missed Dander. He'd only had a month to play with the cat before leaving for camp. He couldn't wait to snuggle with him again.

The Lowrys were waiting at the gate with Sam's parents. Sam called them aunt and uncle, even though they really weren't. Uncle Adam had been best friends with Dan Spencer since they were Sam's age. Sam really liked Aunt Jeanie. She made the best brownies on the block and always let him and Kevin stay up late when he slept over. She was always tired though, which was understandable what with Kevin being the youngest of seven kids. A proper Catholic family, Dan would say, which always elicited comments from Faith about her girlish figure.

"Come here, Sam." He ran into his mom's outstretched arms and squeezed her tight. Dan ran fingers though his hair, which had turned almost auburn in Maine's summer sun.

He missed his folks more than he realized. "I love you guys."

"We missed you too, Sam," Dan Spencer said.

After hugs and waves, and collecting luggage at baggage claim, the Spencers and Lowrys separated. Sam piled into the back of the Beamer, counting the minutes until he could hold Dander again. As Dan was pulling out of the parking garage he asked, "How's Dander? Did she, I mean he, miss me?"

"First, tell us about camp, Sam. Your letters left much to our imagination," Faith said.

Camp Sacquenuckot required a letter addressed home every Monday and Thursday. No letter, no lunch, but they didn't read them and had no way of knowing how short Sam's were. About half of his read, "Dear Mom and Dad - I'm hungry so I'm writing you. Bye. Love, Sam."

So, Sam knew his mom would have a ton of questions. Dan Spencer, on the other hand, wasn't nearly as curious. Sam figured it was because he'd gone to Camp Sacquenuckot too, a long time ago with Uncle Adam. His dad knew all about camp. He'd hiked to the top of Mount Katahdin, done the island swim, ridden the back trails of the Northern Forest, gone fishing in the lake, made shepherd's pie over a campfire, and gone snipe hunting under a full moon. Faith Spencer didn't know any of it. She'd spent her summers modeling in New York City. She always used to say that if she hadn't met Dan, she might have been the next Cindy Crawford.

Sam almost hadn't made it to camp that summer. Surprisingly, Dan objected, and rather strongly at that. Sam

185

tried every trick he knew. He begged. He pleaded. He cried, but his dad still steadfastly refused. In the family tradition of open communication, Sam's camp attendance became a regular topic at the dinner table for weeks. Sam knew he'd won when his mom came downstairs one Sunday morning dressed for church. The night before, Sam heard loud noises coming from their bedroom. Dan wrote the check to Camp Sacquenuckot that morning. Sam could tell his dad wasn't happy about it.

"So tell us more about Francesco." Sam could see his mom's eyes questioning him from the rear view mirror.

Sam's favorite of the two counselors in the cabin, Francesco was an exchange student attending Bates College. "He was really cool, Mom. He's from Italy, some place named Perugia. He said some famous murder happened there. He'd tell us ghost stories about Fruity Rudy and Foxy Knoxy when we camped out. Peter was okay too, but he was from Pennsylvania. He was a beast, like he had hair everywhere." Sam giggled.

"The ghost of Foxy Knoxy?" Faith's brow arched in the mirror. "That not quite how CNN tells the story. Francesco sounds like quite a character. Tell us more about your summer. Who were your best friends? What were your favorite activities? Did you see the great white skunk?"

Sacquenuckot was Algonquin for skunk. The first day of camp, Director Chuck told the legend of the great white skunk that had guarded the North Forest since the dawn of time. In 1948, when Founder Damon was hiking near Mt. Katahdin, he fell into a crevasse and got lost in the caves below, where the great white skunk appeared to him. He followed it out of the caves to the valley where he founded Camp Sacquenuckot.

For the kids who couldn't pronounce Sacquenuckot, and some of those who could, the camp was nicknamed Camp Skunk, or Camp Suck a Nuck, or Camp Suck my

Dick by the older kids, but if they got caught saying that they weren't allowed to swim in the lake for a day.

"Oh man, Mom. There's so much to tell you. I had eight kids in my cabin. Five were from New York and Boston. This one kid, Petah –"

"Like in the Hunger Games?" his mom asked.

"Sort of. You know, Peter, but he said it Petah. He talked funny. He came from a place named Lawn Giland somewhere in New York. He said a lot of words funny. He put buttah on his toast and he got a splintah in his foot from the cabin's wood floor."

Dan and Faith both laughed.

"So, Mom. Where did Dander sleep when I was gone? Did sh ... he sleep on my bed or with you and Dad?"

"Not with us," his dad muttered under his breath.

"I want to hear more about the activities. You mentioned swimming in the letters containing actual sentences."

"The lake is totally awesome, Mom. I went swimming every day, sometimes twice I day. I got to go sailing, they have sunfish and minifish and catamarans which are really cool pontoon boats. I got to go snorkeling too. I can swim really fast with my flippers on. And we had a swim team and I won a big race. And we played water polo. And we went skinny dipping at night and this one guy in my group, Richie, he ..." Sam's face reddened "... he had hair on his privates and he's only ten years old like me. We called him Brussel Sprouts."

Faith covered her mouth with her hand, but Sam could tell it was to hide a smile. Dan though, scowled into the mirror, sending shivers down Sam's spine. "It's not decent."

"Everyone matures in their own time," Faith reassured Sam after a nasty glance for Dan. "It'll happen to you too, sweetie. Just give it some time."

"Mom!" Sam was just old enough for the conversation to embarrass him.

"We can talk about anything, Sam. It's called open communication, remember? So, was the waterfront your favorite?"

"No," he said quickly, glad for a change of subject. "Horseback riding was. Being smaller than the other kids was an advantage. I rode almost every day and Skunkface Bob taught me all about horses."

"Skunkface Bob? Who's that?" Faith turned to face Sam in the back seat.

Sam's face lit up. "Oh, he's the riding instructor. We call him Skunkface cause his beard has a white stripe in it. He's been at Camp Skunk forever. He was there when you went, wasn't he, Dad?"

Dan Spencer kept his eyes on the road and tightened his grip on the steering wheel.

After it became obvious Dan wouldn't answer, Faith broke the uneasy silence. "Your father never mentioned anyone named Skunkface Bob. Trust me; I'd remember a name like that. But, he doesn't talk about his summers at Camp Sacquenuckot very much."

Dan pulled into the driveway. "Grab your things, Sam. I'll fire up the grill. The Parkers will be over soon. Anna's excited to see you."

"You knew Skunkface Bob, didn't you, Dad?"

"Yeah." Dan Spencer made a queer face. "I knew him."

"Isn't he awesome? He taught me how to brush the horses down, how to put on a saddle – did you know the horses try to trick you by holding their breath so the cinch is loose - how to post and how to jump. I won a blue ribbon!"

"A blue ribbon! I'm so proud of you, Sam. Aren't you, Dan?"

Dan grunted.

"Yeah. I'm going to give the ribbon to Dander to play with."

Faith's face fell. "Sam, there's something we need to tell you. About Dander. He's gone, I'm afraid."

Sam's lip started to tremble. "Gone. What does that mean, gone?"

"He just –"

"Wandered off," Dan finished. "The cat just wandered off, just like it wandered into the Parker's back yard this spring. I told you, Sam. I told you nothing good would come from it. Cats are horrid beasts. They always let you down."

Sam burst into tears. All summer long, he'd been looking forward to his reunion with Dander. He ran into his bedroom and cried into his pillow until Faith called him down to the backyard for dinner. Dan Spencer, Anna, and the Parkers were waiting. Sam was so sad over the loss of Dander that when his dad raised up a mug of frosty root beer to toast his return, Sam barely heard him.

***

Sam's second summer at Camp Suck a Nuck went much like the first. Instead of Peter the Beast, Nicky, a waterfront instructor who swam at Michael Phelp's high school shared the bunk duties with Francesco from Perugia. He spent as much time as possible in the stables with Skunkface Bob, who treated Sam like a favored nephew, always doing nice things for him like giving him extra riding time or slipping him candy. From Skunkface, Sam learned the art of dressage, and practiced the jumps, turns, and gaits required for competing in shows. When Sam wasn't riding, he swam in the lake, learned to play tennis and shoot a bow, and fired rifles at the range. In the evenings, he and the other boys roasted marshmallows over campfires and listened to more of Francesco's Foxy Knoxy ghost stories.

"I can't wait to see Tiger," he said to Kevin Lowry as the plane parked at the jet way. Over Dan Spencer's objections, and with Faith's support, Tiger had replaced the wandering Dander. A striped tabby barely ten weeks old when they picked him up from the shelter last Halloween, Tiger tripled in size by the time Sam left for camp. The kitten proved quite the hunter, initially by retrieving catnip-filled toy mice from under the living room couch and then real ones snatched from Sam's back yard and the Parkers'.

After last year, Sam was nervous about seeing Tiger again. He had prayed every night before going to sleep that Tiger would remain safe throughout the summer. He'd thought about it long and hard, and decided that his dad was right. Dander had been a stray. For all Sam knew, the mangy white cat might have wandered back to his home. Maybe a little boy lived there who missed Dander as much as Sam did. Thinking so made Sam feel better.

He didn't think Tiger would wander off like Dander. Sam loved Tiger with every ounce of his being before leaving for camp. He fed him, played with him every day, and slept with him every night. Tiger knew no home other than Sam's and had no reason to wander off. Sam pictured the tabby rolling on his Spider-man bed cover and crossed his fingers.

As soon as the plane door opened, Sam ran down the jet way and into his mom's waiting arms.

"Sam!" Faith planted a big kiss on his cheek and hugged him for what seemed like forever.

Finally, he pulled away. "Mom, that's enough. Geez, I'm eleven years old, remember?"

"Hey, Sam. I'm glad you're home." Dan pulled him close and tousled his hair.

Sam studied his dad. He wore jeans and an old T-shirt with writing about some guy named Jim Beam, not a suit.

His eyes were bloodshot and he hadn't shaven. "You growing a beard?"

Dan's hand fingered his chin. "No, son. Just a long, lazy weekend."

"I think you'd look cool with a beard, Dad. Can I touch it?" Sam ran his fingers up Dan's cheek, against the grain.

"No he would not," Faith said in a tone daring disagreement.

Well, if his mom didn't like the beard, that settled it. Sam expected his dad to shave by morning's light. He turned his thoughts to his snuggly tabby. "Hey Dad, how's Tig–"

Before Sam could finish his question, Dan started down the concourse without even a glance back, weaving crookedly between luggage-toting passengers. He nearly bumped into several.

Faith grabbed Sam's hand and lugged him after Dan. "Your father's in a hurry. The Parkers are due in half an hour."

"Bye, Kev," Sam shouted to the rapidly receding Kevin Lowry. "I'll call you tomorrow!"

At the car Faith held out her hands. "I should drive, Dan."

"Whatever." He fumbled in his pockets for the starter and dropped it in her outstretched hand.

Sam was astounded. His mom never drove the Beamer. "Why are you driving?"

"Your father's had a long day. Buckle up, Sam."

"Okay." Something weird was going on. "Mom? How's Tiger?"

"You first, Sam. I want to hear everything. Your letters were even shorter this year. One time, you mailed us an empty envelope."

Sam felt his stomach sink. Last year, his parents had avoided his questions about Dander too. "Please, Mom. Just tell me, is he okay?"

He saw tears welling in her eyes. "I'm sorry, Sam. Tiger, he … he didn't make it."

A lump caught in Sam's throat. Somehow, he'd just known what his mom was going to say. First Dander and now Tiger. He loved them both so much. "What happened?"

Faith lowered her voice. "He wandered off and a car nailed him. It was over quick, Sam. Tiger wasn't in any pain."

Sam lowered his head into the crook of his elbow and let the tears flow shamelessly. Losing Tiger was almost like losing his best friend. "Oh no, not Tiger."

"Yeah, it was a bad day all the way around," Dan growled. Then he leaned his head against the window and within seconds he was snoring.

Sam picked up his head. "What's with Dad? He's acting weird."

"Nothing to worry about, Sam. I told you he's had a long day. The truth is he's had a long summer. He'll be fine."

"I don't get it. He always shaves. He's always telling me cleanliness is next to Godliness. He was walking funny in the airport too and he always drives the Beamer, not you. What's going on?"

Faith rolled down her window and lit a cigarette, astonishing Sam. He'd never seen her smoke. "Don't worry, Sam. Everything will be all right. I'll get your father straightened out. Just remember, he loves you very much."

"I'm not a little kid any more, Mom. You can tell me what's going on. Open communication, remember?"

She took a deep drag and flicked the half-smoked cigarette out the window rather than use the car's spotless ashtray. "Your father has a new job, Sam."

Sam gulped. His dad had been a sales big shot at the company for so long he could barely imagine him doing anything else. Whenever Sam closed his eyes and tried to picture Dan, what came to mind was the image of him in a dapper suit, driving the Beamer, and flashing a magazine smile. "What happened?"

"He and a co-worker had a ... difference of opinion. One thing led to another and the situation spiraled out of control. Your Dad didn't mean to hit him, Sam, no matter what you might hear from Kevin Lowry or anyone else. He's been wound tight since you left for camp. He missed you terribly."

Sam thought he might burst like a dam. "Do you mean .... it was my fault?"

She corrected herself quickly. "Oh no, Sam. Not at all and I mean that. You had nothing do to with this whatsoever."

"Really?" he sniffed. He wanted to believe her.

"Really, Sam. It's just that your father loves you so much. When you're away at camp, it's hard on him."

"Does Dad still have a job? Are we poor now?" Sam couldn't shake the feeling that he'd caused his dad's problems. If he hadn't insisted on going to camp ...

Faith laughed off his worries, as if they were impossible. "No, Sam. We're not poor. We're just fine. Your Dad still works for the company. They know how valuable he is and so they just moved him to a new spot. Now he doesn't have to manage people. He can focus on selling, which is what he's really good at."

She pulled into the driveway. Sam could hear Anna's nasal laugh from the Parker's backyard. She sounded like a beached seal. Still chubby, Anna's allergies hadn't gotten any better. "I guess that's good. How long ago did it happen?"

"You'd been gone only two weeks. It happened ... the same day Tiger met with his accident. We'd have written you about it, but I wanted you to have a fabulous summer."

Sam's dad awoke with a start. "Are we home?"

"Yes, Dan. Go fire up the grill, please."

Later on, what Sam remembered most about that night was the beer. His dad drank three of them.

***

The night before Sam left for his third summer at Camp Sacquenuckot, the Spencers held another back yard barbeque. They invited Anna and her parents and all nine Lowrys. Kevin had filled out over the winter and was excited about playing junior high football in the fall. Sam was too small to play, unless he ran back punts, which Faith wouldn't let him do because she was too afraid he'd get hurt.

Sam didn't mind. Football was Kevin's thing, not his. He'd rather go riding, but he hadn't been on a horse since last summer. He missed Bomber, his favorite stallion, almost as much as Skunkface Bob. "Did you have a favorite horse, Dad?"

Dan Spencer wheeled around, beer in hand and red in the face from laughing at one of Uncle Adam's stories. Since the fight at work, Dan had been changing before Sam's eyes. These days, he popped a beer the second he got home from work. Sometimes, Sam thought he already smelled of beer. At the dinner table, Dan and Faith argued about something called a sales quota, which apparently Sam's dad wasn't hitting. Sam gathered that missing your quota didn't make the big shots at the company very happy. Once, Faith called Dan a "former big shot" and he stormed out of the house. Sam hadn't seen him again until the next night. Dan swore all the time now too, words even Sam didn't know, words that made Faith blush. Dan never made the sign of the cross anymore and hardly ever went to church. "You say something, Sam?"

"Who was your favorite horse at Suck a Nuck?"

Dan drew back his arm as if to strike Sam, who instinctively covered his face with his hands. "It's Camp Sacquenuckot," he snarled.

Sam dropped his guard, determined to hide his terror from his dad. "What's the big deal? All the kids call it that, unless they say Camp Suck my Dick."

Dan lost what little restraint remained to him. His open hand slapped Sam's cheek hard enough to echo across the yard, which became instantly quiet. Sam felt everyone's eyes turn upon him. Mrs. Parker pulled Anna close and told her not to look, while Mr. Parker moved to block Anna's view. The Lowry boys, who were crouched at an imaginary line of scrimmage, called timeout. Faith was in the kitchen with Aunt Jeannie and hadn't heard, but Uncle Adam had. Of all the people in the Spencer back yard, only he looked at Dan with anything resembling understanding.

"Goddamnit, boy, I told you never to say that. That's even worse than Suck a Nuck." The person speaking sounded like the boogeyman, not Sam's dad.

Sam couldn't believe it. That his dad was willing to strike him hurt Sam far more than the actual blow. With all eyes still upon him, he ran into the house, upstairs, and into his bedroom, where Peanut slept on his bed. Like Tiger and Dander before him, Peanut was the happy recipient of Sam's eternal affection. Sam threw his arms around the calico and sobbed into its belly. Peanut purred, reassuring Sam that all was not lost.

Dan's knock sounded on Sam's door. "Sam? Can I come in? I want to apologize."

"I ... I guess so," he sniffled. The slap still stung.

Dan Spencer opened the door and walked over to the bed. Peanut, who had figured out early on that Dan didn't like him, took off like a rocket.

"I'm so, so sorry, Sam. I should never have hit you. I know it's unforgiveable, but can you ever forgive me?" He went to wrap his arms around Sam, but lost his balance and toppled over onto the bed. The scent of beer made Sam want to gag.

"Sure, Dad." Sam knew from listening to Faith talk on the phone to Aunt Jeannie that it wasn't Dan's fault. The blame fell to the big shots at the company. They had it in for Dan. When he'd heard the whole story, Sam hadn't blamed his dad. He would have hit the guy too. It wasn't fair. The other guy had gotten off with a warning, but they'd demoted his Dan. "I know you didn't mean it."

Dan pushed himself up from the bed and steadied himself on the bedpost. "C'mon, let's go downstairs. I'll make you the best burger you've ever had, one with the works. Lettuce, tomato, onion, cheese, bacon and my special ingredient, a slice of fried bologna. You'll love it."

"Sounds great, Dad. Almost as good as Sacquenuckot shepherd's pie."

Sam made sure to use the camp's real name this time. He didn't want to upset his dad again, but even mentioning camp wiped the smile from Dan's face. "Let's just enjoy the night, Sam. "

"Okay. And Dad?

"Yes, Sam?"

"Thanks for sending me to camp. I know it's not easy." Money was tight since his dad hit that guy. Mom said this new job didn't pay nearly as well and the bonus wasn't nearly as steep. Sam's parents had always talked about him attending St. Mary's, a good Catholic school, but in the fall he would start junior high in the Fairwood public school system. St. Mary's charged an arm and leg, money his dad didn't have. Sam felt guilty about going away to camp with his folks struggling so, but Faith insisted. Camp builds character, she'd said. Dan had long since given up arguing the point.

The burger was as good as Dan promised, but the altercation had a left a bad taste in Sam's mouth. He wanted to go back to his room and cry into his pillow. No one else could enjoy the evening either, not with sound of Dan's strike still echoing in the yard. The Parkers said good night as soon as the sun set and the Lowry's weren't far behind. By the time everyone cleared out, Dan was slumped over in his chair next to half a case of empty beer bottles.

Sam was lying in bed staring at the ceiling when he heard Faith call out from the hallway the next morning. Peanut had curled up in a ball of fur nestled between Sam's head and shoulder. "Get up, Sam. We have to leave now to make your plane."

Sam threw on the clothes he'd laid out the night before and grabbed his backpack. Faith had a banana, a glass of orange juice, and a blueberry muffin waiting for him. After gulping down breakfast, he piled into the Camry's back seat. They'd gotten the Camry for Christmas. It wasn't nearly as nice as the Beamer, but, as Dan explained, it did have lower payments.

"Where's Dad?"

"He's sleeping. I'll drive you to the airport." Faith looked very unhappy. The only time he'd ever seen her like this was when Granny died. Her make-up was smudged and her eyes were swollen. It suddenly occurred to Sam that his mom had been crying.

***

Sam turned sixteen and got his driver's license a month before leaving for his seventh summer at Camp Sacquenuckot. This year, he would be a counselor in training, CIT for short, which meant he'd be assigned to a particular age group or activity. He hoped they'd put him to work in the stables.

The Maine landscape buzzed by during the six hour bus ride from Portland to Camp Sacquenuckot. The time couldn't pass quickly enough, as far as Sam was concerned.

He couldn't wait to feel Bomber's powerful legs carry him over the forest's winding trails, to feel the rush of cool lake water engulf him, to lead the younger campers on yet another unsuccessful Snipe hunt. At camp, he could forget about home. At this point, forgetting was welcome relief.

"So, what are the odds you'll see Bruce Lee at the end of the summer?" Kevin Lowry asked. Sam had sprouted into an almost average-sized kid over the past few years. Kevin had really bulked out. They were both entering their junior year at Fairwood High and Kevin had already earned a starting spot on the offensive line. Sam and Kevin were still thick as thieves, even though they didn't see each other as much as they used to. After Sam's parents sold the house, they'd moved into a much smaller one in a different neighborhood.

"What do you think?" Bruce Lee was the Spencer's newest feline addition. A Siamese with attitude, Sam's dad liked Bruce Lee even less than the other cats.

"I wouldn't take that bet," Kevin responded.

"Yeah, me either." Sam's track record with cats hadn't improved over the years. After his third summer at camp, he came home to the news that Peanut had wandered off. The next year, he learned that Maudie, a tabby reminding him of Tiger, fell victim to the wandering curse. The summer after that, his fifth at Sacquenuckot, Sam added Weasely, the big orange tomcat acquired during his Harry Potter phase, to the long list of Spencer wandering feline fatalities. Last year, he'd lost Pixel, a cat with an exceptionally poor sense of balance. Sam was surprised the shelter hadn't turned them down yet. All those news reports of overcrowded shelters must be true.

Kevin nudged Sam with his elbow. "Your dad was in rare form last night."

Sam groaned. "Don't remind me."

Following tradition, the Spencer family held a barbeque for Sam's last night home. Uncle Adam, Aunt

Jeannie, Kevin, and the two older brothers still living at home joined them, along with a tray of Aunt Jeannie's famous brownies. Faith invited the Parkers, but they begged off. Sam missed Anna. They had played every day as kids, but her folks didn't want her coming to Sam's neighborhood. He couldn't blame them. Anna had worked off her childhood chubbiness and her allergies were under control too. Now fourteen years old, she'd sprouted into a tall, pretty girl with designs on becoming a model like Sam's mom could have been.

Dan Spencer had proven well up to the challenge of ruining Sam's last night home. He drank whiskey instead of beer and tied on a big one before the grill was even hot. He'd really laid into Sam.

"What the fuck are you going to camp for, Sam? Why don't you get a real job and earn some money, for fuck's sake? This CIT bullshit is just that – bullshit. I pay them for you to work your ass off the entire summer? Gimme a break?"

Dan swore virtually non-stop these days and never, ever went to church. Faith nagged him constantly, and the more she did, the more Dan drank and swore. After the company fired Dan three years back, everything spiraled down. Now, Dan sold tools from behind a counter at Sears, they lived in a crappy little ghetto house surrounded by crack heads and forget the Beamer, they didn't even have the Camry anymore. Faith drove Sam to the airport in the rusted out Kia they bought on eBay for $300.

Sam refused to feel guilty about leaving for the summer, or the camp tuition. After everything his parents had put him through, they owed him that. Camp wasn't just a fun summer getaway. It kept him sane. After ten months in the asylum he called home, camp was a necessary respite, a break from all the madness and heartache.

"Just relax, Sam," Kevin said. "Catch some shut eye. We'll be at camp before you know it and then you won't have to think about all the shit back home for another eight weeks."

When the bus pulled onto the bumpy, gravel-packed road leading to the camp, Sam woke up. Relief flooded him like a warm, sunny day at the sight of his beloved Camp Suck my Dick. The younger kids piled out of the bus first and went off with the group leaders to meet other kids their age, old friends from summers past and new acquaintances.

Sam and Kevin were the last to disembark and by then, the area had cleared out. Only Director Chuck, Skunkface Bob, and Mary Larry, the best group leader, remained. Larry earned his nickname when he was still a camper by playing Mary Poppins in the summer theatre production. This was his eighth season as a counselor, counting his CIT summer, and he still couldn't shake it. At this point, Sam wasn't even sure Larry wanted to lose the nickname. He lived in New York, went to a theatre school in Chelsea, and sung at gay bars on free nights, often in drag and billed as Mary Larry or sometimes Merry Larry. Mary Larry was proud of his stage reputation, but Sam thought it ridiculous. He just couldn't understand how Larry enjoyed pretending to be a woman. Larry sat him down last summer and tried to explain that he wasn't playing the part of a woman. He was a woman, deep inside, where it counted most. Sam just couldn't relate, no matter how hard as he tried.

Director Chuck was a man for whom tradition and loyalty mattered. He attended Camp Sacquenuckot as a kid and his teaching job was perfect for continuing as a counselor. When the camp nearly went under some years back, Director Chuck borrowed against his pension to save it. He barked out instructions. "Lowry, you're with Larry. He's got the Badgers this year. Spencer, you'll work in the stables during the day and bunk with the Groundhogs."

Sam broke into the biggest grin he'd worn in weeks. Mary Larry and Kevin headed towards the Badger bunks at the northern end of camp and Director Chuck trotted back to the office. The Badgers were the group for ten year old boys, the age Sam had been his first summer away. Each age group had a name: Polecats for the six and seven year olds (the older kids called them the Stinkies), Muskrats for the eight year olds, Badgers, Weasels, and so on.

Skunkface Bob clapped him on the shoulder. A big man, he towered over Sam. "Spencer. Good ta see you agin, boy. You're fillin' out, but not too much like Lowry. That un's too big. We like 'em small, the horses and me."

As far as Sam knew, Skunkface Bob had been born in Camp Sacquenuckot's stables and had never ventured farther than the back trail. He and his white-striped beard occupied a spot in Sacquenuckot lore for as long as anyone could remember. When Director Chuck bought the place, Skunkface Bob came with it. What Skunkface lacked in formal education, he made up for with his extensive knowledge of horses. Everything Sam knew about them came from him. The past few summers, he and Bomber had taken home half a dozen blue ribbons. "I'm glad they put me with you, Skunkface."

"Yep. Me too. C'mon, let's head out to the barn. Mr. Quiver's will be glad to see ya."

"He's still alive?"

"Sho nuff, but he cain't move so good no more."

"How old is he?" The Siamese cat was ancient. Even if Bruce Lee miraculously didn't wander off, he'd be lucky to live half so long as Mr. Quivers.

"Shoot, you know I don't count so good, Spencer. Twenty something, mebbe thirty? I wasn't much older than you when he was a kitten."

"Did my dad know Mr. Quivers?" In all the years Sam had been coming to Sacquenuckot, not once had his dad opened up about his camp experiences.

Skunkface Bob thought for a moment. Sam could see a crooked smile peeking out from beneath his beard. "I think so. You remind me of your dad, Spencer. We're going to have fun this summer."

***

Sam took his time getting off the plane, waiting until the flight attendant told him he had to leave. He didn't know how he could face his parents, not after everything that had happened. He hadn't told anyone except Kevin. He trusted Kevin enough to tell him the truth, but was afraid to let anyone else know. Not Director Chuck, not Mary Larry, and definitely not his parents. His tormentor had made it perfectly clear what would happen if he spoke up.

Faith stood with open arms, as she did every year, ready to give Sam a big welcome home hug. She looked the same as she had after that first summer at camp. Time and Dan's mistreatment hadn't dulled her beauty in Sam's eyes. Kevin Lowry still thought she was hot as ever too. These days, Kevin called her a MILF.

Dan, however, had completed his metamorphosis from sales exec to … something else. The man who taught Sam to walk, to ride a bicycle, to throw a football, and to read the Bible, had vanished from the earth. The person next to Faith bore no resemblance to the father Sam remembered. This man leaned lazily against a square column, wearing loose-fitting jeans and an untucked, short-sleeved Oxford exposing a hairy paunch. A Sears nametag was pinned to the pocket. His eyes drooped from too little sleep and he stank like the counselor's den two hours after Taps put the kids to sleep.

"Dan! Sam's here. Snap to it!" Faith hugged Sam like she never wanted to let go, then kissed him on the cheek like he was ten years old again, but he wasn't a kid any more. His childhood was over. She whispered in his ear. "I'm sorry your dad's so … he's always at his worst the days you come and go from camp. I think it's because he loves you so much."

"Hi, Dad." Sam didn't know how he felt about seeing his dad in such a state. Part of him wanted to hit Dan, both to show how angry he was and to free him from the nightmare that had become Dan's life. Since that first summer Sam had gone to camp, Dan Spencer had been spinning ever closer to disaster. If he really cared, shouldn't his dad have found some way to carve out a better life for Sam and his mom?

Dan issued a series of burps. "Hi, Sam. C'mere. Give your old man a hug."

Sam kept his eyes closed while embracing his dad. If not for the stale beer odor, Sam could have almost pretended that he was hugging his Beamer-driving, big shot, dad of old. After a few seconds, he pulled away.

When he opened his eyes, Faith was wagging her finger at him. "How was your summer? Do you know why I have to ask, Sam? It's because you only wrote us two letters. They should make CITs write home too. No letter, no lunch. I like that rule."

He hadn't even wanted to write that many. He couldn't tell them what happened in a letter. He didn't know if he could ever tell them. "Sorry, Mom. The kids kept me busy."

"Don't worry about it. You're home now. You can tell us everything."

"Sure, Mom. Later, okay? I'm kind of tired." In a few days, he hoped she'd stop asking.

Faith tried to hide her disappointment. "Whatever you want, sweetie. Let's get to the car. I'm sure you're anxious to get home."

Anxious wasn't the word Sam would have used.

He sat quietly in the back seat for most of the ride home. The rattle from the beat up, old Kia was so loud that he had trouble hearing himself think. When they were almost there, Faith glanced into the rear view mirror and caught his eye. "I'm afraid have some bad news, Sam."

He braced for the inevitable Bruce Lee update. He intentionally hadn't asked. He no longer cared whether Bruce Lee had wandered off or not. "What is it?"

"No barbeque tonight. The Parkers said they'd love to, but Anna has a gymnastics meet, and Aunt Jeannie said football comes first. Sean and Keith are both playing at different local colleges this year. I'll be lucky to see Jeannie once before the seasons end if I don't take in some games."

Sam uttered a silent thanks to God for answering his prayers. "It's okay, Mom. I'm not in the mood for a party anyways."

"Are you feeling all right?" Faith stretched out her arm, placing the back of her hand against Sam's forehead while keeping her eyes on the road. Dan was snoring, with his face smushed up against the passenger window, but Sam thought he was partly awake. "I don't feel a temperature."

"Let him be, Faith," Dan yawned.

"I'm fine, Mom. Really, I'm just tired."

She pulled into the driveway and put the car in park too quickly. The car came to a stop with a jolt. "Okay. There's one more thing. In fact, I'm surprised you didn't ask. It's about Bruce Lee. He ..."

"He just wandered off, just like the rest of those good for nothing cats," Dan, now fully awake, interrupted. "Good riddance, I say. Goddamned Siamese. They're the worst. All like mizz ..." His dad's words trailed off into a mumble.

Faith swiveled, turning her cold stare on Dan. "Be nice and show some respect. Sam really cared for Bruce Lee."

"It's okay, Mom. I'm kind of used to it."

"Oh, Sam. That's horrible!" Her gaze softened.

"It's true," his dad snickered.

"I'm sorry, Sam. I can't believe this keeps happening either. If you'd like, we can get another cat. Isn't that right, Dan?"

"No!" Sam shouted louder and more vehemently than he'd intended. Then he realized that he meant every last decibel. "I don't want another cat. I don't ever want a cat again. Never, as long as I live."

Sam's mom shrank back from his ferocious reply. Dan sat up and turned sharply towards him, his visage more sober than Sam had seen in years. "What did you say?"

Sam glared back defiantly. "I said I don't want a cat. You were right, Dad. They're no good."

Dan's eyes grew moist. The corners of his mouth drooped into utter sadness.

"What's with you, Sam?" Faith huffed. "Honestly, sometimes I just don't understand you. When you're ready to act like a human being, come inside and we'll have dinner." She slammed the car door shut and headed towards the garage.

Dan didn't exit the car. Instead, he returned Sam's glare with a penetrating gaze of his own. It felt to Sam like a blade cutting away armor, leaving him bare. Sam couldn't have broken away, even if he'd wanted to. Dan's stare held him fast, while it searched his soul for answers. Finally, after what seemed like forever, Dan broke off the staring contest.

"Mr. Quivers?" Dan whispered.

Sam sensed a new bond form between them, a burgeoning camaraderie that must remain forever unspoken. He nodded.

A pool of tears formed in Dan's eyes. "I'm sorry, Sam. I just couldn't …"

Suddenly, everything made sense to Sam.

***

205

Faith Spencer glanced at the ribs, slaw, and diminishing pile of fries on Sam's untouched dinner plate for what seemed like the thousandth time.

"Stop it, Faith. Just stop it." Dan tapped his fingers against the table.

"What?" She reached over and took another of Sam's fries even though she had a plate full of them.

"You know exactly what I mean." Dan didn't know what he'd do if she did it again. He was ready to explode. Damn it to hell, how had he managed to screw everything up so bad? His silence had condemned Sam to a lifetime of misery.

"He didn't even stay for dinner." She put Sam's fry back on his plate. "Sorry. I'm just worried. He didn't seem himself."

"Don't take it so personally. He's sixteen." Faith could never know the truth about him and certainly not about Sam. She would never understand. Dan felt nauseous it had come to this. He'd thought he could put his past behind him. For years, he'd done just that. Then Faith, his nagging, interfering wife, enrolled Sam at Camp Sacquenuckot. That's all it took to shatter his elaborate illusion, a registration slip and a stray white cat.

He'd been dreading this day ever he'd sent Sam off for his Badger year. Each year since then, Dan's summers became more and more unbearable, not knowing if this was the year he'd look into Sam's eyes and see himself staring back. He could have taken Sam out of danger at any time the past seven years by breaking his silence, but even after so many years and with his son's life at stake, he couldn't.

Faith nibbled on one of her fries. "I just don't understand, Dan. It's his first night home. We haven't seen him for two months and, I know it sounds petty, but he's been with Kevin every night at camp. Why did you let him go?"

"I —"

"I mean, really! You know how much I've missed him. Christ, I talk about it every day. How could you not know? Did he seem different to you? He seemed different to me. Do you think he's okay?"

Dan polished off the last of his ribs. If he concentrated on the sound of his chewing, he could almost drown her out. "Mmghgf," he mumbled. Let her noodle on that instead of Sam.

She leaned forward in her chair, like a harpy spreading her wings, a sure sign she was getting angry. "Are you even listening to me? I swear to God, you have to stop drinking. I mean, it's like you're not even here most of the time."

To show his contempt for her nagging, Dan downed the last of the beer and went to the fridge for another. Usually, he tuned her out. Tonight, she was getting under his skin. He had to calm her down. The last thing he needed was Faith peppering Sam with questions when he came home. "Give him some space. He doesn't want his parents smothering him."

"Smothering? I'm his mother. You call one dinner after a two month absence smothering? I don't ask for much, Dan. Sure, I want a safer car, and I can't wait to move out of this dump, but all I really want right now is to have dinner with my son and make sure he's all right."

He resumed his place at the table and emptied half the bottle in a single swig. Dan knew exactly why Sam had bolted for the Lowrys. He'd known the moment he'd looked into his son's eyes. He didn't blame Sam for a second. When he'd been in Sam's shoes, he'd run to Adam. Truthfully, he was glad that Sam wasn't here.

Dan thought he'd prepared well for this day. He had answers for every question Sam might ask and some that he wouldn't, after practicing the conversation in his head dozens of times. He'd come to envision this day as his epiphany, the day he confessed his sins to Sam and was absolved of them. But now that the day had arrived, he couldn't face his son with the truth. It had all gone terribly off script. His guilt was immense, far worse than he'd expected. Knowing that something had actually happened made for infinitely worse guilt than worrying about something that might happen.

"Dan! Dan, I'm talking to you."

Faith's voice sounded like the buzzing drone of a toy airplane. "Shut up, Faith. Please, can't you just shut up?"

She aimed her finger of death at him. "How dare you talk to me like that, Dan Spencer. I'm your wife. You will not address me in that tone."

He guzzled down the rest of his beer, pushed his plate away, folded his arms on the table and laid down his head sideways, facing away from her. "Whatever. A little quiet, PLEASE."

She slammed her fist against the table hard enough for Dan to feel it rattle through his arms. "Look at me, Dan Spencer. You want a little quiet, fine. You just call up Adam and tell him to send Sam home the moment he gets there. Something's going on with him. If you weren't so drunk, you'd have noticed. This family needs some open communication time."

"Leave it alone, Faith," he said without looking in her direction.

"Are you out of your mind? Something's wrong with Sam. We need to talk about it, to work it out. Like we always used to, before … things got so bad. Why did you ever hit that man, Dan? Why? If you hadn't, things could have been so different."

He lifted his head, a little angry now. "You just can't help getting your digs in."

"What happened to the man I married? You used to be so … gallant. And look at you now. Such a loser, you can't even get it up for your hot wife." She undid two buttons on her blouse, daring him to take her.

208

The shame from his childhood rushed back like a hurricane. A gust of memory carried Dan back to Camp Suck my Dick's stables. No one else was there, just him, Skunkface Bob, and cats, dozens and dozens of cats, stalking the rafters, like shadows in the night. Some perched on bales of hay, golden-eyed gargoyles, stone and uncaring to the vilest of deeds. Dan remembered strong arms enveloping him, straw scratching the back of his neck, and most of all, the haunting caterwauling that echoed through the stables like a soundtrack for a horrific romance. Mr. Quivers, a huge hulk of a Siamese not yet grown into his full size, conducted the vulgar symphony of Dan's shame not more than two feet from Dan's head, watching everything with unfeeling eyes of amber.

That night rippled through Dan's life, buried in every choice, every decision he made. The path he carved in the world, his family, his career, everything, it all hinged on that night with Skunkface Bob. He'd been a boy that night, but what happened defined him as a man. Trying to escape it was like running on a treadmill. That night would always be with him. Shame had swallowed him like a net. Shame that he'd allowed it to happen. Shame that he'd liked it. The more he sought to escape, the tighter his shame ensnared him.

In sending Sam to camp, his shame turned to guilt. He could live with his shame. He'd proven he could take his secrets to the grave, but allowing Sam to relive his shame was unforgiveable. The thought of Sam spending time in the stable with Skunkface Bob, with all those cats, with Mr. Quivers watching, drove Dan to rage. He had to kill all Sam's cats. They were sacrifices to expunge his guilt. The one time he fought the urges; he punched O'Donoghue and nearly lost his job. He ran over Tiger that very afternoon. On purpose.

"You're pathetic, Dan. I thought you might care, since this is about Sam, but you don't even care about him. Do you care about anything, Dan?" She stuck her tongue out.

It was as if she'd zapped him with a cattle prod. Dan leapt out of his chair. He grabbed the cleaver he'd used to cut the ribs with both hands and waved it at Faith. He felt the veins on his neck throbbing. "Shut up, goddamnit. Just shut the fuck up."

Faith's eyes went wide. "Dan, put that down. You're scaring me."

She'd ruin everything. She'd let all their secrets out and ruin everything. He couldn't let her do that. He had to protect Sam. She was just another cat. "You goddamn better be scared."

***

Kevin pulled up to Sam's house right before midnight. The only light in the house came from the kitchen. Sam undid his seatbelt. "Thanks, Kev. See you tomorrow."

"No problem." Kevin gave Sam's shoulder a squeeze. "Hey, Sam."

"Yeah?"

"Don't worry. It'll all be cool."

"Yeah, right. Thanks, dude."

Kevin's Mustang roared off and Sam trudged up the driveway, still unsure of what he would do. Discussing it all evening long in the Lowry's attic with Kevin hadn't helped. He might say nothing. Pretend, just like his dad did, that he was the same Sam who had left for Maine that June. Sam didn't think he could do that. Moreover, he didn't know how his dad had done it. His mom already sensed he'd changed and his dad knew beyond any doubt. He might talk to his mom first, or maybe his dad. Or maybe talking to them at the same time was his best move. Sam couldn't make up his mind. Every option led to certain disaster.

Sam looked through the window into the kitchen. His dad was sitting with his back to the door at the still uncleared table. Sam's plate had a full serving of ribs and slaw, but half his fries were missing. His mom must have had eaten them. She ate off his plate when she was nervous. Aunt Jeannie used to complain jealously about Faith's fast metabolism. Sam's mom could eat McDonalds every day and still qualify as a MILF. Half a dozen beer cans and a half empty whiskey bottle rested on the table near Dan.

Sam put his nervousness aside and opened the door. Dan turned around and, to Sam's relief, was wearing a huge grin. He'd thought his parents would still be mad. "Sam! I'm glad you're home. Sit down and eat some dinner. I saved it for you."

Sam's eyes darted around the room and into the living room beyond where the television was playing Fallon. "Where's Mom?"

"She's not here." Dan Spencer leaned back in his chair and started humming Camp Sacquenuckot's alma mater.

Something about his manner made Sam freeze. A lump formed in his throat and his heart pounded like Dander's had the first time Sam held him. "Where is she?"

Dan locked fingers behind his head before saying, ever so calmly, "Oh, she wandered off."

MAXIMUS SHOCK

13

Collected tales of Madness and Terror

Maximus
SHOCK

An OMP Magazine

Issue
No. 13

It exists!

SHARKORPION

EMIR SKALONJA

To my sister Ema, my metal concert going partner!

"I got...six more shells," Roger said as he cocked the shotgun.

"Well, that's good because we're all out of flares. Besides, I don't think anyone's coming to help us any time soon. I'd say that we're fucked, but that's an understatement." Lisa rummaged through her now soaked backpack and found nothing of importance that could improve their situation.

"We were fucked the moment we set foot on that boat. Should've just taken the money and disappeared. That's how it's usually done, isn't it?"

"You had to be the righteous bastard, Roger. I told you but you wouldn't listen. The government doesn't give a shit what happens to us or any one of the other contractors. They asked for a monster and we delivered it to them. That was the end of our deal. They asked, we made it. Half shark, half fucking scorpion." Lisa shoved the backpack aside and got up. She walked a few steps and looked at the bigger island they found themselves across from.

"Don't go too far just yet," Roger warned and stood up too, readying his shotgun.

"I mean, I feel like we're in some bad science fiction movie, you know, from the fifties; monsters attacking unsuspecting civilians and no one has a single clue of what the hell is going on. Who comes up with a hybrid of two animals, a scorpion and a shark for that matter?"

"We didn't think it was strange when the dollar signs flashed seventeen million and were given a grant for any future endeavors," Roger said and stood next to her. "We should go."

"What's the point?"

"Well for one, we have a better chance of surviving on that island across from here. It's bigger, there's higher ground. We just have to take our chances and get over this little bit of water. I'm surprised the thing hasn't jumped out yet. We're easy prey here.

The island they barely made it to after their boat was destroyed was a tiny one, a mere few hundred yards in each direction. There was a bigger (or so it looked like) island directly in front of them, some hundred yards of water separating them from it. They were somewhere in the Pacific, off the coast of Mexico. They couldn't have been that much further from San Diego, Roger thought as he stepped into the water.

Lisa joined him. She went in a little deeper and gripped the makeshift raft they made earlier, just enough to support the two of them and to keep Roger's shotgun on.

"Alright, let's do this fast."

"You don't have to tell me twice,"

They both went in now and pushed the raft made of palm leaves and tree bark tied with some heavy-duty twine Lisa found in the backpack when they first washed up on the shore.

They pushed lightly at first, trying to not disturb the fairly still ocean and attract the creature. They kicked their legs lightly under the water and pushed the raft faster as they went.

***

"Almost there," Roger said, "just keep going, honey, we can do it."

Lisa was panting now, short controlled breaths, as if she had been in labor and not lost somewhere in the Pacific Ocean. That was how she dealt with stress, and in this situation, it was more than acceptable, Roger thought. This bizarre and deadly trip was nothing but a nightmare and they saw their entire crew simply torn to shreds by the creature they created and brought to life; Sharkorpion, they called it. He sighed and shook his head as he thought of the half shark, half scorpion terror.

If only those arrogant government fools let them do their jobs and not meddle in science, none of this would have happened. Bryan, it was all his fault; a big shot from Pentagon that was put there to oversee his and Lisa's progress wanted the animal tested before it was ready, before the glitchy sensor chip was fixed and the monster could be controlled properly. But, the suits were eager to put it to use in combat, Roger just wasn't sure what the damn rush was. Like he thought it would, Roger watched the chip short in Sharkorpion and there was nothing they could do when it broke through the barriers keeping it contained. It freely disappeared into the ocean.

At least the tracker was still fully functional.

A splash came from their left side and Lisa turned first to see what it was, and Roger knew it was Sharkorpion. It had to be. Damn it, it was about time the bastard showed itself. He looked to his right and saw the stinger sticking up and curling from the water. It moved slowly at first, then picked up the pace.

"Oh shit, Roger, here it comes!" Lisa exclaimed. It wasn't a scream per se, but her voice was an octave higher and it sounded like along the lines of, *Shit, we better get the hell out or we're fucking dead.*

They kicked faster. Roger knew they only had seconds before the monster caught up and started devouring them. The worst thing of all was that Sharkorpion preceded all of the attacks with its stinger, paralyzing their victims, then chewing them up all while they were fully aware. That was a shitty way to go, Roger thought as he did his best to keep the shotgun dry.

"Almost there," he said. "Keep going! Keep going!"

The water splashed behind them and the stinger flew through the air and missed mere inches from Roger, pushing him to the left, knocking him into the woman and almost sinking the gun.

He was relieved when his feet touched the sand. With all his might, he pulled Lisa out of the ocean and pushed her onto the beach, then grabbed the shotgun and blindly fired off a shot. He didn't miss entirely as part of the blast radius caught one of the creature's pincers. The monster roared and retreated back into the water, its stinger still sticking out.

"Roger, run!" Lisa shouted from the back. "Hurry while it's still in there."

"Run," Roger responded, not taking his eyes off of the submerged hybrid they created. "I'll catch up to you as soon as possible!" He slowly walked backwards and saw the Sharkorpion emerge again, the stinger vibrating, pincers clasping violently. Half of the monster's body was that of a great white shark, the tail end of it morphing into a giant stinger. Thick and scaly scorpion legs protruded from the sides, and right by its gills, a pair of pincers. Roger was appalled by the sheer size of the animal. It had to be the length of at least two full grown men, easily; he had no doubt about it.

Its head swayed as it bellowed and shrieked.

Roger fired off another shot but the animal shielded its head with the pincer, which absorbed much of the bullet impact. The scales and the shell crumbled from the monster's appendage and it screeched in pain. It moved to the side and some distance away, trying to avoid another attack.

The damn thing *thinks*, Roger thought as he observed it in awe; if Roger recalled correctly studied the charts and watched the thing's intelligence increased. On top of that, it got the best of the both worlds, best traits from two nearly perfect predators, with the ability to breathe under water and walk on land just as freely.

"Run dammit!" Lisa now screamed.

Snapping from his trance of awe, Roger finally turned and ran in Lisa's direction. He grabbed her by her arm and pulled her along as they headed toward a thick grove of tall palm trees.

As they ran, he noticed that the ground started to become slightly elevated, and that was good, for

if they had fight the thing before being rescued, they'd want to face it from a higher vantage point.

He glanced over his shoulder and saw the creature roaming around on the sand. That was good; they had put some distance between and now could plan the next course of action.

They made their way further up the hill and he was relieved to see that the woods were still dense, and palms close together, making it hard to navigate, especially for the creature. He stopped them by a tree with a large base that provided for good cover.

"Let's take a break here," he said as he put his back against the bark and looked down onto the beach. "It looks like it's slowly moving toward the line, there. I don't think it will be able to come up this way. At least I don't think it will."

"Well what the hell are we going to do now?" Lisa asked exasperated.

"Catch our breath, then go further into the island. See how big it is, see if there's anything on the other side."

"And if there isn't? If it's completely devoid of any human life?"

"Well then, we're royally screwed. Even more than we are right now." He examined the shogun and pumped it, empty casing flying out of it and landing into the bushes. "For now, we wait here a little while longer and see what the thing's going to do. Like I said, the trees should prevent it from coming all the way up here. We're alive so far, that's something."

"Yeah, some comfort," Lisa rolled her eyes. She sat down behind him, the beach in her view.

She saw a long, thick piece of wood protruding from the bushes nearby, jumped up and grabbed it and sat back down. The stick was sturdy. She observed it for a moment, felt it all over, then pulled out her knife from holster and started to cut it down into a point, slowly creating a spike that was about three or four feet in length. "Hopefully, this will come in handy," she said.

Roger to turned to see what she was doing, and nodded in approval. "We can use just about anything right now."

She smiled at him, but he didn't notice it as he turned away to see the creature make its way in between the trees. It maneuvered somehow and its determination sent chills down Roger's spine. Still, he believed that it wouldn't be able to climb up all the way, but he was wrong before. He saw the monster use the pincers to clear the path before it, using them to gnaw on the wood in its way. Then it stopped for a moment and moved the side

"What is it doing?" Lisa asked.

Roger watched it move to their left and for a moment it disappeared from their view. Reappearing higher up on the hill and there, as far as Roger could see, the palms weren't as clustered as they were around them. He swallowed hard and slowly got up.

"We have to go…now," he said quietly, as calmly as he could. He pointed at the creature closing in on them then started dragging her again along his side.

"It just doesn't give up, does it?" she asked fearfully. "It's going to kill us, I know it. We're just postponing the inevitable. I mean, it's an island it's not like we got somewhere else to hide."

"Just run for now," Roger comforted her, trying not to show his own fear through his voice. "That's all we can do the time being. As long as we're on the move, we'll be fine.

As they ran, he kept looking to the side to see the beast easily keeping up with them. It moved just as fast if not faster. It bellowed now and then, as if to show them that it was there, that the time of their deaths was drawing near. It taunted them, Roger thought, like a perfect hunter it was. But they created it; therefore they should know its quirks, its faults. He tried to think of some, tried to remember the data and the countless spreadsheets and graphs but nothing came to mind. It was designed and created as a perfect killing machine, a weapon for the government.

The further to the top of the island they got, Roger noticed that the trees were becoming a few in number and they were being spread further apart. And, before he could process the information, the creature attempted to ram them from the side. But to their good fortune, the beast hit the tree that they were passing by.

It scared them, terrified them as they came face to face with it. Roger almost lost the grip on his weapon as he fell. Lisa was ahead of him by a few feet, and he saw her clench her makeshift weapon and raise it ready to strike.

Sharkorpion stood there by the tree and clasped its pincers closed and open several times, and its mouth chomped only a foot or two away from Roger. He pointed his weapon at it and without taking his eyes off of its monstrous, grotesque jaws, he spoke to Lisa. "You need to run now. You need to run and not look back, you understand?"

"Roger-"

"It's not open for discussion. You are to run and run as fast as you can. I'm going to stall it here. If I kill it, I will join you, if I don't...well." He exchanged a brief glance with her, smiled nervously then stared the creature down again. "I love you," he said, "And I'm sorry for everything."

"I love you too," she returned the sentiment as her eyes welled up in tears and then turned and ran.

Roger was now alone with the Sharkorpion and watched it move left and right as it tried to find the best angle to impale him first, then eat him.

"C'mon, you ugly bastard," Roger said as the thing jabbed its stinger but just missed him. He rolled to the side and fired off a shot, hitting the tree bark, but still managing to hit one of the legs. He heard it snap and break and the thing shrieked as it attacked again, missing him the second time around. He rolled to the other side now and fired off another shot and hit the creature again, destroying its right pincer. The appendage fell on the ground and Sharkorpion retreated a few feet, as if to regroup and plan the next course of action.

Roger used this brief interlude to get back to his feet and as he did, he stepped a foot closer and fired off another shot, this time hitting the thing's head though the distance he fired the shot from wasn't enough to do much damage save for a mere flesh wound. Still, Sharkorpion retreated yet again and shrieked its unnatural voice that Roger felt came straight from the darkest depths of Hell.

"Now I've got you!" Roger exclaimed joyfully and stepped in front of the tree, out of the cover and pumped the weapon again, ejected the previous casing and pointed the gun at Sharkorpion. "I'm sending you back from whatever fucking Hell we brought you from."

The shotgun blasted twice more and the first one only grazed the animal's side and the second was blocked by the other pincer.

He squeezed the trigger again but the gun clicked dry. Nothing came out. No explosion, no recoil came, just a soft sound of the gun dry firing.

"Shit," he said quietly, realizing his defeat. He lowered the gun and took what was coming.

The beast skittled to him and jabbed the stinger straight through his stomach, yet it didn't puncture his body all the way. The force knocked him down and the tip stayed only inches deep in him as he felt the poison being pumped inside.

Within seconds he felt himself lose the control of his body, numbness overcoming every inch of him. The beast retrieved the stinger and he felt the gaping hole right where his belly button was. He knew he had to been bleeding out bad, but couldn't tell or feel just how much. From the corner of his eye he saw the river of red run down the hill.

Then his gaze met the mangled face of the creature. He saw the fragments of the shell from the last gunshot he fired off, and damned himself for not stepping closer to finish the job properly and instead firing from that distance.

The thing grabbed one of his legs with its one remaining pincer and ripped it off, cutting the bone and tossing it aside like garbage. He saw his blood spray the animal hybrid in its ugly face before it proceeded to swallow his other leg and chomp on it. It opened and closed the large jaws in quick, powerful bites until it made its way all the way to his torso and took one last bite at his pelvic area.

Darkness slowly came over his eyes and the next thing he knew, and most certainly the last, everything went black.

Sharkorpion continued to gnaw on the corpse, creating a bloody, mangled mess.

***

Lisa went back immediately after she noticed the gun shots subside and the creature shriek. What worried her was the fact that Roger didn't call after her.

She hid behind the tree and realized she was too late. Sharkorpion had been chewing on the corpse of her now dead husband. His legs were gone and all around him were the remnants of his organs and a giant pool of blood.

Tears welled up in her eyes and quietly and clenched her weapon tighter. It was just a stick, she thought, but it would serve its purpose if she just did it quickly enough. She peeked from behind the tree and saw the creature was still feasting and that it would be preoccupied for some time. Now Roger's arm was gone, sticking out at its elbow from the animal's jaw as it chewed it up.

Leaving the cover of the tree Lisa ran to the side until she was at an angle, not directly behind the animal but just slightly to the side. She then prepared herself; sighed deeply, wiped the tears from her face, and bolted. She ran as fast as she could and before the creature could notice her, she was airborne.

She jumped on its back and without giving it a single opportunity to start knock her off just yet, Lisa impaled it with her stick, first in the spine, then in top of the head. She stabbed as hard and as fast as she could, blood squirting her in the face and then all over her

The thing shrieked and changed a dozen different tones of its unnatural, Hell-born vocal range until it finally bucked her off and she fell on her back. The impact was hard on her. She wasn't a twenty something year old girl party in medical school staying up until the Witching hour. She was forty-three and she felt that fall deeply all over her body. If she didn't know any better, she'd think something was definitely broke.

Sharkorpion moved maniacally, jabbing the stinger at her aimlessly, missing her every time. She rolled down the hill in an effort to avoid being stabbed or trampled. Lisa's momentum picked up, then was abruptly stopped when she slammed into a tree.

Weakly, she slowly lifted her head to see the animal's speed decrease until it came to a full stop. The stick was still protruding from its head, blood gushing all over its body from the stab wounds.

It gave one last shriek and fell dead.

Lisa stayed there by the tree for a moment longer, trying to gather her energy as her body ached all over. She then rose and slowly started to limp up the hill toward Roger's mangled corpse.

She came within an arm's length to it, but couldn't get herself to come any closer and behold the grotesque sight of her dead husband. He had been entirely butchered, from his legs and arms, to his pelvic area, where the only thing remaining was his torso with one arm and his head. The blood was still freely flowing, soaking the ground beneath him.

His face was frozen in terror, looking up at the sky past the thicket of leaves.

She closed her eyes and mouthed, "I love you."

She walked around Roger's lifeless body and further up, until she came to the very top to a clearing. From this vantage point she could see the rest of the island, down the hill they came from and the other side that showed not much else. It was all the same, more palm trees, a sandy beach and hundreds of miles of perfectly blue ocean.

The sun was at its highest point and she shielded her eyes as she tried to look up at the sky, then across the land every possible way. It wasn't that big, perhaps half a day of walk in each direction. She stood at the top of the hill and stared long and hard until the look on her face turned into nothing but emptiness.

She continued to look around the desolate place.

There was nothing there.

MAXIMUS SHOCK

14

Collected tales of Madness and Terror

Maximus SHOCK

An OMP Magazine

Issue
No. 14

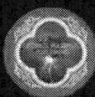

A WOLF IN SHEEP'S CLOTHES

Nature bites back!

Matt Hay

To Tange, Pauline, Anja, CB and Rich Christie -
Thank you for your support.
It has meant so much and kept me focussed and motivated.
You are all amazing.

CHAPTER ONE: MAKE A BEAST OF MYSELF

Alone, he ran through the dark, lush forest, the trees whistling in the light breeze as his legs stretched out, his woollen fur damp with the light drizzle in the air. The pain was still stabbing through him as the memories of the last few hours replayed through his tortured mind. Tears ran down his cheek which chilled in the cold wind sending further shivers through his body. Regret followed with a realisation that he was responsible for the senseless deaths of all those people.

This wasn't who he was, it wasn't who he wanted to be. When the violence started, it was difficult for him not to react, not to kill them all, but they had to pay for what they did to his family. It wasn't fair, why had they killed everyone? His friends, his mother, his flock, all needlessly died. Why couldn't they have just left them all in peace? Why did it have to end that way?

Sorrow turned to anger as the path softened ahead. The beautiful coloured fall leaves stuck to the wool of his coat as they fluttered from the sparse woodland around him. It pushed him faster than he had ever ran before, his paws barely touching the sodden soil covered in a treacherous carpet of autumn droppings.

Earlier that day, the memories of the rich grass glistening as the morning sun that shone on the overnight dew came flooding back to him. It was too inviting not to feast on, the fresh smell had carried over to him and soon, he found himself gorging on the undisturbed meadow.

The unbridled joy became a fleeting feeling as disaster struck during their tragic breakfast. A group of humans stealthily crept up behind them to slaughter his loved ones, shattering the life that he once knew. Using large shiny tools, they struck at his flock, killing friends and family alike. Cowering at the back of the herd, he watched in horror as his mother was slain just a few yards away. Aghast, he yelped as the metallic weapon slashed down separating her head from her delicate, fleecy body, leaving it lying in the blood-stained field staring blankly at him. Grief overtook him as he howled at her death, his haunting sadness echoed through the meadow. His long snout pointed towards the heavens where her final journey started, every blade of grass vibrated in time to his sound of his overwhelming sorrow.

Reality soon brought him back to his senses as he heard further slaughter nearby. Pained bleating and slashing sounds echoed through his heart as each death struck a further blow to him until he could no longer take any more. Lowering his head, he scoured around to identify where the bloodshed was coming from. Three figures were holding down Ramshorn, the patron of his flock, as the fourth one was sliding a long knife along his throat, blood seeping down his exposed neck. A low growl rumbled from the pit of his stomach as the anger raged through his body pumping adrenalin into his enlarged form, pushing him into action.

Long, sharp talons extended out from his feet gripping the tender earth below. Shining, white incisors shot from the roof of his mouth as the remainder of his teeth grew into a ferocious set of fangs. Spiked hackles protruded through his fluffy white coat as the rest of his body transformed into a lupine figure whilst retaining his ovine form.

Flexing his newly formed muscular legs, he rushed towards the slaughter, teeth gnarling in disgust at the senseless carnage ahead. The distress of his mother's death was still at the forefront of his mind. A new feeling of fury grew through the once placid animal as he replayed her final moments.

"I will destroy you!" he roared before leaping at the first man holding down Ramshorn, severing his exposed arm and spraying the warm blood onto his clothes.

A piercing scream was heard as the pain shot through the hanging limb of the bearded beast. Ripping the arm from the socket, he released it before rising to sink his incisors into the jugular, killing the attacker as the crimson stream released into the summer air. A snarl of satisfaction emitted from him as he gracefully landed and continued striding towards the remaining people who had terror etched over their faces.

"You will pay for your destruction!" he roared as he paced towards the second of the thugs who was standing facing him with a large double-bladed axe in hand. Deftly, he avoided the crude swing as he rammed into the bulky male, dislodging him from his feet to the green killing field below. Slashing upwards, he raked into the tender cheeks of his victim before swatting his giant paws against the cranium, driving it into the ground, ending his life in an instant.

Quickly, he dispatched the remaining murderers with relative ease as they struggled to keep up with his enhanced agility. Their slothful swings missed him as he struck with deadly force, removing the danger from the remainder of the tribe as his brethren cowered behind him in terror at his brutal actions.

A feral urge came over him, a sudden pang of hunger, a longing for the taste of meat. This was something that he had never experienced before as he loped over to the carcass of the fallen fiend before ripping the flesh off its limbs and ingesting it in his stomach.

After he had finished his unexpected meal, he moved to join the remainder of the sheep, jolting to a stop as he saw the looks of fear and horror aimed at him. He knew that he could no longer be with them, his time as part of the flock was over as he ran off to escape the nightmare he had caused.

Back in the present, he shivered due to the temperature dropping as the edge of the woods drew near. Ahead, a couple of fields separated by a long country lane appeared. Choosing to ignore the farm animals grazing in the pastures, he strode down the path hoping to find shelter from the wet weather before the impending rain soaked through him.

A large building appeared in the distance, it was brown, with big heavy doors, he remembered Ramshorn once calling it a barn. It surprised him how much he missed the wisdom of the old ram, his teachings were often long-winded but always useful, his advice would have been welcome now. Tiredness caught up to him after the stress and emotion of the morning coupled with the long run through the woodland. The door lay open ahead as he longed for a comfortable place to rest his weary head.

Once inside, a strewn pile of straw looked appealing in the corner as he crawled his way over to the inviting bed, flopping on top of it and passing out into a restful slumber.

CHAPTER TWO: THE CHASER

A cockerel crowed in the distance, the sound echoing through the barn where he lay. Stirring, his head turned slightly before one eye opened to survey his surroundings. Satisfied that nothing else was near, he closed his eye and snoozed back off again. A few minutes later, the infernal bird sounded out again, this time more aggressively. With both lids now opened, he stretched and groggily made his way to his feet, shaking off the straw that had attached itself to his blood-stained fleece. A surprise greeted him as he noticed that his legs had grown significantly overnight to long, thick, muscular limbs. Upon further examination, he had developed large padded paws which were furnished with significant, sharp talons.

The events of the previous day had haunted his dreams, causing him to feel less rested than normal. Thirst and hunger consumed him as he scoured round the building to see if there was anything that would fulfil his basic needs. Unfortunately, all he could see was the hay that he slept on and he didn't fancy eating that.

Hastily, he exited the barn into the bright morning sun which temporarily blinded him as he struggled to find his bearings. Around him, chickens and pigs were playing in the courtyard of the farm with the main building to his right. The hens looked content; clucking away whilst playfully nudging the hogs who grunted back at them, enjoying the shenanigans.

Houses normally meant people and he was keen to avoid them after the pain of yesterday's events. This encouraged him to return down the lane that he had emerged from last night.

As the route widened, he dropped into a loping run, finding the going easier with the enhancement to his body as he padded back up the lane. New smells overwhelmed his senses as he salivated to the fresh beef scent teasing his nostrils from the field to his left. Overcome with the need for bovine meat, he leapt over the hedge to his left and crept towards the herd of cattle ahead. He could make out seven of them, grazing on the grass at the edge of the field. Strangely, his taste for it had gone and a hunger for fresh meat replaced it, almost engulfing him.

Flexing his new muscles, almost tasting his breakfast, he crawled in closer, trying to maintain the illusion of his previous form to prevent panic erupting within the herd. A large black and white Fresian had peeled off from the others and was lying, soaking in the sun, not paying attention to anything in the field. Locked in on the target, he began the process of stealthily hunting down his prey, ready for the next kill.

One of the cattle turned and stared at him, eyeing him up and down suspiciously, with a look that said *what the fuck is a sheep doing here*? Momentarily pausing due to the unwanted attention, he pulled his teeth and claws in and looked sheepishly back at it.

"Baa," he bleated to try and distract it.

"Moo," replied the cow with a deep booming voice, flipping its head up and down in annoyance.

Dropping his head in deference, he nodded in response to the larger animal to try and put it at ease. Sniffing, the cow turned around, returning to chew on the fresh grass, happy that the strange woollen intruder was harmless.

Watching, waiting for it to settle, he concentrated once again on his prey. The juicy, milk laden udder looked very tasty. Licking his lips in, he crept in for the kill, closing in on his unsuspecting victim. He extended his claws, lengthening out his powerful legs before baring his razor-sharp teeth in anticipation of his meal. His body enlarged as huge, spiked hackles rose through his fleece coat. Thick, ivory horns grew through his skull as he stood tall and menacing, looking all the seven feet of his new feral state. His large red eyes were blazing, heightened senses now awakened as he pounced upon the prone beast. His teeth sank deep into the jugular of his prey, ripping out the throat and leaving a fountain of blood spraying onto the grass. Overpowering hunger took over as he tossed the tough flesh into the air, catching and devouring it whole before licking his lips and moving down towards the big juicy milk sacks, full and inviting, almost begging him to taste the sweetness.

Slashing downwards, his talons pierced through the soft covering, a blood-tinged white liquid spurted out in front of him. Hypnotised by the crimson tainted treat flowing before him, he extended his long tongue and lapped it in to satisfy his thirst. As the cream splattered down his cheek, he bleated in delight at the sweet taste.

Finally, he turned to the remainder of the corpse before him and bit deep into its succulent belly, ripping out slabs of meat and placing them on the ground beside him. Holding the steak in his paws, he gratefully chewed on the tender beef, filling his newly expanded stomach.

His bloodlust now fulfilled, he focussed on the rest of the cattle who were cowering in the corner of the field, shouting for their lives. The large black Fresian, who tried to intimidate him earlier, could not hold his gaze, fearing that he would be the next target. The Wolf-Sheep smirked, knowing that he would take great pleasure in killing the arrogant animal. The superiority complex etched on their sneering faces was typical of their race, always laughing at his flock blissfully playing in the sun, sneering at their peaceful ways. It was time to end that mocking laughter.

Lowering his head, the Wolf-Sheep charged into the crowd, taking aim at the neck of his tormentor, trying to rip out his throat. However, he missed as his right horn stabbed into the eye of the herd leader. Screaming in pain, the cow tried to lash out with its hooves at him, missing as he managed to remove his horn in time and deftly dodge the incoming kick. Countering, he sank his teeth into the flank of his foe, ripping the cartilage out of its leg. He watched with satisfaction as it sank to the ground, writhing in agony as the bone of its knee popped out on impact with the ground.

Ready for the kill, he turned to pounce at his prone prey to finish the kill and move onto the next of the herd. However, as he leapt, a loud bang echoed through the meadow and moments later, he felt a sharp pain shooting though his side. Blood seeped down his body, staining his fluffy coat as small metallic fragments stuck to his open wound. Howling in pain, he spun round trying to locate where the blasts had come from, narrowly avoiding another

229

bullet as a whistling noise spun past his ear, missing him by inches.

Fear surged through him as he struggled to locate the marksmen as more shots rained in on him causing him to scurry for cover. Some of the bullets hit him, others missed, but more pain thundered through him with blood matting his coat as he moved to avoid the incoming shrapnel. In the distance, he could hear those damn cows laughing at him as he ran back to the safety of the woodland beyond.

CHAPTER THREE: BE A KID

Screams of excited children reverberated through Anna's head as she sat on a small wooden bench, typing messages to her friend Tasha on her smartphone. They were chatting about what happened on Tasha's hot date last night. Smiling at each message that arrived, she thought back to when she was single, when her life had no worries and she was chatted up every night by a different bloke who was only interested in her body. In some ways, she missed those days, with the freedom to do what she wanted still a huge attraction but mainly she was happy with her life now. Anna was happily married to her husband Chris and their beautiful four-year-old daughter Pauline, who was currently sliding down the chute, shouting in glee along with the other kids at the playground. She smiled as she watched Pauline squealing with joy as she went down again, her beautiful blonde hair flowing in the gentle breeze.

They'd had a tough few months with Pauline. At first, she thought that it was a phase that her daughter was going through. She kept disappearing to her room in a tantrum, shrieking at her in a rage. Over the last couple of weeks, things have been stranger than normal, with toys disappearing into thin air and ornaments moving from one end of the sideboard to the other. Initially, Anna thought that it was her imagination, then she blamed the dog, but the more it went on, she thought that there might be a ghost in the house and it worried her that Pauline was in the same house as something supernatural.

Buzzing, she unlocked her phone again to read the latest musings of Tasha, sighing as she read the complaints about men don't offer to pay for the dinner anymore. Texting a return in sympathy, she sat back, thinking that Tasha just didn't get life at all. Tasha seemed to think that life was one big joke and that the Earth revolved around her.

Shaking her head, she looked up as the hum of the noise reduced to almost a murmur as the children had all stopped to stare at the far end of the playground. Gazing over, she saw a huge woollen figure limping its way towards the kids. It was the strangest sight that she'd ever seen. It had long, muscular, furry legs, a thick, red fleece and a large tail that drooped as it walked. It looked to be part sheep and part wolf but she couldn't be sure. It seemed to have a strange dye over its coat which was unusual as she couldn't remember any of the local farmers using that colour on their flock.

Anna watched as a large group of the kids had left the main playground area and were running across the grass excitedly towards the creature. She knew that most of them were used to handling farm animals as they were often taken there on local trips by their school or they had a relative that worked on one.

Worried, Anna scanned the crowd looking for her daughter, hoping that she hadn't been caught in the mad rush with the other boys and girls. Despite, her frantic searching, little Pauline was nowhere to be found. There was no sign of her beautiful little blonde haired girl anywhere.

"PAULINE!" she screamed at the top of her voice, panicking, "WHERE ARE YOU!"

Standing up, she continued to shout and look around, but Pauline was not within sight. Anna's legs felt like jelly but she forced them to move as she broke into a jog towards the beast, all the time trying to locate her missing daughter, becoming more frantic with every passing second.

The main group had now reached the sheep and were busily trying to stroke and poke its body with their dirty little digits. Anna could see that the creature was getting agitated, it worried her as she thought that it might react and snap at one of the little brats.

Horrified, she watched as one of them climbed onto its back, helped by the arms of the cheering little terrors. She watched speechless as the child bounced up and down, pretending to be a jockey as the other kids continued to spur her on. Incredulously, she came to a halt, her mouth hanging open in surprise as she recognised the rider as her daughter Pauline. What was her precious flower doing up there?

"Pauline!" she yelled again, *"Get down from there, it's not safe!"*

For a moment, it was as if Pauline didn't hear her shouting as she kept jigging on top of its back. Pauline continued to yell excitedly, smiling and giggling with her friends who were egging her on as they continued to torment the poor creature by hitting and kicking it.

Pauline's head suddenly jerked around and she locked onto Anna's eyes. Pauline had a vacant look upon her face as her stare passed through Anna. A small smile crept over the little girl's cheeks as she started to mutter to herself, her hands waving about in strange gestures.

The beast snarled, bared its teeth and growled at the children as it rose into the air with Pauline still on its back. Horrified, Anna watched helplessly as it lashed out with its claws. Slashing through the arms and bellies of the excited kids, cries of joy turned into frightened screams as they fell to the ground in agony or ran scattering to avoid the wolf-sheep who was busily trying to clear the area of the terrified boys and girls.

Aghast, Anna sprinted to attempt to rescue her poor daughter from the ferocious monster that was maiming and killing the innocent lives around it. She was fearful that if Pauline was to lose her grip that she would be trampled or even killed in the ensuing melee. This spurred her on to run faster, nearly falling over the litter bin that had been knocked over in the chaos.

She was making good progress until the incoming children slowed her path to her precious Pauline and she could only watch as the Wolf-sheep broke free and raced off into the woods beyond. Pauline continued to run after it, but it was too fast and she soon lost sight of them. She sank to her knees in despair at what had just transpired.

Her daughter was gone, taken by a freak of nature as Anna's imagination was playing games with what had happened to Pauline. Images of dark caves or nests on the top of cliffs flooded through her mind as she punched the soft turf in anger.

After a couple of minutes, she rose to her feet, looking at the carnage around her and was shocked to see the other children covered with scratches and head wounds after the short devastation and destruction by the monster that now had her poor Pauline. The carnage fuelled the rage inside of her as threw her jacket to the floor and stomped on it.

Scrabbling in her red leather handbag, unable to find her phone, she panicked before realising that she put it in her coat pocket when she went after Pauline. Anna picked up the crumpled clothing and fumbled about, looking for the device, hoping that she had not smashed it in temper. Relieved, she fished it out and dialled the emergency services requesting an ambulance and the police.

Walking over to the injured children, she assisted the other adults who had run over to tend to their little ones, waiting for help to arrive on the scene.

The Wolf-Sheep ran to escape the devastation that he had caused. An anguish seeped through his soul, the pain of injuring innocent young ones tortured him as he bounded back through the safety of the woods. He was aware of the little girl on his back but didn't know why she was there or why he continued to carry her.

Memories came flooding back of what had happened but he couldn't remember doing most of it. There was no recollection of her climbing on top of him or that he lashed out and maimed all those poor children. The guilt surged through him as the sight of their scratched faces and gouged arms flooded his vision. It upset him but the feel of the child on his back was calming as an inner peace settled within.

Unusually, he found that he quite enjoyed her being there, even though it irritated him, it almost felt as if she belonged upon his back, like she was a part of him. He'd never felt anything more natural than her being up there riding him, merrily bouncing away in time with his stride as he glided along the woodland trail.

The first time he saw her, there was a glow around her just before she climbed on. He knew that she was special as none of the other children shone like that. She was such a sweet innocent soul, he felt her aura, the special bond between them. The happiness was overwhelming, he'd never felt such joy in his life.

There had been a huge pain in his side from where the shot had wounded him but he felt no pain now. The blood still ran down his leg and onto the mud below. He knew that no harm would come to him whilst the child was with him and he would ensure that she was protected.

The trail in front narrowed before widening into a large clearing which had a bright light shining on it, reflecting off the blades of grass. It highlighted a path towards the edge of the clearing which seemed to vanish over a cliff. Nearing it, a glimmering coloured bridge appeared. It was beautiful, shining with so many different vibrant shades which surrounded him as he stepped onto it. It enveloped him as he strode over the bridge to the other side and an inner peace flowed through him. It was as if he was walking on thin air.

CHAPTER FOUR: I AM STILL ALIVE

The area was swarming with emergency vehicles as medical professionals tended to the wounds of the injured children, their mothers standing by in tears, watching as their loved ones were either treated or put on a stretcher and taken away to the local hospital. Anna observed as the carnage started to clear and the police officers interviewed people to try and ascertain what had happened. One was stood taking notes with her, nodding furiously as she talked. He was a tall chap with dark hair protruding from under his peaked cap.

"So, miss," the policeman said as he looked up from his notepad, "Your child ran towards a creature that was the cross between a wolf and a sheep and with the help of her friends, she climbed onto its back, bounced up and down on it, and then it ran away with her still on him after it injured the other children. Have I got that right?"

"Look, officer," she replied, "I know that it sounds ridiculous when you say it like that, but it happened exactly the way that you described it. Ask the other people, they all saw it too. I just want to find my missing daughter."

"I totally understand," he said, "If it was me, I'd be worried too. Look, I have statements from everyone around here, why don't we have a poke about the woods and see if we can find her?"

His radio crackled loudly on his belt. Fumbling about, he carefully removed it from the clip, putting it up to his mouth to speak, "Charlie Alpha, this is DS Taylor, repeat that over."

"DS Taylor," crackled the radio, "This is Charlie Alpha, what is your status? Over."

"Charlie Alpha, this is DS Taylor, eye witnesses report a strange beast that is a cross between a wolf and a sheep terrorising the kids and running off with a little girl. The girl's name is Pauline and I've got her mother here with me now, I'm about to take her into the woods to look for the missing child. Requesting back up. Over."

"DS Taylor, this is Charlie Alpha, Sorry, we have no-one to spare. We are stretched to the limit just now. Over."

"Charlie Alpha, is there no-one that we can spare? I desperately need help here, Over."

"DS Taylor, I understand that. DC Smith won't be available for about another hour, apart from that we have no-one. Over.

"Charlie Alpha, I understand, if you could let me know when someone frees up. I'll have to go after this thing on my own. Over."

"DS Taylor, Understood, roger, over and out." The policeman puts his radio back in his belt and turns to Anna.

"I don't think it's wise to go in there unarmed," he said, "You don't know what this creature is like. I've got a rifle in the van. I'll just get that before we head off, give me a couple of minutes."

Taylor disappeared for a few minutes and returned with large brown gun and small satchel filled with ammunition for the rifle. They both headed out towards the entranceway of the woods to look for signs of which direction the creature had ran off .

DS Taylor stopped just before the opening to bend down and examine the muddy ground below. After a few seconds, he motioned Anna over to him.

"Look down here," he said, brushing away some loose grass. Anna bent over to look at where he was pointing.

"The marks here," he said, "Indicate that there was a large creature that was moving at pace, heading off in that direction." Anna followed his arm as Taylor signalled to the north, towards a track that headed deep into the woods.

"If we follow that path," he continued, "We should see more clues to where they are headed. I'm keen to get moving, I don't want us fumbling about in the dark as it might scare the wolf thing and that's the last thing I want to happen. Pauline's safety must come first."

They trudged along the uneven dirt track, travelling towards the heart of the forest. It was slow going at first as they had to avoid the fallen branches and litter that the local thugs had strewn across the path. Broken bicycles lay with their spokes protruding out, ready to spike themselves into the unaware rambler.

After half an hour of struggling over the rough ground, the path opened up into a small clearing, lush with grass, highlighted by the warm glow of the afternoon sun. Several openings went off in different directions which had them looking round for clues to their next destination.

After several minutes of carefully searching the undergrowth, DS Taylor spotted drops of blood in the grass at the edge of a small trail to the far-right hand side of the clearing, next to it was a small patch of wool soaked in blood.

"Anna," called DS Taylor, "Come over here and have a look at this."

She hurried over from the other side of the clearing, almost falling as she rushed to see what the bulky policeman had for her.

"Look," he continued once she reached him, "Do you see this material here; it's like fleece from a sheep. You don't see that every day."

"The creature that took my Pauline looked like a sheep from a distance," explained Anna. "Oh, God, please say that's not her blood."

"I'm sure it's not", replied DS Taylor. "Look, there is no time to waste, let's go down this path and find them."

They headed down the clearing, deeper into the woods as the terrain was rockier the further along that they went. Anna was getting anxious as the reality of the situation was hitting home. She was scared that she would never see her lovely Pauline again, worried that she could be injured or ill and petrified that she could be dead, killed by the horrific animal that took her. The memories of Pauline playing with her in the park, the smile on her face as the swing went higher, the joy beaming from her as she went down the slide, all flooded into Anna's mind as a small tear released down her cheek. She remembered the first time that she took a step and the laughter from Pauline when she fell over just after. The thought of never experiencing any more moments like that spurred Anna to hurry on, moving ahead of the cautious policeman and racing on through the deep woodland.

"Slow down," puffed DS Taylor, "You don't want to injure yourself. You're no use to your daughter if you're lying on the ground with a sprained ankle."

"You are right," replied Anna in frustration, as she eased off the pace, "I need to be in a fit state to deal with whatever we face, I can't do this alone."

A frown of anguish had formed on Anna's face as they had walked down the path without any further sign that they were moving in the right direction. Subconsciously, her fist was pounding into her hand as the tension and trepidation grew with each passing moment as she continually scanned around her, hoping to see her baby alive and safe. Hope began to dissipate as there continued to be no sign of the child. A faint glimmer still remained though, enough left to keep her going. It seemed like an eternity since they first entered the forest.

Relief flushed over Anna's face as they exited into another clearing, rich with thick green grass with pure white daisies scattered within it. Lain, spread out close to the edge, was an enormous, bloodied, woollen creature with a soft blue glow surrounding it.

Putting her finger to her lips, Anna crept up to DS Taylor and whispered softly in his ear.

"That's it," she pointed to the beast, "That's what abducted my Pauline. I'm going to have a look behind it to see if she is nearby, cover me with your gun please."

Tiptoeing carefully, she crept towards the slumbering sheep-wolf as DS Taylor raised the rifle and kept it pointed at the creature, watching carefully for any movement towards the silent housewife, finger steady, ready to react at the first sign of danger.

Concentrating fully on what lay before her, Anna stealthily flanked around it to try and get a better view, hoping to see if her daughter was alive. Nerves shot through her as she shortened the distance and more of the creature came into her vision. It was massive, as big a sheep as she had ever seen, but there were a few noticeable differences that chilled her. The natural ovine shape of his mouth disguised the long jawline and the sharp, bone white fangs underneath. Large furry hackles protruded through the fleece on its back and long hairy legs with huge padded paws displayed long sharp talons which were caked in a combination of mud and rancid flesh. She'd never seen anything like it before.

A few steps later and she was able to see the outline of a child lying, snuggled against it. The little one looked peaceful, as it slept cuddling the monster. Straining her eyes, Anna tried to see if the kid was breathing and more importantly if it was her Pauline.

A gentle movement momentarily stopped her heart as relief washed through her, settling the uneasy queasiness that had formed in the pit of her stomach. Praying that this was Pauline, she stood very still, watching for further movement, hoping that no harm had befallen what she thought was her daughter.

The body slowly rolled over to reveal the face of her only child, her beautiful Pauline. Relief flushed through her, followed by an overwhelming joy as she yelped in jubilation as the sight of her daughter alive.

The noise stirred the lifeless beast as it raised its large, furry head to survey the area, searching for the source of the disturbance. Anna watched as it slowly stood and began to pad its way towards her.

A gunshot rang out as the bullet exploded from the rifle that DS Taylor was carrying. Time seemed to slow down as it passed through the body of the wolf-sheep, like it was an apparition haunting the woods, into the skull of her precious Pauline. Anna wailed in horror as Pauline slumped to the ground, the blood pouring from the large bullet hole in her head. Anna could hear the roar of anguish from the shocked policeman and the clatter of the gun hitting a stone after its fall.

"*No!*" screamed Anna as she sprinted past the wolf-sheep towards her fallen daughter, momentary joy turning to despair as her little girl lay in a bloody heap before her. Anna watched in anguish as the last breath slowly exhaled from Pauline's lips.

Just as Anna reached her, a ghostly figure rose from Pauline's corpse to stand before her. The spectre was a faded mirror of her child with a blue glow surrounding it. Anna howled in grief as it placed its hand on her shoulder sending a shiver down her spine as the incredibly light touch seemed to steady her shaking body.

"Mother," whispered the Ghost in a rasping voice, "It's ok, I'm at peace now, I'm where I want to be."

It pointed over the wolf-sheep.

"He'll look after me, mother, he's my friend. We're now bound to each other, linked. I'm safe now. I have to leave you. I love you, mummy."

Anna sank to her knees and cried as she watched the ghost of her daughter walk over to the mysterious beast as it lay down to let her climb on top of it. She watched as it carefully rose and the ghost of her daughter extended her hand and waved as they rode off back into the heart of the woods. She screamed in agony as the pain of losing her only daughter overcame her.

"I love you, Pauline," she cried as she picked up the corpse of her fallen child and kissed it gently on the forehead.

Anna slowly rose to her feet and carried Pauline's body back towards the burly policeman, who was standing in shock, as white as a sheet. DS Taylor offered to carry the child but Anna couldn't bear him to touch her deceased daughter so she brushed him off with an emphatic shake of the head.

Anna strode back through the trees still carrying Pauline's body with DS Taylor trailing in her wake, her only thought was to get Pauline back home to her final resting place.

The Wolf-sheep watched with the hand of the child placed on his woollen coat as he felt sadness of the woman as she carried the shell of the little girl who stood beside him. The tears flowed from the child as she cuddled into his fleece but he could not feel any wetness. Despite the sadness, he felt the belonging and knew that the child would remain with him as his companion. As the humans disappeared, he turned and comforted his grieving friend.

Collected tales of Madness and Terror

An OMP Magazine

Issue
No. 15

Maximus SHOCK

MAXIMUS

SHOCK

15

Last Stop, or ...

LAST CHANCE

Jeffrey Kosh

Ray Nix heard the sudden noise and snapped out of the story he was reading. Someone had knocked on the windowpane and that unexpected sound caused him to lose grip of his paperback; the worn mystery thriller fell to the floor and then, like a snake looking for a rock to hide, it slithered under the counter. Ray ignored it and looked to his left.

There was no one there. Just the rain.

The monotonous afternoon drizzle had finally turned into a full-blown storm and it was now violently unleashing its fury into the parking lot, pummeling the pumps and the tiny gas station building with chubby drops of water. A strong wind had also decided to join the fray and was now siding with the downpour in that late evening assault.

Seeing that it was dark outside, he hastily reached for the switch to turn on the big sign and exterior lights. He did that more to cast away his fear of shadows than to attract clients, for he wasn't expecting visits at this time of the year. Off season in Prosperity Glades was Dead season.

'Stupid rain,' he thought. Then he bent down to retrieve the book and found it hiding in the dark, amid dirty crumbs, dust bunnies, and innumerable candy wraps. *'I really need to take more care of this place; look at all that shit down here!'*

Ray always thought that when confronted with the untidy state of his workplace, but then he would instinctively forget once he got back to his seat. Fact was, Ray hardly loved his job. He dreamed of more enticing and adventurous experiences; of traveling the world and seeing exotic places. He wished he could leave that stupid road and see new ones. But that required money. And courage. And Ray had neither.

He had always been a coward.

People in town said he was scared of his own shadow. When his name came up in conversation, that is, for most of the time they just ignored his existence. And he couldn't blame them, after all. He certainly looked unthreatening with his lithe figure and gaunt features, his curly – and often unruly – blonde hair, his fair skin that easily got reddish into the hot Floridian sun (not that he saw a lot of it, for Ray worked every day and rarely left his workplace or his home), and a bent posture that made him look like a living scarecrow. He wasn't truly ugly. But neither was he handsome. He was plain. Dull as dishwater. In a way, he really resembled the route where the *Last Chance* gas station sat: easily forgotten.

More, he was quite prone to panic, had a submissive attitude, and seemed to attract bullies like a lightning rod. His passive character caused discomfort in people. Which often turned into pity and then revulsion. Folks got angry at him for the flimsiest things, and even those possessed by a caring nature found themselves irritated by Ray's lack of spine. There was something in him that made even total strangers – such as the rare customers of the station – feel uneasy. All it took was a moment of eye contact, a fleeting conversation. Then, that discomfort would turn into contempt and condescending tones. Ray figured that some of them might feel remorse for treating him this way, but then, once they had lost sight of the station they would probably completely forget about him.

Exactly like they would forget about County Road 312.

312 was dusty, scrubby, and irritating to the eye. Once part of US 27, in the County of Prosperity, it had been almost cut off from the main system by the construction of the new junction at Reservoir Road. It used to go from Waynesford to the intersection with Country Road 313 – now Trail 238 and leading to nowhere. Not as desolate and completely forgotten as 313, 312 was still an unremarkable strip of macadam surrounded by swampland. With the exception of a couple of homesteads, *Last Chance* was its only feature.

Sighing, Ray glanced outside at the raging rain. It was so strong now that it had completely curtained the window and nothing could be seen, except for the haze emanating from the single light bulb above the pumps. Returning upon his stool, he struggled a little to find a comfortable position, then he finally let himself drift back into the story. Books allowed him to experience other places, lives and emotions. Reading was his only way out: an escape pod from his perennially sinking ship.

The thriller was about a professional assassin that loved his job too much. Written in the point of view of this murderous man, it had gripped him so much that Ray hadn't even noticed the darkening of the sky and the coming of the heavy rain. In this particular scene, the assassin had opted for hacking the head off his target with an ax rather than strangling him as ordered in his contract. His descent in total madness slowly progressed with each trophy head he collected.

Bizarre, but fascinating. Ray wondered how it would feel to do such a thing. What kind of person would collect human body parts and get a kick out of it? He certainly couldn't do it. Not because of the vileness of the act itself, but for he would never have the courage to physically attack another person. He had never stood up to anyone in his life. His father included.

Douglas Nix had been a terrible demanding man before finally dying in the same way he had lived all his life: in violence. A former vet, he had seen a lot of action on the field, and once he had left the army with a dishonorable discharge for striking his commanding officer, he had become a bitter paranoiac who saw enemies everywhere. He blamed everyone for his misfortunes: the army, the mayor, the gas company ... his wife. Helen – Ray's mother – decided one day she had had enough. He was just three when it had happened. She had jumped inside the cabin of Matt Finch's truck and had fled to some place up north. From then on, Douglas had vented his frustration on his son.

Ray shivered at the memories of the pain he had endured under his father's whipping belt and, instinctively, his eyes left the book and shot to the back window, searching for his house. Through the heavy rain he couldn't see it, but Ray knew it was there, brooding in the dark. That ugly one-story shack, along with the gas station, was his world – and his prison.

His thoughts were swept away by the sudden appearance of a shadow from the threshold to the garage. "Still reading, uh?" said the shadow.

Ray's eyes bulged out when he realized who the voice and the shadow belonged to. "Brad!"

"Yeah, me. Who *was* you expecting? The Tooth Fairy?" The man emerging from the garage access was big, with a military buzz cut and strong facial features. His eyes were dark and piercing, like those of a raven.

"What are you doing here? You should be at the hospital! Oh, my—"

"HOSPITAL!" Brad cut him short. "You call THAT hospital? Fairview is a goddamned nuthouse: a place where you're locked up to keep you away from *normal* people; not to cure you."

Hearing his angered tone, Ray instinctively shrank into his seat and lifted his hands in a mimicked apology. "I-I-I, I'm s-s-s-sorry, Br-ad. I didn't w-w-w-want to call it like th-at. Are y—"

Brad slammed both his palms on it, causing Ray to almost fall off his stool. "Stop doing that! I hate you when you stutter." His face was tense. Then, his lineaments relaxed. He moved around the counter and snatched a packet of cigarettes from the wall stand. "Do me a favor, would you? Take a deep breath and calm down. I'm not here to hurt you."

Ray was still under shock. Brad was supposed to be spending the rest of his life at Fairview. There was no chance he would be released. He had done some very bad things; things that Ray didn't want to recall, but they involved cutting blades and blood. A lot of blood. So why was he here now? There was only one answer: he was on the loose.

"Don't be scared, bro. I'm not here to punish you. And you know it," said Brad while fiddling with the packet's wrap. He neatly removed the thin film, then rolled it into a tiny ball and threw it into the trash bin under the counter. "I don't blame you for what they did to me. Actually, I must confess, I wanted to be stopped." He plucked a cigarette out of the packet and stuck it into his mouth.

"Really?" Ray couldn't believe his own ears: for the first time Brad was admitting he was ill. "Were you released?" Ray hazarded, even if he knew that was not possible.

Brad chuckled while lighting his smoke. "You jokin', right? You know they would never let me out, Ray. I'm sick. I'm dangerous. I know it; they know it." He took a deep drag of it, as if this were the first after a long time – and it probably was – then released a dense cloud. It slowly drifted to the ceiling, where it vanished like a ghost.

"I cut the ropes, bro," he continued. "I had to. And surely there's my face on an APB now. But I didn't escape because of me. I had to do it because of you."

What was he talking about? He did it for him? "B-b-b-but, Brad, wh-wh-what if they come here. You know I'm not good at lying, and this will be the f-f-f-first place they are going to check. A-a-a-an——" Ray stammered again.

"Please!" Brad's eyes transfixed him. "I told you to stop, for chrissake. It goes to my head and bangs there like a fuckin' jackhammer." He took another deep drag. "Look, no uns are gonna come over. Trust me. Not immediately.

And I'm not planning to stay here for long. I just need a couple days."

"Sorry, Brad. I'll try." Ray closed his eyes and forced himself to relax and focus on his speech. But it was not easy; not with a homicidal maniac who had just escaped from a psychiatric hospital standing in front of him – even if that maniac was Brad. Or especially *because* it was Brad.

"I'm here for you, bro. I'm here to help you," Brad said abruptly.

"Help me? They're going to lock me up as well for aiding and abetting a wanted man. That's your idea of helping me? And why? I don't need your help; I'm not in danger."

"Oh, yes you are, boy." Brad killed the cigarette by crushing its smoldering end between his thumb and his forefinger. "You are in danger of wasting your life. I wasted mine and will not allow you to do the same."

"What are you on about?"

"You're gonna leave this shitty place – with my help – and you're gonna make a new life somewhere better."

"Oh, Brad, you know I can't do that."

"I know you don't have the balls to do it, bro. That's why I'm here: to kick your ass out of this miserable life. A life you didn't want for yourself, but that your nice dad built for you. If you really had the balls you would have left years ago."

Ray really wanted to bark back at him, to tell him that wasn't true. He never had a chance to. His dad first, then the illness, then Brad himself, and last, the very town of Prosperity Glades had conspired to trap him here. Brad was right: he had never grown a pair.

"You know the truth, do you?" Brad insisted. "You hate this place, because you hate the way people look at you; the way they feel pity for you. Still, you are afraid of leaving your *safe* world to jump into the unknown. It's like with the girls, uh? You want them; I know you're no faggot; but you just can't."

Suddenly, Brad grabbed him by the arm and pulled him off his beloved stool. He forced him to look at his own reflection on the wall mirror. "Look at you! You think you are a monster, but you're not! It's just that you don't take care of yourself."

Ray closed his eyes. He didn't want to look. He hated his own reflection.

"Look at you, I said!" Brad shouted.

Slowly, Ray opened his eyes. What he saw in the mirror made him scream.

***

The rainstorm had caught Casey completely unaware. Yes, it had sprinkled for most of the day, which was quite common in Florida. But that shitty downpour had exploded out of nowhere. There had been no warnings such as a lightning striking in the distance or the sudden rumble of thunder. No, that evil bastard had jumped on her like a predator out of a bush. Because of it, she had missed her exit to Prosperity Glades, and had ended up on this desolate road. The rain – and the darkness – had made her progress quite hazardous, but Casey had been in a hurry and could not afford to waste time. And because of her rush, she had not seen the large and jagged pothole yawning at the edge of the worn macadam in time. The wheel on the passenger side had crashed hard into it – which caused a deep slash into the external rubber that had almost sent her old *Toyota* into the canal if it wasn't for her keeping her cool and managing to regain control of the car. However, the damage had been done, and immediately afterward, the automobile had started to shimmy, forcing her to pull over.

Under the lashing rain, she had headed to the trunk to get the spare. And when she had pulled it out and dropped it on the muddy pavement, instead of bouncing, the damn thing had landed flatly against the road.

"Fuck!"

She had pushed the poor thing around, but it wouldn't roll; it had just slithered like a flaccid slug. She had no way to fix it. And she had no cellular phone.

So, she was now seating inside the vehicle – with the emergency lights flashing – and waiting for the rain to stop, or at least calm down a little, in order to undertake the hell of a walk down to the gas station she had passed fifteen minutes ago. She had been here for almost an hour and the one car that had passed by hadn't even slowed down to check if she needed help.

She glanced at her watch: 11.25 PM.

Frustrated, she slammed her fists on the dashboard. "Fuck! Fuck! Fuck!"

Everything was conspiring against her. She could clearly say goodbye to her date with Mike at the Rough House. Damn! She had worked so hard on it! She had met him at a rest area on the US 27. Casey had immediately spotted him among the other truckers (he was exactly the kind of guy she was looking for) and so she had done her best to catch his eyes. Something she was very good at. With her shapely body, wrapped in a flimsy halter top that barely covered the bottom of her breasts and a tight pair of faded denim cutoffs, she rarely went unnoticed. Plus, she was a pro at conversation: she was a selfless, superb listener, and had a voice that made you hang on every word. She seldom talked about herself, but let others lead the dance. Or so they thought. And every time, she would hook the guy immediately. Mike wanted a quick fuck on the road, but Casey had been very good at delaying his urges. She wanted a hot meal and a room where to spend the night, not just his money. So, he had suggested meeting at the Rough House, a biker's bar in Prosperity Glades. He was friend to the manager and the guy would certainly arrange a room for them. He had seemed so eager to put his hands on her. Casey liked that. She couldn't wait herself. But that fucking rain and that fucking clunker had ruined everything. Damn it!

Casey swallowed hard. She knew that allowing rage to ride her was not a good thing. She was to stay cool if she wanted to get out of that ugly situation. Using her charms – and her body – always worked. Especially for one like her. One who lived on the road.

Her thoughts were swept away by a pair of headlights that popped out of the raging rain just around the curve. A vehicle was coming right into her direction. Ignoring the rain, she opened the door and jumped onto the road, waving and yelling at the approaching station wagon. The occupant saw her, but instead of slowing down, they pushed harder on the gas and dodged her by a nick, honking the horn in protest.

"Fuck you!" shouted Casey at the tail of the fast-leaving car. "You short-dicked asshole!"

Frustrated, she decided that she had had enough: she retrieved her bag from the backseat, kicked the door closed and nervously started her long trek to the gas station. The fuck with the car; she would find another way to travel. After all, it was not even her car.

She had barely covered one hundred yards when a tow truck pulled out of nowhere, scaring the shit out of her. With its headlights off, she had not seen it coming out of a side trail.

The driver, a country man wearing a trucker's hat, leered at her as he leaned across the cabin and rolled down the passenger window. "Is that your car yonder?"

Casey looked at him suspiciously, then immediately forced herself to smile. "Yes. Got a flat. And the spare is flat, too. I'm desperate." She hugged herself under the merciless rain. "I'm sure I'm gonna catch a virus or something."

Immediately, the driver jumped down the truck and walked around to open the passenger side door for her. "Come on in."

Casey hesitated. The guy looked creepy: his clothes were encrusted with dirt and oil stains, and his skin looked even worse; his breath smelled rancid and his teeth stood out like a neglected picket fence of brown and yellow. And what about those wild blue eyes that seemed to drill into her own soul?

Her gaze dropped to her feet: her cowboy boots, filled with dirty water, were going to give her a case of bad blisters if she were to walk down to the station. In addition, she felt the need growing.

"Thanks, I really appreciate it." She climbed on board.

"I can give you a lift down to Last Chance, if you want. Or you can come down my place for a simple, but good munch. And you can use my phone, too."

Casey considered. "I would appreciate a warm meal. And the phone. Thank you." She crossed her legs as she noticed his eyes exploring her.

Yeah, old boy, look at the merchandise.

The man pulled the truck back onto the road. "Sure." He gave her his cemetery-like smile.

"What's with the people around here? No one stopped to check if I was okay in more than an hour—"

He cut her short. "That's because of the scare they have about here. Folks are a bit spooked, y'know?"

"Scare? What scare?" Casey felt her hair prickling at the back of her skull.

"Yeah, seems that some people is going missing round a'here. Then, the cops found them bodies. A big mess, if you ask me." He cracked another smile and put a hand on her leg. "Don't be afraid, miss. You were lucky to meet me."

Casey moved closer to the door of the truck. Her hand fiddled inside her bag. She could not wait anymore.

As she plunged the large blade deep inside the man's throat, she whispered, "I'm not afraid. I'll be more careful with you. And, yes, I was lucky."

***

The sound of a sputtering old tow truck awakened Ray from the torpor he had fallen into. He looked around for Brad, but saw no sign of him. Where was he? Oh, God, he had to find him immediately and stop whatever he was planning. Ray could call the sheriff, of course, but he was struggling with the idea of betraying Brad again. He was the one who had sent him to the asylum all those years ago. He couldn't do this to him again.

Still, Brad needed to be stopped.

But there was no time to think about that now; someone had cast a shadow on the main entrance, and soon a figure wrapped in a dark raincoat walked in, dripping water on the floor. "Shitty rain!" the visitor exclaimed pulling down the hood. She was a young woman.

And what a woman.

Ray could see she was one of the most attractive chicks he had ever seen: a cascade of silky blonde hair framed her heart-shaped face. She had small, but full lips – *the color of mature cherries*, Ray thought – and sparkling blue eyes. But the best came when she removed that oversized raincoat: her hourglass shape was enhanced by the revealing clothes she wore. And her skin ... oh, that ivory skin ...

"Hey there, can I get some hot coffee, please?" she said. But Ray did not hear it; he just stood there, mouth agape and eyes bulging, staring at that wonderful smooth skin of hers.

"Hey! Are you deaf or what?" she snapped, causing Ray to immediately lower his eyes.

"I-I-I-I'm s-s-s-sorry, ma'am. I-I-I- wa-s dayd-dreaming," he mumbled, willing his eyes to stay on his shoes. "It hap-pens to me, sometimes."

"Well, can I have your total attention, now, Mr ..." she looked at the patch on his chest, "Mr. Ray?"

"Ray, Ray Nix, ma'am."

She fidgeted, hands on her hips. "So, Ray, are you going to give me that coffee or not?"

"Of course! And it's on me." He filled her a cup of the daily brew. "A way to apologize for my discourtesy."

She looked at him weirdly. "Discourtesy? Is that a word?"

Ray decided to change the subject. "Nasty rain, isn't it? Are you going home?"

She stared at him coldly. "Why you askin'?"

Embarrassed, Ray lowered his gaze again, then held out the coffee mug like a priest offering a sacrifice to his god. "N-n-nothing, ma'am. Just trying to have a *convertation.*"

She exploded into a vulgar laugh. Ray was shocked at hearing that vile sound coming out from such a lovely woman. It was true what Dad used to say: *women are all bitches inside*. Still, she was so attractive ...

"Listen, Ray. I'm not here to have a ... *convertation* ... especially with you." She was looking at him like all other women had so far: like he was a piece of discarded chewing gum stuck under their shoe. "I'm here because I need some coffee, to fill up the tank of that wreck out there, and then zoom out of this horrible road." She took the mug and sipped the dark liquid. "And I need the toilet," she added.

Ray felt stupid. And weak. And worthless. He could only ever dream of a girl like that, he knew it. No beautiful woman, of sane mind, would fancy one like him. He was a freak, and people didn't like freaks. That was exactly what Dad used to say, too.

The girl ungraciously put the almost full mug on the counter with a smirk of disgust. "My, this shit tastes like motor oil! Give me the toilet's key, Ray. I'll be back in a zip."

He felt rage growing inside him. She had no right to treat him like that. No, she had no right. Yes, it was true he was socially awkward, but people had no right to be disrespectful. And this girl? She was here wetting his floor, drinking his coffee, and insulting him! How dared she? He felt the urge to slap her on the face, to yell at her that she was only a whore. He wanted to see her cry. And apologize.

But he couldn't.

"There ain't no key, ma'am. I don't have a toilet. I have outhouses. To the left. Behind the picnic tables."

Again that disgusted face. She huffed, then grunted a 'Great!', and finally left the office forgetting her raincoat on the counter.

Ray hated her, but could not avoid staring at her swinging hips while she turned around the corner and disappeared into the shadows.

She was lucky: the rain had just stopped.

***

Casey felt a bit of remorse for treating the gas attendant the way she had. After all, the creep was just trying to be kind. But he had made her nervous with his way of staring at her and all those questions. Still, she brushed the guilt aside; the guy was going to be a stiff soon. She didn't really want to kill him; he was not her type. She loved to hunt down those she considered potential rapists, abusers, woman haters.

Ray didn't fit the profile.

She sloshed through the muddy picnic area in direction of the outhouses. But she didn't really need the toilet. She was just looking for the right spot where to dump the body of the farmer she had killed. Even he had not been her type, at first. She used to study her victims before striking, and the country man had originally seemed genuinely concerned about her. But then, he had had to touch her legs. Filthy animal!

She spotted a large plastic box just at the corner of the main building. It was one of those big dumpsters used to make compost, or to store recyclable parts. Its lid was half open. She peeked into it and immediately recoiled. It stank worse than a Florida Skunk Ape. It could be a nice resting place for the sweet farmer, but better to check out the whole area. The cops on her tail were getting wiser and she really needed to be more careful.

Hey! Was that a garage? Maybe there was a car inside. No, the damn place was locked. Maybe she could access it from within the building, but first she had to get rid of poor Ray. Again, she felt sorry about that. But the guy had to go. She had stopped at the gas station in the hope to use the bathroom to change her clothes. Comes out the creep had no restroom and now she had no other choice than to kill him and move away fast.

She promised him a quick death.

Then, she noticed that there were some storm doors leading to a basement. And they were open. Now, that was a better place to hide the body. Probably there were oil drums down there and large boxes. Maybe even some tools. Stealthily, she stepped into the dark room. A waft of air carried the stench of rot to her nostrils, but she ignored it. But she could not ignore the constant hum of the power generator. It came from somewhere in the basement and the more she descended into it the more deafening it became. Casey palmed the walls, feeling for a switch, but found none. The only thing she could see was a tiny red light coming from the generator. Not strong enough to brighten the room. She moved around, bumping into boxes and

255

other stashed paraphernalia. Yes, that would indeed be a good place to hide the farmer's and Ray's bodies.

Time to get rid of Ray.

She turned on her heels and her eyes caught a flash high above her head. It had looked like the glint of metal, but now it was no longer visible.

When it appeared again, Casey knew it was too late for her.

The heavy ax buried itself in her head, glinting in the moonlight.

***

Ray considered going out to check on the girl. Twenty minutes had passed and she still had not come back. What if she had had an accident? Surely she wasn't deserving of his worriment, but this was *his* property and it was under *his* responsibility. He still felt bitter about the way she had spoken to him and his only wish now was that she left his place as soon as possible and disappeared forever from his life. Like all the others.

"Where are you goin', bro?"

Brad's voice froze him on the spot. There he was again, standing on the threshold of the garage, with a grin on his face; the same, identical one he wore on the day he had done *that bad thing*. He looked like he had just finished a workout, for his skin was reddened by exertion and he was breathing heavily.

"A girl," Ray said. "She asked to use the outhouse, but it's been more than twenty minutes and—"

Then, he saw the blood on Brad's hands and arms. And on his clothes, too.

"OHMYGOD! What have you done? WHAT HAVE YOU DONE, BRAD?"

Brad's grin turned into the largest Cheshire cat smile.

"I just helped you, bro. Now, you'll have no excuses: you'll have to leave this cesspool."

***

Doctor Eugene Ramis was in a foul mood. Fairview had called in the middle of the night. The nurse had said it was urgent, but had not disclosed any information. He had the feeling he knew what it was all about. And he didn't like it. He didn't like it at all.

He was now climbing the stairs to the State Hospital for the Criminally Insane, being careful to not slip on the wet marble steps. Atop, at the entrance, he recognized the figure of Doctor Alan Fleet.

His gut feelings were instantly confirmed.

"It's Nix, right?" he said, offering his hand to the younger man. Fleet shook it lightly and nodded gravely. Without saying a word, he led him inside, toward the maximum security ward. Their steps resonated heavily along the large green corridor, in an atmosphere of dread and distant shouting. They then passed through two guarded steel gates and Ramis soon found himself in that world where there could be no mingling of inmates and where the natural light never shone; it was replaced here by gridded light bulbs – of the industrial type – and their soft glow did nothing to cast away the elder psychiatrist's baleful feelings. The final corridor was about twenty yards long, with cells on both sides. Some had observation windows; others had regular bars revealing their content of human despair. The psychiatrists ignored all of them and went straight for the last one on the right. Its door was ajar, and there was blood on the floor.

For the rest, the cell was empty.

"Jesus Christ, Fleet! How did Nix manage to escape?" Ramis had been expecting trouble, but not *that* kind of trouble.

"It's Kelley's fault; the new one," replied Fleet, shame in his voice. "We told her a zillion times to not let her guard down with this one. But it seems she wasn't really listening.

"Where's Kelley now? I want to talk to her."

"She's in the infirmary. Had to be sedated. Pain was killing her more than the wound." Fleet looked contrived. Ramis had always insisted to not let any newbie in here.

"How far?" Ramis demanded brusquely. At first, Fleet did not seem to understand what he was referring to. "Nix," he added.

Fleet swallowed hard, cleared his throat, and visibly shaking, said, "We don't know. We're looking everywhere. We're sure Nix hasn't left the hospital, but is hiding somewhere. Problem is: we don't know where."

"But what about the guard? Possible there was no one on duty while Kelley visited Nix? Are you kidding?"

Fleet passed a hand over his face. "Nix was lucky. There was a major issue in Mixed Ward. A stupid card game turned into a total riot and all the wardens on duty had to be summoned to quell it down. It was a real mess, sir. We have three inmates in intensive care and at least another dozen injured. Bailey, the guy who usually works here, was bitten. Nastily. He's in the infirmary, too."

"You are conscious there are going to be hard consequences about this, right?" He felt bad for Fleet. He really liked him, and appreciated his dedication to his. But this mess, this dangerous act of negligence, was going to cost him dearly. There was no excuse for letting a person like Nix escape confinement.

"I know, sir."

They left the maximum security ward in direction of Medical. Ramis was relieved to leave that gloomy place behind, but not enough for his mood to improve. Nix was a killer. A dangerous one. One of those individuals completely detached from reality. Ramis had classified the inmate as a certifiable Axis I diagnosis, and due to the tremendous trauma suffered at a young age, the patient was unlikely to recover. Dr. Ramis himself had provided that Nix would never leave the maximum security ward.

They were halfway to their destination when a nurse rushed out of the reception office.

"They found Nix!"

***

Brad and Ray moved toward the old tow truck. The rain had stopped falling more than half an hour ago now, and the usual Floridian heat was slowly turning the accumulated water into dense vapors. It was Fog Season, a common phenomenon in winter.

"Why you had to kill her? Why? In the name of God, Brad ... why you had to do that?"

His whiney brother kept going on and on, and Brad was really tempted to hit him in the face. Just to shut him up. He didn't understand. He never would.

"You're sick, Brad. You know you should be at the hospital. You're not right in the head! Dad was right about y——"

Brad slapped him hard. "Don't you dare talk about *him*! Don't you dare!" Just the thought of the old man made him sick. He felt like vomiting. "Shut up and give me a hand with this, you stupid. We need to move this clunker to the back, then we'll prop the girl."

Ray rubbed his face, more shocked by the fact Brad had slapped him than by the actual pain. "Y-y-you ... hit me," he stuttered.

Brad rolled his eyes. "So, what? You deserved it."

"BUT YOU PROMISED!" yelped Ray.

"Yeah, I promised I would never hurt you. I promised to protect you. And I did it, didn't I?"

"B-but you hi-hi-hit m-m-me!"

259

"YOU STARTED TALKING ABOUT THE OLD MAN!" Brad could not hold it anymore: he grabbed his younger brother by the shoulders and slammed him against the tow's driver door. "Who was there for you? TELL ME! Who made *him* stop? And who's supposed to be in the nuthouse for admitting killing his perv father? Tell me, Ray. Yeah, I'm not right in the head, you're right. But *he* made me! He made me what I am."

Ray was crying now. Brad felt remorse for hitting him, but he had to understand. Instinctively, he hugged his younger brother. "Look," he said softly, "I apologize. But I really want you to have a life, bro. I'm sick, but I'm the stronger one. Once I'm sure you're outta here I'll let them catch me. I don't care."

"I-I-I'm s-s-s-sorry, I didn't w-w-want to ..." cried Ray.

"It's okay. It's okay now." But Brad was lying to himself. His mind went back to the day he had killed his father. There had been so much blood. He recalled how he had felt. Free and sad at the same time. He had loved his dad, but there had been no other choice. Ray had been in danger; he had risked his own life, for crying out loud! The man was ill. He had never recovered after mum left. He had blamed everything on Ray. And then, when he got drunk ... it was even worse. He had forced Ray to dress like a girl and ...

NO! It was too much.

Brad forced that memory out by banging his head against the truck's metal, as if he were trying to transfer it from his brains to the inanimate thing.

Ray had stopped crying and was now looking at him in befuddlement. "I'm sorry, Brad. I know you love me."

Brad feigned a smile to reassure his brother that he was okay and opened the tow truck's door.

He heard his brother's scream before he actually saw the mangled body stowed at the feet of the passenger's seat.

***

Jaime had been driving for hours. She was tired and in urgent need of coffee. The heavy rain that had surprised her at the outskirts of Prosperity Glades had worsened the drowsiness caused by the monotonous and hypnotic to and fro of the windshield wipers. She took the first exit to a secondary road in the hope of finding a diner, a bar, a roadhouse – anything that could supply her with an essential dose of caffeine.

Plus, it was safer for her to stay away from the major arteries if it was going to keep raining like that. True, it was not Hurricane Season – and there had not been any major warning – but a downpour was always a cause of big concern for the authorities. The terrible visibility conditions were often the source of deadly accidents; long neglected telephone and power lines could give away, leaving entire neighborhoods and rural areas in sudden blackouts. And then, there were those that took advantage of the chaos to commit crimes or violate the law. That meant the entire law enforcement community was put on maximum alert. She was doing her best to *'Protect and Serve'* her county by staying on the lookout for potential rotten eggs that could trouble the good folk of Prosperity. But she had her ways, and the Sheriff Department would not understand.

The FBI would not understand.

She had given up on being understood a long time ago.

The State Patrol cruiser thumped a couple of times when it left the well-groomed asphalt of the freeway and met the wreck that was Route 312.

And there, she spotted the gas station.

And two men holding a corpse.

***

Doctor Ramis could not stop thinking about Nix's troubled past. His patient had been apprehended after an extensive manhunt that had spanned six different states and had involved the collaboration of federal, state, and local law enforcement agencies. The individual had been hard to track because the modus operandi changed from crime to crime. Nix had killed women, men, and children indiscriminately. Of course, as it was discovered later, there were reasons for this.

At the age of fifteen, Nix had already suffered enormous psychological damage. Douglas Albert Nix – the father – was a deranged alcoholic with pedophiliac tendencies who used to vent all his frustrations and enacted sexual fantasies on his own child. The absence of a maternal figure – the mother had walked away when Nix was just three – meant the child had no other role model than the abusive father. Nix had endured mistreatment after mistreatment, violent act after violent act, and rape after rape until one day the child's mind had started to disconnect from reality. The breaking point, the final trauma that caused Nix to take refuge into a dissociative disorder, had been the very moment the patient had finally gained liberation: the murder of Douglas Nix.

The syndrome had set in and the patient had reveled in it. It is fact that when faced with intense trauma, a child's mind can fracture. These fractures can be an excellent way to forget about the pain; a way for the system to restart itself and fix what wasn't functioning. And while it may appear that the individual is stable, the defective, and sometimes delusional, fantasies are still dormant – but when triggered by external stimuli, they may resurface. Violently so.

In the last five years Nix had retreated into a docile mood by taking refuge into one of these fractures. However, Dr. Ramis had insisted for Nix to be kept inside the maximum security ward; he *felt* something was amiss and that the patient was just simulating stabilization. He had just been proven right.

A cold shiver ran down his spine as he prepared to meet the escapee.

***

Jaime saw the two men freeze as the cruiser's flashlights came to life. The smaller one stood there, his eyes bulging out, his frame shaking, while his hands refused to let go of the arms of the dead man. The bigger one, however, easily snapped out of the initial shock: immediately, he lifted his arms in surrender, releasing his hold on the corpse's legs, which in turn thumped to the ground.

"You! Yes, you," ordered Jaime, while exiting the car and training her revolver on the smaller guy. "Hands up. You, listenin'?"

The douche was making her nervous, and that was not good. She knew what would happen if she lost control.

"Ray, do as she says, please," said the bigger one. Then flashed a knowing smile at her.

"You, shut up. Keep your hands up and move – *molasses–like* – to the truck. And I mean it: go faster than a slug and I'll give you one straight between the eyes." She turned her face to the guy called Ray. "Put down that fuckin' body!"

The tone of her voice seemed to shake him out of his trance; he let go of the corpse and the head of the dead man slammed violently to the ground, producing a sickening sound. Dark fluid soon mixed with the mud.

"I-I-I-I didn't ki-ki-ki-kill him!" he said, while raising his arms. "Tell her, Brad!"

"Bullshit!" she roared. Those two fuckers were not exactly what she was looking for, but one couldn't complain when one had a body to dispose of stashed inside

263

the trunk of a stolen State Patrol cruiser. And these two murderous idiots, while none of them fitted the profile for a new identity, could be a shortcut to her next life. All she had to do was to make it look like a robbery gone wrong.

"He's not lyin'," said the bigger man. "And you know it." Again that grin.

"Okay, Big Boy, I sincerely advise you to take that smirk off your face." There was something weird in that guy ... no, not just him ... both. They looked familiar, even if Jaime could swear she had never met them before.

"You know what?" said the one named Brad, lowering his arms, "I'm fuckin' tired of this show, and I think it's time for the grand finale." He turned to his freaky partner. "Ray, look behind the mask. Don't you see? Don't you recognize her?"

"SHUT UP!" she hollered. "I swear I'm gonna blow your head off!" But something was happening. She felt dizzy, her vision became blurred, and her legs started to shake. The sound of dripping water and the voices of Brad and Ray faded away, soon to be replaced by a strange buzz. And a new, disembodied voice.

Are you listening to me, Kay? –

Kay? Who the fuck was Kay?

Her surroundings became clouded, as if someone had pushed her underwater, but she could still see the blurred shadow of Brad. Closer. His voice was distant, as if coming from another world.

"Been waiting for you, sister. But the first time ... well, you weren't really yourself, were you? Now, this is closer to what you are. What you became." He said something to his ... *brother?* How did she know they were brothers? Scared, and almost blind, Jaime lifted her gun, and pointed it at the approaching indistinct form.

"See, Ray? She is Casey ... the same girl I killed minutes ago."

"B-b-but that's impossible!" protested the other one.

Jaime cocked the hammer.

"Ray, look at the body." Brad voice was closer. It still sounded like it came from behind a wall, but she was able to locate its origin.

Then Ray started to scream. His voice was definitively male in the beginning, but then it turned more high-pitched ... like the scream of a hysterical woman. At first she couldn't understand what he was saying over and over, but then the word *'Dad!'* became clearer.

And that disembodied voice resounded again. No, there were two of them, now.

What's going on, Dr. Ramis? –
Please, be quiet, Fleet. –
Can she hear what you're saying? She looks absent. –
I don't think I'm talking to Kay now. Who are you? –
The sound of shuffling paper, then more voices in the background. Yelling.

"You see the truth now, Ray? I promised to protect you. And I'm doing it. She will not take hold of you anymore. Dad is dead, Ray! You killed him. We killed him! We——"

A loud explosion rang when Jaime finally pulled the trigger.

And then, a second shot was fired.

***

Kay Nix had been hiding in the boiler room when she had been found. The guards had no idea how she had managed to get that far, but it was not important: there was no way she could actually escape Fairview. Oddly, she had not resisted; and they had taken her to the infirmary, where she had immediately been strapped to a restraining chair.

She had not said a word.

Dr. Ramis suspected what was happening inside her. Since the time of the final trauma, Kay had been sharing her mind with at least eight different personalities. She switched from one to another when certain circumstances made one personality stronger than the others.

The one that called herself Casey was a charmer on a mission: to kill potential rapists. Of course, in her delusional state, any kind of flirt, even the most innocent one, was perceived by her as sexual harassment. She had lured and killed at least three men around Prosperity Glades.

Then, there was Brad. He was the brute. He reacted to the world in an aggressive way and his killings were impulsive, and prompted by fury. Ramis believed that Brad had been created by Kay as an imaginary, overprotective old brother, and it was Brad that had killed Douglas Nix by burying an ax inside his head. He was also responsible for the death of five other persons.

There was Farmer Doug: an old pervert with a passion for tow trucks and molesting children. Of course, Kay had never physically abused the three children she had abducted; she had simply killed them. But in her own mind, Farmer Doug, who was the personification of her real father, had raped and tortured them for years.

And then there was Margot, a sweet and caring nurse for the elders. She was a positive personality, and had never hurt anyone. And Angelina, Terry, and Kathie: all minor personalities that posed no threat.

Finally, there was the darkest one: Jaime Doe. Jaime was the most terrible construct born to justify Kay's constant need to experience new lives, and her murders. Jaime was conscious of sharing the same body as the other identities, and she had become some kind of evil puppeteer that used all of them to her advantage. Jaime was an identity thief. She was driven by the need to become someone else. When she fixated on a target, she would study them for weeks with the aim of taking everything away from them: their wealth, their name, their past. Once she was sure she had assimilated everything about her victim's behavior, she killed the real person and moved somewhere else, assuming their identity. The problem was that like a vampire, she was never sated. As a kid that dreams of becoming a cop, or an astronaut, Jaime easily fell in love with the prospects of a new life.

However, after originally being apprehended something had snapped inside Kay Nix's mind. Jaime had vanished and all the remaining personalities had fused into a new one: that of a timid and remissive boy named Ray.

And as Ray, Kay had never been a source of problems in Fairview until that night.

The day before, Dr. Ramis had observed a sudden change in Kay's attitude, and suspected one of the more dangerous female identities had managed to take control, and by the same, had set all the other identities loose. He had scheduled in an emergency re-assessment of the patient, but it had been too late.

And now, she was sitting there, silent.

And Dr. Ramis was not sure who he was talking to.

***

They were looking at him. Those strangers. And they were talking to him. But he would not talk back. He would listen to them and show them he was no longer dangerous. He would do as his brother had said.

His brother had sacrificed his own life to allow him to finally get one. And he would be forever grateful to him. Thanks to him he was now free.

267

By silencing Jaime's voice forever, Ray Nix had finally seized his one last chance at a life.

"Are you ready for the scariest, most terrifyingly spooky tale that Helston has ever known?" asked Toby, staring from face to face.

The whispering youngsters stared back; expectant grins and more than one grimace of apprehension spreading across their faces.

"Shouldn't we wait for Scott, though, sir?" asked Peter. He was the newest, and youngest, member of the group. His oversized jumper hung from his thin frame halfway to his knees, but his mother had insisted he would grow into it.

Toby hadn't given the second scout leader much thought, but it was a valid point and he looked around the campsite. Their shadows danced on the ground from the rising flames and he was nowhere to be seen in the meagre light. Neither was their small bus for that matter.

"He must've popped back for something," Toby surmised, "I'm sure he'll be along at any moment."

"Maybe he's getting marshmallows!" exclaimed one boy with much licking of lips.

Toby hushed their excited murmurs and continued his tale, "How many of you knew that our town was once actually called Hell's town?"

Mouths gaped at the secret knowledge being revealed.

"Oh, yes," Toby moved his arm in a wide arc, indicating the surrounding darkness, "Rumour has it The Devil himself once walked in the forest trails that surround our sleepy town. Taking the souls of unwary travellers back to the deepest, darkest depths of Hell to feast on for all eternity."

Kyle, one of the braver boys, frowned and said, "But my dad told me it was because a yeoman called Helsford used to own the woods and all the surrounding land. It then became known as his town, and they shortened it to Helston."

269

Toby stared him down and nodded knowingly, "That's what they want you to think so that the awful truth is forgotten and Lucifer can stalk these lands once more."

Huffing and folding his arms in a sulk, still the young boy's eyes took in the surroundings with a fearful respect. The eleven other scouts were totally immersed in the unfolding yarn. Sitting on benches formed from fallen tree trunks that had been carefully carved with a seat and backrest, Toby smiled inwardly at their eager faces. He had always loved the campfire tales that his scout leader would regale them with in the darkness; the nervous tingle in the pit of his stomach as each fable would build to its horrific climax.

"What happened, sir?" asked Peter, breathlessly. He was desperate to know, but scared in equal measure of the coming fable.

A loud pop from the fire caused them all to jump as sparks danced lazily into the sky on the heat currents.

Toby laughed with as much of an evil tone as he could muster, "You see? They want the secrets to stay buried. That was a warning to you all! Should we just forget it and sing jolly tunes to be on the safe side?"

"We aren't afraid of any Devil!" stated Billy defiantly and the rest nodded their agreement. There was no way they were going to miss this.

"I don't know, boys. I think maybe it's for the best that we don't stir up any trouble with the ghouls and demons which prowl the night," Toby apologised and stood up, pretending to search behind the chair for his guitar.

A chorus of denial erupted amongst the group and it was exactly the reaction he had been fishing for. Composing himself to hide the huge grin, he turned back to the boys with a look of concern.

"If you insist, but don't say I didn't warn you," Toby cautioned with a wagging finger.

Seating himself, he held out his hands to the fire for warmth before starting. He nearly laughed and ruined the whole thing when he saw the boys leaning slowly closer, their wide eyed faces a picture of nervous anticipation.

"The year was seventeen twelve; a time of deprivation, disease, and superstition. Science was slowly pushing at the boundaries of understanding, but for rural England the darkness still held unknown terrors. A farmhand by the name of Edward returns to find his daughter in a state of ill health. She was feverish, but cold to the touch in spite of the warm fire of their small homestead."

"I don't know what to do, Edward," sobbed Mary into his shoulder, "Every day she weakens."

"Calm yourself," Edward whispered, "The doctor has promised us he will consult with his peers and get back to us within a week."

"She won't last that long," replied Mary, pulling away and wiping at her eyes.

Edward knew she was right and looked towards the bubbling cooking pot to hide his fear. Ever since Millicent awoke three days ago, she had been lethargic. This had worsened during the following days, and each morning the condition worsened. Mumbling while in the grip of her delirium, the young girl had spoken of ill tidings and witchcraft. Edward and Mary had dismissed the notions as the wild fancies of youth. In the darkest hours of night, a name would accompany the ramblings; Lavina. Neither her parents, the physician, or anyone in the surrounding cottages had heard of anyone called by that name.

"I hate to countenance the idea," whispered Mary so quietly that Edward had to ask her to repeat it.

She turned from the simmering broth and looked directly in his eyes, "What if there is another, otherworldly explanation? We've scoffed at the notion as peasant superstition, but our ancestors knew better."

"What would you have me do?" Edward demanded, slamming a fist into the table.

"Anything!" screamed Mary in reply, *"Call the reverend, see what he thinks of the terrible dreams she is beset with."*

"We have to trust in medicine!" Edward exclaimed, standing abruptly and spilling the dining chair over.

He stormed from the living area into Millicent's tiny room. Sitting on the side of the bed, he gently caressed her clammy hand and brushed strands of hair away from her brow. She was calmer during daylight hours and it was only the onset of dusk that brought with it the more disturbing symptoms. As the man of the house he felt unable to explain to his beloved wife of his inner fear; that if his daughter was in the thrall of some dark malady, what could they possibly do about it? They had no money to pay, no status to demand the clergy take action. All they had was each other and their love.

Mary entered with a small bowl of stew, *"See if she will take food. I tried earlier, but she wasn't hungry. She hasn't eaten properly in days."* This brought a sob and she quickly left the room before breaking down again.

Edward wiped at a solitary tear and shook Millicent gently by the shoulder, *"Poppet, would you like some rabbit stew? It's delicious; mummy has added extra onion by the smell of it."*

Coming to, her eyes fluttered open, *"No, thank you, Daddy."* It was the faintest whisper, like a gentle breeze through a corn field. His mother's sweet voice on her death bed had been the same; a mixture of sadness and defeat.

Throat tightening with grief, Edward croaked, *"Rest now, darling. I will check on you presently."*

"Anything?" Mary inquired hopefully.

"No," Edward replied, pouring the broth back into the pot. He tried to swallow but his mouth was bone dry and the lump in his throat wouldn't budge.

272

Sitting back at the head of the table he tried to eat his own meal but the flavours were bland and unsatisfying. He knew it wasn't the cooking, merely an extension of his anxiety at knowing life had no meaning if he lost his only daughter. Complications during childbirth had ended any possibility of his wife producing a male heir to the family name. He didn't blame her at all and it was only by the mercy of God that she and the baby had pulled through.

"I'll go and see Father Norris after supper," Edward finally conceded.

Mary flew from her seat and embraced him tightly, "Oh, thank you. I only pray that he can help."

"As do I."

Before the meal was over someone started hammering on the front door and Edward was taken aback when the caller turned out to be the father himself. A light drizzle had coated the man's coat so Mary dutifully hung it by the fireplace to dry out while the men settled at the table over a small measure of whiskey.

"Thank you," nodded the priest to them both, then spoke to Mary directly, "I think you too may need a drink, my dear."

"Why are you here, Father?" Edward begun, "Not that I am complaining, I was coming to see you this evening as it happens."

"I had a feeling you might but I didn't want to tarry. You see I ran into Dr Jennings in town and we got talking. Your poor Millicent came up and I asked after her health. I didn't think anything of it until he mentioned the word Lavina."

A chill crawled up Edwards spine at the mention of the name and the sight of the priest crossing himself, "What of it?"

"I'm so sorry, my children," said the priest with genuine sorrow, "I fear that what I may have to tell you will make little difference anyway."

"You're scaring me, Father," Mary gasped, biting her fist in anguish.

"Do you know what is happening to our daughter?" Edward demanded.

"I may do, and that is the moral dilemma I have," Father Norris was nearly in tears himself, "Because if I do, then Millicent is almost certainly going to die."

"For the love of God, man, make some sense. You are scaring us out of our wits." Edward was clenching his glass hard enough to risk shattering it.

"You should be afraid," he whispered, terrified eyes darting between them.

"But why? Millicent only has a fever!" Edward shouted. He stood up and started to pace the small room, trying to mentally prepare himself from what was likely to come.

"A fever that has no accompanying increase in temperature, is that correct?"

"In a way, yes. She is actually getting colder as the days go by, though," confirmed Mary.

"Is it worse at night?"

Edward didn't want to reply and instead looked at the ground, answering without words.

Shaking his head, Father Norris replied, "Then it is as I feared. To understand what is happening to your little girl I need to take you back nearly fifty years and several towns over. It has never manifest this far away from the source which means she is growing in strength."

"Who is? What are you talking about?"

"Lavina is who I am talking about. Her full name was Lavina Marth, and she died nearly half a century ago," explained the Father.

"And this is who Millicent is dreaming about? A lady from the past?" Mary was perplexed.

"If only it were a simple dream," he sighed.

"Please stop talking in riddles," Edward begged.

274

"My apologies. Lavina was a beloved member of the church and wider community when she was alive. Rumour had it she was a gifted healer and people would travel the length and breadth of the country to seek her counsel. Some say she was a white witch, though I hesitate to use such a term."

"So what has she got to do with Millicent's illness?" Mary asked.

"To understand, you must also appreciate she was beautiful. It is no exaggeration to say she was probably one of the most attractive females in all the land. Her beauty ultimately became her downfall, though. As the years passed, time inevitably took its toll on her appearance and with each new wrinkle or grey hair, so she cut herself off from outside contact. She would shun all who attended her and, in the beginning of her descent into madness, would chase off any trespassers with threats of horrible curses."

"Poor woman," sympathised Mary. She too was feeling the passage of time and noticing the first ashen tinges to her brown hair.

"Save your pity," snarled Father Norris and she flinched at his tone, "I'm sorry, but you will see why in a moment. No man, or woman, may defeat time. From the mightiest king, to the lowliest slave, all must eventually succumb and meet their maker. The townsfolk would hear her screaming and wailing every time she caught sight of her reflection as she collected water from the lake. In her addled mind, she felt God had abandoned her to the slow creep of grotesquery even after all her acts of kindness. In spite of the assurances of the local clergy that her reward would await in Heaven, she sought a pact with the Devil himself to gain immortality. The contract was sealed with blood, but to maintain her youth she would forevermore need to feed on the innocent children of the surrounding towns. Street urchins would never be missed, and for years she committed the most heinous acts of butchery without

275

discovery. Now, being the Great Deceiver, Satan had played a trick on Lavina. For a while it worked, but it is alleged that once she developed a taste for child flesh, He reneged on the bargain. Her kindness had infuriated Him while she was working for God and this ultimate blasphemy was a great joke on all that was holy. Her last reported sighting was from a hunter out collecting the bounty of his snares. She was monstrous, with running sores and inexplicable growths forming all over her twisted body."

Edward was aghast. "What became of her?"

"It was assumed that she died of her afflictions. It was certainly apparent from the increase in activity of petty thefts by the local street orphans. A search party found her cabin and scrawled notes alluding to her infernal dealings, but no sign of the missing children or the witch herself. They burned it down out of hand and its ruin stands there to this day. No plants will grow within thirty yards and the animals are always silent in its presence."

"I don't see what this has to do with us, though," complained Mary. She hadn't expected to be regaled with a story of child cannibalism.

"Please bear with me," Father Norris urged, "After about six weeks, strange reports started to circulate about children falling ill with no explanation. Over the course of thirteen days they would sicken and die, regardless of any attempts to treat the ailment. Obviously the doctors of the time knew a great deal less than our current advances have revealed. It didn't transfer from person to person via fluids or bodily contact, so they simply put it down to a previously undiscovered disease."

"How many children have died?" Edward felt compelled to ask.

"From what Millicent is suffering from? Over five hundred."

"Dear God in Heaven," Mary gasped and slumped back into her chair.

"*We certainly could use His aid,*" *agreed Father Norris, "Every month, without fail, a child falls into a fever that they never recover from. It has never been this far away from the source though, which can only mean she is growing in strength."*

"*Who?*" *said Edward with confusion.*

"*Lavina.*"

"*But she is dead,*" *Mary added.*

"*Her body is, yes. But her spirit still stalks the night to feast on the children. In place of their flesh, she absorbs their souls.*"

"*Preposterous!*" *shouted Edward.*

"*But it all matches what we have seen and heard. She mumbles about the children and Lavina while she nightmares. It is awful,*" *Mary started sobbing and left the room to check on her daughter.*

Edward sighed, "If this is all true, what can I do?"

"*Nothing, and that is why I am so heartbroken for you both. If Lavina's earthly remains could be found, she could be laid to rest in hallowed ground. It's the only thing that could possibly break this curse, but the problem is no one has ever been able to find her lair. After the cabin burned, a militia searched for weeks, mapping every valley and cave in the area. They found nothing.*"

"*Then why come at all?*" *Edward said, crushed by the hopelessness of their cause. He couldn't deny the possibility of an entity attacking his child, only lament his lack of power over the outcome.*

"*I felt you deserved the truth. I have also brought a map which will lead you to the site of her cabin if you felt so inclined. Edward, I know you are a strong and proud man who will do everything he can. Perhaps you will find something the others missed. Some chance is better than no chance,*" *said the Father and he squeezed Edward's hand reassuringly.*

"Father, how can I truly know if this is happening to Millicent? What if I leave and the doctor returns with some news and I miss it?" Edward pressed, aiding the elderly man in putting his coat on.

"Lavina is a creature of pure evil. Her presence is said to be a shadow within the shadows so when the witching hour is upon you and all is darkness, look into Millicent's room. Then you will know."

"Can you not just bless us?" Edward asked in desperation.

"It has all been tried; prayers, holy water, even exorcisms. We need her remains to have a chance at banishing this malignance from the world," said the priest with sorrow, before disappearing into the night.

On the table was a crudely drawn sketch which showed a route covering about one hundred miles in a north easterly direction. Moving to the doorway, he watched Mary as she cradled the pale form of their daughter and a steely resolve settled in his heart.

As darkness fell, Mary retired to bed and Edward watched the dying embers in the hearth. Judging it to be well past midnight when the red glow diminished to nothing, he stood on unsteady legs and paused outside the bedroom. The next few seconds would confirm or dismiss the ravings of their beloved reverend and fear caused his hands to tremble as they reached for the latch. On creaking hinges the door swung inward and the room was almost pitch black. Straining his eyes, the gloom receded somewhat and he could finally make out the crooked shape that loomed over the bed. It was as the priest had warned; a black taint on the more mundane shadows from the moon. Tiny wisps rose from Millicent's open mouth and into the thing in the room. In slow motion, what appeared to be the head turned in his direction and stared without eyes.

"You leave my daughter alone, you abomination!" Edward roared and swung his fists at the being. The blows

passed through the darkness with no effect and, almost nonchalantly, the witch resumed her meal.

"What's going on?" asked Mary fearfully, holding out a wooden crucifix.

Edward tried to press the holy symbol on the wraith but it showed no sign of discomfort. Prayers went unheeded as the life force was slowly drawn from their child.

"Enough!" Edward growled, "I will end you, fiend."

As he tore room to room, loading a bag with belongings, Mary followed, "What are you doing? It's the middle of the night and I don't want to be alone with that thing."

"It means you no harm, only Millicent. I can't sleep knowing that witch is gorging on our daughter's soul, so I am setting off now. I will be at her godforsaken cabin within three or four days if I can beg the loan of a horse."

Within the hour, Edward was provisioned and on foot towards town. He had a couple of favours owed by the local stable hand and even in the dead of night they were obliging due to his plight. The miles and hours disappeared in a blur of open fields and the rhythmic sound of horse hooves on packed dirt. In the back of his mind, the radiant smile of his wife and little girl kept the loneliness at bay and spurred him on.

On the fourth day Edward stabled his mare to rest her and headed into the surrounding woodland. Speaking to the locals revealed they too had been under threat of the evil in the night for many decades. One thoughtlessly commented that it was a relief to have a period without their own children being taken. Edward could forgive the slight; these people had been through so much death it had changed them completely.

It was noon before the sounds of nature faded into silence and he reached the cross on the parchment. Edward pressed through a dense thicket, scratching his arms on the abnormally large thorns sprouting from the brambles.

Reaching the clearing beyond, the circular growth enclosed the whole area. Whether it was nature trying to contain the evil, or the evil attempting to conceal itself he couldn't guess. Time and the elements had erased much of the charred remains and were it not for the malevolent power, the vegetation would have long since buried the location in lush greens. Instead, the soil was shades darker than it should be and barren of even the smallest weed. Sat in the centre of the desolate sphere were the charred spurs of the thicker cabin timbers protruding from the ground like filthy teeth. All the smaller wood had been consumed utterly and a thick blanket of mulched black material lay on the ground from the decades old ash.

"There is something here," Edward whispered to himself.

He had sensed it the moment Father Norris explained the absence of life. Only a lingering malignance could corrupt the very ground he stood upon. Carefully surveying the area, nothing immediately presented itself and Edward considered the militia had been right in their estimation that the lair was elsewhere. Stepping onto the black crust, the glassy shell gave beneath his feet and a dark ooze splashed up onto his foot. Ignoring the vile smell, he walked around what was once the floor of the cabin, trying to think. Sighing with disappointment he made to leave but something creaked beneath his feet. Jumping up and down replicated the sound and it could only be unsupported wood. Kneeling down he frantically scraped the congealed mess and revealed a depression around a square trapdoor. In the intervening years enough moisture had made it through to weaken the hatch and with a few solid stamps the whole thing broke away and dropped into the darkness below. Why this had been missed was a mystery but Edward looked Heavenward and said a small prayer. It remained to be seen if fates were smiling on him this day or if he had just discovered her cold store.

"Please, please, please," Edward begged as he set about igniting a flame to use on the lantern.

Holding out the sputtering flame, the steps had been carved into the earth and water had eroded them to little more than a ramp. If he made it down without injuring himself, he still wouldn't be able to climb back out so he took a rope and tied it to one of the remaining fangs of timber. Sliding on his bottom down the mud, a small nook revealed itself and his stomach fluttered with fear. It had shelves buried in the wall, covered in decayed matter. It was just her pantry.

"I'm sorry, Millicent," Edward moaned, sinking to his knees.

All of his hopes had rested on this expedition and now he was lost. If a militia had scouted the whole area to find the remains and been unsuccessful, he stood no chance. Looking up from the ground, below the lowest shelf was a tunnel three feet in diameter. It couldn't be seen from a standing position and he dared to hope. Holding the lantern at arm's length it revealed a chamber beyond and he forced his way through the accumulated mess which had gathered on the ground, partially blocking the passage.

"Oh my Lord," Edward muttered at the sight.

The chamber was small, measuring twelve feet by eight feet. The smooth stone walls bore the marks of water erosion which was unusual because the closest river was at least half a mile away with the lake itself a mile further. This chamber must have been hollowed centuries ago before a shift in the water course redirected the stream. A small hole in the corner dropped away as far as the lantern could illuminate which probably went to a deeper, inaccessible water source. The true horror lay in the neatly arranged small bones with a skull perched atop each pile. In the centre of the room was a man-made altar comprising neatly arranged rocks. There was no disguising the cruelly twisted skeleton which lay on the top, nor the knife which was embedded between the ribs where she had driven it into her own heart. A flaking tome lay at her side and the open pages revealed hellish imagery and incantations in an alien tongue. It wasn't English or Latin, but something much worse. Just looking at the scribblings gave Edward an agonising stabbing pain in his head and he looked away before he passed out.

Opening a burlap sack, Edward carefully placed the bones inside. The hunter had been correct in his description of her as each part of her skeleton was twisted and covered in knotty growths. Her skull fared no better with extrusions and what appeared to be small horns sprouting from the white dome. Whatever hair she may have had before the transformation was not evident in the chamber and he surmised it must have fallen out. Guilt twisted his heart at the thought of leaving the poor children behind but at least now he could alert the relevant constable and have them laid to rest. Although unable to carry their innocent remains to safety, he refused to leave them alone with the blasphemous book and snapped it quickly shut, before placing it under his arm. The leathery material of the cover seemed to writhe and it took all of his fortitude to keep it held tight. Extinguishing the lantern, he climbed into the light and tossed the dreadful manuscript onto the floor, liberally soaking it with kerosene before using the small fire he had built to ignite it. A howling wind broke out in the glade, lashing fiercely at Edward and the book in an attempt to blow out the consuming flames. Combined with the liquid it only aided the inferno and in minutes a peace had settled on the area. The remaining pages fluttered into the air ablaze, destroying the taint forever.

"Good riddance!" Edward spat onto the fire with a hiss.

A bird warbled and was swiftly answered by another's mating call; a melody not experienced in half a century.

Edward was satisfied that in time nature would reclaim this land and wash any lingering taint of evil from the soil. The brambles had lost their unnatural power and the interwoven thorny branches gave way easily. In less than an hour he was back on the road with his trusty horse, driving her on to previously untapped levels of endurance. She seemed to sense the urgency and galloped without complaint. The four day journey was cut in half and at twilight Edward was hammering on the door of the vicarage.

"I have her," he panted, having run from the stables.

"Truly?" Father Norris was amazed, "Then we mustn't tarry. I have everything prepared but in truth I never thought you would be successful."

Together they stood at the open hole in the graveyard, it's mud piled to one side. A makeshift wooden cross had been made with the name Lavina Marth carved into it and an estimated date of her birth and death.

"Was that really wise?" Edward nodded at the tomb marker as he lowered the bones, "People loathe this creature and will probably desecrate the grave if they know she is at rest here."

"I understand, but if we hope to save her eternal soul her remains must be treated with dignity."

Edward wasn't convinced but he wasn't a man of the cloth so was untrained in these things. After saying a prayer, Father Norris poured a small measure of holy water onto the sack. An ear piercing shriek tore the gloom and a dark apparition rose into the air.

"That's Lavina!" Edward shouted and he could feel the mental poison under her undead gaze.

Pouring the remaining liquid on the bones it screamed in its torment and Father Norris finished the rite, "You are no longer bound to this world. Your body lays in holy ground and is blessed by our Holy Father. Begone!"

In a blur of shadow, she was gone into the night with a mournful wail.

"Is it over?" Edward asked.

"She has lost her power, but I fear she will be unwelcome in either Heaven or Hell. She is doomed to walk in the darkness, a soul trapped in purgatory for all eternity."

"Did Millicent make it?" asked Peter expectantly.

Toby smiled and looked around the gawping faces, "Indeed she did. After a week she was fighting fit and lived to the ripe old age of eighty-nine."

A round of applause broke out among the youngsters and Toby bowed. They were enthused by the story of good prevailing over evil and clapped each other on the back.

"I must warn you all," Toby continued, "Lavina still roams these woods, screaming and wailing when people die."

"You mean like a banshee, sir?" offered Kyle.

"Yes, exactly," Toby patted him on the shoulder, "They say she watches their souls rise to Heaven and vents her despair into the night. If you hear her, someone is about to pass on."

"Whoa," exclaimed the youngsters.

Toby glanced around and was confused to see Scott still hadn't returned. He had all the equipment, including the tents and food. Surprisingly he wasn't hungry despite having eaten nothing since setting off that morning.

He turned in a circle and decided to take action, "I'm heading out to the road to flag someone down. I must have left my mobile phone on the minibus too."

"Don't leave us alone," Peter said and was instantly derided by the older boys.

"Enough of that!" Toby warned them, "I will be back in a few minutes at most, the road is just through those trees. Don't leave the fire for any reason whatsoever until I return, do you understand."

"Yes, sir," they all agreed.

Although termed camping, the road was only a hundred yards away and the nearest habitation was only a short walk further. It was more like staying in your back yard than camping proper, but they all got some enjoyment from being out with nature. Toby strode off with purpose and was quickly lost to the night. Without an adult present the boys started to discuss the spooky tale and puffed up their chests to show how unafraid they were.

Kyle laughed at them all, "I saw you all pissing your pants. I was the only one who didn't believe a word of that crap."

"Yeah, right. I saw you holding Peter's hand," argued another with a grin.

Arguments started while they tried to convince each other they were the bravest until an inhuman howl echoed among the trees in all directions. Shrieks and screams of differing volumes assaulted their ears and they all huddled together in fear.

"Toby, stop it!" shouted Kyle through streaming tears.

The night was alive with mournful wailing and they all jumped in fright when Toby appeared from the opposite direction he had been walking. He pulled them all close as the din rose and fell in pitch, looking around frantically for the cause.

"Sir, is it Lavina? Is she going to kill us all?" sobbed Peter.

"No, don't worry. That was just a made up story I was told when I was younger. There are no such things as witches and banshees," Toby tried to reassure them but he was petrified and the words stuttered out.

"How did you appear behind us, sir?" Kyle asked, "Did you get lost?"

285

As the responsible adult he thought for a few moments before answering. The boys trusted him so he told the truth, "No, I walked in a straight line away from the fire but I couldn't find the road. The noises started and I saw a light which I thought may be a house. As I got closer I could see it was you and the fire. I must have walked in a circle." The last part was a lie, he knew he had walked in only one direction.

"What is it?" they all cried out.

"It has to be animals," Toby replied, "I must have disturbed them as I passed."

Ears pricked in an attempt to discern if they carried a bestial quality. No one wanted to articulate that each cry carried a distinctly human quality. Minutes passed and the piercing amalgamation abated. In place of the unending cacophony, they could start to identify individual traits in some of the screams. A female inflection here, a deeper, bass tone from a male cry there.

"Is it people?" Peter asked, looking up into Toby's eyes.

"I…" he gaped, "I don't know."

"I think I just heard my name," exclaimed Joshua.

Concentrating with all their might, they could finally make out individual words buried within the howling. The boys all looked at one another as they recognised their names but Toby was walking away from the group, straining to make out a familiar voice. It sounded just like Scott and he cupped hands to his ears in an effort to further isolate the voices.

Just lay still, don't struggle. You are on your way to hospital.

But what about the others? Toby and the boys, are they alright?

You were the only one who made it out of the wreckage alive, sir. The crash threw you clear before it burst into flames. I'm so sorry.

CHECK OUT THE OMP WEBSITE FOR
A COMPLETE LIST OF OUR TITLES

WWW.OPTIMUSMAXIMUSPUBLISHING.COM

BOOKS ARE AVAILABLE IN BOTH PRINT
AND ELECTRONIC FORMATS

RICKY FLEET
HELLSPAWN
SERIES

10.35 AM, September 14th 2015. Portsmouth, England.

A global particle physics experiment releases a pulse of unknown energy with catastrophic results. The sanctity of the grave has been sundered and a million graveyards expel their tenants from eternal slumber.

The world is unaware of the impending apocalypse. Governments crumble and armies are scattered to the wind under the onslaught of the dead.

Kurt Taylor, a self-employed plumber, witnesses the start of the horrifying outbreak. Desperate to reach his family before they fall victim to the ever growing horde of shambling corruption, he flees the scene.

In a society with few guns, how can people hope to survive the endless waves of zombies that seek to consume every living thing? With ingenuity, planning and everyday materials, the group forge their way and strike back at the Hellspawn legions.

Rescues are mounted, but not all survivors are benevolent, the evil that is in all men has been given free rein in this new, dead world. With both the living and dead to contend with, the Taylor family's battle for survival is just beginning.

Book 1 in the Hellspawn series.

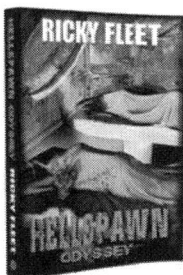

Kurt Taylor and his family have battled the living and the dead and now find themselves on the run, their home reduced to ashes. With unimaginable horror lying in wait around every corner, the onset of winter and the plunging temperatures only add more danger to their precarious existence. They decide to forge ahead and try to reach the protection of others who have hopefully survived the zombie apocalypse. If this fails, their only choice would be to try and reach an impregnable fortress, a sanctuary that has stood for a thousand years.

Standing between them and salvation are the villages and cities of the damned, a path that will test their spirit and resilience unlike anything they have faced before. More companions are rescued from the jaws of death and join them in their perilous journey. Mysterious attacks befall the group and it becomes clear the dead aren't the only things that lurk in the darkness.

Tempers fray and personalities clash. The group starts to fracture and Kurt is forced to commit acts that cause him to question his own morality. Can they survive the horror of their new existence? Will they want to?

The Hellspawn saga continues.

BALLYMOOR, IRELAND, 1891

Patrick Conroy, a young American student of medicine in Dublin, decides to take a break from the hustle and bustle of the big city and spend a month in the quietude of the wild and beautiful Glencree valley, County Wicklow. However, surrounded by local legends and myths, he is soon dragged into an ancient mystery that has haunted the village of Ballymoor for centuries. Set on the background of the tumultuous years preceding the War of Independence, and colored by Irish folklore, the Haunter of the Moor is a ghost story written in the style of Victorian Gothic novels.

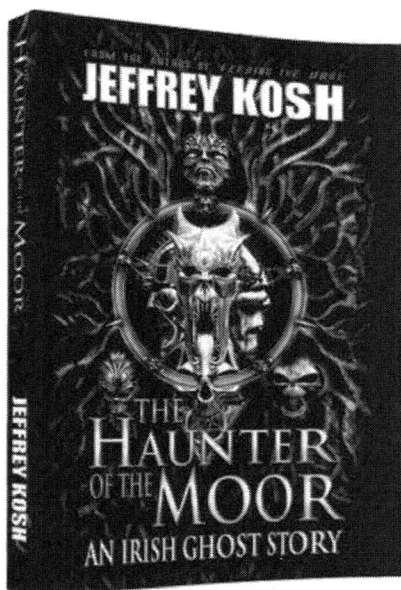

To Fight Evil with Evil

England, 1392.
As the Black Death quickly spreads through the kingdom, the little hamlet of Blythe's Hollow suffers under the yoke of a sadistic Lord. Desperate, the villagers decide to seek out the magical help of a local witch, causing the wrath of the Church. Torture and murder befall on those accused of being in league with the Devil, adding more sorrow to the beset folk of Blythe's Hollow. Yet, one man will rise against the tyranny; a man willing to learn Black Magick to fight back.

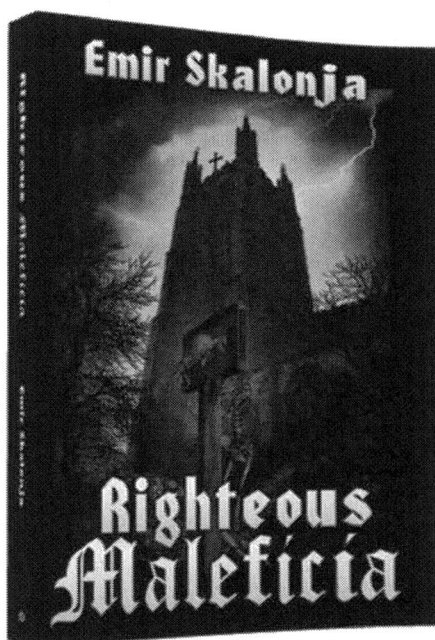

A modern dark urban fantasy, telling of two powerful families who uphold a secret duty to protect humanity from a threat it doesn't know exists.

Though sharing a common enemy, the two families form a long-standing rivalry due to their methods and ultimate goals.

Forces are coalescing in a prominent Central European city criminal sex-trafficking, a serial murderer with a savage bent, and other, less tangible influences.

Within a prestigious, private university, Lilja, a young librarian charged with protecting a very special book, finds herself suddenly ensconced in this dark, strange world. Originally from Finland, she has her own reason for why she left her home, but she finds the city to be anything but a haven from dangers and secrets.

Book One in a planned series.

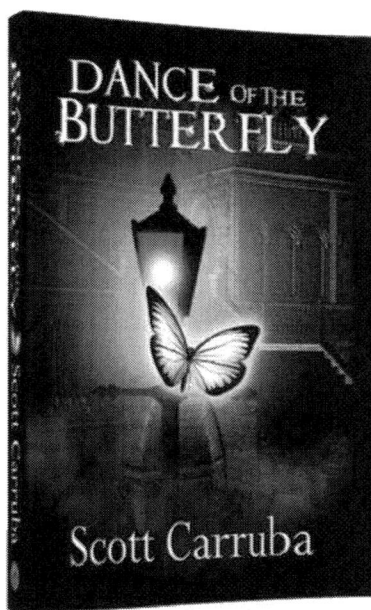

DANCE OF THE BUTTERFLY

Scott Carruba

Meet Mason Ezekiel Barnes, former NFL tackle turned successful author of the naughty ninja adventure series Mia Killjoy. Mason is obsessed with winning a Pulitzer and is thwarted by his fellow author and nemesis, the twerpy little gnome Conrad Bancroft.

Perk Noir is full of comedic relief, pop culture, NFL, jazz, a little touch of romance, and flashbacks of Lightning and his family during both the first half of the 20th century and later during the Civil Rights movement. Mason and Shelly and their adventures is a fun filled thrill ride that will appeal to all readers, there is something for everyone at the Perk.

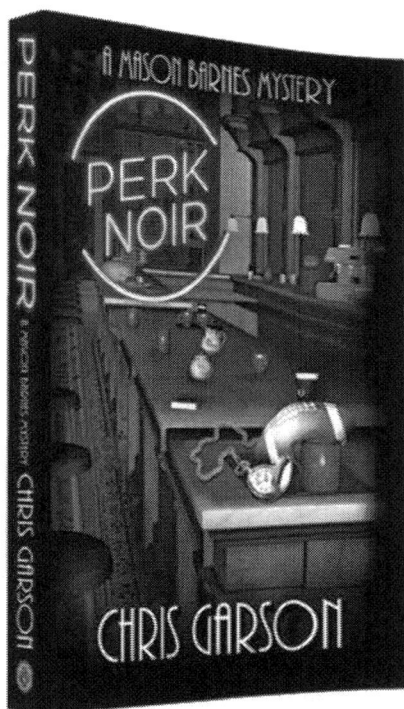

Two hunters pursue the same prey.

Fate has forged the slayer, Trey Thomas and the Sandrian vampire, Adalius, two natural enemies, into an uneasy alliance against an evil more powerful than either have ever faced. Only together do they stand a chance of defeating Anna; if they don't destroy each other first.

As they pursue Anna, the apprehensive Lycan watch as a confrontation looms on the horizon between vampires, the New Bloods and the Old Guard, which threatens to plunge the vampire world into civil war and trigger an all-out supernatural conflict which in the end could destroy them all.

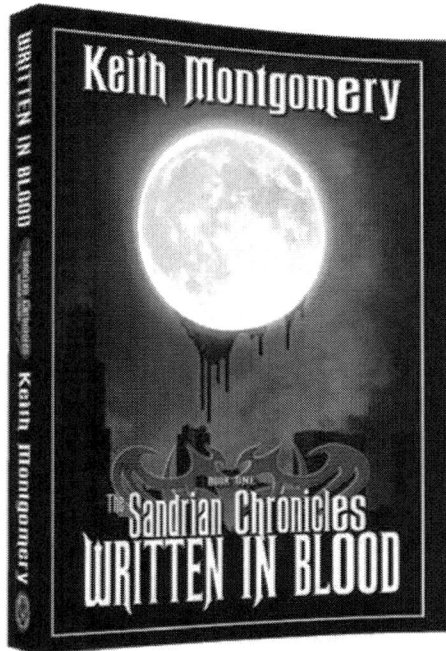

WRITTEN IN BLOOD

Keith Montgomery

Keith Montgomery

The Sandrian Chronicles

WRITTEN IN BLOOD

GIDEON'S PASSAGE

BEN LAFFRA

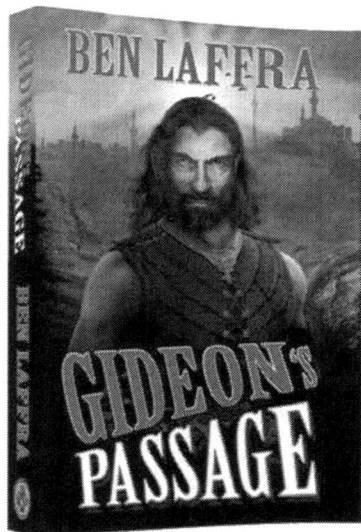

Killing is the sole province of the religious fanatics, an axiom as true today as it was some five hundred years ago; and no nation, region or person is immune.

Europe had clawed its way out of the Middle Ages with the dawning of the renaissance, only to be plunged once more into darkness, as the dogs of war circled to destroy its resurgence during the 16th century. The Islamic successor to the Roman Byzantines, the Ottoman Caliphate, flexed its muscles to conquer much of Western Asia, North Africa and South-Eastern Europe. Christian Europe shuddered when the once invincible bastion of the Knight's at Rhodes were defeated; and now trembled as the Ottoman army rattled the very gates of Vienna. No Christian army, it seemed, could withstand the ferocity of the Azabs, the Akıncı, the Sipahis, the Janissaries, and ruthless Iayalar's of the all-conquering Islamic hordes.

This then is the cauldron into which Gideon de Boyne is unwittingly thrust with his small army of dedicated Christian warriors. On the hostile island of Crete, at the doorstep of the Ottoman Empire, Gideon must face not only the overwhelming force of Muslim warriors but his own inner conflicts of the futility of war and his very Christian beliefs.

Will he succeed and come out of it unscathed?

Made in the USA
Middletown, DE
16 February 2017